STEVEN HOPSTAKEN &
MELISSA PRUSI

STOKER'S WILDE

This is a **FLAME TREE PRESS** book

Text copyright © 2019 Steven Hopstaken & Melissa Prusi
stokerswilde.com

FLAME TREE PRESS
6 Melbray Mews, London, SW6 3NS, UK
flametreepress.com

Distribution and warehouse:
Baker & Taylor Publisher Services (BTPS)
30 Amberwood Parkway, Ashland, OH 44805
btpubservices.com

Thanks to the Flame Tree Press team, including:
Taylor Bentley, Frances Bodiam, Federica Ciaravella, Don D'Auria,
Chris Herbert, Imogen Howson, Matteo Middlemiss, Josie Mitchell, Mike
Spender, Cat Taylor, Maria Tissot, Nick Wells, Gillian Whitaker.

The cover is created by Flame Tree Studio with
thanks to Nik Keevil and Shutterstock.com.
The font families used are Avenir and Bembo.

Flame Tree Press is an imprint of Flame Tree Publishing Ltd
flametreepublishing.com

A copy of the CIP data for this book is available from the British Library
and the Library of Congress.

HB ISBN: 978-1-78758-173-9
PB ISBN: 978-1-78758-171-5
ebook ISBN: 978-1-78758-174-6
Also available in FLAME TREE AUDIO

Printed in the US at Bookmasters, Ashland, Ohio

STEVEN HOPSTAKEN &
MELISSA PRUSI

STOKER'S WILDE

FLAME TREE PRESS
London & New York

WHITE WORM SOCIETY ARCHIVIST'S NOTE

These materials cover the involvement of Bram Stoker and Oscar Wilde in the 'Greystones' and 'Black Bishop' incidents. It has taken many years of painstaking investigation to compile them. In some cases, items were sold to us or given freely by the principals; in others, bribery, chicanery, or outright thievery was required. To paraphrase Mr. Stoker, such is the life of a White Worm Society archivist.

All letters, journal entries, transcripts and news items have been placed in chronological order where possible. In most cases, materials that do not pertain to the cases at hand have been eliminated; however, we have retained some exhibits that reflect more upon the personal lives of the participants. The insight these writings provide into the minds of their authors deepens our understanding of their involvement in the fight against supernatural evil and how it may have been impacted by events transpiring in their personal lives.

Spelling of writings from the original authors have been retained; however, punctuation has been updated in accordance with White Worm Society international style rules.

Viewing of this collection is restricted to members of the White Worm Society. Removal of these materials from the library is strictly forbidden.

LETTER FROM OSCAR WILDE TO FLORENCE BALCOMBE, 1ST OF NOVEMBER 1876

Archivist's note: Wilde, like most educated Victorians, was a skilled and prolific letter writer. Unlike the correspondence of today, his letters could run upwards of twenty pages, double-sided. Here he begins to relate the events of the Greystones Incident. While no doubt some of the dialogue has been fabricated, we know from other sources that the events depicted are more or less accurate.

My dearest Florrie,

I am counting the days until we are together again, my golden flower. I bitterly regret that I haven't had the opportunity to visit you while I am home from Oxford, but the last few days have been the most traumatic and dramatic in all my twenty-two years. I can scarcely put these events to paper, as my mind still reels with the memory of what I have seen – what I have done. But I shall do my best in the following narrative. It is a tale of supernatural terror, illuminated only by the tarnished light of a full moon. A tale in which I am the hero, of course, since I am the narrator. But no matter how flattering a light I cast upon myself, I swear to you that every word is true.

This story is not for the faint of heart. I fear your delicate nature may, in fact, make you swoon from the words. So, my dear Florrie, please be seated. This is a story to be read in the light of day with company in your presence, not on some stormy night alone in your room.

Dare I continue?

I do!

It all started a few nights ago when Mother hosted an informal dinner party. Our special guest for the evening was none other than the remarkable Captain Richard Burton, the noted explorer and adventurer.

As he was a friend of my late father, Captain Burton makes a point to drop by whenever his travels bring him to Dublin. It had been several years since I'd seen him, so I should not have been surprised to notice how age had at last begun to diminish the great man, if only slightly. He is, perhaps, less formidable a figure, his bearing less commanding, his stride a bit slower. Nevertheless, he is still a vibrant personality, always ready with a fascinating tale or the occasional bawdy joke, and it's easy to see how he earned the nickname Ruffian Dick. His dark eyes still make one feel that he knows all one's secrets at a glance, and his thick, dark hair has not receded an inch, a virtue which I consider worthy of emulation.

Along with him was his lovely wife, Isabel, who is a bit of a flirt when she has had a glass or two of claret and is one of the few women I know who can (and will) quote the *Kama Sutra*! She has travelled widely with her husband and perhaps it is this experience that lends her the enviable ability to find something interesting in everyone she meets, a talent that would be put to the test that evening, for also joining us were my older brother, Willie, and one of his most tiresome friends, Bram Stoker.

Like Willie, and unlike Burton, Bram is not remarkable in any way. Oh, I suppose his appearance is striking. He is well past six foot, strong as an ox, with a red-bearded face that frightens small children but that, mysteriously, women find handsome.

He was educated at Trinity so he speaks proper English, though he hasn't lost his Irish brogue as I have worked so hard to do. In fact, the angrier he gets the more Irish he becomes. When he becomes flustered, which is often if I can provoke it, I am only able to pull out the occasional swear word from his Celtic stream of obscenities.

Bram is a civil servant and can converse endlessly on any subject as long as it is dull and uninspiring. That night he regaled us with tales of railway timetables and an extraordinary new method for filing documents.

Willie met Bram at school, where Bram showed some small talent as a writer. (I suppose this puts him one up on Willie, who has never shown talent at anything.) At Trinity, I attended the reading of his paper, 'The Supernatural as Introduced by the English Poets', which I thought showed promise, despite his monotone drone. In more recent years, he has published several short stories, which make up in clumsy moralising what they lack in wit. However, any poetic inkling he may once have possessed has been crushed under the weight of bureaucratic manuals and file cabinets, as was evident that night as Mother tried to get him to shut up and let Captain Burton talk.

"How astonishing to learn there is so much more to filing than memorising the alphabet," Mother said, interrupting Stoker's treatise on folder-tab placement. She quickly turned to Burton and patted him on the hand. "I have just reread your book of Hindu tales, *Vikram and the Vampire*, Richard. It is so engrossing and has helped me immensely with my own work." (Did you know, Florrie, that Mother is a noted expert on all things supernatural? She writes under the *nom de plume* 'Speranza', which is quite convenient when I do not wish people to know of her unusual interests. But you, my dear, I wish to know everything about me!)

Stoker's face had reddened to match his ginger hair and beard. No doubt he realised he had been dominating the conversation at a table shared with one of the world's greatest lecturers. I almost felt sorry for him.

"Thank you, Lady Jane," Burton said. "That is a great compliment coming from one with your expertise."

"Yes, quite a good read," Willie chimed in. "I find Hindu vampires to be much more civilised than European vampires."

"Yes," Burton said. "But then they are purely whimsical folk tale inventions, and not real creatures, like Eastern European vampires." He relished the last bite of his steak and kidney pie as Stoker's eyes widened.

"Excuse me," Stoker asked. "Are you saying that European vampires are real?"

"Oh, yes, quite frightfully real," Burton said. "Horrible creatures. Drooling, rotting, mindless things you would not want to meet up with on a dark night. Killed three myself back in the Crimean War. The battlefields brought them out like rats. They prey on the dying, you see."

Stoker seemed amused, and was about to respond, but a kick from Willie kept him from pressing the matter further. How I wished I was in kicking range myself!

"But vampires are old news, I'm afraid," Isabel said, her eyes twinkling. "These days, my dear husband has turned his sword to fighting werewolves." She raised her glass slightly, in a teasing but affectionate toast to her husband, then drained it.

"My dear wife mocks me, but it is true that I am currently investigating, at the request of Her Majesty the Queen, the recent killing down in Greystones."

"And you believe it was a werewolf? What an interesting coincidence!" Mother exclaimed. "I happen to be writing a book on werewolf lore at this very moment!"

"What good fortune! I thought I might beg permission to look through your folklore collection for a way to track and kill the beast."

Stoker could not contain himself any longer. "You cannot be serious," he protested. "Surely that poor girl was killed by a pack of wild dogs."

"If only it were so," Burton said. "The killing occurred under the light of a full moon." He lowered his voice as if the werewolf itself were listening. "An upstanding constable saw the creature running right down the main street. And, unbeknownst to the general public, a similar killing took place in Wexford the full moon before. A fisherman had his throat torn out, and strange, wolflike tracks were found nearby."

"In what way were they strange?" I enquired. The servants clearing away our plates did their best not to appear frightened and hurried back to the kitchen whispering.

"Bigger than any dog, or wolf for that matter – not that there has been a wolf seen in Ireland in decades. But the tracks went on towards town and in mid-trail—" here Burton paused for effect, "—they turned into human footprints."

Mother gasped with delight. "Oh, a chill just went up my spine! Do tell us more!"

"Wexford must be fifty miles from Greystones, at least," Stoker said.

"Wolves in Canada have been known to go three hundred miles in a fortnight," Willie said. "Still, I have to agree with Bram. It must have been a wolf or a monstrous dog."

"A large dog with deformed feet," Bram added, "that when stepping in mud leaves a humanlike print."

Burton took out his pipe and started to fill it. (The captain has never been one to feel bound by the rules of etiquette.) "Maybe so, but I shall be heading down to Greystones by train tomorrow to see for myself."

"Oh, could we accompany you?" Mother asked excitedly. "It would be perfect for my book."

Willie scolded her. "Mother, a werewolf hunt is hardly a place for a woman of your...." He trailed off, possibly thinking it best not to finish his thought.

"Of my what, child? My age? My girth?"

"Your dignity," he improvised, forcing a smile.

Mother wagged her finger at him. "If your father were alive he would be the first to say, 'Jane, melt down the silverware and grab your gun!'" She banged her fist on the table to make her point.

"If any woman can stare down that beast," I said, "it is Mother!"

Isabel laughed uproariously at this and added, "It will leave Ireland yelping, with its tail between its legs!"

Mother did not enjoy us laughing at her expense. "I am serious, Richard. I have spoken to Gipsies and witches at length about werewolves and my information could be invaluable to your hunt."

"I welcome your research, Speranza, and you are welcome to escort us to Greystones, but the hunt should be left up to the men. What say you, Oscar, Willie, Bram? Shall we track this creature down?" He waved his pipe as he said this and the swiftness of it caused sparks to fly, nearly catching Stoker's beard on fire.

"Er, what?" Willie said, turning a whiter shade of pale than usual.

"I have to be back at work on Monday," Bram said, brushing ashes from his whiskers. "Perhaps the next one."

"Nonsense, lad," Burton said, chuckling. "Just tell 'em you're with me. I daresay the Burton name still counts for something. And if it doesn't, well, a word from Her Majesty will have you back behind your desk – or your manager's – in a trice."

"Count me in," I said loudly. "As you yourself once wrote, Captain Burton, 'Do what thy manhood bids thee do.' No hell beast is going to terrorise Ireland on my watch!" (I must admit I had had a few clarets myself.) "And besides, how many times in a man's life does he have the chance to go on a monster hunt with one of the greatest soldiers and explorers the world has ever known? I shall regale my eventual grandchildren with the tale on stormy evenings in front of the fire!"

Burton looked pleased at that. Willie and Bram glanced at each other and I could tell my words had hit home. Breathes there an Irishman with soul so dead he doesn't long for a bit of adventure?

Willie pounded his fist on the table, exclaiming, "The Wilde boys reporting for duty, Captain Burton!" I raised my glass to him, and he drained his.

All eyes turned to Stoker, who muttered something unintelligible in Irish before saying, "At your service, sir. Let's go kill a…werewolf."

Burton leapt to his feet and in that moment I could once again see the fearless young adventurer, entrusted by his Queen with the protection of her subjects, and I would have willingly followed him into a pit of vipers. "That's the spirit that made the Empire great! We leave on the first train in the morning!"

So, the very next morning we boarded a train for Greystones. I had no idea one could take a train to Greystones, or why anyone would want to go there if not to hunt a werewolf. Stoker, of course, not only knew of the train but had memorised its entire schedule, so we were in good hands there.

I was having second thoughts about being on a hunt with Burton. He has been known to pull out his pistol with the slightest provocation. Rumour has it he shot the Marquess of Queensberry's parrot for singing a song insulting the Queen.

And frankly, I am quite surprised I was invited along. When Willie and I were lads, Captain Burton took us hunting and I shot his dog. It was an accident, I assure you, and the dog pulled through, living to hunt another day. Still, it's not the sort of thing a man forgets.

Mother and Isabel occupied their own private car. Mother was poring over books of folklore, researching the habits and weaknesses of werewolves, while Isabel was weaving us all necklaces of wolfsbane. I was doubtful as to the effectiveness of a dried herb against the claws of a ferocious beast, but Mother assured me that it had been known to work in the past, as cloves of garlic have repelled vampires. These things must be true because I have never heard of Italians or the French being attacked by vampires or werewolves and they are positively swimming in garlic and herbs.

Bram, Willie and I kept Captain Burton company in another private car, where he regaled us with a tale in which he slew a giant snake monster in the jungles of India.

"The locals worshiped the thing," he informed us. "So, we had to fight our way through them before we could get close enough to chop its head off!"

Stoker could barely contain himself; his face was becoming red as he held back his comments. I have to admit Burton's tales were getting more outrageous with every breath, but I egged him on if only for the possibility of seeing Stoker's head explode.

"How ghastly," I gasped. "But you did kill it after you dispatched the natives?"

"It wasn't as easy as all that," he said. "The thing had the power to cloud men's minds. As we approached, my own men began to fall under its spell. They bowed down before it, praying in some foreign tongue. Luckily, Sir Reginald Farnsworth and I had taken a gin and tonic only moments before, which seemed to have protected us from its influence."

"Gin to the rescue," Willie said, laughing, and took a swig from his flask.

"Perhaps it was the tonic," Stoker muttered.

"It took the two of us forty whacks to get the head off. Then the thing still managed to slither off into the jungle before it died!"

Stoker sunk into his seat as if he wanted to slither away himself and said, "I suppose you have its head hanging over your fireplace?"

"Heavens, no. Frightful thing. Full of poison!" Burton became quiet for a moment, and it seemed to me he had slipped into a particularly vivid, especially dark memory. He continued, his voice thoughtful. "I've seen some truly horrible things out there in the far reaches of the Empire. As we bring civilisation to the wild, some of the wild slips into civilisation. Who would have ever thought a werewolf would come to Ireland's shores? I fear there are even more terrible creatures right behind it."

"Well, I say we send it back into the wild, whimpering like the craven cur it is," I said, raising my own flask for a toast. "We shall make these shores safe for mad dogs and Irishmen once more!"

Burton seemed cheered by my remark, but I felt disquieted. What hope was there for our expedition if our leader was relying on my meagre courage to buoy his own?

I would like to say that Greystones is a charming, picturesque fishing village. I would like to but cannot. It is a squalid shantytown that smells of rotten fish and rotten sailors – many of them pirates, I suspect. If I were a werewolf, it is just the sort of place I would seek out.

Remote, rocky and shrouded in mist, Greystones hardly looked the part of a busy seaport. Only a single ship of any size was in the harbour that day, a Russian schooner called the *Demeter* (which will play a part in this tale later on).

Apparently, the village was quite isolated until recently. Stoker told us that the railway line was put in a few years back to bring trade from its tiny harbour to the surrounding area and on to Dublin. The scheme seems to have enlivened the place, but in a most unwholesome way. Rather than the bustling, cheerful harbour town officials may have imagined, it feels shabby and grim and has an air of danger that I suspect is only partially attributable to the recent killing.

It is big enough to have an inn, if one could call it that. We secured the only three rooms and I was forced to share with Willie and Stoker. (The first of the horrors I faced on that trip!)

Florence, dearest, the tone of this letter has been light so far, I will admit. However, let us both remember that a horrible deed had been done in this village. A young woman was savagely killed. The mood of the villagers was sullen and fearful. Some businesses were closed and houses boarded up. Only the fishermen and Russian sailors were out on the streets that day.

When we entered our rooms, we found that our windows and doors were already framed with the yellow flowers of wolfsbane. The innkeeper herself warned us to leave on the next train.

"The love of God has left our village," she informed us. "I would leave meself if I could sell this place."

Captain Burton wasted no time in gathering information and asked the woman many questions about the recent killing. She told us that the girl had worked as a barmaid at the Blue Moon, one of the local pubs.

We started there. I doubt a gentle, well-bred soul like you can imagine what the place was like. I myself have scarcely seen anything like it. Walking into its smoky, dimly lit confines, it was not hard to imagine the Blue Moon playing host to all manner of villainy and wretchedness. It bore the marks of violence and debauchery – a deep gouge in the wall here, a puddle of some unidentifiable substance there. I was quite glad that we were visiting in the morning whilst the place was quiet.

Nevertheless, there were already several sailors sullenly hunched over their drinks or passed out at the filthy tables. The place smelled of stale

ale and whisky, which was actually a welcome relief from the smell of fish that permeated the outside.

In the faint sunlight that managed to filter through the grimy windows, the patrons eyed us suspiciously, and I could not blame them, for we stuck out like diamonds in a bin of coal.

We sat at the bar and Burton ordered a whisky while the three of us ordered gin and tonics, which seemed to annoy the bartender.

"We don't got limes," he said. "Nor tonic." He plopped down four glasses, splashing three with gin and one with whisky, then slid them to each of us, spilling much in the process.

"We are here to enquire about the recent tragic event," Burton said.

"We don't need no outsiders sticking their noses into our business," the bartender grumbled. "The constable has formed a hunting party and they're out searching for the beast even as we speak."

A tall, wiry sailor weaved his unsteady way to the bar and tapped Willie on the shoulder. "Hey, boy-o. Where'd you get those fancy clothes? Let me buy you a drink." Willie ignored him and moved closer to Stoker for protection. Stoker stood taller so the sailor could see his full height and bulk. The sailor scowled and slunk away.

"I have been asked by Her Majesty the Queen to lend a hand here," Burton said. (Perhaps he had forgotten that invoking the Queen does not always endear one to Irishmen.) He continued, "I am a skilled tracker and hunter."

One of the regulars at a back table laughed. "Of what? Rabbits?"

Burton pulled out a pistol and pointed it at the man. The smile quickly flew from the miscreant's face. "Of wolves, Bengal tigers and nefarious men," Burton said, his gaze as clear and steely as one imagines it was when he was a young man fighting for Queen and country. The man averted his eyes and Burton returned the pistol to his belt. (I remember my father telling me that at Trinity, Richard had challenged another student to a duel for laughing at his moustache. Clearly, he is not one to waste time in conversation when more expedient methods are at hand.)

"Well, you best get tracking then," the bartender said. "There ain't no wolf tracks in here."

"But this is the last place the poor girl was seen alive?" Stoker asked.

"Far as I know," he said. "'Cept by the beast what murdered her."

"Tell us about the girl and that night," I said, getting into the spirit of the investigation. "Was there anything out of the ordinary? Any strangers hanging about?"

"Aye, there was a shipload of sailors in that night. From that Russian schooner still in the harbour," the bartender said, lowering his voice. "Too much time on their hands, that lot – their ship is after needing some repairs. Some took a fancy to her, but then most men did. Polly was a pretty little thing. But she could take care of herself."

"When did she leave?" Willie asked.

"I don't keep my eye on the clock and it wouldn't do me much good if I did because it's broken. But it was late, maybe two in the morning. There was a full moon that night and it was starting to set. She wanted to get home before it did. She liked having the light to see her way." The man's eyes clouded over and he suddenly felt the need – undoubtedly the first in years – to bend to the task of polishing glasses.

"Where was she found?" Burton asked.

"In a grove of trees near the old mill at the end of town," he said. "At least that's where we found most of her."

"Could you draw us a map?" Burton asked, handing him a pencil and paper.

He reluctantly agreed.

"And wasn't there a witness?" Stoker asked.

The bartender handed Burton the map. "That would be Mrs. Goode. She owns the pie shop down the street."

And where that witness led us, dear Florrie, ah, there our tale grows still stranger and more chilling. But I fear I must, as many a good showman before me, leave you in suspense for the time being. Rest assured, I shall write again soon. Think of this account as a serial, such as Mr. Dickens used to write. Our next instalment promises adventure, blood and, if I may say, a fair show of derring-do from yours truly.

I sign off now, as I must depart soon for a luncheon with some of my old school chums and I wish to post this today. I can't bear to go one more day without letting you know how often and how fondly I think of you. The memory of your sweet face and the tender moments we have shared have seen me through darker times than you can imagine, my beloved Florence. I remain, as always,

Yours truly,

Oscar

FROM THE JOURNAL OF BRAM STOKER, 29TH OF OCTOBER 1876

Archivist's note: These entries are from one of the seven journals believed by Stoker's wife to have been burned upon his death. They were saved from the fire by one of the White Worm Society's operatives, embedded as a servant in the Stoker household. Shorter entries are handwritten; longer passages to come later are typed on a Remington 2 typewriter, the first commercially produced machine to type both upper and lowercase letters.

Stoker was said to have perfect memory recall, something we would call photographic memory today. This would serve him well as a clerk, and later as a theatre manager and writer. It also serves us well, for his journal entries contain precise physical detail and dialogue not usually found in such materials.

Greystones: 10:30 a.m.

I do not know how I get myself into these things. Apparently, I have been kidnapped by Richard Burton and the Wilde family. It is becoming increasingly clear that I will never understand the lives of the idle upper class.

I fear that I will not make it back to work on Monday and will lose a day's pay, if I'm not sacked outright. Such is the life of a petty sessions clerk.

I have recently decided to live a more pious life. I made a promise to myself and God to increase my devotions and self-discipline. However, I am afraid being friends with Willie Wilde and his family is going to make that difficult. It is not yet noon and I have already drunk too much gin. *Is milis dá ól é ach is searbh dá íoc é.* (It is sweet to drink but bitter to pay for.)

As I write this, Willie and his brother Oscar (a more vain and irritating seeker of attention you'd be hard put to find, though admittedly he has shown promise in his academic pursuits) are arguing about the proper spelling of wolfsbane. For you see, we are on a werewolf hunt in the charming fishing village of Greystones, where a young barmaid was savagely killed.

I could tell from the moment we got off the train that Greystones is filled with salt-of-the-earth, hardworking people. The fresh sea air is invigorating, and I could see myself settling here someday and living the life of a simple fisherman or innkeeper. But such rustic, honest pursuits are miles distant from the dark business we undertake today. After questioning the landlord at the Blue Moon, where the unfortunate lass worked, we have regrouped back at the rooming house to plan our next move.

While I am under the firm belief that the recent tragedy was the work of a large, rabid dog, Captain Burton is convinced that the perpetrator is of the lycanthropic variety, and the Wildes, whether through genuine belief or bemused tolerance of a longstanding friend's flights of fancy, are playing along with this delusion.

I am almost certain the Wilde brothers do not believe in werewolves any more than I do and are just along for the diversion. They are also quite amused at my scepticism in the face of Burton's addled imagination. I have long been an admirer of Captain Burton, and it is a sorry sight indeed to see the noted explorer and diplomat tipping on the verge of madness. Sorrier still, he is taking me down with him!

11:15 a.m.

It has been decided that Willie and Captain Burton will attempt to pick up the beast's trail, while Oscar and I question a woman who claims to have seen the creature fleeing the scene of the attack.

Although I have met Oscar on a few different occasions, this is the first that I have spent any significant amount of time with him. To say he is annoying is an understatement. He has affected a London accent, and from time to time will slip into speaking French, Italian or Greek as if to prove his intellectual superiority. Alas, he merely comes off as a pompous twit.

He also finds himself exceedingly witty and humorous, often laughing at his own bawdy jokes. Furthermore, I suspect he may be a poof. At least he dresses the part, often wearing frilly velvet shirts and a purple top hat. When first I met him, I thought perhaps he was going to a fancy-dress party as the Mad Hatter.

Ah, the Hatter calls. Off to play detective, while my livelihood surely disappears like the Cheshire Cat.

6:00 p.m.

My head is pounding and I am visibly shaking. *It* has happened again – one of those spells has come over me. It has been many years since I have experienced such a thing. I had all but convinced myself that the other incidents were nothing but childhood flights of fancy. Most children see fairies in the woods, do they not? However, today it was strong and vivid and I fear I may be losing my sanity!

To make matters worse, I experienced the latest hallucinations in front of Oscar. He claims to believe my visions, even more than I do myself, but I am not certain he isn't just humouring me.

It happened after we questioned the woman who says she witnessed the creature fleeing the woods. Mrs. Goode, a plump and motherly lady, runs a pie shop down the street from the Blue Moon. (I shall attempt to recreate our conversation as best I can from memory; I find that remembering what was said helps me to think more clearly on the subject.)

"It was horrible," Mrs. Goode informed us. "All hairy, with fangs and claws, but it ran upright like a man." Oscar was busy savouring the smell of the pork pies cooling on a table next to the window. It was up to me to keep the investigation moving.

"Let us be honest; it was dark. How can you be sure of what you saw?" I asked.

"'Twas a full moon," she countered. "I could see with no trouble at all. Nothing wrong with my eyes. It was as close to me as he is." She pointed at Oscar, who was eating one of the pies.

"Do you partake in drink, madam?" I asked.

She took offence. "I've been known to have a sip of brandy or cider on occasion, but that night I was sober as a bishop!"

Apparently, she hadn't known the bishops I had. I pointed out the window at a passing sailor. "Tell me, dear woman, how many stripes are on that sailor's shirt?"

She squinted. "Er, four?"

"There are no stripes," I exclaimed, with too much vigour I suppose, for she cowered back in fear. "And yet you claim you clearly saw a monster by moonlight, as it ran into the forest?" I was surprised to find I was actually good at detecting and wondered if there could be a career in law enforcement in my future.

"I don't think I care to answer any more of your questions," she said, staring at me coldly. "You will kindly leave my shop."

Oscar came forwards and took a coin from his pocket to pay for the pie. "This is surely the most delicious thing I have ever put in my mouth," he said. "And I make it my life's mission to only put tasty things in there!"

She lit up at this and replied, "An old family recipe."

He smiled at her in a way that was, I'll admit, most winning. "Pardon me, madam, but I must correct you there," he said. "It is an old family *treasure*. With pies like these, your shop must be a smashing success."

"Well, I do all right," she said. "Course, if I didn't have some regular custom after fifteen years of business in a little village like this, I daresay it would be time to hang up my rolling pin."

"Fifteen years!" Oscar exclaimed. "Why, whenever did you open for business? When you were five? My good woman, I fear you are having me on, and me, a humble visitor to your fair village. I ask you, is it kind to tease a stranger so?"

The woman actually blushed. "Now, sir, who's teasing who?" she said, with a bit of a giggle. "I've earned every one of my years, and I'll not let you deny me any of them."

"Well said, madam," Oscar replied, bowing slightly. "But that makes me wonder whether, in all those years, you've ever seen this wolflike creature before? Or heard tell of its like? Any other brushes with the supernatural? Do you, perhaps, have the second sight?"

"Nay, I'm a good Christian woman and haven't been bothered by those beyond the veil." She thought for a moment while Oscar finished the last bite of his pie, then added, "But when I was but a girl, I did hear the cry of the banshee, right before my parents died."

Oscar gasped. "So, you *are* connected to otherworldly things! If I were you, I would keep the Lord's cross at hand and wolfsbane at your door. Thank goodness you are a good Christian, free of sin, for that will keep you safe and on the road to heaven."

Then a remarkable thing happened. The woman's brow furrowed and she frowned as if a pain had suddenly overcome her. Oscar noticed this too and pressed the matter further.

"Have I said something to upset you, dear lady?"

"No…I must be getting back to my pies." She turned as if to avoid meeting Oscar's eyes.

"Madam," Oscar said with real concern in his voice. "If there is something burdening your heart you can certainly tell me. I am not one to judge, being a sinner myself, and I know how confession can uplift the soul. Pray tell me, what did you really see that night?"

Mrs. Goode wiped her hands on her apron fretfully. "I…was only trying to protect my brother. Danny's a good man when he doesn't drink, and he raised me when our parents died."

"If you know something, you must tell us," I ordered her. Oscar held up his hand to silence me and approached the woman, who still had her back to us. He gently took her by the shoulders and turned her around.

"We are not the authorities," Oscar said. "We are just trying to keep others from being killed. If you know something, if your brother is involved, his very soul may be at risk."

She gazed at him for a moment, fear and worry etched upon her face. "That night," she said, her voice trembling, "I saw Polly go by from my bedroom window. She was with my brother, who I know fancies her and walks her home from time to time."

"When was this?" I asked.

"Late. I had woken up from a bad dream. I'm not sure of the time."

"Why didn't you tell the constable this?" Oscar asked. "It sounds innocent enough."

Tears welled up in her eyes. "They were arguing about something. I couldn't hear what they were saying, but then he grabbed her roughly. She broke away from him and ran into the woods at the end of the street."

"I see," said Oscar.

"He ran after her…into the woods. And that's the last I saw of her."

"But you didn't see him attack her?" Oscar asked.

"Nor did you see a creature," I added.

"Nay, I didn't see him do anything to her, and I'm sure he didn't.… He couldn't!" she cried. "But I made up the story of seeing the creature because one *has* been seen – by none other than the constable himself, though not with poor Polly. It must have been the beast what did her in, and I saw no need to distract the police by dragging Danny into it."

"So," Oscar said, "you saw her run into the woods at the end of the street, not down by the mill as you claimed earlier?"

Her head hung down in shame. "No. They found her body at the mill, so I told them that's where I saw the creature."

"Thank you for telling us the truth," Oscar said, giving her a small kiss on the cheek. "We will look into the matter and protect your brother if he is innocent."

"Thank you, sir." Mrs. Goode wiped a tear from her eye before exclaiming, "Oh, my pies!" She rushed off into the kitchen.

Just as I was starting to think Oscar was not the cad he appeared to be, he stole a pie, wrapping it in a towel and putting it in his pocket.

"Let us depart, Stoker. Captain Burton and Willie are looking in the wrong place!"

He rushed out and I followed. We headed down to the end of the street and into the woods.

"Shouldn't we try to find Burton and Willie before we go getting lost in the forest?" I protested. "We are hardly equipped for a hunt."

"The beast, or man, is far from here by now. We must gather evidence. Find the abduction spot to find the beginning of the trail. My God, but this is exhilarating!"

Before I could stop him, we were rushing headlong down a deer trail into the thick of the shadowed woods.

"She must have run down this very path," he said. "With that sweaty man hot on her heels." He stopped to catch his breath; I'm sure this was the fastest he'd moved in many years.

"Really, we must get the others," I said. "And not trample over the trail!"

"Yes, I expect you are right, Stoker," he said, fanning himself. "I lost my head there for a moment."

It was then that my spell began. The woods took on an eerie, green glow as if lit by fireflies. My head began to throb and my heart to race. I must have looked a fright because Oscar noticed.

"Stoker, are you all right? You look as though you've seen a ghost."

"It's nothing," I said. "I just need to sit down and rest a moment."

I sat on a nearby log, hoping it would all go away quickly like it has before. However, this time it was different. Despite the green tint to my vision, I seemed to be seeing more clearly than ever. My hearing was sharp. I swear I could hear Oscar's heartbeat and the heartbeats of small animals in the brush.

Upon looking at the ground, I saw as plain as day the footprints of a wolf; they shone a bright, unearthly green as if they had been burned into the ground.

"Do you see those footprints?" I asked.

"Where?" He looked down and I could tell he saw nothing.

"This way," I ordered. I leapt to my feet and dashed down the trail, compelled to follow the prints into the dark heart of the forest. As I ran, I felt invigorated. A scent of blood overwhelmed me and made my mouth water. I ran faster and faster down the trail, leaving Oscar behind. I felt as though I too were a wolf and my prey was only a claw's length in front of me!

I entered a clearing and saw a vision. A dream – no, a nightmare – being replayed in front of me, through me! It was suddenly a moonlit night and a pretty young woman with ginger curls was cowering in fear at my feet. I was the beast and she my prey, and, oh, how powerful I felt! I was consumed with lust like I had never felt before. I lunged at her and a scream pierced the night and I had one delicious taste before Oscar burst into the clearing.

"My God, Stoker," he yelled. "Have you gone mad?"

I awoke from my trance and the daylight returned. I was hunched on all fours over a patch of grass that was matted and covered in blood. I had found the spot where she had been killed!

"You were growling like a dog and clawing at the ground," Oscar said with more than a bit of concern in his voice. "What has got into you?"

"What, indeed," I said, getting back up on my unsteady legs. My mind groped for a plausible explanation, but Oscar had seen too much. There was nothing for it but to tell him the truth. "I'm afraid you have witnessed some sort of spell, the nature of which I cannot explain."

"Has this happened to you before?" he asked.

"A few times when I was a child, first when I was eight years old. I saw what I thought was...."

"What?"

"You will laugh," I said, regretting saying anything in the first place.

"I will not. I promise."

"I saw a leprechaun," I confessed. "I was on a school picnic and there he was, plain as day, sitting under a toadstool. When he realised I could see him, he put his fingers to his lips as if to say *shhh*. And then he scurried off into the woods."

"How wonderful!" Oscar exclaimed. "Mother always told me leprechauns are real, and I believe most of what she says when she is sober."

"I have always chalked it up to a childhood fantasy," I said. "But then once, when I was much too old to believe in these things, I was deep in the woods and came across a beautiful pond. I sat down to read a book on its bank and looked up to see a ring of fairies circling my head."

This time he did laugh.

"Sorry, but I just pictured it. You with a halo of fairies! But I do believe you. After all, I just witnessed it myself – you were channelling the creature!" he exclaimed with glee. "I have seen this sort of thing at Mother's séances. You must have the gift of second sight!"

"It is a curse, not a gift," I said. I looked at the trampled ground in front of me, spattered with blood and gore. "This is where he attacked and killed her. I could see it as if it were happening at this very moment." I did not tell him that I *felt* him killing her, or that I, shamefully, enjoyed it while in the throes of the vision.

"Did you see anything else?"

"I did not. You broke the spell. Thank God."

"Try and visualise it again," he said.

"I have no control over it, and if I did I would not willingly bring it on!"

"Bram, you must try. Lives are at stake!"

Knowing he was right, I stared at the unholy ground and tried to let the surroundings envelop me.

"Is it working?" Oscar asked, peering into my face.

Through clenched teeth, I said, "Perhaps it would if you could manage to go a few minutes without hearing the sound of your own voice."

"Right, sorry," Oscar said, and backed off a few paces. I tried again to calm my mind and go where the infernal curse would take me.

Then I was in the vision once more. This time I was able to keep my wits about me and back away from the creature's feelings. This made the vision blurry around the edges, but I dared not fall into his depravity further. I – or rather, he – heard a noise and turned to see a man looking on with horror. The man turned and ran. The creature turned back to his prey, picking her up in limbs that were an amalgam of human arms and the hairy forelegs of a wolf, and loped off into the forest with her. Then I felt a shudder and saw that the arms holding the unconscious woman were fully human and the vision vanished once again. Perhaps I can only have a vision of the creature when it's a wolf. I nearly fainted and Oscar helped steady me.

"He was interrupted," I said. "By a man. But I didn't get a good look at his face." I did not mention to Oscar that I could, in fact, smell the man as the creature could. The memory of the man's scent burned into my brain as if the creature were storing it away for later recall.

"That man must have been Mrs. Goode's brother," Oscar said.

"Or the brother is the werewolf and he scared away another man," I countered.

Oscar looked troubled at this. Clearly, he had grown somewhat fond of Mrs. Goode and didn't relish the thought of the pain this would cause her. "What else did you see?" he asked.

"The monster took her deeper into the woods to…finish her off undisturbed. That is all I can recall."

"This is the start of our trail," Oscar said, looking down the path where the creature had crashed through the underbrush. "We must get the others and start the hunt from here."

As he turned to go, I stopped him with a hand on his shoulder. "Please, Oscar, do not tell anyone else about my visions."

He looked at me curiously. "But why ever not? You should be proud.…"

"I do not wish to be seen as a mental defective," I said, more hotly than I intended. I took a deep breath. "My headmaster took the strap to me for lying when I told him of seeing the leprechaun, and my schoolmates laughed at me for weeks. I do not know why these visions have plagued me so, but I do not wish to give them more credence. Promise me you will tell no one."

"All right, I promise. It will just be our little secret. I do so love keeping secrets." Oscar smiled, but I could see the concern on his face and turned away from it. As my eyes lingered for a moment on the spot where the beast had seen the horrified man, it suddenly struck me why the creature was storing the man's scent.

"Quickly, Oscar, we must find Mrs. Goode's brother. If he was the man witnessing the attack, I fear his life may be in danger!"

We returned to the pie shop where Mrs. Goode informed us that her brother, Danny Sharpe, lived on the family farm, not far from town. She was adamant about coming with us, but Oscar talked her out of it, saying that there were some things best discussed among men and assuring her that we hoped to help her brother.

Captain Burton had been kind enough to leave a pair of pistols for us at the inn, which we took with us for protection. However, as much as I would have liked to deny it, we now were surely dealing with some supernatural beast that ordinary bullets might not kill. What we would do when we found it, I did not know.

All was strangely quiet when we arrived at the farm. Not even the squawk of a chicken or lowing of a cow broke the unnatural silence. The tingle I feel before the onset of a vision was prickling my skin as we approached the house.

"Mr. Sharpe!" I yelled. "Do you have a moment? Your sister sent us to speak with you."

There was nothing but silence and we both looked about us uneasily.

"Are you sensing anything, Stoker?" Oscar whispered.

"No, but as it is broad daylight and not a full moon, the creature would be in human form, and I suspect that would make him harder to detect."

I did smell blood but was not sure if it was a clue, my imagination or just one of the smells normal to a farm.

I drew my pistol and Oscar fumbled through his pockets for his. For a moment, I suspected he had forgotten it, but he soon produced it from beneath his coat, almost dropping it in the process. He looked at me sheepishly, then gestured towards the house.

When we entered into the kitchen we saw Mr. Sharpe seated at the table. He was dead, his head thrown back with a large wound in it. On the table in front of him was a letter. A pistol lay on the floor under his right hand.

"Dear Lord!" Oscar exclaimed. He turned away and looked as though he might be sick.

I picked up the letter and read it aloud. "I am sorry for what I have done to that poor girl. May God have mercy on my soul."

"Well, there you have it," Oscar said, leaning against a wall. "Neatly wrapped up in a confession. Too neatly, I suspect." He pulled a silver flask from his waistcoat pocket and took a swig to steady himself before offering it to me.

I accepted and took a small swallow of gin. It went down smoothly but did nothing to ease the aching in my head. "Perhaps," I said, handing the flask back to Oscar. "But I am still not sure he wasn't the werewolf."

"Use your voodoo, Stoker. Can you see anything in this room?"

I stared at the dead man, trying to let the feeling come over me, but my head ached and I was weak still from the last vision. I breathed deeply, calming myself, and after a moment my external senses stilled and my inner sense – my demon sense? For that is what I begin to fear it is – awakened. The smell of the man filled my nostrils as it had done before. "I see nothing. But I am now certain this was the man I saw fleeing from the creature."

"How do you know? You said you didn't see his face. And even if you had," he said, gesturing to Mr. Sharpe's ruined features, "you would be hard-pressed to identify it here."

My eyes met Wilde's. "I am certain. You must take my word for it."

He nodded slowly. "I do. So, that means the werewolf, in human form, killed this man and falsified the confession."

"It would appear so. But can we convince the others? I do not want to tell them about my visions, and even if I did I doubt they would take them as true."

Oscar smiled slightly. "Have you learned nothing of my family?" he said. "But as you wish. Let us go. We need to tell Mrs. Goode of this tragic turn."

There you have it. I finish this entry in the hotel, waiting for the return of the others with a foreboding of what is yet to come. Should I not survive the hunt for this terrible beast and these be my final words, tell my family I love them. *Dia idir sinn agus an t-olc.* (God between us and the evil.)

LETTER FROM OSCAR WILDE TO FLORENCE BALCOMBE, 2ND OF NOVEMBER 1876

Archivist's note: Only text not covered in Stoker's journal entry is recorded here; unnecessary paragraphs have been eliminated.

My dearest Florrie,

As promised, this is the second letter relating the tale of the frightful mystery in which yours truly played an integral part. The most important part, really.

When we last left our story, Richard Burton, my brother Willie, Bram Stoker and I had just questioned the barman of an unsavoury pub in the fishing village of Greystones.

{Two pages already covered by Stoker's journal omitted.}

Our discovery of the point of attack in the forest turned out to be not as useful as I had hoped. Captain Burton and Willie returned at dusk, having followed the trail to a dead end.

"We tracked the beast to the beginning of town," Burton said. He sat down at a table in his room, and Isabel helped him pull off his boots. "But once the creature was on the cobblestone, there were no more tracks to follow. I spoke to the constable. He says he will let us use his dogs to continue the search tomorrow." A clap of thunder dashed all our hopes as it was followed by a burst of rain that would surely wash away any scent.

"I was worried about you, dear husband," Isabel said, giving him a heartfelt hug. "You're not a young man anymore. Perhaps we should leave the hunting to the townspeople."

This ruffled the captain's feathers a bit. "I daresay I'm better equipped to handle this creature than a bunch of shopkeepers and fishermen," he said.

Mother was looking out the window at the street below. "Perhaps he has fled town. That's what I would do if I were a werewolf," she said. "Wouldn't be smart to hang about until the next full moon." The rain continued to tap on the roof and we all listened to it quietly for a moment.

"I think we are going about this all wrong," Stoker said. "We are hunting the animal, but we should be hunting the man."

"The trail has gone cold there too," Burton said.

"He might not even know he turns into the monster," Willie pointed out. "Isn't that true, Mother?"

"Yes, it was described to me by the Gipsies as such. We must keep in mind the man is as much a victim as that poor girl. He is cursed and cannot help what he is."

Stoker's face grew pallid. He appeared for a moment to be in a trance. "No, he remembers," Stoker said.

"How can you be sure?" Burton asked.

Stoker seemed at a loss to explain.

"Surely he must suspect," I said. "He just happens to be in the same place someone is killed every full moon? I'd wager he wakes up naked and covered with blood. He must know, even if he blacks out."

"Ask yourself, what would you do if you suspected you were such a creature?" Stoker asked.

"I'd slit my own throat," Willie said. (Self-sacrificing to the hypothetical last, my brother.)

"At the very least I would chain myself up on the full moon," Isabel said.

"Exactly," Stoker said. "As would any decent person. This man does not and, in fact, has committed cold-blooded murder as a man in the hope of covering up his own crime. No, we are looking for a man who enjoys what he becomes. And is good at hiding his true nature."

"But just how does he do that?" I asked. "Wouldn't other people start to see the connection? The townspeople are going to be watching each other the next full moon, and anyone not accounted for is going to be a suspect."

"He must travel," Stoker said.

"Or he has only recently been bitten," Mother speculated.

Stoker smiled bitterly. "With all due respect, Lady Wilde," he said, "our killer seems far too organised to be a newly turned werewolf."

I suddenly had an epiphany. "He must be one of the sailors! If the other murder in Wexford is any indication, it must be someone who goes from port to port. A murder here, a murder there. Who would think to connect them?"

"Yes, by spreading the killings all over the world, there is less likely to be a pattern seen by the authorities," Burton said.

"A good theory," said Isabel. "But wouldn't there be deaths on the ship? How could a sailor be certain he wouldn't be out at sea during a full moon?" Isabel has quite a keen mind, though I appreciate it more when it is not puncturing one of my theories.

"True," I said. "There is no way a sailor has any control over where his captain...." At that moment, my brain caught up with my mouth, which it often never does. "Unless he *were* the captain!"

"The ship in the harbour wasn't supposed to be in Ireland two full moons in a row," Willie said. "Remember, the barkeep said the ship had to pull in here for repairs."

So, it was decided we should try to track down the captain of the *Demeter* and put a few questions to him – or a few bullets in him, should his lupine nature emerge.

"At least there is no full moon tonight," Mother said. "It will be easier to bring him in as a man than a wolf."

Burton loaded two of the pistols with his meagre ration of silver bullets. He handed one of the guns to Willie.

"Here now," I protested. "I happen to be an excellent marksman. Why would you give him the gun with the silver bullets?"

"Because you shot my dog," Burton said.

"I was ten!" I exclaimed. "And, apparently, I'm good at hitting canines. The wolf won't stand a chance."

He ignored my request. "Just make sure you hit him in the heart," Burton said to Willie, "as I am uncertain about the purity of the silver."

"What?" Willie asked.

"I melted down some candlesticks, wedding presents from my

cousin Cecil. I think they were pure silver, and probably have enough in any case."

"Perfect," Willie said. "I could be hunting a werewolf with pewter bullets."

"They're at least silver plate, surely," Isabel protested.

"All Bram and I have are lead bullets!" I said. "So, you'd better not miss!"

And with that, we were off to where we thought we'd be most likely to find a sailor: the pub.

As you'll remember, I thought the Blue Moon was a den of iniquity in the daytime. At night I cannot begin to describe the depravity! (Or rather, I expect I could describe it quite vividly, but would not in a letter to a lady. No, do not beg me so, your mother would never forgive me!)

Oh, all right, just a little.

Two more ships had arrived in port that day, and sailors and some of the less savoury townsfolk crowded the bar and every table. The room was so filled with smoke I could scarcely see my flask in front of my face as I took a drink to brace myself. A saucy, raven-haired barmaid was telling an off-colour joke to a group of patrons. I shan't reveal the punch line, but they all laughed uproariously and one of them patted her in a spot that wasn't her shoulder. Across the room, a dapper-looking gent neatly dipped his hand into a drunken sailor's pocket, then quickly slipped whatever he'd found there into his own.

Captain Burton pushed his way to the bar and talked with the landlord for a moment, as Bram, Willie and I hung back. I could not hear what he was saying over the noise of the rowdy patrons, but at one point he slipped the man a five-pound note.

Burton made his way back to us. Just in time too, for more sailors were pouring into the overcrowded room.

"He's playing cards in a room upstairs," Burton informed us. We threaded our way through to the stairs, which were clogged with more drunken sailors.

Captain Burton shouted, "Make room!" waving his arms – and his pistol – impatiently.

The crowd readily parted and Burton led the way up the stairs, followed by Stoker and me. Somewhere along the way, we lost Willie to the throng.

At the top of the stairs, Burton gestured down the dimly lit hall. "Around the corner to the left," he said, and Stoker and I flanked him as he led the way towards our brutal quarry. A clatter behind us made us all wheel about, weapons at the ready, but it was only Willie, who, having escaped the mass of sailors on the stair, stumbled as he cleared the last step, dropping his pistol onto the floor. Pulling himself up, he straightened his clothes, adjusted his hat and retrieved his gun. "Carry on," he said, gesturing us forward.

After we'd assembled ourselves into a suitably intimidating force outside the room in question, Burton threw the door open then immediately braced himself and sighted down the barrel of his pistol at the group of sailors around the table. Most dropped their cards, their eyes wide, but a few seemed more accustomed to having pistols pointed at them and stared back boldly.

"Don't move, you scurvy pirates!" Burton commanded. Such is the authority in his voice, when he chooses to employ it, that they obeyed. "We are here to speak with the captain of the *Demeter*."

A thin, bearded man facing us smiled a gap-toothed grin. With a jagged scar on his cheek and a wild mop of hair, he looked the part of a pirate and I daresay, should anyone ever decide to produce a biography of Blackbeard for the stage, he would make a convincing lead!

"I am Captain Abramoff. What can I do for you gentlemen?" he asked in perfect but accented English. He laid his cards down on the table. "Now that you have so rudely interrupted my game." He rolled his *R*'s as Russians often do.

"Where were you the night the girl was killed?" Burton asked, his gun now pointed straight at Abramoff.

"As I told the constable, I was on my ship. My crew can testify to that."

"Then you won't mind giving us a sample of your handwriting," Stoker said.

The captain looked puzzled for a moment.

"A man's handwriting is as recognisable as a leopard's spots," Burton added.

The captain's grin grew broader. "I would be happy to."

Then suddenly the table exploded upward, sending mugs, cards and coins flying. He flung it at us with such a force it pushed Burton and me back. A gun went off, blasting a hole in the ceiling. The sailors scattered and the captain leapt over the table with a speed and agility I can only describe as beastly!

Stoker grabbed him, but though he is certainly the largest and strongest of our lot, the captain threw him aside like he was a rag doll and bolted into the hall. Willie was close behind.

"Shoot him!" Burton ordered, as we clambered to our feet and dashed into the hall. Sailors dropped to the floor and covered their heads as Willie wildly tried to take aim.

Willie fired but missed, succeeding only in scattering plaster dust as his bullet added another hole to an already scarred wall. The captain disappeared around the corner, tossing a sailor into our path as he went. A door slammed as we followed, dodging the sailor. When we rounded the corner, he was nowhere to be seen. This part of the hallway was empty, with a closed door on either side.

"We'll take them one at a time," Burton whispered. "Oscar, open that door, and Willie, you take aim. Bram, this one shall be ours." He positioned himself in front of the door, his pistol held at the ready.

I crouched at my door and Stoker at his. I slowly and carefully turned the doorknob, holding my breath.

I flung my door open and Willie fired into the room.

"Willie, you fool!" Burton shouted. "Wait until you see the whites of his eyes!"

"Er, I'm out of bullets now," Willie said fearfully. Luckily, the beast was not in that room. Even more luckily, Willie had fired high, missing the sailor and the woman entertaining him! They cowered in fear under the bedclothes.

At his door, Burton shouted, "We have you trapped, Abramoff! Come out with your hands raised and you'll get a fair trial." We all held our breaths, listening. We heard laboured breathing and the sound of cloth ripping.

Boom! The door shattered into kindling, sending shards of wood flying into our faces. A snarling, furious beast charged out, knocking Burton away before he had a chance to get off a single shot. Burton hit the opposite wall and fell, unconscious.

The remnants of the ship captain's clothes hung from the beast's hips and shoulders and coarse dark fur covered him from head to foot – or should I say paw. Pointed ears stood up from its head and it rotated them as a dog might to catch every sound. An elongated wolf's snout had replaced the captain's leering grin, but his black eyes still glittered out of the monster's face. It stood upright like a man on two crooked legs and howled. The sound was deafening in the cramped hallway and the woman in the room behind us screamed, or perhaps that was Willie. Then the creature dropped to all fours and crept forward, growling menacingly as it backed Willie up against the wall. Willie trembled with fear.

We heard a sailor yell from down the hall, "Captain's loose again!" The rumble of a mass exodus sounded from the bar below, as seemingly every sailor in the pub poured out into the street, leaving us to fend for ourselves. Willie and I were too scared to move, fearing the slightest motion might provoke a killing blow. The beast was snarling and foaming at the mouth. I could smell its foul breath and its drool dripped onto Willie's shoes. Had he been in any condition to notice, I'm sure he would have been quite annoyed at the mess.

Then, from seemingly nowhere, Stoker appeared with a chair. He swung and smashed it across the creature's back. The beast broke off its advance on Willie and wheeled to face Stoker.

As its red-rimmed eyes met Stoker's, it froze with what I swear was the same puzzled look I had seen on the captain's human face just minutes before. It seemed to be thinking, plotting its next move.

"Back!" Stoker yelled, holding a broken chair leg over his head like a club.

I was certain the werewolf would rear back and pounce on Stoker, but instead, it tucked its tail between its legs and slowly backed away. It seemed to be afraid, like a dog whose master was scolding him and was about to strike him with a switch.

From the corner of my eye, I could see that Burton had regained consciousness and was struggling to his feet. He raised his pistol as he stumbled forward.

"Step aside, Bram!" he said, and as Stoker did so, the wolf dodged and Burton fired, hitting the creature in the shoulder. It yelped, turned and ran down the hallway at an unnaturally fast sprint.

It crashed through the window just as Burton got off another shot. His bullet hit the sill, missing the creature by no more than an inch.

As this point, Willie fainted, hitting the ground like a sack of potatoes.

"Let's go after it!" Stoker shouted.

"There are lanterns in these rooms, grab them," Burton said. "He won't get far. And he'll be leaving a trail of blood to boot."

"How are we doing for ammunition?" I asked, helping Willie to his feet. He had smashed his nose in the fall. It was bloodied but not broken and I held my handkerchief to it to staunch the bleeding.

"I have four bullets left, but not to worry," Burton said. "It only takes one to the heart to finish him off."

"Hmm, yes," I muttered. "Pity one to the shoulder and three to the wall wouldn't do the trick."

"Give us a drink, Oscar," Willie pleaded. I reluctantly gave Willie my flask and he greedily drank the rest of my gin.

By the time we exited the pub, the creature had already disappeared into the woods. Stoker led the way into the dark forest, which grew even darker when the moon became shrouded by clouds. Our lanterns did not offer much light or comfort.

Stoker forged on as if he were a hound who had caught a scent.

I must end here, dear Florrie, but a third letter will follow soon!

Archivist's note: A third letter mentioned by Wilde pertaining to the hunt was never found. See next entry.

FROM THE NOTES OF SIR RICHARD BURTON, DATE UNKNOWN

Archivist's note: Isabel Burton donated these notes to the White Worm Society in her will and they were added to our collection upon her death in 1896. They appear to be notes for a longer memoir that was never written. An excerpt is included here to fill in missing material pertaining to the Greystones hunt of 29th of October 1876 that is covered by neither Stoker nor Wilde.

The Night of the Werewolf!

I have hunted in the dense jungles of India and the scorching deserts of Arabia, but nothing prepared me for the hunt of my life in a tiny forest in Ireland!

The Queen herself had dispatched me to hunt down a terrible creature that had been terrorising the fishing village of Greystones, Ireland.

My hunting party consisted of William and Oscar Wilde and Bram Stoker. We determined straight away that the creature was a werewolf. And, through brilliant deduction on our part, we had further ascertained that it had come in on a Russian schooner. The creature's human form was no less than the captain of the ship himself!

Who knows how many natives it had killed on its trips around the globe? Nor did we have any way of knowing how the man came to be cursed thusly. I am told the bite of a werewolf is all it takes, so it is a wonder we aren't knee-deep in the things – a werewolf plague, as it were – for biting is surely one of the things they do best. However, it seems the werewolf seldom inflicts a wound that isn't fatal, so perhaps that is what keeps their numbers down.

We confronted the captain at the local pub, hoping to capture him in his human form. But alas, unbeknownst to us at the time, some werewolves can change at will. This was one such creature. He transformed into a wolf quickly and I managed to wound it with a silver bullet to the shoulder, but it escaped into the darkness.

So, there we were on a cold Irish night, in the forest, hunting a wounded monster. We had no dogs, and only four silver bullets in two pistols. I was sceptical we could follow the blood trail in the dark, but as it turns out Bram Stoker was a natural-born tracker. I had never seen a white man with such skill. By only lantern light he was able to see wolf tracks and droplets of blood. We followed him, and he was so focused it was as if he were in a trance, similar to what I have seen in the eyes of Indian trackers in Punjab.

The trail led us out of the woods and to a farm. A dog began to howl somewhere in a farmhouse far down the road – a long, agonised wailing, as if from fear. The sound was taken up by another dog, and then another and another until, borne on the softly sighing wind, a wild howling began. It seemed to come from all over the country, as far as the imagination could grasp it through the gloom of the night.

I stepped over the bloody remnant of a goat's head.

"It has fed," I told the others quietly. "Maybe it will be more docile."

"I wouldn't count on it," Stoker whispered. "Perhaps it fed because it needed strength to heal."

There was no light from the farmhouse. That meant the owners were either not home or dead. Or I suppose they may have been sleeping. Farm folk are early risers after all. In any case, it was dark.

A horse in the barn whinnied and snorted in what sounded like fear.

"He's in the barn," Stoker said.

"Bram, you and I will go in through the front. Willie and Oscar, see if there is a back entrance. And for God's sake, remember you only have two silver bullets. Make them count." Willie nodded and he and Oscar went off to the back of the barn.

I set down the lantern to make myself a less obvious target and entered through the double doors, which were open slightly. Only moonlight from the loft window illuminated the interior. It was dark and, damn my old eyes, I could barely see a thing.

"Do you see him?" I whispered.

"No," Bram said. He froze in his tracks. "I'm not sure he is in here any longer."

Before I could ask him why he thought that, a whooshing sound cut the night. Bram took the full force of a shovel to the stomach and was thrown backwards by the blow. I saw a shape run by in the shadows. He was in the form of a man now! I took aim at the naked man but he disappeared in the pervasive darkness and I dared not waste a bullet.

I turned to check on Bram, a foolish thing to do I know now. The man must retain some of the beast's supernatural speed, for suddenly a pitchfork pierced my leg with incredible force! I fell to one knee, pivoted around and fired into the darkness. I did not hit him, but it was enough to keep him from advancing on us.

Willie and Oscar rushed from the back of the barn with guns drawn. "He's in human form!" I shouted.

We could hear his footsteps running away from us and Oscar fired his pistol towards the sound. We could hear our quarry scurrying up the ladder and into the loft.

Willie came to my aid. Bram was getting to his feet, holding his midsection.

"Leave me," I ordered. I handed Bram my pistol, with its one remaining silver bullet. "I'll be all right. Finish the bastard off."

A pair of red eyes pierced the darkness of the loft. The creature snarled and growled in pain as he once more transformed into a wolf.

Stoker took aim and fired up into the loft, but his angle was all wrong and it went high.

"Damn!" He tossed my empty pistol down and pulled out his own. Willie was trying to aim. "Where is it? I don't see it!"

The wolf leapt out of the loft and Willie fired, missing it. The creature landed on all fours near us. Stoker shot it several times, but the ordinary lead bullets bounced off it as if it had an elephant's hide.

Willie, trembling, aimed at the creature. So, there he stood, terrified, certainly, well aware he had but one more bullet with which to kill the beast, but he bravely stood his ground, awaiting the proper moment to fire.

Oscar threw his lantern at the beast, smashing it onto its back. This proved to be a smart move, as it did momentarily catch the creature on fire. (I do not know, specifically, if fire would kill a werewolf, but then fire kills most things.)

The wolf then did a remarkable thing. It laughed. A deep, guttural sound, but it was recognisable as a laugh. It stood up straighter on its crooked back legs and shook out the flames as if it were a dog shaking off an unwanted bath.

It was then I saw its front paws were more like deformed hands, something you might see on an ape. Willie stepped forwards to shoot, but the beast jumped at him and grabbed the barrel of the gun, yanking it from his hands. It flung the gun with such force that it smashed against the wall of the barn into pieces. It backhanded Willie, striking him to the ground.

Bram charged the creature, but it simply grabbed him by the throat and held him up as if he were a rabbit. Bram pounded on the beast with his fists and kicked at it wildly, but it held its grasp firmly. He turned Bram this way and that and sniffed him. I was sure its next move would be to bite off Bram's head!

But then it spoke! A raspy, almost unintelligible voice asked, "What are you?" It snarled and leant in closer, sniffing at Stoker. "I was wrong to be scared of you. You are weak like a human, but you smell like… something else. What bewitchment is this?"

While it was preoccupied with tormenting Bram, Oscar had snuck up behind it. I saw the glint of something shiny in his hand. It was his silver flask. In one swift move, he pushed the flask against the middle of the creature's back, put his pistol up to it and shot through the flask!

The bullet must have forced a piece of silver into the creature. It dropped Bram and howled in horrible pain. It whirled around and took a swing at Oscar, but he had already backed away out of its reach.

It dropped to all fours, gasping and choking. Blood and foam came from its jaws. It rolled onto its side and fell silent.

Then an incredible transformation took place. We watched as it turned back into a human being! Where there had once been a powerful wolf, now there was a frail, naked man. He was still living, for his chest moved with breath and his eyes slowly opened. They held a look of defiance.

Bram bent down before it. "This curse that has afflicted you is gone. May God have mercy on your soul."

The man laughed and said, "Whatever you have, perhaps that is a curse. My wolf…this was a gift." He choked and blood came to his lips as he breathed his terminal breath.

I returned to England and reported to the Queen herself that the creature had been put down. Had I known then it was a portent of horrible things to come, I would have never gone off to India and left England unprotected from supernatural forces. Fortunately, my companions on that fateful hunt were there to take up the mantle as defenders of the Empire.

LETTER FROM DR. VICTOR MUELLER TO LORD ALFRED SUNDRY, 5TH OF NOVEMBER 1876

Archivist's note: Several letters were found hidden in the secret compartment of a desk purchased from Lord Sundry's estate after his disappearance in 1880. Some letters were written in code, which we quickly deciphered using Babbage's Difference Engine number 3.

Dear Lord Sundry,

I regret to notify you of Captain Abramoff's demise. It was beyond my control, I assure you. Please inform the Bishop and offer him my sincere apologies for the delay this will cause.

As you know, it took me years to track Abramoff and months of planning to become part of his crew. I grew to be his friend and confidant and was well situated to abduct him as soon as we reached a port that would be convenient for our purposes.

However, before we reached such a locale, the ship had to pull into an Irish harbour for repairs. He became careless, and after he killed a barmaid his true nature was discovered. He was hunted down and killed by Captain Richard Burton and his men.

This is a setback to be sure, but I am optimistic I can obtain another specimen. Abramoff himself told me there were others of his kind in Romania.

I witnessed one of the men accompanying Burton ward off an attack by Abramoff, which is no small feat. From his signature in the guest book at the local inn, I have ascertained that he is Abraham Stoker. Has not Stoker's name come up before in our research? Perhaps it is a just a coincidence that Stoker was a member of the hunting party, but it seems unlikely a man with his gifts would have been chosen at random by Burton.

I will investigate Stoker further, as it will be a profitable use of my time until I can secure passage to Romania. There I shall begin my hunt anew.

I give my word to the Black Bishop that I will do my utmost to bag him a live werewolf, unharmed. However, as you know, a hunt like this could take several years. I am fully aware that we are on a strict timetable, and that the door closes on Saint George's Day, 1880.

I am confident I will be able to fulfil the Bishop's request long before then.

Sincerely,

Dr. Victor Mueller

LETTER FROM LUCY MAYHEW TO FLORENCE BALCOMBE, 22ND OF MAY 1877

Archivist's note: Victorians would often write letters back and forth throughout the day. For a ha'penny, a child would deliver a letter and sit outside waiting for a reply. In this way, an entire conversation could be conducted almost in real time. The exchange below is here because of the importance of Florence Balcombe and Lucy Mayhew to the Black Bishop events to follow.

My dearest Florence,

It is with trepidation and a heavy heart that I must impart some information I have come across in this past week. As you know, I am not one to listen to or pass along gossip. However, my affection for you is stronger than this aversion and so I must tell you that I have heard from a reliable source that your betrothed's family is facing calamitous financial difficulties. As such, Oscar may not be able to provide you the lifestyle you deserve.

From what I am told, after Dr. Wilde's scandal and subsequent death, Lady Wilde's fortunes have continued to decline. She is now so destitute she is selling off the household silver, furniture and paintings. In fact, a cousin of mine has just purchased a painting by George Whistler for, as he put it, 'a song'. And from what I gather about town, the Wildes owe every shopkeeper so much they no longer have any credit available to them. I fear your Oscar may be heading to the poorhouse before he heads down the wedding aisle.

I tell you this only for your own good, as I do not want you, my dearest friend, to be dragged down with him. You have always been like an older sister to me and I could not live with myself should this marriage lead to your ruin.

As always, your friend,

Lucy

LETTER FROM FLORENCE BALCOMBE TO LUCY MAYHEW, 22ND OF MAY 1877

My dear, dear Lucy,

Thank you for your concern regarding my future happiness with Oscar. I am aware of his financial situation and, while it does cause me some apprehension, I feel our love will overcome such obstacles.

Furthermore, I feel he has great potential to be a good provider through his artistic endeavours. I know that stands to be seen, but I have read his writing and find him to be as brilliant and insightful as he is witty. And while his passion is for more intellectual pursuits, he also has a talent for popular storytelling. Why, just for my amusement, he once conjured the most engrossing supernatural tale you can imagine! At the very least he could make a living as a writer of penny dreadfuls (though I doubt it will come to that).

My father, at first, did not approve and threatened to withhold my dowry. He feared Oscar was no more than a rapscallion trying to get his hands on Father's military pension. But upon meeting Oscar, Father was as charmed by him as I am and has since given his blessing.

Being my oldest and dearest friend, you know of my dream of being an actress upon the stage. Oscar has written scenes for me and has coached me in my acting. Together I think we can live the lives of vagabond artists, perhaps poor in material possessions but rich in our love and fulfilled by our art.

Again, thank you greatly for looking out for my interests. I am, as always, grateful beyond measure for your friendship.

With love,

Florence

P.S. Who is that gentleman I have seen escorting you about town? He is quite distinguished.

LETTER FROM LUCY MAYHEW TO FLORENCE BALCOMBE, 22ND OF MAY 1877

My dearest Florence,

The gentleman you have seen escorting me on occasion is Robert Roosevelt. He is a congressman from America and a recent widower who is in Dublin to attend to trade business. I am showing him the city as a favour to my father.

I do find him charming for an American, and he has spoken of his fondness for me. However, I must put such gossip in its place, as there is nothing but friendship between us. The death of his wife is too fresh in his heart, and his stay in Dublin is but brief as he is off to London soon.

Though, as fate would have it, my Aunt Agatha has invited me to stay with her in London, so perhaps I shall see him while I am there.

As always, your friend,

Lucy

FROM THE JOURNAL OF BRAM STOKER, 17TH OF DECEMBER 1877

5:03 a.m.

I had another dream last night, about that terrible weekend in Greystones. Though it has been over a year since I last was stricken with my 'second sight', I am in constant apprehension it will return.

The dream would be a nightmare for any decent person. I am a wolf lost in pure, primal violence. I tear into flesh, lapping up blood and taking joy in the scream of my victim. I wake up laughing and euphoric, which quickly turns to shame as I return to myself.

The words of the werewolf still ring in my ears. *"What are you?"* It is a good question.

Since my 'awakening' at Greystones, I find it ever more difficult to keep to the righteous path and have fallen to the darker things in life. I have been carousing with the other clerks far too frequently, and now I find myself going to the theatre almost nightly. I have convinced myself theatre is ultimately good as most, if not all, plays have a moral message at their centre. However, this preoccupation with frivolity is causing my duties to suffer, and if I aspire to rise above Petty Sessions Clerk Inspector I would do well to focus on more sober, industrious pursuits.

My recent activities also leave me with no time for writing my poetry or stories. A letter came the other day from Walt Whitman in America. He continues to encourage my writing, for which I am humbly grateful, though I fear I will disappoint my mentor with my feeble attempts at art.

Instead, I spend my nights writing theatre reviews for the *Dublin Mail* (for which I receive no payment, not even the cost of a ticket), and – too infrequently – working on my manual of petty sessions clerk duties, which I have already promised to a publisher. The editor grows impatient and I fear that I may lose that interest if I do not finish it soon.

And yet tonight nothing could keep me away from the theatre, as the great Henry Irving will be performing *Hamlet*. I eagerly await Irving's every visit to Dublin and I shall spend the day in anticipation of tonight's performance.

11:06 p.m.

Mr. Irving's *Hamlet* fulfilled my every expectation. I was mesmerised by his performance, as was the rest of the audience. When he takes the stage, the limelight seems to ignite a fire in him. His presence and command of the dialogue are stunning. Shakespeare's words are brought to life like I have never seen before and I feel as though I have been offered a glimpse into Hamlet's soul.

I have been greatly impressed by Mr. Irving before, but his Hamlet surpasses any of his previous roles. He is not a robust or handsome man; he has sharp features and a thin frame, and appeared frail, despite his young age (in his forties, I would think). However, once the words started to flow out of him, he projected the strength and vitality of a man twice his size.

I find myself inspired. Dare I dream of casting off the daily grind of the clerk's life and working in the theatre one day myself? Not as an actor, surely, but perhaps as a director or writer. To help bring stories to life for enraptured audiences – what an adventure that would be!

Likely this is nought but a foolish dream, which will be forgotten tomorrow as I attend to my usual duties.

FROM THE JOURNAL OF BRAM STOKER, 20TH OF DECEMBER 1877

12:13 p.m.

Just as I have given notice to the *Dublin Mail* that I will no longer be available to write reviews, the theatre life comes knocking on my very door. Henry Irving himself, having read my favourable review of his performance, has invited me to take dinner with him at the Shelbourne Hotel!

He writes, *I have read many reviews, both praising and condemning my performances, and I have to say, Mr. Stoker, you alone have articulated the realism I try to bring to acting.*

I am beside myself with pride, which I know cometh before a fall, yet I cannot say no to meeting such an enormous talent. I have sent a reply that I accept his invitation. Now, as I write this, my hand shakes. I am anxious about our dinner conversation. What could I possibly say that would interest such a man of the world? I think back to my dinner with Richard Burton, where I fear I almost put him to sleep with my banality.

As I fret about this I fall further behind in my duties, writing and social obligations. Christmas is but days away and I have not yet shopped for gifts for my family or friends. Nervous anticipation preoccupies my mind and I cannot sleep.

LETTER FROM DR. (WILLIAM) THORNLEY STOKER TO BRAM STOKER, 27TH OF DECEMBER 1877

Dear brother,

Thanks once again for the oranges, very delicious. My cook is candying the peels as I write this.

I enjoyed seeing you at Christmas dinner and am sorry I was called away so suddenly. I would have loved to hear more about your adventures in the theatre. But such is the life of a local doctor.

A harrowing Christmas night that was for my young patient. She was found unconscious just off Baggot Street. Her throat had been punctured and she had lost much blood; however, we were able to save her and she is doing well. We gave her a blood transfusion. A new technique is making them much more successful, as she can attest to. The new theory is that there are different types of blood distributed among the population and matching up the right type from person to person is the key to success.

The poor thing cannot recollect who attacked her. It was gruesome – she had been stabbed in the throat with an ice pick or awl. Who would do such a thing? The streets of Dublin are becoming increasingly unsafe. Too many foreigners about if you ask me.

But enough of this dark subject. Happy New Year, brother, and I hope all is well with you.

Best regards,

Thornley

P.S. I heard from Willie Wilde that his brother Oscar is engaged, and she is a great beauty at that. Glad to hear that wild Wilde boy is settling down.

LETTER FROM DR. MUELLER TO LORD ALFRED SUNDRY, 28TH OF APRIL 1878

Dear Lord Sundry,

I have word that the mummy you purchased from the collector in Cairo has shipped. It is quite a perfect specimen and will be accompanied by its well-preserved organs in clay jars.

See bill of sale for £50. The shipping costs are around £60 and will need to be paid on delivery, which I expect to take no more than eight days.

I hope it serves your purpose and once again offer my apologies for not as yet procuring you a werewolf. I continue the search, as do my agents abroad.

I have returned to Dublin to keep an eye on Mr. Stoker as you requested. You were right to be concerned. Irving is here and up to his old tricks.

Yesterday I covertly followed him and he, in turn, was covertly following Stoker. Curious, is it not? It is even more curious, knowing that Stoker was a member of the party that killed our werewolf. Does Stoker know his true nature, and is he actively trying to thwart your plans?

Count Ruthven arrives in a fortnight and will use his special skills to investigate the matter further.

Sincerely,

Dr. Mueller

LETTER FROM LORD ALFRED SUNDRY TO DR. MUELLER, 6TH OF MAY 1878

Archivist's note: On the 2nd of June 1880, the White Worm Society and the Queen's Guard raided Dr. Mueller's Edinburgh laboratory, only to find that he had fled the country. This letter was found among his papers left behind.

Dr. Mueller,

It is indeed troubling that Irving is making contact with Stoker at this time. We run the risk of missing our window of opportunity should Irving reveal Stoker's destiny too soon.

By all means, discreetly investigate Irving and Stoker. I am a bit concerned that Ruthven is tasked with this, however. In the past, he has shown little restraint in his methods. Make it clear to him that the Black Bishop would be most displeased should any harm come to Stoker or if our plans are exposed in any way.

Lord Sundry

FROM THE JOURNAL OF BRAM STOKER, 1ST OF JUNE 1878

2:00 a.m.

I scarcely know where to begin this entry, so much has happened tonight. It is the small hours of the morning and, were I sensible, I would go to bed and delay any attempt to record this evening's events until I've rested, when I shall surely be more coherent. But I am certain I shall not be able to sleep. Thoughts are spinning through my brain like dervishes and perhaps by writing them down I can quiet my restless mind.

I attended a party tonight celebrating the engagement of Oscar Wilde to Miss Florence Balcombe. I had heard about the engagement but, knowing Oscar, had assumed that it would end – most likely with an overly dramatic speech from him and tears on the poor girl's part – long before it reached the stage when caterers would become involved. But people will insist on surprising one, and the appointed hour approached with no last-minute cancellation.

I arrived at the Wilde residence unfashionably on time, as is my habit, try as I might to convince myself that a later entrance would present a more advantageous appearance. Lady Wilde greeted me warmly and pointed me in the direction of Willie and Oscar, who were indulging in glasses of champagne, I am sure not their first of the evening.

"Stoker!" Oscar exclaimed as I approached. "My brother-in-arms. How good of you to come. Werewolves and other creatures of the night will surely fear to menace our guests now that we three mighty hunters are reunited. Ah, if only Captain Burton were here."

I looked around, alarmed, but nobody was near enough to hear. "Oscar, I wouldn't for the world miss the opportunity to meet this unfortunate girl you have surely tricked into marrying you. Congratulations, by the way," I added, shaking his hand before accepting a glass of champagne from a passing waiter.

Oscar grinned. "You are right, Stoker, I see no reason why she would want me, and yet she does. And I shall be eternally grateful for it. To love!"

I couldn't help but smile as Willie and I joined him in his toast. He seemed so genuinely happy and in love that I would have scarcely recognised him if not for the pomposity.

The evening progressed and more guests packed the house, making it uncomfortably crowded and boisterously noisy. The bride-to-be had not yet made her entrance, which I supposed was customary at these things.

The food and drink flowed copiously. I would not have thought they could afford to host such an event, but Willie had confided in me earlier that his half brother, Henry, had died and left them some money. Up until that point I had no idea there was a half brother Henry. I had heard through others there were two half sisters who were tragically killed in a fire, but not one mention of this brotherly benefactor. I suspected that he, like the sisters, was illegitimate and therefore an embarrassment to the Wilde name.

I mingled with the other guests for some while until I noticed Lady Wilde greeting a familiar figure: Henry Irving! I knew he was back in Dublin, of course, and he and I have already arranged to meet for supper after his Tuesday night performance in *Henry V*. I was not aware, however, that he knew the Wildes. I made my way over, hoping not to appear over-eager.

I need not have feared for he greeted me with genuine enthusiasm. "Bram!" he cried, clasping my hand. "How good to see you! Lady Wilde told me you'd be here."

"She said not a word to me," I said, glancing in her direction. She beamed.

"I was keeping it as a surprise," she said. "I met Mr. Irving last week, and was instantly charmed, of course." She smiled at Henry. "I knew the two of you were acquainted and lured him to my party with the promise that he would know at least one other person here."

She excused herself to attend to her duties as hostess and it was on me to keep Mr. Irving entertained. I was scarcely up to the challenge. Not being well-suited for small talk, I did my best discussing the news of the day and books I have read. There were many lulls in the conversation, however, and I became increasingly anxious that I was not equipped to entertain someone who entertained others for a living. I finally said as much.

"Nonsense," he said. "You are quite pleasant company. I find you a remarkable fellow, Bram. Quite frankly, I get a bit tired of always having to perform in public, even when I am not on the stage."

Willie pushed his way through the crowd with two glasses of wine. He nearly sloshed us as he rammed into me.

"Quite the crowd," he yelled over the din. "You both look like you could use a drink."

I took a glass just to keep it from spilling on Mr. Irving.

"No, thank you," Irving said. "I never drink wine. Dulls the senses."

"Really? I suppose I've had too much wine to notice," Willie said, downing the other glass in one gulp. "So, Mr. Irving, you're an actor?" Not for the first time I wondered why I bothered to associate with him.

Irving smiled. "I dabble," he said.

"My brother writes plays," Willie said, depositing his glass with a passing servant and taking another. "Some are almost good. Bram here is a writer as well. Not just theatre reviews. He has had some stories published."

"Is that so?" Irving asked. He looked at me to elaborate.

"Just some melodrama written for local magazines," I answered.

"He's being humble," Willie said. "He's working on a book. Already has a publisher for it."

I was mortified. I had specifically asked him not to talk about the book – a book that had filled me with terror these many nights as my deadline looms.

"H-hardly a book," I stammered. "I mean it's not for a general audience. It is a procedures manual for clerks. That is my current occupation. Petty sessions clerk."

"It's going to be used across the Empire to train clerks," Willie said. "You should see how this man runs an office and manages files. He's brilliant!" I wasn't sure if he was making fun of me or genuinely trying to brag me up to Irving.

"Is that so?" Irving's eyes lit up. "I've been looking for someone to manage my theatre in London."

Willie jabbed his finger at me. "This, this is your man!" His speech was slightly slurred. "He loves the theatre and is a stern taskmaster. Why, he cut the staff in half at Dublin Castle just through his efficiencies. Got a medal for that, he did."

I was both annoyed and touched by Willie's praise. I knew then he was trying to be a good friend, but it was unfortunate that it took drink to bring it out.

Willie seemed suddenly to remember something, took out his pocket watch and looked at it through squinting eyes. "Ah, speaking of theatre, it's time for the leading lady's entrance. I must find Oscar."

And with that, he disappeared back into the crowd.

"I am quite serious, Bram. I would like you to come and work for me in London."

I was stunned. "I am flattered by the offer, Mr. Irving, but urge you to take some time to consider. I am not certain that I am worthy of such a position."

"Nonsense. It takes a special kind of temperament to manage a theatre troupe; one must have a head for detail and a degree of business acumen, but it helps to also have a passion for the art form. I know you well enough to see you have just such a nature. Come to London with me, Bram. I'll pay you twenty pounds a week."

As I am making eight pounds a week as a clerk, and have thought that a rather nice sum, twenty sounded like a king's ransom. Could I possibly provide value for such a salary? I felt he was making an offer he might come to regret, and tried to say so, but he interrupted before I could get out more than, "I couldn't possibly—"

"All right, twenty-two. You drive a hard bargain. Further proof that you're just the man I need overseeing my affairs!"

Before I could even truly comprehend the idea, Lady Wilde appeared at the top of the stairs and rang a bell to get everyone's attention. The crowd became quiet, with still a rumble of anticipation and echoing gossip.

"My dear friends, I am so pleased that you have joined us here tonight to celebrate this happy occasion. My dear son Oscar is a lucky man indeed, as you will all soon see. With that, may I present my future daughter-in-law, Miss Florence Balcombe."

The crowd fell even more silent as she appeared at the top of the stairs. It was the first time my eyes beheld her, and they were rewarded with a sight of exquisite beauty, and a warm, tender smile that surely signified a soul equally as lovely. The crowd gasped at her beauty, or perhaps that was only me. She seemed a woman who could inspire daring acts of bravery or passionate lines of verse. The candlelight and gaslight radiated more brilliantly in her presence. She was resplendent in a green and white gown, and as she descended the staircase her soft auburn hair framed her angelic face, and her green eyes lit up the whole room. It was as though she had stepped out from a master's oil painting or had broken free from a sculptor's block of translucent marble. Surely Oscar Wilde could not have captured this beautiful creature's heart. Knowing the family, I would suspect Lady Wilde had hired a witch to cast a love spell.

And then, suddenly, there he was, Oscar, pushing his way through the crowd to meet her. He joined her several steps from the bottom and took her hand. A jealousy I had no right to feel rose within me as I saw her smile warmly at her fiancé.

Willie grabbed a glass of champagne and flicked it twice with his finger to make it ring.

"A toast to my brother and his fiancée." The crowd raised their glasses. "Here's to their health, peace and prosperity. May the flower of their love never be nipped by the frost of disappointment, nor the shadow of grief fall among their family and friends."

Many gave a 'hear, hear', and drank their toasts down with great enthusiasm.

Giving his brother a thankful nod, Oscar raised his glass and declaimed, "A woman begins by resisting a man's advances and ends by blocking his retreat." The crowd chortled at his witticism (which I'm sure I have heard somewhere before, but Oscar offered no source for the quotation, so perhaps he wrote it himself).

He continued, "I know many of you thought this day would never come and are still thinking it a dream." He gazed at Miss Balcombe tenderly. "And I say yes, it is a dream, a wonderful dream that I hope never to wake from." He raised his glass. "To my lovely Florence, whose smile shines upon me as the sun shines upon the barren moon." He kissed her hand and the ladies in the room cooed from the romance of it.

"The wedding will be in September, and I hope you all can attend,"

Oscar added. "For tonight, please follow my example: eat, drink and be merry!"

"He does know how to work an audience," Irving remarked, startling me. I had forgotten he was there, had forgotten anyone was there save for the auburn-haired goddess on the stairs and the fortunate man who stood where I felt I might give anything to stand.

"Yes," I replied, my voice emerging in a choked whisper. I cleared my throat. "He has ever been so." Irving deftly nabbed a glass of wine from the tray of a passing waiter and handed it to me with a curiously sympathetic smile. I accepted gratefully and forced myself to sip rather than gulp.

Willie made his way back to Irving and me. "Well, that went off splendidly, and my official duties are done, save for ensuring no one drinks so much he'll embarrass himself. Rather like putting the fox in charge of the henhouse, that. In any case, can you believe it? Oscar settling down right at the peak of his debauchery? Whatever is he thinking?"

"She is quite striking," Irving said.

"Her father's in the military, a colonel, I think," Willie said, watching Miss Balcombe and Oscar mingling. "Not a penny to her name, of course, so I don't think she'll keep Oscar in the life to which he would like to grow accustomed."

"Perhaps it is love then," I said.

"Must be," Willie said. "Or perhaps he loves the idea of her as if she is a poem or piece of art he can collect."

"It sounds as if you two bachelors are jaded at the very notion of love," Irving said. "Or perhaps it is jealousy?" I glanced at him sharply. His smile was knowing, but not unkind, and he gave me a quick pat on the shoulder.

Oscar was dragging Miss Balcombe through the crowd, making introductions, and they were coming our way.

"I've been jealous of my brother his whole life," Willie admitted. "He's one of those people that have all the best things fall into his lap. Not his fault, I suppose, but it does grow tiresome to watch him succeed with such little effort."

"Perhaps he only makes it seem effortless," Irving mused.

It was finally our turn to meet the bride-to-be. I found myself all a-flutter, like a schoolboy approaching a girl at his first dance.

"My darling Florence, may I present the actor Henry Irving, and Willie's school chum, Bram Stoker."

Mr. Irving took her hand and kissed it lightly, with a graceful panache that caused her to blush. I myself thought I might swoon at the sight of that blush, which would have been a ridiculous consequence of a kiss in which I did not even take part.

"It is a pleasure to meet you, Mr. Irving," she said. "I have seen you perform several times and always eagerly await your visits to Dublin."

"It is my pleasure to entertain you," he said, releasing her hand.

"Florence has ambitions to the stage herself," Oscar said. "I am tutoring her in acting, and I must say she is coming along nicely."

"You would look lovely under the limelight, my dear," Irving said, and was rewarded with an excited smile.

She seemed about to pursue this line of conversation with Mr. Irving but thought better of it and turned to me. "And Mr. Stoker, Oscar speaks highly of you."

"Really?" I was surprised to hear this, of course, and wondered if perhaps his remarks had been sarcastic and she too innocent to notice.

"Oh, yes. He has even written you as a character in one of his fanciful tales. A fearless hunter of werewolves. It is a very invigorating story, despite the lurid subject matter."

"Is that so?" I shot Oscar a look I hoped would burn through his forehead. He smiled back at me blandly. "I had no idea Oscar held me in such regard."

"And yet," Willie said, "I bet Oscar himself was the hero of the tale."

"Naturally," said Oscar. "Aren't we all the heroes of our own stories? Who would cast himself as Polonius if the role of Hamlet were open?" he added, with a nod towards Irving.

"They both end up dead by play's end," retorted Willie. "I'd far rather be Oberon."

With that, Oscar bade us farewell and yanked Miss Balcombe back into the crowd for more introductions. The poor creature was beginning to show signs of exhaustion from all the attention.

Lady Wilde made her way over to us, accompanied by an odd-looking young man. He was very thin and tall with a pale, feminine face. At first, I thought him to be a woman in man's clothes, such as one may see in a burlesque show. She introduced him as Count Ruthven.

"It is a pleasure to make your acquaintance," he said in a thick, unidentifiable accent. He was drenched in some dreadful cologne that was so sickly sweet it turned my stomach.

"Count Ruthven and I have corresponded for several years. He knows a great deal about the supernatural in Eastern European culture and has been generous in sharing this knowledge. He is currently on an around-the-world tour," Lady Wilde explained.

"Is that so?" Irving asked. "How exciting. I love to travel. Where have you been so far?"

"Italy, Greece, Spain and Portugal," he said. "It was getting dreadfully hot there and I thought I would head north for some more refreshing air."

"You've come to the right place," Willie said. "You can get chilled to the bone even in August here."

"I am quite used to the cold as my home is in the mountains," he said. "I took a ship here from Portugal and we hit a terrible storm…"

I suddenly went totally deaf from a ringing in my ears.

I began to feel dizzy. At first, I thought it was from the smell of the count's perfume, perhaps combined with too much drink. But then I knew it was another of my spells. It had been nearly two years since I'd had one, and I had all but forgotten the sensation.

As Ruthven spoke about his sea voyage, he gestured with his hands, and an ever so faint green light came off his fingertips like smoke off a cigarette. His breath smelled of rotting meat, overpowering the cologne. My heart pounded and blood rushed to my ears at the thought I might be in the presence of yet another werewolf. Why hadn't this sensation come upon me sooner in the Count's presence? Perhaps the wine inhibited my ability.

I shook off the spell and the blood left my ears.

"…and I am not looking forward to my crossing to England tomorrow. I just do not like boats," the Count concluded.

I stumbled a bit and Mr. Irving steadied me. "Are you all right, Bram? You look pale."

His touch completely brought me back, and I regained my composure quickly. "I'm fine. Not used to so much drink, I'm afraid."

Lady Wilde waved over one of the servants and asked him to bring me a cup of strong Earl Grey tea.

"I have followed your career closely, Mr. Irving," the Count said. "I have seen you several times in London and on the Continent. Normally I am an enthusiast of the opera and have not enjoyed so much the theatre I have seen. But I find your performance very intriguing. It is like the opera without the music, yah? Much passion and fury."

"That is gratifying to hear," Irving said. "Theatre, like life, should always be undertaken with passion. Where are you going when you get to England?"

"I am meeting old friends in London," he said.

"I am heading back to London soon myself," Irving said, taking a calling card from his jacket pocket. "You should come by the Lyceum Theatre and I will give you a tour."

Ruthven accepted the card. "Thank you. I might just do that."

With that, Lady Wilde led him off to meet more of her guests. Mr. Irving watched them cross the room. "Does that man strike you as a little strange?"

Willie offered, "Quite."

"He didn't look well," Irving said. "I hope he hasn't brought some foreign flu with him from his travels."

Willie wiped his hand on his jacket. "Dear God, you're right. He did look sickly. His handshake was cold and clammy. I'd best get some gin to fortify myself."

He left us to find more drink, and Mr. Irving asked a servant for his hat, coat and walking stick.

"I must be off. I have two performances tomorrow. Please think about my offer, Bram. This could be an exciting adventure for you: a home in London, a life in the theatre. You were meant for greater things and this could be your ticket to them."

"Thank you. I will consider it carefully, Mr. Irving."

"Please, call me Henry. We will discuss this further when we meet on Tuesday. I hope by then you will have made your decision. The right decision."

He smiled, shook my hand and left.

I found the nearest empty chair, grateful that it was in a quiet corner, and sat down to get off my shaky legs. The servant brought me my tea and I sipped it slowly, hoping it would clear my head. I closed my eyes and breathed deeply.

A soft voice said, "Mr. Stoker," startling me. I stood quickly, sloshing tea onto my lap, and looked up to see Florence Balcombe.

"Please, do not get up on my account," she said, taking the seat across from me. "I desperately need to get off my feet as well."

Her very presence cleared my mind and strengthened me. Funny, I had been so nervous around her earlier.

"I have seen you before, you know, at Trinity," she said, smiling.

I was surprised. "S-surely, I would have remembered meeting you," I stammered.

"We did not meet. I saw you win in a foot race. I was impressed a man so big and strong could also be so swift-footed."

Now it was I who was blushing and she seemed to find it amusing.

"You are not like Oscar's other acquaintances," she said. "You don't offer the pretence of being an artist, yet I know you are a writer. I've read some of your stories. 'The Crystal Cup' I found most inspiring."

"You are too kind, Miss Balcombe, but I am gratified if it offered you some enjoyment."

"Are you working on another story currently, Mr. Stoker?"

I was chagrined to admit that I was not. Eager to offer her something of interest about myself, I quickly changed the subject. "It has been an eventful evening, first with your engagement and lately for me as well. Mr. Irving has offered me employment at his theatre in London. He would like me to manage his entire company there."

To my great satisfaction, she seemed genuinely impressed. "Why, Mr. Stoker, that is very exciting news indeed. Congratulations. I am sure you will be a great success."

"In truth, I am reluctant to take the job as I have a good position here as a clerk. I have already advanced quickly in the civil service and feel confident that, with continued diligence, I could progress swiftly up the ranks. But the theatre is a passion of mine. And when would another opportunity like this ever present itself?"

"If you would like my honest opinion, I would say, never."

"So, your advice would be to take the position, then?"

"I, too, love the theatre, and confess that I would not hesitate were I in your position," she said. "However, I do not presume to advise you, Mr. Stoker. Only you can make such a decision for yourself. You must look within your own heart."

Her warmth and interest buoyed me, and her mention of my heart – so innocuous on her part – thrilled me far beyond reason. "I am letting fear get the better of me. I would be foolish not to take the job. A life in the London theatre! It sounds like a bit of adventure, doesn't it?" I said, with what I hoped was a rakish twinkle in my eye. "Yes, Miss Balcombe, I think you have helped me make up my mind."

"I am so glad I could be an inspiration to you," she said, with a smile that struck me as altogether admiring.

Lady Wilde interrupted our conversation. "Florence, my dear, there you are. Oh, and Bram, feeling better, dear?" My affirmative reply had barely cleared my throat when she said, "Good, good. Go and mingle, or at least rein in Willie. Now come, Florence, there are still people you need to meet." Miss Balcombe reluctantly got back onto her tired feet and I rose as well.

"I am very pleased we had these moments to talk, Mr. Stoker. I hope you will write to Oscar and me when you get to London and tell us all about your new life."

I am ashamed to say my heart sank when she mentioned Oscar's name. "I will." I forced a smile.

And with that, she disappeared into the crowd.

The appearance of Lady Wilde had reminded me of why I was sitting in a quiet corner with a cup of tea: Count Ruthven. I felt an urgent need to find him. Now that my head had cleared I knew that, if he was indeed a werewolf as I suspected, I could not let him roam freely among the Wildes and their friends. What I would do when I found him I did not know; my only thought was to restrain him somehow until silver bullets could be acquired.

I made my way through the crowd, which was thinning with the late hour. Ruthven was nowhere to be found, but Willie had two pretty girls cornered in the hallway to the kitchen.

"Have you seen Count Ruthven?" I asked him. The girls took this interruption as an opportunity to slip by him and back into the dining room.

"Yes," he said, irritated. "Oscar has taken a shine to him and last I saw was giving him a tour of the house."

I considered telling Willie of my suspicions and enlisting his aid, but at that moment he leant back slightly to peer around me at the fleeing girls and nearly toppled over. Obviously, he was already far too drunk to be of use. I steered him back towards the party – safety in numbers, after all – and resumed my search, continuing down the hall towards the kitchen.

There were no tracks to follow as there had been with the werewolf in Greystones, yet I felt my senses heighten. I was pulled onwards and a clear vision of the wine cellar came into my mind. I glanced about to make sure no one was near, then tried the knob. The door was locked. Remembering that Lady Wilde kept a skeleton key on the ledge above the door, I quickly located it and gained access.

I crept down the stair so as not to startle my quarry, for I was sure then that he was down there. I could smell his sickly scent and a green glow emanated from behind a rack of bottles.

I picked up a shovel that was leaning against the stairs and slowly made my way around the rack. I could hear an inhuman panting and feared the worst.

Finally reaching the end of the wine rack, I leapt around the corner with two hands on the shovel handle, holding it high above my head.

"Back!" I yelled with all my might. To my horror, I saw Oscar with his back to me and his trousers down around his ankles. He had the Count bent over a table and the sounds I had heard were disgusting grunts of ecstasy.

Startled, Oscar jumped away from the Count. His legs caught in his trousers and he tripped, toppling to the ground. He scrambled behind the table, attempting to pull up his trousers without exposing himself further.

Unembarrassed, the Count straightened and took his time reclothing himself. As he pulled up his braces, an evil grin came across his face, as if he were proud to make me witness such a thing.

Oscar stood and dusted himself off. "Er, Bram. Have you met the Count?"

I became enraged at the thought of his lovely fiancée, who was at that moment under this same roof, celebrating her engagement to a man who would betray her trust in such a base and carnal manner.

"You selfish—" I yelled. "This is your engagement party, for God's sake!"

"Bram," he pleaded. "It's just a bit of harmless fun."

"Harmless? You are betraying your fiancée, who is but a few rooms away." I imagined the lovely Miss Balcombe upstairs, being shepherded around by Lady Wilde, mingling herself to exhaustion for this cad. "I have never been so disappointed in a human being in my life! And bear in mind I had no great expectations of you to begin with."

"Bram," Oscar said, in what was clearly meant to be a placating manner. "I love Florence dearly and always shall. This does nothing to—"

Suddenly I took a blow to the back of the head. It did not drop me, but I stumbled and turned to see the Count. He struck me a second time as I heard Oscar scream, "No!"

I collapsed to the ground, still conscious, but just barely. My vision blurred as I saw the Count grab Oscar by the shirt and pull him close.

I attempted to get on my feet but could only make it to my knees.

"Sleep," the Count said to Oscar, who went limp in his arms. He tossed Oscar aside and pulled me to my feet with great strength.

He looked into my eyes. His own were dead and obsidian-black, with no glint of human feeling. I could see my reflection in them and was unable to look away. I felt as if I were falling into an abyss.

"Sleep," he commanded. I could feel him in my mind as if his bony fingers were poking into my very brain. I sensed his expectation that the command would be obeyed as Oscar and who knows how many others before had obeyed. And yet I did not obey.

"Sleep!" He said it with anger this time. He opened his mouth wide and I could see snakelike fangs dripping with saliva. "I wasn't nearly finished with that one yet, but now I find I'm more interested in you. Your scent is intoxicating. I have been forbidden to kill you, I am not sure why. But I shall take a taste before wiping your memory of this night."

With that, he sunk his teeth into my neck!

The pain pushed him out of my head. He seemed shocked by this, and I could feel him pull completely out of my mind. He recoiled in fear as the werewolf had done and pushed me away with great force, bouncing me off a rack of wine bottles, which swayed but did not give way.

He was choking, coughing, then vomited up my blood.

Oscar stirred awake.

I recovered my wits and my shovel and charged the monster.

The demon yanked Oscar to his feet and took refuge behind him. He wrapped his spindly arm around Oscar's neck.

"Stay back, Stoker, or I will snap his neck!"

I remembered his immense strength and knew him capable of it. I backed away.

Oscar struggled and then, unexpectedly, the Count screamed in pain, his grip loosening. I could hear the faint sizzle of searing flesh. He recoiled in horror, letting Oscar go. Ruthven's sleeves were rolled up and on his arm was a cross-shaped burn, still smouldering. I could see that Oscar was wearing a silver cross around his neck.

"Oscar, the cross," I yelled. "It burns him!"

Oscar yanked the chain off his neck, breaking the clasp. He held it in front of him and the vampire, for that's what he most surely was, backed away. The fiend ran for the second set of stairs that led outside and into an adjacent alley. He was but a blur and a gust of wind and was out the door before I could take another step.

"Come, we mustn't let that thing loose on the city!" I cried. I tightened my grip on the shovel and Oscar grabbed a bottle.

"Oh, no, not the champagne," he said, putting it down and grabbing another vintage and a lantern.

Out we went into the night. He was far ahead of us now, making it more difficult to track, but with concentration, my nose could find that nauseatingly sweet scent that I now knew was his natural odour. Like a carnivorous flower, he emanated a honeyed reek to mask his true nature.

He moved swiftly and covered much ground. It was nearly half an hour before we caught up to the beast, and we never would have were it not for the fact that someone – or something – had beaten us to it!

As we approached a dark, damp alley we heard a brief cry, a thump and swiftly retreating footsteps. With a quick, grim glance at each other, we plunged into the alley.

The creature we'd known as Count Ruthven was sprawled on the ground. His head had been cleanly cut off. There was no blood; only dust poured from his wounds. The head and body were decomposing as we watched, looking more like a shrivelled mummy than a freshly dead corpse. We could only stare in astonishment.

Finally, Oscar broke the silence. "A bit of luck, that."

I nodded my agreement, for as we had tracked the thing I'd realised I had no idea how to deal with a vampire. Somehow, I think a shovel and a bottle of Bordeaux would have been of limited use. But someone had known how to kill him. Whoever it was had escaped out the other end of the alley and, by unspoken agreement, we did not give chase.

I bent down and started to go through the Count's pockets.

"Bram, what are you doing? Don't touch that thing!"

"Need I remind you that you were buggering him less than an hour ago?"

Oscar turned away from me, retched and vomited. I couldn't help taking some small satisfaction from the sound.

In the Count's pockets, I found a cigarette case, Henry Irving's calling card (that I had seen him receive earlier), and a chess piece, a black bishop. The body was nearly all dust now; the suit had collapsed completely.

Oscar regained his stomach and I showed him what I'd found.

"Why is he carrying a chess piece?"

"That's not at the top of my list of unanswered questions," I said.

"You saved my life, Bram," Oscar said as if it had just occurred to him. "He would have drunk my blood, perhaps even turned me into…." He nearly retched again but maintained his composure. "Thank you, Bram. Damned lucky for me that you were around. I guess we're even now."

Under the circumstances, I let the comment go unchallenged.

"I say, can't you work your magic vision on that chess piece? Perhaps find out more about him?"

"I'll try." I closed my hand around it and closed my eyes. All I saw was a quick flash of the piece passing into his hand, and then the vision was gone. Opening my eyes, I regarded the piece. "The black bishop is a calling card, of sorts."

"His calling card?"

"No, it was given to him by someone."

"Can you make out who it was?"

"His face is but a shadow," I said.

"You don't suppose that's who took his head off?"

"I do not know," I said. "I can't see it." The chess piece was making my hand go numb. I slipped it into my pocket. We returned to the party, not saying a word to one another on the walk back.

I have now recounted the evening's events in as much detail as I can muster, and yet my mind is still unquiet and I feel no closer to sleep. In the last several hours, I have encountered a monster and a mystery. I have been offered a job in London, working for a man I respect and admire. I have met the most beautiful and intriguing woman I have ever known, a woman who is promised to another. And I have in my possession information that would surely sway her to break her engagement. What I shall do about any of these things I do not know.

I wish I understood why it is given to me to commune with the supernatural and its creatures. I wish I had the means to rid myself of this dreadful ability, though I have to admit that it has saved my life and others'. I wish I knew what to do about the job and the woman and Oscar, who I don't quite count as a friend but who has proven himself a worthy ally on more than one occasion.

Such is *not* the life of a petty sessions clerk.

LETTER FROM FLORENCE BALCOMBE TO LUCY MAYHEW, 5TH OF AUGUST 1878

My dearest Lucy,

I hope this finds you well in exciting London. I am most joyful to hear of your engagement to Robert! Will he whisk you off to America, or will you both live in London? I am happy that one of us is going to have an exciting and fulfilling life.

I wish I could be happier that we are both engaged. My own engagement, I'm afraid, is off to a rocky start.

Oscar is on a trip to Greece with some school chums and his former literature professor, while I plan the nuptials on my own. His mother is of great help in these matters, and I suppose men never participate in the planning of these things, but I can't help but feel neglected.

Oscar normally is a copious letter writer; however, his letters from Greece are short and infrequent. One's darker nature imagines him being seduced by some Greek siren. Is it not odd that a man should disappear for months before his wedding?

However, to be truthful, I myself have felt the bond of our engagement weakening. I have struck up a friendship with Bram Stoker. (It's possible you met him at the engagement party. He is a dear friend of Oscar's brother.) Though I can assure you it is strictly platonic, I have been spending more and more time with Bram. We go on long walks by the river and we talk of the most interesting things.

Like Oscar, Bram has literary aspirations. He has published stories and poems and is being mentored by the famed American poet, Walt Whitman.

I will miss our walks and talks. Bram leaves for London in December where he has secured employment as manager of the Lyceum Theatre.

Can you imagine how exciting and interesting his life will be?

Oscar talks of us moving to London after we are married. I hope we do. I would love to see you again and have you show me all that great city has to offer.

I must go now, but write back soon.

Love,

Florence

FROM THE JOURNAL OF BRAM STOKER, 23RD OF AUGUST 1878

11:15 p.m.

I continue to make preparations to leave for London. I have given notice at Dublin Castle and have trained my replacement clerk. I have also finished my petty sessions clerk manual and delivered it to the publisher. I have a tidy sum that should help me get settled before I start my new position at the Lyceum.

There are nights I lie awake and fret that I am not up to the task. The only thing that bolsters my confidence is Florence's encouragement. I do not wish to let her down. As of late, she is all I can think about. Oh, how I wish she were not engaged to the reprobate Oscar.

It is a wonder I can sleep at all, for I also must worry about vampires and my supernatural 'gift'. I have not had any spells since Oscar's engagement party. Perhaps they have run their course like a fever.

I have sworn to Oscar to not reveal his indiscretion. In exchange, he will not tell the world of my demonic visions. Yet, can I trust him to honour that bargain? I am certain he sees it as just another chapter in the story of Oscar Wilde. What a thrilling tale it would make at one of his salon readings!

To make matters worse, he has gone off carousing with his school chums, and his mentor, a 'confirmed bachelor' known to take a fancy to his brighter students. They are in Greece, where I'm sure the wine is flowing; what are the chances he can hold his tongue when there is a story to tell and a crowd of eager listeners?

Yet I must confess, I am sorely tempted to tell his secret as well. It is something I now feel Florence must know. As a friend, I should tell her that her fiancé has been unfaithful. What kind of marriage could she have to such a scoundrel?

To be honest, I may not have the best of intentions for violating

Oscar's trust, for my romantic feelings for Florence continue unabated. Do I only wish to break up their engagement for my own selfish motives?

These are the difficult moral dilemmas that keep me up at night.

Even if Florence were to end things with Oscar, would she fancy me? I fear there is no time to court her properly, even if she does.

Why must my life be so complicated when I have strived so to keep it simple? Why must my happiness at moving up in the world be tarnished with the thought of losing the love of my life forever?

LETTER FROM OSCAR WILDE TO ELLEN TERRY, 11TH OF DECEMBER 1878

Dear Miss Ellen,

Will you accept from me a poem, which I have written for you as a small proof of my great and loyal admiration for your splendid artistic powers and the noble tenderness and pathos of your acting? My hope is that it gives to you some small measure of the joy and inspiration that have edified my soul while watching you perform.

I am given to understand that congratulations are in order, as you are joining the repertory company of the Lyceum Theatre. I remember it was just a few months ago that you were lamenting to me that your ingénue days were behind you. And now, here you are taking the stage of one the most respected theatres in the world, acting alongside the great Henry Irving. Rumour has it that *Hamlet* will be the next production, and I for one am giddy with anticipation of your Ophelia. Now do not mistake me, Ellen, I would sit enthralled through Mr. Irving's portrayal of David Copperfield, but compared to his Hamlet you will appear little older than a babe in arms.

However, I must warn you about the nefarious types you will encounter there. I am speaking of the new theatre manager, Bram Stoker. He is a cad of the worst sort, having stolen away the fiancée of another. (I am embarrassed to confess she was mine.) He has swept her off to London without a proper courtship and after a hastily arranged marriage, and I shudder to think of my delicate flower sharing a breakfast table – let alone anything else – with that great, bearlike oaf.

Despite my broken heart, I worry about my dear Florrie and hope you will befriend and watch over her. She is very innocent and knows not of the ways of the world as you and I do.

As if this betrayal were not bad enough, Stoker attracts dangerous elements to himself like flies to honey, moths to flame and society matrons to gossip. Twice in his company I have found myself fighting for my life – and worse, his! I will not go into the lurid details here but suffice to say keep your eye on him and your wits about you. I should take it somewhat amiss if any harm were to come to you through your unfortunate association with that scoundrel.

On to more pleasant topics. I shall be moving to London myself soon, having completed my studies at Oxford last month. I shall be lodging with my friend Frank Miles at 13 Salisbury Street, London. Frank is a brilliant portrait artist, and I do hope you will sit for him one day. He can capture the essence of a subject in a way that no other artist can match, and I can think of no one more deserving of that particular immortality than you, my dear Ellen.

I hope to see you often upon the stage, now that I shall be so near.

Your loyal subject,

O.W.

P.S. I must ask of you one more favour. I will be sending to you a silver cross. It was a gift from Florence to me. Please see that it is returned to her. Tell her to wear it at all times as protection from evil. Superstitious, I know, but it will give me some comfort knowing it is around her lovely neck.

LETTER FROM FLORENCE BALCOMBE TO JAMES BALCOMBE, 20TH OF DECEMBER 1878

Dearest Father,

Saints be praised, here we are, settled in London at last!

I wish you could see our house, Father. We have six comfortable rooms on a tree-lined street in the Bloomsbury neighbourhood, near to the theatre district. Please do not fear that this attracts an unsavoury element; Bloomsbury is pleasant and sedate, and quite safe. You will be happy to know the head of Scotland Yard lives just around the corner!

We are settling into married life quite nicely and are becoming acquainted with our neighbours and surroundings. We have engaged a housemaid – Mrs. Norris, a capable woman of some experience – and you would laugh to see how she defers to me as the lady of the house. I am doing my best in that capacity. Mother warned me that running a household is more difficult than it appears and she was right. Even in a home as small as ours, there are many details that must be seen to and I sometimes fear that I will never become adept at juggling them all. But I persevere! As we become established in our new society we shall be expected to entertain and I wish nothing more than to make a home to which my husband will proudly invite his friends and colleagues.

As for my social life, you will be happy to know my good friend Lucy Mayhew lives but across the back garden with her Aunt Agatha, and I see her often. She is a dear reminder of home, and we have been a great help to one another, two Dublin girls learning the ways of London. I, of course, also have married life to adjust to while Lucy, though engaged, is as yet unwed.

Father, I know you have had your qualms regarding my marriage. It was sudden, true, and I realise that you feel my choice was capricious and careless of the feelings of others. Please know that I took my previous engagement very seriously and deeply regret any pain caused by its conclusion. I shall always be fond of Oscar but decided, ultimately, that marriage to him would not make either one of us happy in the long term. I feel that one day he will realise the same.

I hope that soon you too will agree and will overcome your reservations about my husband. Bram is a fine man and he loves me deeply. Lest you worry that he whisked me away to London on a whim, please remember that he is here at the behest of one of the finest – and most successful – actors on the London stage. He is earning a substantial salary and his prospects are good for a long and rewarding career. It pains him deeply that we did not have an engagement of proper length, for he is very traditional when it comes to social conventions. It was I who concluded that a lengthy engagement was not practical, and pleaded with him for our married life to start straight away.

I miss you terribly and think of you often. As my first Christmas away from home and family approaches, I know my homesickness will deepen. Please remember me this holiday and raise a glass to your loving daughter,

Florrie

P.S. I almost forgot to mention, I had tea today with the actress Ellen Terry! She is ever so nice and has taken me under her wing. Under her tutelage, you just may see yours truly upon the stage in the coming new year!

LETTER FROM ELLEN TERRY TO OSCAR WILDE, 23RD OF DECEMBER 1878

My dear Oscar,

Thank you for the poem and the much-needed flattery. No amount of skill on the part of the actress can make up for the loss of youth, but your letters always make me feel young again. And you provided a welcome diversion from the day-to-day drudgery of theatre life and a recent harrowing encounter, which I shall relate shortly.

But first, I must answer your assertions regarding Mr. Stoker's moral character. I can attest he seems very much in love with Florence and appears to be a fine husband. I have met the young woman in question and believe her to be quite happy in her new marriage, excited to be in the bustling heart of London and, aside from an overly romanticised view of life in the theatre, adapting to her circumstances quite remarkably. (I hope you truly do wish her the best, Oscar, and that this is good news to you.) I do perceive the naiveté to which you alluded, but she is young.

Perhaps Mr. Stoker's pilfering of your fiancée was his only fall from grace. Our acquaintance has been brief, but he appears to be a quick learner, a shrewd manager and conscientious to a fault. He has already whipped the stage crew into shape (no mean feat, I assure you) and set Mr. Irving's affairs in good order (possibly an even more challenging task). Though he only started on the 14th of December, under his direction all the sets have been built and the parts cast for our next production.

I am looking forward to playing Ophelia once again, but despite your over-abundant (nevertheless, most welcome) praise, I am quite nervous at the prospect. No, I am not being maudlin about my age again, Oscar; it is simply that I wish to make a good impression on Mr. Irving, and I am afraid this 'natural' style of acting he demands is very intimidating. One must actually feel the emotions being portrayed. Now I ask you, how is that acting? However, I am up to the challenge!

But not all is well here. I must thank you for your advice to keep my wits about me. At first, I took your warning about Mr. Stoker and the company he keeps to be, quite frankly, petty jealousy. (Do not resent me for that, dear Oscar. I thought no less of you for it. It would be a very natural reaction on your part.) However, since meeting Mr. Stoker my life *has* been put in danger.

Perhaps it is merely a coincidence, and I must add that he was nowhere near when the event took place, but I have heard of those born under unlucky stars who attract bad luck just as surely as killing a spider will bring rain.

The incident happened just last night.

I am staying in a dressing room at the Lyceum until I can secure my own accommodations. The theatre is a different place at night. During the day there is so much activity and noise – with sets being built, actors practising swordplay and the like – but at night it is eerily quiet. The only sounds you hear are rafters creaking as the old building sways ever so slightly in the wind and the occasional rat scurrying about. It does make one uneasy.

In general, I am not totally alone, as the property master, Mr. Arnott, has a room in the basement, and Mr. Irving often works in his office until sunup.

Last night, however, Mr. Irving was out dining with a friend and Mr. Arnott had gone off to Leeds to acquire props.

I had not yet dressed for bed and was going over my rehearsal notes from Mr. Irving (which are always quite copious) when I heard footsteps in his office overhead. This did not set me to worrying, as I often hear him pacing about and so I thought nothing of it. Then I remembered that he was out. Still, I thought, nothing to worry about, it could be Mr. Stoker, who often works late in an office adjacent.

But then: the sound of breaking glass!

What to do? Surely it must be a burglar. At first I thought I should stay quiet and wait for him to leave, but I felt cowardly doing so. I made my way stealthily to the property room and acquired a sword; a prop, true, but real enough to crack the skull of a criminal.

As I climbed the staircase to Mr. Irving's office, I had second thoughts about confronting a burglar on my own. I considered going outside and yelling for the police, but just as I started to turn back, the intruder threw open the door and bolted down the stairs to make his getaway. I recognised him straight away. It was the young lad who runs errands for Mr. Irving. He had a large book clutched in his hands. The boy was shocked to see me standing there, especially brandishing a sword.

I recovered my wits first and resolutely blocked his path, commanding "Stop!" in my most forceful stage voice. I might have been more aggressive in my stance than I should have been considering he's no more than ten years of age, but then he had given me quite a start.

"Blimey!" he screamed. He shielded his head with the book, which was more than up to the task, being quite large. "Don't chop me, mum!" I recognised the book. Mr. Irving keeps it in his office, under a glass case.

"Why are you stealing that book?" I demanded.

"I'm not, I'm just borrowin' it!"

"Give it to me," I ordered. I lowered the sword, and this proved to be my undoing. The little urchin took that moment to push past me down the stairs. His shove made me drop the sword right onto my foot. With a throbbing foot, I could not give chase and he was out the door in a matter of moments.

I hobbled out just in time to see him hand the book off to someone in a hansom cab in exchange for a coin, and flee around a corner. I flagged down a police officer, but by that time the child and the cab were both long gone. I know him only as Dennis and so I was of limited use as an informant. I related the incident to Mr. Irving this morning and he will pursue the investigation from here. He seemed quite vexed, naturally, and told me that the book was worth more than one hundred pounds! "And so much more," he muttered, almost to himself. It must have some sentimental value to him, poor dear. I do hope he can recover it.

So, that was my adventure. I must admit, I found it exhilarating! Perhaps I should hope that Mr. Stoker is as dangerous as you say so that I shall have further opportunities for thrilling escapades, though hopefully my foot will be spared in future.

I am so happy to hear that you will soon be a Londoner. I look forward to seeing you much more often.

Until then,

Ellen Terry

FROM THE JOURNAL OF BRAM STOKER, 5TH OF JANUARY 1879

9:00 p.m.

I look at my last entry in this journal with dismay as I realise how long it has been since I have troubled to set down my thoughts and experiences. I have been so busy that I have not felt I had the time to spare. Nevertheless, I resolve to make more of an effort, for I realise how quickly one's memory of specific events and people can fade, and my life now is so rich and interesting – to me at least – that I know I shall want to recall it with as much detail as possible in years to come.

My work at the Lyceum fills my days with challenges, problems, tasks and duties ranging from the mundane to the glamorous. Well, not truly glamorous, perhaps, but tangential to glamour, as when I had the opportunity to play host to none other than Alfred Lord Tennyson when he paid a visit to the theatre last week. I am pleased to say that we got on immediately and were soon engaged in a lively conversation that ranged from the great man's own works to those of Edgar Allan Poe to boxing. He has a keen wit, as one would expect, but is also a strong and strapping man for his age and was apparently quite the athlete in his youth. We are considering staging one of his plays and I fervently hope that we do, as there are few authors for whom I carry stronger admiration.

I am also more engaged than I had dared to hope in the creative aspects of the theatre, as on an evening last week when I sat up all night with Mr. Irving working on our upcoming production of *Hamlet*. I felt a true member of the company then as he read scenes aloud and we discussed how to stage them to best convey their theme and meaning.

That night was exhausting and exhilarating in equal measure. I feared that Mr. Irving, being some years older than I, would overtire himself, but he seemed to take it in stride. Shortly before dawn he declared it a good night's work and woke his driver – who had been dozing in the auditorium – to take him home for some well-deserved rest, bidding me to also get a few hours of sleep before the next work day began. I imagine after years in the theatre he is accustomed to odd hours and is as comfortable working all night as most of us are toiling away the daylight hours, and indeed, since that night I have observed that he rarely makes an appearance at the theatre before late afternoon and often works late through the night, though he usually does not require my services at this time.

Of course, I have many other duties that, while less artistically fulfilling, are necessary and no less gratifying. Managing a theatre with the reputation and ambition of the Lyceum comprises myriad details. I estimate that I write upwards of fifty letters a day on matters large and small, and overseeing the staff and stage crew provides numerous opportunities to chide poor performance, intervene in petty squabbles and hear improbable excuses for tardiness. I endeavour to lead by example and hold myself to a higher standard than I expect from my staff. I feel that even in the short time I have held my position I have gained a measure of respect even from those to whom I have been forced to issue reprimands.

The actors require more diplomatic handling for they are temperamental artists by nature. Still, they are a jolly bunch and dedicated to their craft. By and large, I like them immensely. Ellen Terry, our leading lady, has earned my particular respect and gratitude, having made me feel welcome at once. On my first day at the theatre I expected to be greeted by Mr. Irving but, finding him unavailable, felt somewhat at a loss. It was Miss Terry who took me by the arm and gave me a tour, introducing me to all and sundry, providing a running commentary on the theatre's history and the professional resumés of various cast and crew members, and discreetly relating the occasional bit of gossip. I soon felt as though we had been friends for years, though I imagine an actress of her calibre is bound to have a talent for making one feel that way.

Knowing we are new to the city and have made few acquaintances, she has even extended her friendship and hospitality to my dear Florence. They have taken tea together and I know Florence was thrilled. She aspires to the stage herself and while I have cautioned her not to assume that my position at the Lyceum can secure her a role – indeed, I have resolved not to mention her name when discussing casting decisions with Mr. Irving for fear he would think that I am abusing my station – I see no harm in her discussing the profession with Miss Terry.

I am pleased to note that Florence is adjusting nicely to life in London and that Ellen Terry is not her only friend here. Lucy Mayhew, one of Florence's oldest and dearest friends, lives nearby – we share back gardens, in fact – and they see each other often. It does my heart good to know that she has someone to talk to for I have observed that the first years of married life entail many changes and adjustments, more so for the wife than for the husband. The difference between a Miss and a Mrs. is vast, as a wife assumes new duties in managing a household and attending to the needs of her husband. This change is even more profound in Florence's case, of course, as I have stolen her away from her home and family. I remind myself to be patient with her and any bouts of melancholy or sudden shifts in mood.

FROM THE *LONDON TIMES*, 8TH OF JANUARY 1879

BRITISH MUSEUM ROBBERY BAFFLES SCOTLAND YARD

Unknown assailants broke into the British Museum on Saturday night and, after overpowering a guard, made off with a Roman artefact.

It is the specificity of the item taken that has museum curators scratching their heads.

"They could have stolen priceless paintings or jewellery, yet what they have taken was of little monetary value," said Theodore Hyde-White, head curator. "They knew exactly what they wanted, for it was in a crate down in storage, and they had to move other crates to get to it. All of the other crates they left unopened."

The inventory of what is missing consists only of a single bronze spear tip. It was brought back to England during the Second Crusade, along with dozens of similar items.

Police suspect it may be the work of religious zealots who may have confused the piece for a holy relic.

"It may be a sect seeking the Spear of Longinus," explained Hyde-White, "which is believed to be the spear that a Roman soldier used to pierce Christ's side. But this spear is most likely from an earlier period."

Police have no leads and are seeking the public's help in apprehending the thieves.

"What they have stolen may be of little value," said Detective David Naughten of Scotland Yard. "But they did assault a guard and we don't take these things lightly."

Anyone having any information is encouraged to contact Scotland Yard immediately.

WHITE WORM SOCIETY BLACK BISHOP REPORT, 9TH OF JANUARY 1879

Operative: Anna Hubbard
Location: London, England

Reports continue to come in from our operatives that something is afoot in the world of the occult.

A ten-year-old male street urchin was apprehended in our own library stealing valuable books of the occult. He apparently entered through a coal bin chute during the night and picked the lock on the library doors. Fairly impressive burglary skills for a child, I must admit.

Under questioning, he told us that it was not the first book he had removed from the shelves. The young thief claims he was approached by an upper-class gentleman who arranged payment and collection of the materials. He has given us a vague description of the man, which we are following up on.

The boy was paid a handsome sum for pages torn from specific books as well as several volumes from the shelves in the west wing.

He was given locations and descriptions of the books, but he cannot read so was unable to tell the titles he removed. We are checking the shelves and compiling a list of the missing volumes. One of the missing books appears to be *The Vellum Doyle Manuscript*, which is most troubling since that book comes from the Other Realm. A difficult volume to translate, to be sure, but it could be most disastrous if they do.

Furthermore, he told us he was also paid to steal a book from the Lyceum Theatre that was part of the collection of the owner, Henry Irving. The boy remembers the book was very old and had a picture of a dragon on the cover. From this description, we fear it may be the book *The Munich Manual of Demonic Magic*.

We have operatives looking for the stolen volumes and are infiltrating occult societies to track down any rumours of their whereabouts. The street urchin is now one of our operatives and it is hoped that the gentleman will approach him again for further larceny.

I shall further investigate Henry Irving. This is not the first time his name has come up in our investigations and research.

– End Report –

FROM THE DIARY OF OSCAR WILDE, 10TH OF JANUARY 1879

Archivist's note: While Wilde was in prison for gross indecency in 1895, his wife, Constance, sold his diary to the White Worm Society to raise money for his defence. Oscar Wilde's diary was written in Pitman Shorthand and is transcribed into long-form below.

Dear yours truly,

I am sorry that it has been so long since I have written in our diary. I see here the last time I did I was only thirteen years old! I assure you many exciting things have happened to me since then; many I have forgotten and many I wish to forget!

But here we are with a new year, and with it a resolution to write in the diary every day, giving you something to read in our old age. I do hope I shall find an opportunity to recount some interesting and noteworthy experiences to reflect upon when I am you.

To begin, you should know that I have moved to London and am currently sharing a flat with Frank Miles. My plan was to find accommodations of my own, however, my current financial situation is not as sound as I would like it to be. Also, the simple fact is that Frank needs me. He is quite mad with his art, you see. Unless he has drifted out of our life by the time I am old, which would make me quite sad, you will remember that Frank is a painter and a brilliant one at that. At present, he is the very model of the starving artist. This is not because he lacks money for food; it is simply because he forgets to eat! So, I make sure he has three proper meals a day, takes the occasional bath and, with much coaxing, goes out to socialise with friends from time to time.

Frank is obsessed with becoming the best painter he can be. He will spend days looking at something before he begins to paint it. This is fine when his subject is a bowl of fruit, but it can be quite unnerving for a human model.

The other day he sat down to paint a dead pigeon he found out on the street. He studied it for days until it had grown (pardon the pun) quite foul. Then in a burst of frustration, he cut it open with a knife to study the entrails, explaining that he needed to see what was inside in order to paint the outside properly. Egad, I hope he doesn't follow suit with one of the poor models sitting for his portraits!

For it is the portraits that are his bread and butter. People pay him quite handsomely to paint them. I swear he manages to capture the subject's very being. He has a technique with his brush strokes that makes the portrait's face glow as if there were warm blood flowing under the skin and just a bit of perspiration on the brow. His paintings almost seem alive, as if they are the real people and the models mere sketches.

There are patrons, clients and models coming into the flat day and night. One never knows who will be sitting for him. One day it is a count, the next a prostitute he's brought in out of the rain simply because her eyes intrigued him.

I must admit I do like the activity. There is never a dull moment in the Miles-Wilde household! (Perhaps I should refer to it as the Wilde-Miles household. Yes, that sounds much more rakish!) And as luck would have it, it seems that mostly attractive people pay to have their portraits painted. I must have seen half the beautiful people in London come through our doors.

As for me, I am a work in progress. I have been doing some writing and some thinking, and also some translations of Herodotus and Euripides, which I have hopes of publishing. I have been toying with the idea of going abroad to continue my studies, but London is so vibrant and exciting that I am reluctant to tear myself away from it. I yearn to make a name for myself here, to set the world on fire with new ideas and new aesthetics. Is there any city more important for arts and culture and the life of the mind? This, I feel, is my domain, the place I am meant to be. The moment is mine to seize.

FROM THE JOURNAL OF BRAM STOKER, 12TH OF JANUARY 1879

9:37 p.m.

An extremely upsetting day today! I have been agitated all evening by the day's events, which were capped by a row with Florence in which she listed all my faults, which it seems she has been cataloguing since the beginning of our marriage.

I deserved it. I was quite abominable to her. She was merely trying to coax me into pleasant conversation over dinner, but I was in no mood for it and spoke rather sharply to her, asking her to please let me eat my meal in peace.

"I am stuck in this house all day, only to have you come home and speak to me that way," she snapped. "Am I to always bear the brunt of your foul moods? I am not one of your stage crew, I am your wife."

I offered an apology, but the outburst had released something that has apparently been building steam in her for some time and her complaints continued: I work too much. I am often morose or distracted. We do not have the social life she imagined we would in London. She has not enough to occupy her days.

I knew not what to say other than to offer another apology and a promise to try to improve. (Though in truth I have no idea how to accomplish this; I cannot shirk my work responsibilities nor introduce her to social contacts I do not have.)

She seemed about to launch into another litany of grievances, but instead she sighed and looked somewhat abashed. "The shameful truth is, Bram, I am vexed nearly as much by your good moods as the bad. For they remind me of all the excitement of the theatre, a world which I do not share with you. A world you know I wish to be in. I recall you promising me that it would not bother you in the slightest if I should pursue an acting career."

I told her that I will do my best to hold that promise, but as the theatre manager it would be unprofessional of me to put my family up for parts that should go to professional actresses.

This made her go silent and she withdrew soon after to attend to some correspondence, apparently again angry with me and my shortcomings.

I returned to the theatre for an evening rehearsal, only to find the gaslights are not functioning properly. I have sent the actors home and am frustrated that the gas company cannot dispatch anyone until morning.

I should return home as well; however, I shall wait until Florence is likely to be asleep for fear my foul mood will be a contagion and lead to another argument. I hope that writing in this journal will quiet my mind, and shall help the process along with some brandy.

Now for what put me into a foul mood in the first place.

The encounter earlier was a small thing, really, if judged by duration. I was coming home for my supper and had just crossed the Strand.

It was quite cold and there was a feeling in the air as if it might snow, and so most of us were bundled up against the chill, with scarves wound tight around our necks and faces and hats pulled down as far as we could manage.

As I hurried up Wellington Street to catch my tram, a feeling came upon me that I have not experienced in many months. Fleetingly but strongly, I felt the presence of something supernatural and malevolent. I stopped short as a wave of dizziness passed over me, and the man behind me cursed as he bumped into me. Muttering an apology, I whirled around, scanning the crowd and catching a glimpse of the familiar green glow enveloping a man hurrying in the other direction. I attempted to follow, but the tide of foot traffic proved difficult to swim against and I soon lost him in the crowd. I know nothing of him – not even what form of monster he might be – save that he was wearing a black coat and hat, as were ninety per cent of the men on the street, myself included.

If he frequents the neighbourhood it is possible I will see him again at a more opportune time to investigate. But I do not know if I wish for this to happen. I know that a good man does not let evil walk the streets while doing nothing to challenge it. If I saw a street crime in progress, would I not step in to try to stop it? How much greater is the responsibility to rid the world of a monster who might terrorise and murder countless innocents, most of whom have no knowledge of its very existence much less the threat it poses?

But is it my obligation to chase down every evil creature that prowls the world? Can I not simply enjoy my life, my work, my marriage, without these intrusions from the netherworld? This is the first such incident to trouble me since my marriage; what would Florence say were she to know about this curse and the danger in which I place myself when I heed its call? Is not my responsibility greater to provide a secure and stable home life for my wife and family?

I have no answers to these questions and asking them has only served to upset me further. Another brandy when I get home, perhaps, in front of the fire, and then I shall try to sleep. The morning may bring greater clarity.

13th of January, 4:45 a.m.

Monster!

My hand shakes so badly, I can barely keep pen to paper.

Werewolves and vampires exist. I have known this for some time, of course, but now it has become obvious that I somehow attract their attention. They are drawn to me like flies to a rotting corpse.

What else could it be? One encounter, bad luck, but two, now three must be some sort of curse.

After my last journal entry, I headed for home. The cloudless sky made the night even more bitterly cold and I was not dressed properly for it. Instead of snow we'd had rain, which had frozen and made my walk treacherous. The surrounding buildings were encased in ice, and I felt as though I was too. I was chilled to the bone and worrying about frostbite when my vision lit up like the Northern Lights.

A loud ringing in my ears deafened me and gave me a feeling of vertigo. It was all I could do to remain standing. But this time I was determined to take control of the vision rather than fight it. I imagined taking the reins of a horse and tried to control the vision in the same way. It seemed to work and I must admit it made me feel powerful. My fear passed through me and I gained a clarity I have never felt before.

I quickly turned and looked behind me. A man...a thing...was following, but upon my turning to look he disappeared into the shadows. A green glow betrayed his position but was not enough to allow me to see who or what was there.

"Who goes there!" I shouted, with as much authority as I could muster.

He pulled himself further back into an alley to avoid my gaze.

It was foolish of me. I had no weapon with me, not even a cane or umbrella.

My fear returned and I turned and walked towards home quickly. I could feel his presence still and wanted to break into a run but feared I would lose my footing on the icy ground.

Then I realised I was leading this creature to my home. I looked around for somewhere else to find refuge. A pub, or church, any place with people.

All the buildings were dark. The nearest pub was blocks away and behind me. Then I remembered there is a newspaper office a street over. They must work late into the night. I would go there.

I quickened my pace, then heard a scream. Not a woman's scream, but a man's loud groan, as if he were being beaten or stabbed. I am ashamed to say I thought of running away. But I knew I must summon the police.

"Help! Help," I yelled, hoping some constable was nearby and would come running. "Police!"

Then I felt an excitement in the lower part of my stomach that suddenly radiated through my entire body. It was the same feeling that I had when the werewolf's violence took me over. I was both repelled and drawn to the violent emanations.

My second sight was making my whole body throb. As I tried once again to harness it, a surge of bravery and strength flowed through my veins. I felt more animal than human, like a large jungle cat chasing down its prey.

I ran towards the sound and promptly slipped on the ice, in a manner assuredly unlike any jungle cat. I don't remember getting to my feet but I must have because I found myself standing at the alley entrance where I had seen the monster moments before.

In the shadows I could see a man lying on the ground, the creature feeding at his neck!

The vampire looked up at me. The moonlight lit his bloodied face as he hissed and bared his dripping fangs.

He leapt up before I could take a step back and grabbed me by my coat. He swung me around and threw me into the alley, where I landed on top of his victim, who turned out to be a constable. Though I was stunned I had enough presence of mind to see a billy club in his hand. I grabbed it.

The creature was on me, but I swung and bashed him in the skull. That surprised him more than hurt him, but it was enough to make him stumble back and let me get to my feet.

The constable stirred! He moaned and got to his knees.

The creature leapt over my full height and landed on the constable. He snapped his neck, killing him instantly, and turned his attention back to me.

He grabbed me once again. I struck him repeatedly on the head with the billy club, but he merely absorbed the blows. He slammed me hard against the wall of a building and a great heap of icicles rained down on us. He batted the billy club out of my hand and it clattered and slid away down the alley.

My strength was no match for his. I could no longer fight him off and became motionless like a stunned mouse in a cat's claws, my mind racing for some way to escape.

"I'm not supposed to kill you," he said peevishly.

Had I not known he was a monster, I would not have been able to tell. Like Count Ruthven at Oscar's engagement party, this one looked human enough to walk among us. His fangs were no longer visible. Except for the blood smeared around his mouth, he could pass for any tradesman you would see on the street. Strangely, this all went through my mind as he held me against the wall.

"But I suppose I could take a pint or two," he continued, opening his mouth. His fangs grew before my eyes, glistening with saliva. His breath smelled of rotting flesh and sickly sweet honeysuckle flowers.

He sunk his teeth greedily into my neck, then – like Ruthven had – backed away, choking and spitting.

I fell to my knees and my hand brushed against an icicle. I grabbed it and, with all my might, jumped to my feet and plunged it into his neck.

I stumbled out of the alley and found my footing. A carriage was going by and I staggered into the street and blocked it. The driver pulled the horses to a stop just before running me over.

"Oy, watch where you're going," the driver scolded. "I could've killed ya."

The vampire zoomed by me at such a speed the driver didn't seem to notice him. I watched him vanish quickly into the darkness. The driver then saw my wounds and helped me find a policeman. I led him to the alley and told him the partial truth – that I had heard his colleague scream, come to help and been attacked myself. I described the perpetrator honestly – minus the fangs – and the officer deduced that he must have been in the grip of some sort of murderous mania, perhaps drug-induced. The wounds on my neck were evidence enough of that.

I sit here now, at home in front of the fire. The puncture marks on my neck are healing remarkably quickly. I wish I could say the same for my bruises and scratches. But there is more to trouble my mind. While I am grateful to be alive, I can't help but worry about the vampire's words: *"I'm not supposed to kill you."* Why not, and by whose orders?

To explain my injuries, I told Florence I fell from the scaffolding at the theatre. She tended to my wounds and we once again apologised to each other for our earlier row.

She fell asleep in my arms. It made me feel safe momentarily, but when I drifted off I was awakened by nightmares. Nightmares that now will follow me throughout my day. I fear there will be no more sleep for me tonight.

FROM THE JOURNAL OF BRAM STOKER, 14TH OF JANUARY 1879

1:30 p.m.

Took lunch with Willie Wilde today at the Langham hotel.

He was hard to track down. A few weeks back he borrowed twenty pounds from me and then apparently disappeared off the face of the earth. I found out from a mutual friend that he is working as a freelance reporter (which is hard to imagine with his atrocious vocabulary and spelling skills), and that he is living with his mother, who has also relocated to London. I was sorry to hear they had fallen upon hard times once again and were barely supporting themselves.

Perhaps that was why Willie seemed happy to see me and agreed to let me treat him to lunch.

I needed to confide in someone about my run-in with the vampire. I also told him that Oscar and I had encountered one at the engagement party (leaving out the more lurid details, although I doubt it would shock him to discover his brother's predilections).

The news that a vampire had been a guest in his own home understandably came as a shock to Willie. He paled visibly, and his hand shook as he took a swig of gin from his flask, then poured the rest of its contents into his teacup.

He suggested I talk to Captain Burton about the situation, which of course had been my first thought as well. When I pointed out that the captain is currently in India, Willie asked, "What are you going to do?"

"Me?" I replied. "I was hoping 'we' would think of something. Willie, you are the only one I can turn to for help. Anyone else would think me quite mad."

"Oscar wouldn't think you mad," he said. "But I can see why you couldn't ask him for help after pilfering his bride-to-be."

Indeed. Oscar would just as soon kill me as any vampire. And truth be told, I do not care to spend time with him any more than he wants to see me. I would have been able to put aside our differences in temperament under normal circumstances, but the situation with Florence makes that quite impossible now.

"Would you be able to track this thing down, even if you did want to kill it?" Willie asked.

I thought it best not to burden him with knowledge of my second sight. Oscar knowing is bad enough. I pointed out that the creature seemed to be tracking *me* down. Willie then suggested that I consult his mother's library, which is quite extensive on subjects such as this. I readily agreed.

"And can I count on you to help dispatch them should it come to that?" I asked.

"Errr, I don't know, Bram. I think killing one supernatural creature in a lifetime is more than enough, don't you?"

I was a bit perturbed at his apparent cowardice. "You were not actually the one who killed the werewolf, though. Perhaps I am talking to the wrong Wilde brother after all."

"I didn't say I wouldn't. Did I say that? I just meant why are you taking the weight of the world on your shoulders? Do your research, figure out how to kill this thing and then we'll go to the authorities and let them handle it. Captain Burton will back us up. They'll have to believe him."

I am forced to admit that even in his inebriated state, Willie was making a great deal of sense.

FROM THE JOURNAL OF BRAM STOKER, 15TH OF JANUARY 1879

2:12 p.m.

Most of what I know about vampires comes from fiction: *Varney the Vampire* and other stories of that ilk. My limited experience with real vampires has shown me only that they are strong, fleet of foot and are turned by a silver cross.

Willie is right: if I am to combat these creatures, I must research the subject further. And so, I paid a visit to Lady Wilde and her extensive collection of folklore and supernatural texts today.

I was uncertain how she might receive me – she lost a daughter-in-law, after all, in addition to Oscar losing a bride – but she welcomed me warmly and asked after Florence. It was very nice to see her again and I apologised for not visiting sooner. I'm sure she sensed that I was concerned that a visit might bring about an encounter with Oscar. Thankfully, he was not visiting when I arrived.

Lady Wilde showed me into a small parlour, its shabbiness somewhat negated by furniture that I recognised from the Wilde's Dublin home, fading reminders of the elegance in which they once lived. I told Lady Wilde of my interest in vampire lore but did not mention that I had been attacked by one. As fond as I am of her, I knew such news would not remain between us.

"You're married now," she scolded. "You should put monster hunting behind you."

I agreed and claimed my interest was purely academic.

"Let's see," she mused. "The folk tales vary greatly. Vampires are mostly thought to be the un-baptised dead or recently executed criminals who come back to life, crawl out of the grave and feed off the blood of the living. A more scientific theory has it that eating tainted beef causes the affliction."

She searched her shelves briefly before pulling out a dusty volume. "The most scholarly work on the subject was done in 1746 by Dom Augustine Calmet. His study of the subject was set off by an increase of vampire reports from Germany and Eastern Europe. Here's an English translation."

I read the work with great interest. Calmet was impressed with the detail and corroborative testimonies regarding incidents of vampirism coming out of Eastern Europe and believed that it was unreasonable to simply dismiss them. As a theologian, he recognised that the existence and actions of such beings could have an important bearing on various theological conclusions concerning the nature of the afterlife. Calmet thought it necessary to establish the veracity of such reports and to understand the phenomena in light of the church's worldview. The Catholic Church roundly condemned the reports and, especially, the desecration of the bodies of people believed to be vampires.

Calmet defined a vampire as a person who had been dead and buried and then returned from the grave to disturb the living by sucking their blood and even causing death. The only remedy for vampirism was to dig up the body of the vampire and either sever its head and drive a stake through the chest or burn the body. As Oscar and I had seen, chopping off the head did indeed turn a vampire to dust, so that much of Calmet's information, at least, is reliable.

Some of the other texts Lady Wilde provided claimed a vampire could not come into a home unless invited and that they were unable to cross running water. There was nothing on the crucifix keeping them at bay, but silver and garlic were mentioned quite often as protection from the creatures.

What I found the most disappointing in the accounts was that none of these vampires looked like Count Ruthven or the one I had encountered in the alley. They were not articulate, nor could they even pass for a normal human. They were half-rotted corpses, reanimated and mostly brainless.

I have learned nothing more on how to detect vampires or exploit their weaknesses.

I thanked Lady Wilde for her help, promised to visit again and left. But just outside on the street, I ran into Oscar in all his foppish regalia. He was dressed in blue velvet with a purple top hat, and before I had even had a chance to take in his ridiculous appearance in its entirety, he came at me swinging a cane.

"You!" he screamed. "How dare you come to my mother's house, you, you scoundrel! I have had the common decency to avoid you, why could you not do the same?"

I stepped aside to avoid the cane and he stumbled forwards and lost the hat off his head.

I thought it best not to engage him further and tried to walk around him. He huffed and puffed and blocked my path.

"I should strike you down," he said. "It is bad enough you corrupted my sweet, young, impressionable Florence!"

"You are being overly dramatic, Oscar, as usual," I said.

"Overly dramatic? You snatched her away, and after I was kind enough to save your life!"

This very notion angered me to no end. I shouted back, "I wouldn't have been in danger if your family hadn't snatched *me* away!"

Oscar glared at me coldly. "You, sir, are no gentleman," he spat. "You not only stole my fiancée, you did so by betraying my confidence."

"I did no such thing."

"Are you denying you told her about finding me in a…compromising situation?" He at least had the decency to look somewhat shamefaced at the memory.

"I am denying it, yes," I said. I lowered my voice, as decorum dictates when speaking of such matters. "I would never repeat what I had seen you doing with the count in the cellar, especially to a woman. Most especially to Florence. If you had any regard for the feelings of others you would have suspected the truth by now. She turned to me for comfort when you were off gallivanting around Greece. That was no way for a recently engaged man to behave. She had her suspicions of your character even without me saying a single negative word about you."

As usual, logic proved no deterrent to Oscar's volatile whim. "Still, you took advantage," he exclaimed. He thought a moment, then added, "You used your voodoo on her! You put some sort of spell on her, for that is the only explanation why a beautiful girl like that would be interested in a low-class brute such as yourself!"

STOKER'S WILDE • 95

He was foaming at the mouth now, all worked up like a tea kettle about to shoot steam out of its top. He was causing such a scene that passersby were stopping.

Willie came out to see what the ruckus was about. He seemed very amused by the situation. "Everything all right, lads?"

"Hardly. Your brother here is about to bash my brains in with that cane of his."

"Shall I get you a cane, Bram, so you two can duel?"

"I *should* challenge you to a duel. Luckily for you, I abhor violence," Oscar said, lowering his cane and his voice. "But if I ever see you on my mother's doorstep again I will give you such a thrashing as you have never had before."

"Consider me frightened off then," I mocked, as if he were a little dog yapping at my heels.

Of course, this only served to antagonise him further. He glared at me and his voice turned icy cold. "Remember, Mr. Stoker, we all have things we wish to hide from the world. I suggest you show more discretion in the future."

I took this as the threat it was: that he could, at any time, tell the world of my curse.

"Oh, Oscar, I doubt he will steal *another* fiancée from you," Willie said. "Come inside before the neighbours have you arrested for disturbing the peace."

I turned and left, determined to avoid any further confrontation with Oscar Wilde. If I never see that twit again, I shall consider it a life well-lived.

FROM THE DIARY OF OSCAR WILDE, 15TH OF JANUARY 1879

Dear future Oscar,

Do you remember the day you nearly came to blows with Stoker? For me, that day was today.

He had the gall to call on my mother as though he has nothing for which he should feel ashamed! I am amazed he could be so brazen after his betrayal, for despite his protestations I am almost certain he told Florence of my momentary indiscretion with Count Ruthven. It did not matter to him that the monster had me mesmerised and I clearly was not myself. What Florrie must think of me!

He swore to me it would be a secret between us, then used the information to destroy our engagement and woo her away. Bad enough that he snatched away my chance at happiness, but the thought of my vivacious, charming Florrie torn from the life of joy and beauty which I could have provided and plunged into the dour, humourless world that he inhabits is almost too much to bear.

Ah, but he knows I have a secret of his as well. He is plagued by visions of the supernatural, and it is his greatest fear that this will be revealed. However, who would believe such a thing? Certainly not levelheaded Florrie, who, no matter how much I tried to convince her otherwise, thinks the werewolf hunt was a fictional account that sprang forth from my fertile imagination. (It is hard to blame her, for my imagination is one of my finest features.)

We, dear yours truly, will need some sort of proof.

FROM THE JOURNAL OF BRAM STOKER, 16TH OF JANUARY 1879

7:13 p.m.

After my vexing day, I slept much more soundly than I had expected to. Still, I awoke with the feeling that my dreams had been troubled, though my only clear recollection of them was of my childhood nanny, Mary, caring for me when I was ill.

Florence was in one of her good moods this morning and I made a point of being cheerful and attentive over breakfast. She kissed me so sweetly as she saw me off that I found myself looking forward to my return home even more than usual.

En route to the theatre, though, I grew uneasy again. On the tram, I endeavoured to read my newspaper but found myself peering at my fellow passengers with trepidation, looking for that telltale green glow. I could not tell if the pounding of my heart was the onset of another spell, or merely the dread of one.

It was with relief that I entered the relative calm of the theatre, where at least I knew that the challenges that awaited me were of the earthly variety. I spent the day productively enough, immersing myself in plan and detail and duty to the exclusion of all troubling distractions. Mr. Irving arrived in the afternoon for our first complete 'stagger-through' rehearsal of *Hamlet,* which I attended so that I could make note of any necessary production details. There was much stopping and starting as the cast and crew worked through details of entrances, exits and other movements about the stage, but I still found it stirring to hear the Bard's words brought to life by so talented an ensemble. Miss Terry as Ophelia was particularly affecting and I told her so after the read-through.

"Thank you, Mr. Stoker, but you are too kind," she replied. "I was merely giving my character some slight shade and colour today. I have much work to do yet before she is truly brought to life."

"And that effort is what makes you a true artist, Miss Terry," I said. "I have no doubt that by the time we open, Ophelia's confusion and despair will be felt all the way to the last row. I will stand in the lobby as the audience files out and shall hear nothing but your name and an assortment of superlatives."

A woman like Ellen Terry is accustomed to glowing reviews, but she smiled and blushed at that, which made me smile myself, a first for the day.

"I only hope to do justice to the text and to the production," she murmured. "Henry is a demanding director and I fear I will not be able to satisfy him."

"I myself have no such fears, and I can tell you with certainty that Mr. Irving does not either." I lowered my voice. "One wonders, however, about our Laertes," I said, with a knowing nod towards young Will Marpole, an actor only recently added to the company to replace another who had suffered a temporarily disabling injury. "He seems a bit over his depth."

"Do not be too hard on Will," she replied. "He will find his way. Or if he does not, Henry will somehow pull another Laertes out of his sleeve."

At that moment, Mr. Irving's commanding voice rang out: "Ellen, a word, please." With a smile and a slight curtsy, she took her leave. I returned to my office to see what crises had occurred while I tarried at our imaginary Elsinore.

As I passed through the theatre lobby later in the afternoon, a slightly rumpled, bemused-looking, middle-aged vicar approached. "Excuse me, young man," he said. "There is nobody at the front. Perhaps you could help me?"

"Certainly, sir," I said, wondering where our box office attendant had got to this time. "Are you looking for tickets to *Hamlet*? Come along to the box office and we'll see what we can do."

"No, no," he said. "I am looking for Henry Irving. He is expecting me, I believe," he said, slightly out of breath. The man was portly and his cheeks red from exertion. "Excuse me, it was a long walk from the railway station."

I had no particular reason to disbelieve the man, but people do on occasion misrepresent themselves in their desire to meet a favourite artist. Already in the short time I have been here, several young men have appeared at the stage door claiming to be suitors of Ellen Terry. I offered him a seat in the lobby and asked his name.

He introduced himself as the Reverend Richard Wilkins, and I went off in search of Mr. Irving.

I found him in his office making notes on his script and informed him of his visitor. He jumped up immediately, exclaiming, "Excellent! I have been awaiting his arrival." As we hurried down the stairs to the lobby, he told me that the reverend is an old friend and a vicar in Salisbury. "We correspond regularly, but our meetings are too rare," he said.

As we reached the lobby, he rushed forwards and clasped the reverend's hand warmly. "Richard," he said. "How glad I am to see you."

"The pleasure is mine, Henry," Wilkins replied. "I only wish my visit coincided with a performance of *Hamlet*."

"You must return for opening night. Have you met my new manager, Stoker?" Mr. Irving asked, and I was surprised to find myself being ushered into the midst of this warm reunion, and even more surprised and gratified at his next words. "He's the one I've written you about. Brilliant man, don't know how I ever managed without him."

I can only surmise that they must write each other frequently indeed if Mr. Irving would bother to tell the man about a new employee.

"Ah yes, Stoker. I should have guessed," Reverend Wilkins said, smiling. "Recently arrived in the city from Dublin, if I'm not mistaken."

"Indeed, I am," I replied. "And enjoying London immensely, though I confess I have yet to explore it fully."

"I'm certain that Henry here has scarcely given you the time," Wilkins said, with a playful look at his friend. "Bit of a slave rider, this one, from what I gather."

"I believe the term you're looking for is 'slave driver', Richard," Mr. Irving replied mildly. "And I deny all such charges. Officially." He smiled at me, which I took as my cue to return to my duties.

"I would certainly testify in your favour, sir," I said. "Nevertheless, I should attend to my work and leave the two of you to your visit." I turned to bid farewell to Reverend Wilkins but didn't get the chance.

"Nonsense," Mr. Irving said. "Join us for tea, Stoker. I'm sure there's nothing that can't wait until later. Or tomorrow." He turned to Wilkins. "Stoker is a newlywed, you see. I do hate to keep him from his evenings with his lovely wife, though admittedly I do from time to time."

I hesitated. "I do not wish to intrude," I said.

"Not at all, my boy," Wilkins replied jovially. "Henry and I will have plenty of time to catch up. Please do join us."

And so, I found myself at a shop down the street from the theatre, taking tea with my employer and his old friend. We were soon discussing Dublin, as Reverend Wilkins had been there just last year. "A lovely city," he said. "I found the people to be a most welcoming and intelligent lot."

"Were you there on business or pleasure, sir?" I asked.

"Business, I would call it, though there are many among the church leadership who would call it my crackpot whim."

I looked at him curiously.

"Richard has some unorthodox views," Mr. Irving commented with a smile.

"They are considered so here and now," the reverend said. "But we must not forget that here is not everywhere and now is not the sum total of time." He turned to me. "I was in Dublin speaking about the supernatural and the danger it poses to our Christian nation."

My mouth went dry, not entirely due to the slightly stale scone I had just bitten into. I took a sip of tea to compose myself. "The supernatural in what form, sir?"

He leant forwards eagerly. "It takes many forms, Bram. May I call you Bram?" I murmured my assent. "I have heard tales – from right here in Britain, mind – that would turn that ginger beard of yours white. Stories, credible stories, of vampires, witches and mummies. Why just a few years ago, I have it on good authority that a werewolf menaced the shores of your fair land."

"A werewolf you say?" My heart was beating wildly and I gripped the arms of my chair so as not to betray the trembling of my hands.

"Indeed. Imagine that, right there in Ireland!"

"Yes, imagine." My mind raced. Here was someone who knew what I knew, indeed far more than I, about the unseen evils of the world. About the monsters who prowl the night. About, perhaps, the elusive menace that had so briefly crossed my path just days ago. Should

I tell him my dark secret? Was this someone to whom I could, at last, unburden myself?

Looking to my right, I realised that here, also, was my employer. A man who has entrusted me with the care of his life's enterprise, who pays me handsomely for it, and who is responsible for my very presence in this city. How would he react to hear his trusted manager spout mad tales of sensing evil, seeing through the eyes of a monster, remembering horrific misdeeds that were not his own? How long could I expect to hold his trust were he to know of my curse?

"Surely such tales are—" I began.

"Utter lunacy?" the reverend finished wryly.

"I was going to say rare, and subject to interpretation," I finished.

"Rare, yes," Wilkins agreed. "Fortunately so, at least so far. But more and more the ancient monsters and pseudo-gods that plague the far-flung reaches of our Empire are reaching the shores of Britain. The faithful among us must prepare ourselves, or many more of us shall fall victim to their evils. Even if such things do not exist, the very idea that people think of them at all should give one pause. In fact, it may be worse if they are merely stories. Why would good Christian people be entertained by such tales?"

Mr. Irving was looking at me intently, but kindly. Had he noticed my discomfort? He finished his tea and said, "Yes, yes, Richard, but perhaps that's enough for now. Forgive him, Stoker, he has the passion of a zealot on this subject."

"No forgiveness is necessary," I replied hurriedly. "It's quite fascinating, actually. Perhaps...." I hesitated. "Perhaps we could speak of it in more depth at a later date."

"Of course, my boy," the reverend replied, smiling. "I should like nothing better."

And with that we returned to the theatre, I to my work and the two old friends to Mr. Irving's office. As I passed on my way home, I heard the reverend's voice raised in prayer. This surprised me, as I have not known Mr. Irving to be a spiritual man. Perhaps he was only indulging his old friend, but I hope he takes genuine comfort and guidance from the prayers.

WHITE WORM SOCIETY BLACK BISHOP REPORT, 16TH OF JANUARY 1879

Operative: Anna Hubbard
Location: London, England

I have taken a position as a cleaning woman at the Lyceum Theatre in order to investigate Henry Irving. We now know he had a copy of *The Munich Manual of Demonic Magic* in his possession. I have managed to get into his library, which I can only safely do when I know he is performing on the stage, for the only access to it is through his office, where he works most nights.

He has a very extensive collection on the occult, but nothing else as dangerous as the volume stolen from his office. There is, however, a membership directory for the Order of the Golden Dawn, which I have never seen before. It would make a valuable addition to our collection and I will try to steal it if I get the chance.

FROM THE DIARY OF OSCAR WILDE, 31ST OF JANUARY 1879

Dear diary,

I have returned to Dublin to oversee the sale of the rest of my father's property. This is a task that should be left up to Willie, but he is off on one of his alcoholidays and is nowhere to be found.

Apparently, our father owned a few cottages that have only come to light after a cousin's death. It is good news as we can use the money. Why my father had these cottages is something of a mystery, although it was most likely to hide away a mistress or two. Whatever the reason, I shall simply accept this as good fortune bestowed upon me by a benevolent universe.

While I wait for the transactions to complete I have taken the opportunity to investigate Stoker's past.

While in Greystones, he confided in me that his 'visions' began when he was seven years of age after a period of grave illness. His mother still lives in Dublin, though not in the house where he grew up.

One morning when I knew Mrs. Stoker was out I knocked at the back door and a maid answered. She looked to be in her late thirties. Her apron was covered with flour and when she opened the door a cloud of it sprinkled itself onto my clothes.

She was taken aback, exclaiming, "Oh, sir, this entrance is for deliveries. You want to go 'round the front."

"My apologies, miss, but it is you I would like to speak with, if you have the time, that is."

"Oh, dear, I don't know if that would be proper...."

"I am not here to sell you anything or to court you, though you are quite pretty."

She blushed and giggled, of course.

"I am a friend of Mr. Bram Stoker, Mrs. Stoker's son. We were children together and I have fond memories of his nanny and was wondering if she is still employed here?"

"She passed a while back, I'm sorry to tell ya."

So, the nanny was no good to me for information, outside of a séance. I could ask Mother to help with that, but her séances never go off quite as planned.

"Are there any staff left who might have known her, from Bram's childhood I mean?"

"No, I'm the only housekeeper now. I don't know of any except for the housemaid who I replaced. She joined a convent."

So, dear diary, it looks like I am off to a nunnery.

FROM THE DIARY OF OSCAR WILDE, 3RD OF FEBRUARY 1879

Dear yours truly,

I am uneasy in holy places, for many reasons of which you are quite aware, and convents make me especially queasy. These poor girls locking themselves away from life. Imagine, dressing drably on purpose! No art on the walls, nor flowers on the table; I have seen stables with better decor.

The maid took the name Sister Agnes when entering the convent. I told the mother superior that I was a long-lost nephew and was allowed to see her. I do not know what I thought she could tell me, or why she would tell me anything at all. What did she know? That Bram was a strange child, I suspect, but that is apparent to anyone who knows him as an adult.

We met in a large room with a long table, the dining hall perhaps. Other nuns were about, sweeping and doing nunnish things.

She was confused to see me but took it in stride. The spiritual life does thrive on serenity, after all.

"All of my nephews are accounted for, and you are not one of them," she said.

"I apologise for the ruse," I said. "My name is Oscar Wilde, and I am a friend of Bram Stoker...."

She quickly sat down at the table across from me. Her face had gone white, which is very apparent when one is wearing black.

"Bram!" she exclaimed more loudly than she wanted to. She lowered her voice and asked, "Is he well, Mr. Wilde?"

"Yes, fine," I said, then added, "physically, at least." Her reaction convinced me that she did indeed have the information I sought, and so I decided to lay all my cards on the table. "He's been having visions, Sister Agnes."

She looked distressed. "What sort of visions?"

"Demonic, I fear," I said, feeling that this would have the desired effect. "I am quite worried about him. He confided in me that he had similar visions when he was a child."

"Oh, saints protect us. I was hoping there would not be any ill effects."

"Whatever do you mean? Effects from what?"

"I have said too much already." She stood to leave and I grabbed her hand.

"Please, if there is anything that can help me understand Bram's condition, I must know." Her eyes were still hesitant. "Sister Agnes, his very soul may be in danger." Appealing to her piety worked for she sat back down.

"It is something that has weighed upon my own soul for some time now," she said. "Yet I cannot bring myself to talk of it in confession. Sometimes I convince myself that it didn't happen at all. Does Bram not remember...that night he was cured?"

I didn't know what she was talking about and decided to lie. "He does not," I said. "Consider me your confessor in this matter. I will keep what you tell me in the strictest confidence."

She smiled ruefully. "No one would believe you if you were to tell, but Bram has a right to know, though he may not want to."

"It might help him control his curse if he understands." (Perhaps, diary, it is my propensity for lying to nuns that makes me so uncomfortable around them. Something to consider.)

She sighed. "Well, I'm not sure I understand it myself. I certainly didn't at the time, but I was just a slip of a girl when I worked for the Stokers. My name was Bonnie then. I shared a room with the nanny, Mary Crone, and it soon became apparent that she did not walk with God. She read books on the occult and practised divination. While this bothered me, I did not feel it was my place to set her down the correct path, for she did, as well, read the Bible daily and attended church twice weekly."

"Did the Stokers know about this?" I asked. Bram does not seem the sort to have grown up in a tolerant household.

"Oh yes. In fact, they would often ask her to do their astrological charts or brew a potion for an ailment. There were five children in the family and they all were very fond of Mary. And despite her ways, she seemed to me a good woman. Over time, I too grew accustomed to her behaviour in these matters and thought little of it."

"How old was Bram at the time?"

"Six. He was a sickly lad, bedridden most days, but cheerful and bright. I would often keep him company, and he would read me stories he wrote. When he discovered I could not read, he started teaching me and I was reading myself in only a few months.

"However, his taste in literature concerned me – books of the occult, tales of pirates and highwaymen. He was especially fond of *Frankenstein*, a book of which I could see some moral value, as it shows the follies of playing God, but it is morbid nonetheless."

I felt glad she did not know of the reading material available in my home as I was growing up.

"One morning I came into his room to find him covered in a sheet. I gasped and dropped the laundry, for it appeared he had passed in the night. To my relief, he stirred and pulled the sheet down.

"'Don't fret, Bonnie, I was just practising being dead,' he said.

"'Why would you want to go and do a thing like that?' I cried.

"'I heard Mother talking with the doctor. She doesn't know I can hear through the chimney flue. He said I only have a few months to live and that I may not see Christmas.'

"Upon hearing this I felt faint. I tried the best I could to hide my sorrow and fear from him. I told him he must have heard wrong and that he'd be out of bed in no time.

"'The only way I am leaving this bed is in a coffin,' he said, without a bit of remorse in his voice. 'What do you think it will be like to spend eternity in a coffin?'"

My goodness, Bram *was* a morbid child! Perhaps he is not so ill-suited to the theatrical life as I thought.

Sister Agnes continued. "Later, I asked Mary if it were true, and she said it was. The blood disorder Bram suffered from was not curable, and he had taken a turn for the worse.

"'There is nothing science can do for him. He's in God's hands now,' she said.

"I wondered how God could do this to such a young, bright boy. In my mind, I could hear my mother chiding me not to question the

Lord's wisdom, but I didn't care. Her voice seemed very far away then.

"Mary told me there might be a way we could save him, but she didn't dare tell the Mister or Missus. 'Tonics and horoscopes are one thing,' she said, 'but this....'"

Sister Agnes looked away, her brow furrowed. I feared she was about to cut our interview short and urged her on gently. "Whatever Mary's idea, it worked, obviously. But at what cost? Please, Sister, I must know." She looked at me sharply, and I hastened to add, "For Bram's sake." She nodded and went on.

"She told me that she knew of a Gipsy woman who might be able to cure him with magic. I scoffed at the notion. 'But it is better than doing nothing,' she persisted.

"So, I was tasked that night to go to the Gipsy camp on the edge of town to fetch the woman and bring her to Bram's bedside. These weren't the Irish Travellers I had encountered in the city, but Romanian Gipsies who had by then mostly been driven out of Ireland."

"Yes," I said. "I've heard of them." My mother, in fact, used to visit their camps often to learn their lore, but I thought it best not to mention that to Sister Agnes.

She continued. "I took the Stokers' horse and carriage, following Mary's directions out of town and down a dark, lonely road. The looming forest seemed more frightening in the moonlight and I feared highwaymen. But soon I heard the music and saw the firelight of the Gipsy camp. As I got closer it was almost too much to take in. People dancing half-naked, singing drunken songs. The smell of spicy foods and unbathed men filled the air and it was all I could do to catch my breath.

"I dared not get out of my carriage and did not have to, as the old woman was expecting me and met me on the edge of the camp.

"'You have been sent by Sister Crone?' she asked. She was wrinkled and grey and looked every bit the witch, dressed in colourful silks and adorned with jewellery that bore pagan symbols. I nodded and she bade me to wait, saying, 'I'll get the master.' I grew even more uneasy.

"She returned shortly with a tall man dressed in a black cloak. I was immediately taken with fear of him and at the same time, I could not look away from his face. He was dark-haired and handsome, his alabaster skin seeming to glow in the moonlight. He was tall and thin, but not gangly as some such men are. His face was youthful and yet not, for his eyes had a wise and weary look, as though he had seen much.

"The horse backed away as he approached and I could not regain control. The man waved his hand ever so slightly and the horse calmed, then bowed his head before the man.

"He did not speak on our way back into town. The old woman looked up at the stars and began to sing a song in a language I did not recognise. The horse sped up, and I could see something running beside us. It was a wolf! I let out a little yelp and the old woman laughed and said, 'There are worse things in these woods than a wolf, my dear.' The wolf stayed with us until we reached the gaslights of the city, then turned back.

"Mary was waiting in the garden. She let out a small gasp when she saw the man but quickly regained her wits.

"The man leapt off the carriage with an eerie silence. Not even his cloak flowing behind him made a sound. And then, in one quick motion, he snatched the old Gipsy woman from the carriage as if she were as light as a wee babe and gently set her on the ground.

"'Do you know who I am?' he asked Mary in a deep baritone voice.

"'Yes,' she said, and I noticed she avoided his eyes. She looked to the Gipsy woman. 'You told me you had a potion.'

"'He is better than any potion. Do not fret, Mary Crone, he means us no harm. Far from it. Sometimes a dance with the devil will bring the angels running.'

"'Invite me in,' he commanded.

"Mary seemed not to know what to do. She glanced back at the house – how safe and warm it looked. She looked at me, but I was no help to her, as frightened as I was. Finally, she made her decision. 'Please, enter,' she said, swinging open the garden door. She told me to put the carriage away and not to come upstairs."

Diary, I fervently hoped young Bonnie had not heeded that instruction. My hope was rewarded!

"My curiosity got the better of me," she continued. "I went up the back stair and into the connecting linen cupboard where I knew I could observe them unseen.

"Bram's room was lit only by the light of the fireplace. In the shadows, I could see a pentagram had been drawn on the floor at the foot of the bed. Bunches of wolfsbane and clover hung from the bed's canopy. Little Bram sat up to greet his visitors.

"His voice was weak but he smiled politely. He was always a well-mannered child. 'Are you a new doctor?'

"'Yes,' the man replied, his voice as rich and intoxicating as wine. 'Let us see what we can do for you. Look deeply into my eyes.'

"Bram did as he was told and, in an instant, he appeared to be mesmerised.

"'Sleep, my child.' The man turned to Mary. 'He is seven years of age?'

"'This very night,' Mary said.

"'Could this be the one?' he asked the Gipsy woman as he touched the boy's ginger hair.

"'It is written that snatching an innocent from the grip of death will protect him from curses, repel the evil eye and allow him to open the doors between worlds,' she said.

"'He will not become....' The man fell silent.

"'Like you? No. If you give and do not take, his innocence will protect him.'

"'It has been so long since I have fed. I fear the act of giving will destroy me. I am weak. It takes all my strength to not succumb to the monster within.' I caught a glimpse of the man's face and saw that his eyes, so difficult to look away from, were anguished.

"The old woman seemed much more certain. 'It has been a long time since you have killed. If you are not the one to break the curse, no one is.'

"I trembled in the cupboard, unsure of what I was seeing. What evil pagan ritual was about to be performed? My mouth fell open in a silent scream as I watched the man bite at his own wrist, causing blood to trickle down his arm. He put his wrist up to Bram's mouth and the boy began to suckle like a pup.

"I fell to my knees, my legs unable to hold me up. I wanted to scream, to wake the household, but nothing would come. I fell forwards and the cupboard door swung open as I tumbled into the room. Blackness enveloped me and I fainted dead away.

"The next morning, I awoke in my bed. With the morning light warming the room, I was sure it had all been a bad dream. For a moment, I was at peace. But then I felt the bandage around my neck."

Sister Agnes's hand went to her neck then, and I wished the nun's habit was just a bit more revealing. (Diary, I am not having impure thoughts, I swear; I just wanted to see the bite marks.)

"I cried out and Mary came rushing in. 'Calm down child, all is well! It was a small price to pay for Bram's life,' she said. It was then I noticed the bandage around her own neck. 'He took just what he needed from us to replenish what he gave to the boy.'

"I feared I would become a monster, but she assured me that one bite would not be enough to harm me.

"At that moment, Bram himself came running into my room. 'What is wrong? Are you all right, Bonnie?'

"'She just had a bad dream,' Mary said.

"But I had forgotten my troubles the moment I saw Bram running. He got better each day after that. The doctor proclaimed it a miracle, but I knew it was not the work of God. But who was I to tell? Would they believe me, or think me mad?

"I left the household that spring and entered the convent."

She paused, spent.

"That is a remarkable story, Sister Agnes," I said.

She smiled sadly. "You don't believe me."

I rushed to assure her that I did. "And for what it's worth, I think you did the right thing."

Her eyes were troubled. "Well, sometimes I think the whole episode was a horrible dream. But then I look into the mirror and see the scars on my neck and know that I have been touched by evil. I have no right even to enter this holy place, but I fear to leave it. In any event, it is your secret and your burden now, Mr. Wilde."

She bade me farewell and I gathered my things and left.

There you have it. What are we do to with this information, diary? I am having second thoughts about telling Florrie of his condition, for it would just upset her unnecessarily and not even I am that sort of cad.

Stoker may be part monster and her life could be in danger. However, I must confess I do not believe this. He saved my life once from a vampire and I admit he at least tries to be a virtuous person.

Should I tell him the tale if he does not remember it? Would he even believe me? Is this the cause of his second sight and would it bring him comfort to know the origin? Or would it only anger him that I investigated his past? I will not bring him comfort, nor do I wish to anger him further, so for now I will keep this to your pages, dear diary.

I put all this behind me and return to London tomorrow, to see where life takes me next.

LETTER FROM ELLEN TERRY TO LILLIE LANGTRY, 6TH OF FEBRUARY 1879

Archivist's note: At this time Lillie Langtry was the mistress of the Prince of Wales and was not yet the famous actress she was to become. She saved the letters from Ellen Terry for her entire life, so one can assume she found them entertaining at the very least. We are not sure how she responded to these letters as Ellen Terry did not save any of her return correspondence.

My dearest Lillie,

I hope this letter finds you well in your little Red House in Bournemouth.

I have settled into my life at the Lyceum quite well, but thankfully I am not there quite as many hours a day now. I have finally secured lodgings of my own and am no longer staying at the theatre.

My needs are modest, and as such I have hired a room, as the return address on this letter reflects. I have become acquainted with Florence Stoker, the wife of our theatre manager, and through her met Lucy Mayhew. Lucy lives with her Aunt Agatha, who, it turns out, would welcome the additional income provided by a respectable young woman lodger. Unable to locate one, she settled for a theatrical Gipsy such as me! She has a cook and a maid who see to all my needs and this lets me concentrate fully on the play at hand.

Lucy and I have become fast friends and she is grateful for the company, for her aunt travels frequently. I am glad to be there, particularly now, as Lucy has recently taken ill. Nothing to worry about, the doctor assures us, nothing more than anaemic blood for which he has prescribed a strong tonic. Still, I feel better being there to check on her daily.

And for my own part, I am relieved to not spend another night in that eerie theatre. As I told you in my last letter, the recent robbery left me quite shaken. I still wonder what was in that book that made it so valuable to a thief?

On my remaining nights there I made sure my door was securely bolted and my favourite prop sword close to hand.

My new director I find to be very off-putting. Oh, not as a director, for there he is patient and helpful, but when not working with actors he is a stern taskmaster. Poor Mr. Stoker. He is at Mr. Irving's beck and call at all times. He is not only responsible for the day-to-day operation of the theatre, but also performs the duties of a personal servant! Scarcely a moment goes by in which Irving is not barking an order at him or making a complaint about how things are being done, all of which Stoker seemingly takes in stride.

Strangely, now that we are in the thick of rehearsals, Irving insists that we work only at night, for that is when the play will be performed and he is of the opinion that we will do well to set our 'performance clocks', as he calls them, to this time.

After rehearsal, when the actors have been let go, poor Mr. Stoker must take down copious performance notes under Irving's dictation. This can go on well into the night, I am told. I wonder how Mrs. Stoker feels about the hours her husband keeps. She is far too diplomatic to complain about it to a member of the company!

Irving himself stays up all night, poring over his books until the sun comes up. He then sleeps most of the day, rising in the afternoon to prepare for another night's work. I suppose a life in the theatre has accustomed him to such hours.

He is an odd duck in many ways. I have never seen him partake in drink (which is extremely rare for theatre people, who, as you know, often do so with gusto). He holds to all the tiresome theatrical superstitions: actors must not wish each other luck before a performance, we must never mention the name of the Scottish play, and all mirrors must be covered when he enters a room.

He has not much of a social life, so far as I can tell. He does attend soirees from time to time if invited by a patron of the arts, but I have never seen him go out with friends. Aside from Mr. Stoker, his closest friend must be a Reverend Wilkins, whom he has known for many years.

I have never seen two friends more different from one another.

Irving is thin, pale and of sombre mood, while Wilkins is quite plump, rosy-cheeked and jovial. He is quick with a joke and, unlike Irving, is not one to pass up a good meal or bit of drink.

I would have never reckoned Mr. Irving for a religious man (for I know he does not attend any church), but when the good reverend visits they spend much time praying and going over religious texts in Irving's office. Perhaps Irving is just humouring a friend, but he does seem in better spirits when Wilkins visits.

As for *my* social life, I am afraid there will be none until the closing night of this play. As we are often reminded, the Lyceum and its company have very high standards and I am consumed by my desire to live up to them. If this is not the finest Ophelia to grace the London stage in a generation, I shall consider it a personal failure!

In particular, I do not see as much of our dear friend Oscar as I would like. He detests Mr. Stoker and refuses to set foot in the Lyceum as long as he works there, though I expect I can persuade him to attend a performance. (Have you ever known Oscar to pass up the opportunity to be seen at an opening night?) He has even talked about challenging Mr. Stoker to a duel! Oscar being Oscar, to be sure, but I hope he can find it in his heart to truly forgive Florence and to at least be civil to Mr. Stoker. If Oscar has any aspirations as a playwright, it would not be in his best interests to keep the manager of the Lyceum an enemy.

Write back soon.

Love,

Ellen

FROM THE DIARY OF OSCAR WILDE, 12TH OF FEBRUARY 1879

Dearest diary,

You'll remember, future Oscar, that I've written about Frank's portrait clientele, comprising the lovely and fashionable of London society. Well, they're all as plain as dinner plates compared to the young man I met yesterday when I wandered into Frank's studio.

It was late afternoon and the sun was approaching the horizon, bathing the model in a rich golden light, and lending a warm glow to his flaxen hair. Frank had posed him standing, wearing an Italian suit that perfectly complemented his tall, lithe frame. In his right hand he held an open pocket watch, and he was looking off into the distance as if waiting for a train, or perhaps a late lover's coach.

When our eyes met, I felt that I was growing pale. He gazed at me, tilting his head slightly – Frank must have been working on another part of the portrait or he surely would have been annoyed at the tiny movement – and a curious sensation of terror came over me. I knew that I had come face to face with someone whose mere personality was so fascinating that, if I allowed it to do so, it would absorb my whole nature, my whole soul, my very art. I did not want this influence in my life.

His still face broke into a playful smile as though he knew my thoughts and found them amusing.

I don't know how to explain it to you. Something seemed to tell me that I was on the verge of a terrible crisis in my life. I had a strange feeling that fate had in store for me exquisite joys and exquisite sorrows, great temptations and momentous choices that would determine what kind of man I would be – and I felt certain I would choose wrong, all the while knowing what was right. I grew afraid and turned to quit the room. It was not conscience that made me do so; it was a sort of cowardice. I take no credit to myself for trying to escape the temptations that await.

Frank glanced away from his canvas long enough to see the look of astonishment on my face.

"Beautiful, isn't he," Frank whispered. "I am afraid he is the property of Lord Basil Wotton. Well, he is his patron in any event. Lord Basil is the one paying for this portrait."

I doubted that the young man could hear what we were saying, but he knew he was being discussed. I regained my composure and turned to inspect the painting, which was nearly complete. It was remarkable, even for Frank. He had managed to capture his subject's elemental nature on the canvas, right down to the spark of life in the young man's eyes.

"Frank," I said, shifting my gaze from portrait to model, "please introduce me to your friend." He remained in pose, except that his eyes darted up and down as if he were trying to take me all in.

"Derrick Pigeon, Oscar Wilde," Frank said, returning his attention to his canvas. "Derrick plays the piano like Mozart, or so I am told. I have never heard him play myself. And Oscar does…what *do* you do, Oscar?"

"Think mostly. And from time to time I write my thoughts down as a poem or a witty letter to a fascinating person," I said.

"Quit grinning like a school girl, Derrick," Frank scolded. "It is most unbecoming and I am but moments away from completing this wretched painting."

"Sorry," said Derrick, staring again into the imaginary distance. "It is a pleasure to meet you, Mr. Wilde. Satisfying to finally put a face to the name…and to the stories, only half of which I hope are true."

"Half are true and the other half I made up myself," I replied.

"That is a relief," Derrick said. "I didn't think any one man could be that bawdy all the time."

"Perhaps not all the time, but I am a work in progress," I said. "And what sort of stories should I be telling about you?"

"Only dull ones so far, I'm afraid. I am quite new to London society and its gossip."

Frank tossed his brush down with a loud clatter and proclaimed the painting finished.

Derrick stuffed the watch back into its pocket and rushed over to see the portrait. He grasped it by the sides and yanked it off the easel as if he were a boy grabbing a present on Christmas Day.

"Careful, the paint's not dry," Frank said testily.

"It is brilliant!" Derrick studied the portrait up and down. "It is like looking into a mirror. Better, for I have never seen my soul in a mirror."

Frank gently pulled the canvas from his hands. "Well then, all the more important that you let it dry properly. We wouldn't want your soul smearing onto your waistcoat." He set it back down on the easel and backed away to get a better look. "What do you think, Oscar?"

"It's marvellous. You have truly outdone yourself this time, Frank."

"It helps to have the perfect model. And to have the light of youth radiating from him," Frank said, and the way he spoke held nothing of flattery or polite conversation; it was a simple statement of fact, an artist appreciating his subject in the same way a butcher might comment that the slab of meat before him was particularly fresh. He turned to Derrick and added, "Your benefactor should be pleased."

"Yes, the old fop should be happy to hang this in his study," Derrick said. His face went all sad, which distressed me more than it should have. "Why is good art wasted on fools? The sooner I can get away from the old letch the better."

Derrick plopped himself down in a big, overstuffed chair Frank keeps by the window. "I suppose I'll be old one day, like Lord Basil. And I'll be the one chasing youth and trying to suck the life out of its marrow."

"Ageing is the only fair thing about life," Frank said.

"What if it were possible to cheat it, though?" Derrick asked. "What if you could remain young forever? Wouldn't that be grand?"

"It might grow tiresome after a few hundred years," I said. "My God, the old men at the club are dreadfully bored and most of them are barely past sixty."

"There is a difference between bored and boring," Frank said, cleaning off his brushes.

Derrick let out a sigh. "The sun is setting and I must be off to perform at one of Lord Basil's mixers." He stood and fetched his overcoat and hat. "You and Frank should come to the Cock and Bull this Saturday, Mr. Wilde. I play there for my friends. Nothing classical, just a good old singsong."

"Please, I insist you call me Oscar. That does sound delightful but getting Frank out of the house these days is a bit of a struggle," I said, not knowing whether or not I hoped he would urge me to come alone if necessary.

"I will come," Frank said. "If only to see Oscar enter such a place. It's fish and chips, Oscar, not escargots."

"You tease, but I am an Irishman after all. I am at home in any pub. Remind me to tell you about the Blue Moon in Greystones."

"Good, it is settled then. I will see you there on Saturday night," said Derrick, cheery once more after his momentary thoughtfulness. He bade us farewell and took his leave.

Frank was already staring critically at the portrait again, and I quietly finished cleaning his brushes to mitigate the temptation I knew he was feeling to deepen this shadow or repaint that trouser cuff. The thing was perfect as it was. When I finished, I suggested tea and Frank agreed. As we left the studio, I looked once more upon the portrait, and for the first time it was Frank who had to remind me to come along and have a bite to eat.

FROM THE JOURNAL OF BRAM STOKER, 15TH OF FEBRUARY 1879

11:31 p.m.

I am shaken, to be sure. For the second time within a month, I have been attacked on the street. There is nothing like an assault upon one's person to make a man feel like a helpless child.

What brought on the attack, I do not know. If it were money they were after, why not say so? A proper highwayman would give the command 'stand and deliver' and the like. These villains asked nothing of me.

I was leaving the theatre to go home for supper, as I often do, before returning for the evening's rehearsal. It was very foggy and a moonless night, a perfect environment for thieves of all sorts.

I do not even remember hearing footfalls behind me, just a sudden plunge into darkness as a burlap sack was pulled down over my head. At first, I feared another vampire attack, but these men were too clumsy and I could struggle against them.

There were at least three of them. Two held me back while the third's grubby fingers tore at my sleeve, trying to get my cufflink, no doubt. I struggled with all my might. Looking back, this was a foolish thing to do, for a few possessions are not worth my life.

In the struggle, I felt the sharp jab of a needle at my wrist. My heart raced as I feared I was being drugged. For what? Did they mean to shanghai me onto a merchant ship? Or worse, to kill me and sell my cadaver to the local medical school?

Just when I felt all hope was lost, a voice cried out, "Stop! You ruffians!" I heard my saviour running towards them, then the sounds of him thwacking them with something.

My would-be abductors released me immediately and ran off. I stumbled to my knees and fell forward, but someone caught me.

He pulled off the sack. "Mr. Stoker!" an astonished voice exclaimed. It was Reverend Wilkins. "Are you hurt?"

"I don't think so. They did jab me with something," I said as he helped me fully to my feet. "But I am all right, just shaken."

"I beat them off with my trusty umbrella," he said, brandishing it like a club.

"That was quite brave of you," I said. "I am forever in your debt."

"Jabbed you, you say? Are you sure they did not drug you?" He took my elbow solicitously.

"It was a hypodermic needle. I felt them pull the plunger back but you stopped them before they pushed it down, I am fairly sure of that." I showed him my wrist, where a slow trickle of blood was evident, then drew my handkerchief to staunch it. "In any event, I feel no effects. Surely it would be a quick-acting agent of some kind."

"Well, to be safe let me walk you home," he said in a fatherly tone.

"I thank you, Reverend, and in return, I insist you stay for dinner."

"Oh, I don't wish to impose upon your dear wife," he said. "Unexpected guests can throw women into quite a tither, I have observed."

I am not sure whether he meant to say 'dither' or 'tizzy', but either way, I replied, "Florence would never forgive me should I fail to bring my rescuer home for dinner. And besides, our cook always makes far more food than two people can reasonably consume. Please, join us."

"Well, if you insist. I was on my way to see if Henry wanted to join me for supper, but he is not expecting me."

"It's settled, then," I said, clapping him on the shoulder, and ushering him along the thoroughfare.

"I wish I had got a better look at them," he said, glancing around as if he might still catch a glimpse of the villains. "But it was so foggy, and my eyes aren't what they used to be."

"I am sure we won't see them again," I said. "With any luck, having an angry vicar attack from the fog will put the fear of God into them."

"Well," he said, chuckling, "I don't imagine I have ever put the fear of God into anyone before. It is quite a novel experience!"

Florence welcomed our guest graciously and gushed her gratitude when she heard of the evening's events. I should not have told her, but there is a small but angry bruise on my wrist and a larger one on my right side where I had been held particularly roughly, so it would not have remained secret for long. After a pleasant but hurried meal, I left them chatting and returned to the theatre to complete my day's work. I encountered no further trouble on the streets. Still, I may do well to arm myself somehow in future. I must remember that London is not Dublin and that not all danger is of the supernatural variety.

FROM THE DIARY OF OSCAR WILDE, 16TH OF FEBRUARY 1879

Dear yours truly,

My head is still swimming from last night at the Cock and Bull, where Frank and I went to see Derrick play piano for a jolly good singsong.

Few are immune to Derrick's charms, it would seem, as by the end of the evening anyone in the crowd would have gladly taken him home for a hot meal or to marry their daughter. There was nothing he could not play, and all from memory too; Irish drinking songs, popular parlour tunes, traditional folk songs, none was beyond his repertoire.

The Cock and Bull is near Dutfield's Yard in Whitechapel, a place I would not normally venture during the day, let alone in the dark of night. Frank, however, has been there many times and has always returned safely. I took along a pistol for protection but felt foolish when I entered the pub and found the crowd to be most jovial. The pub itself was clean and warm, hazy from tobacco smoke, but free of the stale odours one usually finds in such places. I am pleased to note that it bore scant resemblance to the Blue Moon in Greystones! (Do you remember, Oscar of the future, that thrilling tale from our youth? Remind me to write it down so we don't forget. I doubt Florrie kept the letters.)

Among the patrons were prostitutes and criminal types to be sure, but there were many upper-class gentlemen and middle-class working folk. Even a constable or two came in from the cold for a quick nip.

When we arrived, Derrick was leading the entire pub in a rousing rendition of 'I am the Captain of the *Pinafore*', his sprightly fingers dancing along the keyboard, his clear, fine voice rising above all others, his merry smile making a friend of every person in the room from the swellest gent to the lowest pickpocket. I longed for a moment alone with him, but he belonged to the crowd. As midnight approached, however, snow began to fall and the wind to howl, driving many to leave for home. Only a few of us remained around his piano.

Derrick introduced us to his acquaintances. There was Nick Dripp, who spoke with an Eastern European accent. He was short and stocky, with dirt under his nails and a flinty look about his eyes. He struck me as someone who works in an unclean industry, a chimney sweep perhaps, though his clothing belied this impression, being *au courant* and of decent quality.

Dripp was flanked by two equally unsavoury characters, introduced as Mr. Leech and Mr. Coal. Both were brutes like you might see working the docks or in the back of a butcher's shop and neither had Mr. Dripp's fashion sense. Leech was pale and looked as slimy as his namesake. Coal might be mistaken for ruggedly handsome if one were to wipe away a layer of dirt and perhaps comb his hair, an unruly mop as black as his name implies. The three of them had been joining in the general mood of conviviality, but there was a nastiness about them, as though their amusement was at, not with, the rest of us. They could often be seen muttering to each other, stealing furtive glances at one or another of the assembled crowd, and laughing harshly. None of these people seemed to be worthy of Derrick's company and I was curious as to how they had ever met, let alone become friends.

Derrick ordered up a round of brandy and French cigarettes for Frank and me. Frank had taken out his sketchpad as usual and was feverishly trying to capture Mr. Dripp's swarthy face as a charcoal caricature.

"'Hey, vut are ya doin' there?" Dripp asked, straining to see Frank's drawing.

"I am making you famous," he said.

Dripp lurched forward, ripped the paper from the pad and crumpled it up. "I like my anonymity just the vay it is, thank you." It was surprising to hear a word like 'anonymity' come out of his mouth un-mangled. It was like hearing a dog say 'good morning'.

"You'll have to forgive Mr. Dripp," Derrick said as he improvised a soft tune on the keyboard. "He has little appreciation for the arts."

"What line of work are you in, Mr. Dripp?" I asked.

"I'm an assistant to a fine gentleman. Leech and Coal here vork for me."

"Ah, I should have known you were a gentleman's gentleman," I said, hoping he would hear the mocking in my voice. "Your calm, helpful demeanour gives it all away."

He took offence, but not as one would have hoped. "I am not a valet! I run an entire estate. And just vut do *you* do for vork, Mr. Wilde?" he asked, taking care to over-enunciate the *W* in my name – perhaps he thought it was some sort of insult.

"He amuses me," Derrick said before I offered an answer. "Isn't that enough?" At that moment, I felt that it could, indeed, be enough. Mr. Dripp disagreed.

"A monkey could do that," he said. "And probably be content with less expensive cigarettes and liquor."

"Indeed," I retorted. "There is ample evidence of that right here in this pub tonight." I had made sure to slide my hand over the pistol in my pocket before I said this, but Dripp's only retaliation was a loathing glare.

"Ve haf someplace ve need to be," he said to his burly friends. "It's time to go."

With that, Leech and Coal followed their master into the snowy night. On their way out, they let in a gust of icy cold wind that made me shiver.

"Interesting characters," Frank said. "Wherever did you find them?"

"They found me," Derrick said, still playing the piano, seemingly with as little thought or effort as the average person puts into breathing. "Before my current benefactor took me in I earned my living as the musical entertainment in a house of ill fame where they were regulars."

"How the ladies must have looked forward to their visits," I remarked. Derrick just smiled.

"They took a shine to me and would take me out on the town with them. The seedier part of town, of course, but I was grateful for the company when I didn't have a penny to my name. Now I am returning the favour and am hoping to introduce them to a little culture."

"And how is that project going?" I asked.

"Better than expected," he said. "They have made the acquaintance of soap and table cutlery. And next week I shall teach them to waltz. I saw a bear waltz once, so I believe they could do it as well."

"In whose employ are they?" Frank asked. "Surely not your patron, Lord Wotton?"

"Heavens no, he would disown me if he ever found me associating with the likes of them. No, they work for some mysterious foreigner. They're getting his estate ready for his eventual emigration to England."

"From where will he be emigrating?" I asked.

"I'm not sure. Dripp just calls it 'the old country', in that manner that foreigners often do. I always assumed it to be some place full of peasants farming cabbages and Gipsies playing accordions. Dripp gets awfully weepy when he hears accordion music and he often smells of cabbage."

"Well, I do wish you would persuade him to let me draw him," Frank said. "His face fascinates me. I imagine it leering out from a dark alleyway or looming over a prone figure in a deserted warehouse. And with that cheery thought...." He paused a moment to down the rest of his brandy and turn up his collar. "I think I shall depart as well. It's getting wicked out there." He gave me a knowing glance. "Don't keep Oscar out too late, Derrick. His mother is expecting him for tea tomorrow."

"I'll do my best to see he makes it home, although I cannot control the weather."

Frank departed, leaving Derrick and me alone at the piano.

Derrick closed the keyboard and grabbed his brandy snifter. "Come on, I've rented a room upstairs. Please stay awhile longer and play a few hands of cards with me."

The 'room' was more of a suite and very nice. He lit a fire in the fireplace and the room became quite toasty. We never got around to playing cards, and before your mind goes where it should not, dear diary, it was because we became lost in conversation.

We talked of art, music and philosophy. He was quite taken with my theories on aesthetics, and we conversed until the sun was nearly up. By that time the snow had made the roads all but impassable.

I fell asleep in a big, comfortable chair and dreamt Derrick and I were alone on a Greek island. We walked among the ruins of an ancient civilisation admiring the alabaster statues of gods surrounded by the blue Aegean Sea. I could hear the tranquil waves breaking on the shore, punctuated with the occasional faraway cry of a seagull.

I wanted to stay there forever, except for the sudden gathering of storm clouds that blackened the sky. Then, to my horror, a werewolf leapt out of the ruins and tore into Derrick! I fought the beast furiously, to no avail. The harder I attacked, the faster he ripped Derrick apart. I awoke with a start, in a silent scream.

I gathered my wits about me and was calmed by seeing Derrick alive and sleeping peacefully across the room. The fireplace was dark and a winter chill had crept in. I watched Derrick sleeping and thought to myself, how can such terrible things be in the same world that holds such an innocent beauty?

Until we meet again, dear diary, keep my secrets safe amongst your pages.

LETTER FROM THE BLACK BISHOP TO LORD ALFRED SUNDRY, 23RD OF FEBRUARY 1879

My dearest Alfred,

Success at last! Stoker's blood does show the properties we need. My Gipsies tell me that the most effective date will be 6th of May 1880. I am a bit concerned as that will be the last day of the intersection, but they assure me it is our best chance to take advantage of the largest opening. Our timing will have to be precise and we will need to get all our pawns on the board before that day.

I worry we may have to dispose of Henry Irving should he continue to stumble in our way, but please do what you can to keep him safe and in the dark.

You have done fine work, my friend. Soon we will rule over the thousand years of peace and be the guardians of the gates at the Second Coming of our Lord Jesus Christ.

BB♟

FROM THE *LONDON TIMES*, 3RD OF MARCH 1879

MURDER ON THE DOCKS

A ghastly murder took place last night at the east London docks, pier 28. Mr. Leonard Trowl, a stevedore working the night shift unloading ships, had his throat cut as he attempted to stop a robbery in progress.

Thieves boarded the merchant ship *Demeter* around midnight and stole a large crate of unknown cargo. Several sailors on board were assaulted in the brash robbery. A sailor reported witnessing Trowl being killed by the thieves when he valiantly tried to stop them from loading the cargo onto a hearse carriage.

The hearse carriage is believed to have been stolen earlier from morticians Wolfram & Hart, who are offering a reward for its return and the apprehension of the murderous thieves.

The owner of the crate has been notified of the theft but has not come in for police questioning.

Anyone having seen this carriage or with knowledge of the crime should contact Scotland Yard immediately.

WHITE WORM SOCIETY BLACK BISHOP REPORT, 5TH OF MARCH 1879

Operative: Anna Hubbard
Location: London, England

I regret to inform you that my employment at the Lyceum has been terminated. Ellen Terry, an actress at the theatre, caught me trying to steal the Order of the Golden Dawn membership registry. It was all I could do to get out without revealing my cover entirely or ending up in jail. She seemed very adamant about me paying for my crime. However, after a few tears and quite a bit of begging, I was released.

In any event, I think I have learned all I can from Irving's library. He and Stoker should continue to be of interest to us, but I am unable to connect them to recent occult activity in the area.

LETTER FROM FLORENCE STOKER TO DR. (WILLIAM) THORNLEY STOKER, 14TH OF MARCH 1879

My dearest Thornley,

I hope this finds you well. Your brother and I look forward to your next visit, however brief.

I write today of a more pressing matter. My friend Lucy has become quite ill. Her skin is distressingly pale and she suffers from fainting spells. Her physician suspects anaemia but can offer no theory as to its cause.

She is often too weak to rise in the morning, but by early evening is right as rain.

I remember you had some success with a treatment involving a transfusion of blood. Would this be something that could benefit Lucy?

Should you think so, I have included the address of Lucy's physician for you to discuss the matter through correspondence.

Love,

Your new sister, Florence

LETTER FROM DR. (WILLIAM) THORNLEY STOKER TO FLORENCE STOKER, 23RD OF MARCH 1879

My dearest Florence,

Regarding your friend Lucy, I am afraid we are not having much success these days with the transfusions. Some patients take to it immediately and spring back to life. Others, it seems to make worse. Blood from related family members increases the chances of success, but even then, the results can be disastrous for the patient.

So, you can see, this is a treatment we use only as a last resort. I have sent detailed instructions to Lucy's doctor, should she take a turn for the worse. I have also sent him a recipe for a tincture of iron that we have had great success with in treating mild forms of anaemia.

On a personal note, make sure that brother of mine stops burning his candle at both ends and spends some much-needed time relaxing with his beautiful wife.

Hope to visit soon and will try to write more often.

With much fondness,

Thornley

FROM THE JOURNAL OF BRAM STOKER, 12TH OF JUNE 1879

9:24 a.m.

A recent turn of events has put me in a difficult and awkward position. Ellen Terry came to me in quite a terrible state. She confided in me that she has witnessed what she believes to be a horrific crime. If true, it would indeed be the ruin of this theatre and its company; if not, it means Ellen Terry herself may be mentally unstable, something that would trouble me greatly as I have developed the utmost respect for her in these past few months.

She is dramatic; after all, she is an actress and that is at the core of her personality. However, I have found her to be quite levelheaded for a woman and not given to flights of fancy or hysteria. She is very intelligent and worldly and not shocked easily by the darker aspects of human behaviour. She is also possessed of a remarkable memory and keen powers of observation, as her craft requires these skills.

It was last night when I was about to retire when she knocked on our door. She apologised profusely for coming at such a late hour, but she needed to speak with me in confidence, away from the theatre.

Florence had already gone to bed. We had argued earlier about my long hours at work and though I had ultimately placated her I knew the peace was tenuous. I worried that attending to theatre business so late in the evening would only serve to revive our disagreement, so I was reluctant to admit Miss Terry, but I could see by her state that I had no choice.

I invited her in and we withdrew to my study. It was a frightful mess and I had to clear a seat for her. She didn't notice the clutter as she was quite frazzled.

It seems she had found herself alone in the theatre that night. Monday is our dark day, but she had stopped in for some private rehearsal on the set. Afterwards, she had retired to her dressing room to review some script notes and fell asleep, awakening a few hours later in the darkened theatre. She was disoriented for a moment, but not overly alarmed; she had lived at the theatre for a time before she settled in with Lucy and her aunt.

She was startled to hear Mr. Irving's voice as he was escorting someone up the stairs to his office. Upon exiting her dressing room, she caught a glimpse of the person Irving was talking to as they disappeared at the top of the stair.

"It was a woman, a common streetwalker by the looks of her," Miss Terry said, with none of the shock with which most women would have made the statement. "It is none of my business with whom he associates, and I was quite prepared to be discreet and not repeat what I had seen for fear of starting gossip among the company. I gathered my things and was about to quietly exit and hail a cab when I heard a muffled scream!

"At first I thought I'd imagined it. I froze at the bottom of the stairs, straining my ears. And there was another unnatural sound I could not make out."

"Perhaps it was a rehearsal," I offered, but my imagination went in other, less gentlemanly directions.

"Or perhaps it was a scream of ecstasy," she said, completing my thoughts. "I did not want to rush to judgement, throwing open his office door to embarrass us all if that were the case."

I felt a blush creep into my cheeks. (Damn my Irish complexion!)

"But what if the girl were in danger?" she continued. "Or Mr. Irving for that matter, for these poor women often resort to robbery. What if she had stabbed him and it were *his* screams I heard? You can see what a predicament I was in, Mr. Stoker.

"I continued to listen but heard nothing. How long I stood there, I don't know. Seconds? Minutes? I was paralysed with indecision, which is not something I am often prey to. Ultimately, I could wait no longer. I grabbed my trusty sword – the one I used to fight off the burglar several months ago – and headed up the stairs. And there I stood outside the door, again unable to act. Do I knock and give him time to compose himself, or do I throw the door open and gain the element of surprise?"

I feared for her, though she was safe in my study. "That was foolish, Ellen. You should've summoned the police!"

"I considered that, I did. But what if it were a tryst? Think of the scandal to Mr. Irving and the theatre. I gathered all my courage and threw the door open to find…to find the office empty! Neither he nor the girl was anywhere to be seen, yet they could not have exited the office without passing me."

"Perhaps you dreamt it. After all, you were asleep in your dressing room only moments before."

"Ah, a possibility. Yet, there on the back of his office chair was a woman's scarf." She pulled it out of her sleeve as a magician would a bouquet of silk flowers. "This very scarf. Take a close look at this, Mr. Stoker."

She handed it to me to examine. It was wool, once white and now grey. It smelled of stale perfume and gin. On it were several drops of what could have been blood. The spots were already dried and brown from exposure to the air so there was no telling how old they were.

"You suspect foul play," I said. "But where is the girl? How did Irving slip past you?"

"I don't know. Did I stumble upon a crime, or did I dream it and the scarf is but a piece of wardrobe or something left by the cleaning lady? I was hesitant to come to you, but I didn't know where else to turn. You must think me a silly woman…."

"Not at all," I said. "You have shown remarkable bravery and astuteness in this situation. It is worth further investigation. I will look into this discreetly, I assure you, if only to put your mind at rest."

I escorted her through the back courtyard to the rear French doors of her own home. The private garden is accessible only to the rear of the houses on our street and the street adjacent. The only other entrance is a single locked iron gate, with the groundskeeper having the only key. I suspected it was safe enough, even at night, for a woman to cross its scant width, but I knew she felt better having me walk her.

"How is Lucy's health?" I enquired.

"Better, I think. She was up and about earlier today. The tonic the doctor has given her seems to be helping. Your brother's recommendation, I believe?"

"I am glad it has been a help," I said.

She said good night and gave me a little peck on the cheek, which caused me to blush yet again. I was thankful for the cover of night. "I am glad to have you as our manager, Mr. Stoker. I think you will keep us all safe."

On my stroll back, I mulled over the many things that could explain what she had seen. Could my benefactor have done something nefarious? It did not seem possible, yet the story Ellen told me was mysterious to be sure. My one comfort was the knowledge that Irving is not a vampire or other supernatural creature, for with my powers I would know. Still, a man need not be supernatural to be a fiend.

Then, suddenly, it was as if that very thought had brought the curse upon my eyes once again! A green streak of light pierced the darkness in the corner of my vision. I whirled around and looked in its apparent direction. A large birdbath and marble statue obstructed my view. It had been so fleeting I was not sure I had seen it at all, but then a rustling of leaves drew my focus further into the darkness.

My heart raced. It had followed me to my home!

"Who goes there!" I yelled.

The creature burst forth from the cover of bushes and sprinted away from me at high speed. I gave chase, but it was to the garden wall in seconds and leapt over the eight-foot height as an ordinary man might step onto a kerb.

I bolted through my apartment and out the front, but I had lost him (it?).

I stayed up much of the night looking out the back window, standing guard over our neighbourhood, which no longer felt safe.

LETTER FROM FLORENCE STOKER TO PHILLIPA BALCOMBE, 13TH OF JUNE 1879

Dear Mother,

I must share with you some momentous news, which will bring you great joy. You are to be a grandmother, for I am with child. The doctor says I shall deliver by the end of the year, or very early in the next. Bram and I are already discussing names and he has given me a modest allowance to outfit a nursery.

I feel so very blessed, though I must admit the news comes at an inopportune time. As I have written before, I have a small role in the Lyceum's production of *The Merchant of Venice* and am understudy to (the regrettably healthy) Ellen Terry in the role of Portia. I hope to continue until the play closes, or until my condition precludes it, as we are a tremendous success and attendance shows no sign of waning! However, Bram would prefer I leave the cast now. Ammunition for this request is provided by the costume mistress, who has darkly hinted that there are limits to how far she can let out my costume. Add to this the fact that I feel ill often and disagreeable nearly always and I fear I will be dismissed before I have a chance to resign.

I had hopes for a larger role in our next production, but alas, that dream will have to be foregone in favour of the joys of motherhood. Perhaps the one after that, if we have a reliable nanny. If so, I hope that you and Father can come to see me perform. I believe you would be proud of your daughter.

I must go, for it is nearly time to leave for the theatre. I do hope you and Father will be able to visit us when we have the new baby. I miss you terribly.

Yours always,

Florence

P.S. I am sure you realise that my comment above regarding Ellen Terry was only in jest. She is a dear friend, and I wish her nothing but health and happiness. And, perhaps a few days of rest in the country!

FROM THE JOURNAL OF BRAM STOKER, 13TH OF JUNE 1879

2:00 p.m.

It has been several months since I have felt any evil presence, and for that I am grateful.

In even happier news, I am to be a father. This joyous time is somewhat dampened, however, because Florence feels motherhood spells the end to any hope she had of a career on the stage.

This is nonsense, of course, as I pointed out. Several of our female players have children. After the child is weaned and a proper nanny can be hired there is no reason she could not pursue acting on an occasional basis. This did nothing to calm her fears, however. She, in fact, became hysterical today and could not be consoled. My attempts to bring her to a more tranquil state led to her throwing a teacup at me, missing my head by mere inches. I have never seen her in such a state.

"My figure will be ruined!" she screamed. I knew not what to do and sent for her friend Lucy to console her. I left for the theatre and am not looking forward to going home.

FROM THE JOURNAL OF BRAM STOKER, 14TH OF JUNE 1879

5:45 p.m.

After my discussion with Miss Terry on Monday night – and my glimpse of the creature in the courtyard – I found myself unable to concentrate on my duties the next day. As Irving does not come to the theatre until the evening, I had most of the day to investigate the possible crime of the night before.

I checked his office thoroughly. Nothing seemed out of place: no signs of a struggle, no telltale drops of blood or strange tinglings from my second sight, as Wilde calls it.

As the sun set and Irving failed to appear, I became worried he may have been a victim of a crime himself. Perhaps the woman had an accomplice who came in through the window to help her dispose of his body. One reads of these things in the penny dreadfuls and police blotters all the time.

I was both relieved and anxious when he finally entered his office. He could tell by the look on my face that something was amiss and asked me about it quite directly.

I decided to match his straightforward approach and told him what was witnessed the night before, though I substituted myself for Miss Terry. I told him that I had returned to the theatre to collect a book I had left behind, that I had fallen asleep reading, and it was I who thought I saw the events but was unsure as to their veracity due to my drowsy state.

He forced a smile and sat down in his favourite office chair. "I am embarrassed to confess you caught me at a moment of weakness," he said.

I did not wish to proceed but knew I must. "Sir, it is none of my business what you do with your private time, but I need to know if anything more than a crime of the heart took place here."

"Some men drink or play cards. My vice is the company of a young woman from time to time," he confessed. "But I assure you that she left in good health."

He stood and went to a bookcase on the far wall. "As for our quick disappearance." He slid out a book, then pulled down a lever that was concealed there. The case swung open to reveal a hidden stairway. "When I heard someone coming up the stairs I hurried her out through here."

I was greatly relieved, though embarrassed that I had pressed him on so personal a matter, and apologised for prying into his personal life.

"You are a man of honour, Bram. I would have expected no less of you if you had any suspicion of foul play. But I hope I can count on your discretion regarding this matter."

"Of course, sir, as in all things," I said.

We both returned to our duties and said nothing more of it.

The next day I met with Ellen at a café near the theatre. I told her it would be safe for her to return to work that evening and that Irving was none the wiser that it was she who had seen him with the girl.

She listened thoughtfully and thanked me for my efforts, and for saying it was I who had seen the woman, saying it was 'clever and gentlemanly'. "And brave too, for if he were a maniac you could have been his next victim," she said.

I assured her that it is a manager's duty to protect the company and crew. There was an awkward moment of silence as she daintily sipped her tea.

"Still, our Mr. Irving has some strange habits," she finally said. "Do you not think so? Having to cover mirrors when he enters the room if he isn't wearing makeup. That is vain even for an actor."

"It is all part of his artistic temperament," I speculated.

"Ah yes, we mad actors," she said, smiling wryly. I began an apology but she waved it away.

"I have never seen the man eat or drink," she said, taking a bite of a cucumber sandwich.

I quickly searched my memory and realised I too had rarely seen him consume anything, even when we met for supper. He had always an excuse – he had just eaten, his stomach wasn't well, a toothache – and he was so quick to engage in conversation I hardly noticed. He abstained from alcohol he told me, and when tea or coffee was served he usually took only a few polite sips.

"It's not natural for a man not to have a hearty appetite," she continued. "That is why he is thin as a rail, no doubt, and why he often is in a melancholy mood."

"His friend, Reverend Wilkins, confided in me that he had a great tragedy as a young man and it turned him away from God," I said, only then realising how it sounded like gossip. "Only recently has he regained his faith; perhaps that is why he seems overly serious at times. When not working, I can attest that he can be quite jovial and quick with a joke."

"I am glad to hear it," she said, smiling. "And I am glad he has you as a friend to manage his work and life."

"He has been very good to Florence and me. I am happy to repay him in any way I can."

She enquired after Florence and I confided that she was not feeling well.

"When I was expecting I was frightfully ill," she said.

I had not heard her mention a child before, and it never occurred to me she might be a mother. Again, my face betrayed me. It is just as well I am a manager and not an actor.

"Oh, yes, I have two children, Edith and Edward. I am not married to their father, making it all quite scandalous. Currently, they live with their father and have assumed a separate surname to avoid the stigma of illegitimacy." She said this all quite calmly and looked me in the eye with a confident gaze. "Does this shock you, Bram?"

It did, but I did so want to appear modern and liberal in my thinking as I am now working in the bohemian world of the theatre.

As I did not answer quickly, she continued, "Part of being an artist is to throw off society's chains. I believe love should be fluid and taken where one can find it, for there is so very little of it in the world."

I stammered some vague reply. It does make sense when she says it.

The theatre world runs on a different set of rules, I gather. Irving himself has a wife and children living in Italy, I am told. When I am a father I do not think I could bear to be away from my family to pursue a career.

"I do hope Florence feels better soon," Ellen said. "I think she will, as the sickness is only a fleeting thing. In fact, being with child may make her feel important and invigorated. I quite enjoyed it myself, after the morning sickness faded."

I did not tell her that Florence and I are barely speaking to each other or that Florence acts as though she hates the very sight of me, let alone my touch. I wanted to confide in Ellen, but I could not bring myself to speak of such a personal matter.

"Oh, I almost forgot," she said as we got up to leave. She handed me the scarf. "Perhaps he could return this to the girl. I'm sure she would like to have it back, as she is alive and will presumably have need of it again."

I left the encounter with more than a bit of doubt about Irving. Back at my office I examined the spots on the scarf and wondered if they were drops of blood.

Was I blind to his faults to such a point that I could not recognise a monster in front of me? Or, am I seeing monsters everywhere I go because of my past confrontations with the supernatural?

FROM THE DIARY OF FLORENCE STOKER, DATE UNKNOWN, MOST LIKELY THE SUMMER OF 1879

Archivist's note: These pages, written by Florence Stoker, were sold to the White Worm Society by William 'Willie' Wilde in 1898, a year before he died from complications related to his alcoholism. How these pages came to be in his possession is a mystery. They appear to have been ripped from a bound journal, and Willie Wilde claimed he found them in the former Stoker London residence under the floorboards of what would have been Florence's bedroom.

Awakened.

Had that horrible nightmare again. I am giving birth, but something is wrong, blood pours from me, soaking the bed and spilling onto the floor. Bram and Ellen are across the room, unaware I need their help. They are talking and laughing. I call to them, but they do not hear me. For some reason Oscar is there, drinking tea and reading a book of poetry. He too is ignoring me, despite my cries for help. After a great push, the baby is born, but I cannot see its face because it is covered in blood. So much blood.

I gasp myself awake again, the sheets wet with night sweat. I am exhausted from lack of sleep. I feel the baby inside me writhing like a snake in my belly. I am reminded of the time as a child when I suffered from a tapeworm. How glad I was to be rid of it, and how horrified I was to think it had lived off of me for so long. How can a woman have such thoughts and become a loving mother?

Why is Oscar in the dream? Would I have been better off marrying him? Would I be in the condition I am now had I?

Unable to sleep, I get up and go to the French doors that overlook the garden. The moonlight makes all things seem like granite statues and the statues themselves look like glowing moonstone.

Strange, it is so quiet. Even at night, I hear the occasional carriage here in London, but tonight nothing disturbs the silence. I throw open the doors and step out, still in my sleeping gown. I do not even bother to put on a robe. Bram would scold me for immodesty. But there is no one awake to see me, or so I think. I am wrapped in the darkness.

The night air is cool for summer. My body comes alive as the breeze's insistent fingers caress my skin. The baby stirs as if it has become cold and uncomfortable. I do not care.

I walk across the courtyard towards Lucy's house. I see her doors are open as well. The curtains of her bedroom are blowing in the breeze.

It's then I hear a noise. A noise that should startle me, but it does not. It's a sigh, then a moan coming from behind the hedges near the fountain. I know instantly what it is, and that decorum dictates my return home, but I follow the noise and my curiosity instead.

I peer through the hedge. It is as if I have fallen into the world of a painting. I see Lucy bathed in moonlight; she lies on a stone bench. Her nightgown is pulled down around her shoulders, baring her breasts to the night. Her thighs are wrapped around a man. His naked buttocks are muscular and lean and thrusting up and down, back and forth in a slow, rhythmic dance. He buries his face in her neck. On her face is a look of ecstasy I have only seen on religious zealots in passion plays. Her groans are more animal than human. Her lover is eerily quiet and seems intent only on pleasing her. For a moment, I am filled with envy, but it quickly passes and is replaced by a lust of my own. Thoughts of Roman orgies and swarthy men in Bedouin tents fill my mind and stir my loins. I feel no shame. My own clothes feel like heavy chains keeping me tethered to the earth. I want to break free from them and fly into the night!

I am mesmerised; only the baby's stirring breaks my trance. My shame returns and I turn and flee, afraid I might be engulfed by their sin.

I returned to my room, locking the doors and taking cover under my damp sheets, where my thoughts returned to the scene I had just witnessed. I am ashamed to say I touched myself like I wished Bram would touch me. After an intense moment of ecstasy, which I did not know was possible, I felt free of the thoughts once again and fell into a deep sleep. I dreamt it was a warm summer day and I was holding my new, beautiful baby. Bram was by my side and love once again filled our lives.

LETTER FROM THE BLACK BISHOP TO LORD ALFRED SUNDRY, 16TH OF JUNE 1879

Dear Lord Sundry,

I have received your list of candidates and find them worthy of joining our order. All are of fine breeding and pious stock. Please proceed to give them the gift in the order I have indicated. After Saint George's Day, we will have an unlimited supply of dragon's blood; however, as of now, we must ration what we have. I believe we have enough of our red elixir to easily bring fifty into our ranks.

I also agree with you on admitting those of lower standing, as long as they can provide a skill or artistic endeavour to our new world order.

Keep in mind, siring must be kept to a minimum or we will have an exponential increase in our ranks that could not be contained. I am well aware we will need servants, guards and the like, but restraint must be used.

My only concern on your list is Lord Wotton. I have heard rumours of his character that include sexual depravity, namely an unnatural attraction to young men.

I for one do not hold much regard for gossip and if you can vouch for him I will accept your recommendation.

BB 🔱

FROM THE DIARY OF OSCAR WILDE, 21ST OF JUNE 1879

Dear yours truly,

I feel strangely grim and somehow virtuous at the moment – an odd combination for me as I generally feel neither. I have just returned from an interesting – and troubling – gathering hosted by Lord Basil Wotton, Derrick Pigeon's benefactor. It took place at Wotton's gaudy mansion near the Thames in Purfleet.

The house is very large and of all periods back, I should say, to mediaeval times, for one part is of stone immensely thick, with only a few windows high up and heavily barred with iron. The rest of the house is just tacked on and looks quite out of place, as if another house had rolled down a hill and smashed into it.

There are but a few houses close at hand, one being a very large dilapidated structure in full view of Lord Wotton's property, much to his disdain. Derrick tells me that he has been trying to acquire the property, if only to burn it down, but the owners have moved off to unknown parts of Europe. This amuses Derrick to no end, as Lord Wotton laments about it daily, often shaking his fist and shouting obscenities at the empty house.

I, of course, was surprised to get an invitation from Wotton, as I have it on good authority he does not approve of my friendship with Derrick. That authority was Derrick himself; the dear fellow thought I would be flattered to rate the disapproval of 'the debauched old reprobate', as he calls Wotton, and I suppose he's right. It can only be jealousy that would cause him to dislike me and I must say it does please me to be seen as a serious rival for Derrick's attentions. Even so, I thought it best to attend in hopes of striking up a friendship with him for Derrick's sake. One of us must look out for the boy's best interests. As it turns out, there was another reason I was invited, which I shall get to presently.

I had never actually met Lord Wotton but took it from Derrick's description that he would be old and decrepit. I was surprised to find him a handsome and distinguished gentleman, no more than fifty years of age. He dressed stylishly, but not as though he were striving to maintain the illusion of youth, and his full head of hair, slightly greying in a very dignified manner, would make him a fine catch for any well-bred widow of a certain age. He smiled often and acted the genial and generous host, but his eyes – a glittering, flinty grey – betrayed a certain hardness and reminded one that there was little warmth behind the smile.

It was a lavish affair, I will give him that. Wine, champagne and other libations were in abundance, and waiters circled with delectable morsels on trays. There were many lords, ladies and dignitaries in attendance and the lamplight caused an excess of glittering on the jewels adorning the ears, fingers and décolletage of the ladies.

To my chagrin, Henry Irving was there with the Stokers in tow. It's bad enough that Stoker and I move in the same theatre circles, but to find him here was quite jarring. If anyone did not belong at that party it was he. Stoker blundered through the crowd like a big, lumbering ox. One would think he was drunk, but I am sure it was mere clumsiness, as I saw him abstaining from drink that night. He was dressed in a tweed suit that made him look like a burlap sack of potatoes and one could hear his donkey-like braying that passed for laughter throughout the night.

He amused the upper-class guests as an oddity, I suppose, as he always had a crowd gathered around him. Or perhaps he was just basking in Henry Irving's limelight. The wall of sycophants around Irving kept me from having to mingle with Stoker and for that I was grateful.

Florence looked lovely in a pale yellow gown, cut in the lines of the latest spring fashions, and I noted that she still wears the silver cross I returned to her at the conclusion of our engagement. She has put on some weight and it suits her; she was always a trifle too thin in my opinion.

Our paths crossed but briefly. She greeted me shyly, no doubt unsure of the reception she would receive. I confess that for one brief, petty moment I considered prolonging her discomfort. However, though I still regret our parting I find that my heart has, in fact, mended tolerably well and that my fondness for her outweighs my bruised pride. I smiled warmly and kissed her hand.

"Mrs. Stoker," I said, and she blushed. "How lovely to see you. Honestly, it is," I added, seeing that she was uncertain whether to take me at my word.

"And I am so happy to see you, Oscar," she said, clearly relieved. "Your brother dines with us frequently so I hear news of you from time to time. I am glad to hear that you have been writing again. You have such great talent."

I was mildly annoyed that Willie had been bandying my name about and spreading word about work that I am not yet ready to discuss myself. "It is kind of you to feed Willie," I said. "It lifts some of the burden of his upkeep from our dear mother."

At that moment, we were obliged to give our attention to our host. He was introducing the evening's entertainment, which consisted of Irving performing a series of dramatic readings from Shakespeare, which went on and on and on, followed by a much too brief piano recital by Derrick, who played a series of Beethoven sonatas.

As the night progressed, Derrick was able to slip away and take me on a tour of the immense house.

Lord Wotton is a collector of art, everything from Egyptian and Greek statues to contemporary English painters. It is a pity that I had to view this lovely art against hideous wallpaper. I had no idea that yellow roses and frolicking cherubs could sneak up from behind and assault your eyes in such a way. In another room, a Grecian urn pattern on velvet screamed, 'Don't look at the painting, look at me!' Even the urns had patterns on them, naked Greeks pouring water from yet smaller urns. It was enough to give one vertigo. I pointed this out to Derrick and he laughed and pulled me to a far corner of the room.

"I know," he said, "look at this." On one of the urns-within-an-urn, he had drawn yet another naked Greek pouring water from still another urn. "I don't think the old sod has noticed it yet, but I hope I'm here when he does."

"Oh, Derrick," I said, laughing. "He'll chuck you out when he sees it!" And despite my desire to preserve Derrick's livelihood, I was half hoping it would happen.

"No," he replied. "He'll pretend he finds it as big a joke as I do. But inside he'll be seething."

Derrick was soon called back to his piano and I found myself alone in a room admiring a van Dyck (a portrait of some nobleman and his family) when Lord Wotton himself unexpectedly appeared at my side.

"Exquisite, is it not?" he said, admiring it with me. "Van Dyck immortalised so many noblemen of his day. Without his work, their faces would be lost to the sands of time."

In the case of this particular family I couldn't help thinking that might not be such a tragedy, but before I could answer Wotton became perturbed. Next to the painting was a large window flanked by velvet curtains. Outside, lit by the light of the moon, was the dilapidated property that vexed him so. He yanked the curtains closed, which required much effort as they were big and heavy.

"I am sorry for the view of the rat trap adjacent," he said. "It is a travesty that any English nobleman would let his property rot away. To make matters worse, it has apparently been purchased by a foreigner. Can you image such a thing? From what I hear it is one of those oily Carpathians, maybe even a Jew."

"Perhaps the new owner will take pride in the estate and restore it to its former glory," I offered.

"One would hope," he said. "At least he is a nobleman. A count, I think."

"How lovely," I replied, merely for something to say.

After an awkward moment of silence where we both pretended to admire the painting some more, he said, "Derrick showed me one of your essays on aesthetics. I was quite impressed with your ideas."

For the second time that evening I was dismayed to hear someone mention my work. The essay was not ready for a public debut. I had given it to Derrick to read for his opinion with the strict understanding he was to show it to no one. For him to share it with this man of all people was very disconcerting, to say the least. Derrick has often described Wotton as a philistine with no aesthetic tastes whatsoever.

"Thank you, Lord Wotton," I said, attempting to maintain my composure. "It is a subject about which I am quite passionate."

"Lord Wotton is so formal. Please, call me Lord Basil. Come into my study for a moment," he said, waving me towards a set of large oak doors. "I have something I would like to discuss with you."

Inside the study, the walls were adorned with more paintings, some I recognised. One was by my friend James Whistler and several were by

Frank, including the portrait of Derrick, which had pride of place above a large mahogany desk.

"These are all paintings by English artists," he said. He went over to a liquor cabinet and took out a bottle of brandy. "I have many more in storage. I think it is important to preserve our culture."

"Indeed," was all I managed to say before he continued.

"England soon will rule even more of the world than it already does," he said, quite casually for such a momentous pronouncement.

He poured us each a brandy and stepped back to admire his collection. I could not imagine his intention in bringing me here, where this strange turn of conversation would take us next or what I should say. I tried to keep silent and found it an easier task than usual for me.

"There is a new order coming, Oscar, run by the upper class, as is right and natural."

I wondered who was running the current order if not the upper class.

"A new church that prays to the beauty of the world and that is not bound by the moral constraints of frustrated old men. We are going to need art in this new world, and men with new philosophies. Men like you."

"I had no idea I was so important," I said. I realise now there might have been sarcasm in my voice, as I'm told there often is.

"You can be, Oscar. Remember that. It is good to have me as a friend, you know, and you certainly wouldn't want me as an enemy. You could ask my enemies, but they have a habit of disappearing."

My blood ran cold at this remark and he could tell because he laughed and slapped me on the back. Brandy sloshed out of my snifter.

I forced a smile. "I would very much like to be your friend then," I said. "I rather like continuing to appear."

"Good. I am quite glad that you are Derrick's friend. You bring culture into his life and make him think of other things than drinking and carousing with his lower-class acquaintances."

So, he knew about Mr. Dripp and his cohorts. I wondered if he was having Derrick followed.

"I would like to think I am a good influence," I said.

"There is no such thing as a good influence, Oscar. All influence is immoral, from the scientific point of view."

"How so?"

"Because to influence a person is to give him one's own soul. He does not think his own thoughts or burn with his natural passions. His virtues are not real to him. His sins, if there are such things as sins, are borrowed. He becomes an echo of someone else's music, an actor of a part that has not been written for him. The aim of life is self-development. People are afraid of themselves, nowadays. They have forgotten the highest of all duties, the duty that one owes to one's self."

He refilled my brandy glass and continued.

"Courage has gone out of our race. Perhaps we never really had it. We behave 'morally' because we fear what society will say of us if we don't. We attend church on Sunday, piously singing the hymns and murmuring the prayers because we fear God. These twin fears govern our lives. And yet I believe that if one man were to live out his life fully and completely, were to give form to every feeling, expression to every thought, reality to every dream – what a leap forwards that would be! But the bravest man amongst us is afraid of himself. We are punished for our refusals. Every impulse that we strive to strangle broods in the mind and poisons us. The body sins once and has done with its sin, for action is a mode of purification. Nothing remains then but the recollection of a pleasure, or the luxury of a regret."

"Very true, sir," I said. "I believe the only way to get rid of a temptation is to yield to it."

This brought a broad smile to his face. "Yes, indeed. Resist it, and your soul grows sick with longing for the things it has forbidden to itself, with desire for what its monstrous laws have made monstrous and unlawful. It has been said that the great events of the world take place in the brain. It is in the brain, and the brain only, that the great sins of the world take place also."

"Perhaps it is that impulse to suppress and condemn our own desires that makes them so appealing," I said.

"Perhaps." He paused for a moment, then said, "There is another reason we should be friends. The truth is, I rather feel I owe you something, Oscar."

I was truly taken aback by this and dearly hoped that what he owed me was money, or perhaps a case of the rather excellent champagne I had indulged in earlier. "I cannot think what that could be, Lord Basil," I managed to say.

"I knew your father. Did you know that?"

"No, sir, I had no idea."

"A fine physician, your father. Saved my eyesight. I suffered an injury when I was younger, and Dr. William Wilde was the only one who could help. I am eternally grateful – and I take eternity quite seriously," he said.

"I am gratified, Lord Basil, to hear that my father was of service to you. However, I am sure you paid him quite handsomely at the time and can't think what is left owed to me." See how good and virtuous I am, diary? Brushing off rewards as though they were crumbs left on my lap after tea.

"As I have said, it is good to have me as a friend. Unfortunately, I was unable to help your father when he faced his…troubles later on. I regret that, and the hardships your family has been forced to endure since." His steely eyes bored into me like pins affixing a butterfly into a specimen case.

My father's 'troubles' are a subject I avoid, as a matter of strict policy, and I attempted to brush off the conversation but he would not be deterred.

"In my last correspondence with your father, I vowed to help you and your brother re-enter society. As a friend, know that I am in a position to do you favours. How would you like me to sponsor your endeavours?"

"What endeavours would those be?"

"I am thinking of a series of lectures. You would give readings of your essays on the aesthetic movement and the like. I am seeing a tour of Europe, perhaps America. Would you like that?"

Oh, I would! I would! And yet something – that pesky virtue again, I suppose, or perhaps just stubbornness – held me back. "I do so like to talk, and earning a living doing so would be appealing, but leaving London right now is not possible. My mother is not well and I dare not leave her side for travel. Besides, I have only the one essay and it is not nearly enough for an entire lecture."

"Why don't you complete the writing of the lecture while you stay close to your mother, and when she is well, perhaps later this year, we can plan your itinerary? I can offer you the use of my country estate as you work on the project. It is quite secluded and fully staffed. You and your mother would be very comfortable there."

Ah, so there it was. With me off at his country estate, then on a lengthy tour, he would have Derrick all to himself. Clever, I must say.

Then he sweetened the pot. One thing I can say for old Basil, he may be overly accustomed to getting what he wants, but he does not insist on getting it cheaply.

"Of course, there would be a monthly stipend to live on while you write, as I hear your father's untimely death has caused some financial difficulty."

His flinty eyes bored into mine and I felt not unlike a thoroughbred racehorse under evaluation by a potential new owner. I consulted briefly with my soul and determined that it was not for sale. "We have managed to muddle through, Lord Wotton. And I am bringing in some income writing for local publications. Your offer is very generous, but I must decline at this time."

He stared at me as if willing me to change my mind. Finally, he sighed and drained his brandy glass in one gulp.

"That is a disappointment," he said. "But perhaps you will reconsider in time." Then he excused himself to return to his guests.

I cannot help but think that I have offended him by not letting him sponsor me. Perhaps I am now among his enemies. I do not know what is wrong with my thinking lately. Lord Wotton was offering to grant my dearest wish (that I had not yet even thought of myself) and all I had to do was stay away from his protégé. Yet I did not take it. I hope I am not developing a nasty case of morality, as that could lead to all sorts of unwanted behaviour. I like to think I just wanted to put the old bore in his place. And keep seeing Derrick, of course.

Good night, future Oscar. I have much to ponder.

FROM THE JOURNAL OF BRAM STOKER, 21ST OF JUNE 1879

1:15 a.m.

It is with a heavy heart and frayed nerves that I must put to paper a secret I dreaded might be true. My friend and benefactor is indeed a vampire! I had hoped that my suspicions were unfounded, a flight of dark fancy born of my too frequent and too intimate experiences with the supernatural. Alas, the events of tonight have removed all doubt: Henry Irving is one of the Un-Dead!

Florence and I, accompanied by Lucy, Mr. Irving and Reverend Wilkins, attended a party this evening at the estate of Lord Basil Wotton. The night began with much laughter and gaiety. Mr. Irving was at his most charming. (Charming! A word, of course, that can have a magical connotation. Is Mr. Irving's silky personality one of his weapons, a tool to mesmerise his prey? Heaven help me, to what danger have I exposed my dear wife and our future child?)

Despite Florence's condition, Lucy had convinced her it would be good to get out and socialise. While it would be unthinkable in Dublin, in London, it is perfectly acceptable, it seems, for a woman who is expecting to attend such events if she is not too far along. It is even encouraged by the more 'enlightened' in society. Her condition is not obvious, in any event, and she felt well enough to attend. Lucy, who herself has been under the weather, was feeling much more chipper, and although she had looked a bit pale when I had seen her earlier in the afternoon, she seemed quite full of energy when we picked her up for the party.

As I said, all seemed well. Irving entertained our fellow guests with humorous stories of his travels and the characters he has known in the theatre, and I made many a new acquaintance. Not even the sneers of the insufferable Oscar Wilde from across the room could dampen my good spirits.

Florence even managed to make small talk with Oscar, which was more than I could stomach, and it appears he bears her no ill will, or at least he has the decency to be civil to a woman in public. Me he ignored completely, which is just how I preferred it. I could see him from time to time, holding forth to one partygoer or another – or, better yet to his liking, a small crowd of them – going on, no doubt, about his theories on art or music or whatever subject he fancies himself an expert in these days. He was dressed in the height of fashion, of course – how does he afford it? – with a purple cravat and matching waistcoat, and the cut of his suit struck me as quite Continental. Why, when first I saw him I mistook him for a conjurer hired to entertain the crowd.

Nevertheless, I was having a most enjoyable evening talking with Henry Irving and Reverend Wilkins.

Lucy approached us. She was wearing a lovely pale green gown and a crimson silk scarf that Florence and I had given her for her recent birthday, and she looked radiant as she introduced her fiancé, Mr. Robert Roosevelt. He is an older gentleman, too old for Lucy, I think. However, he seems to have the constitution of a much younger man – Lucy has told us he is very athletic – and is overly friendly, as Americans tend to be. He explained to me, Reverend Wilkins and Irving that he is in England trying to sell Her Majesty the latest in destructive weaponry, something called a Gatling gun.

"You should see it in action, Mr. Stoker," Roosevelt said. "One hundred rounds per minute. Put enough of these on the battlefield and we could end war as we know it."

"Isn't war bad enough," Reverend Wilkins enquired mildly. "Do we have to make it more efficient?"

"Actually, Gatling, the man who invented it, was a physician. He was horrified by the slow, agonising gangrene death that current warfare brings. He reasoned that a weapon like this would end wars more quickly and, at the very least, kill soldiers straight away."

"Oh, Robert," Lucy scolded. "One does not talk of such things at parties. It is all so gruesome." Suddenly, Lucy's smile left her face and she swooned, falling backwards so fast that Robert and I scarcely had time to react. I reached out for her and my glass went flying, but she was already out of my reach.

In a quick blur, Henry caught her and slowed her descent to the floor. In the momentary confusion, the speed at which he reacted didn't register in my mind, but it must have triggered something deep within my brain for I was suddenly afraid and alert to my surroundings. Where had Henry come from? Wasn't I between him and Lucy just moments before?

Florence rushed over from across the room to attend to her friend while Reverend Wilkins went in search of a physician.

A crowd gathered to help as Robert stepped in to lift Lucy to a nearby sofa. Henry must have had a sharp fingernail, for as he withdrew his arm from around Lucy he scratched her slightly and a few drops of blood welled up on her shoulder.

Henry was still crouched where he had eased her to the floor, and as she was carried away, I saw him pull his hand back, a small smear of blood on his fingertip. His pupils dilated, turning his eyes nearly black, and his hand trembled slightly as he gazed at it. Then, to my astonishment, his canine teeth elongated to fangs! He moved his hand towards his mouth as if to lick the blood away, then, with effort, recovered himself. He closed his mouth and his eyes, and when he opened them again, both were normal. I quickly averted my gaze so he would not see that I had seen, though I am sure, had he endeavoured to speak with me, I would not have been able to conceal my horror at what I now knew.

"Please, let's give her some room," Lord Wotton told the guests. They obeyed, but I could still hear their concerned voices talking in hushed tones. He found a glass of water on a nearby table and soaked his handkerchief in it, wringing it out before handing it to Florence then discreetly stepping away. "Lucy," Florence said calmly as she loosened her friend's scarf and applied the damp cloth to her forehead, "it's all right, I'm here."

Lucy stirred and opened her eyes. "What happened?"

"You just fainted, that's all." Florence lowered her voice. "And to think we worried I would be the one who would have a fainting spell."

I was relieved to see Lucy revived, then I received my second shock of the evening: there were marks on her neck – puncture marks! How had I not made the connection? The creature I had chased in her courtyard. Her declining health, her pale skin. She is the victim of a vampire! Could it be Henry?

But why had she collapsed now, when she had been so lively earlier in the evening? She had been laughing and enjoying herself mere moments before. I wondered – could the mere presence of a vampire have a debilitating effect on an already weakened victim?

I willed my eyes to use my second sight. The room became hazy and when I looked down at Lucy the marks on her neck gave off a faint green glow. I now could see that some otherworldly creature had been feeding off of her. Brief images of the encounter – encounters, for I was sure there was more than one, flashed through my mind. But I could not focus on the face of the monster.

Forcing myself to remain outwardly calm, I turned my gaze to Henry. He appeared normal to my vision. And yet I knew he was anything but.

"I will have my coach brought around, Bram. My driver will take her home," he said. "Would you and Florence care to accompany her?" I nodded, not trusting myself to speak.

Irving slipped out to call his coach and I was left dumbfounded. As I watched him leave the room he still had nothing of the green light around him, and yet he is undoubtedly supernatural. It was like I was seeing him for the first time. Not as a man, but as a monster. A monster that was slowly killing Lucy!

We escorted Lucy back to our apartment that night. I convinced Florence it would be good for us to watch over her until she is better.

I hadn't a chance to warn Reverend Wilkins. In all the confusion, he left to catch the last train to Salisbury. At least he is out of harm's way.

Can I find the strength to dispatch Henry Irving? If I do, will I be accused of murder? Is there anyone who will believe Irving is not human? Only the Wilde brothers, I am afraid, and I doubt very much they are up to the task of killing another monster. Oscar, at least, would not be eager to help me in any case.

This I must do alone.

FROM THE DIARY OF OSCAR WILDE, 22ND OF JUNE 1879

My apologies, dear diary, for not getting back to you sooner.

A new turn of events has me quite occupied with fret.

Derrick has moved into his rooms above the Cock and Bull on a permanent basis, having quit the hospitality of Lord Wotton.

"I have left that horrid man's house for good," he informed me last night as we met for our weekly game of cards. "And I have found a new benefactor. He is a kind and decent sort, without the lurid intentions of Lord Basil."

I was happy to hear this, for he is not one who could live as a pauper after having spent time in the lap of luxury. I wish I could be his patron, but I am scarcely able to keep myself in the luxury I deserve.

"Who is this new patron?" I enquired.

"I am not at liberty to say," he said, producing a bottle of champagne. He popped the cork and poured us each a glass for toasting. "But suffice it to say, my working days are over and I can concentrate fully on my piano." We touched glasses and drank.

Across the room near the fireplace, a painting, covered by a sheet, was leaning against the wall. He brought it over and pulled off the sheet. It was his portrait, the one painted by Frank. I am sure I would have found myself gazing at it, to the exclusion of all else in the room, had I not had the real-life Derrick before me.

"I stole this from the letch before I left," he said. "I want you to have it, Oscar."

I was touched, of course. "It will be my most prized possession."

He admired it, but not in a narcissistic way. "Frank is an exceptional artist. To think this painting could freeze me in time long after this body has been eaten by worms. Remember how I wished to remain as young as this painting forever?"

"I do recall your fear of growing old."

"What if I told you I found a way? Think of it, Oscar, to be young and beautiful forever."

"Whatever do you mean?"

"An elixir, of sorts, exists to let you live forever, as you are now, or better."

I laughed. "Surely you do not believe in such fairy tales."

"No, Oscar it is real. And I – we – can have it!"

"Who put these ideas in your head? It is nonsense. How is such a thing possible?"

"Have you heard of the Scholomance?" he asked, lowering his voice a bit as if we were speaking of something we should not, as if the very word were illicit.

"I have. Some sort of school of black magic, is it not?" Obscure knowledge of this sort is one of the benefits of being my mother's son.

"It is taught by an ancient order of knights who have harnessed the powers of magic for the force of good. They alone drove the Turks out of Europe and, with the blessing of the pope himself, became the keepers of the dark knowledge of alchemy, the rituals that summon demons to do the bidding of man."

He spoke these words as a preacher would to enflame a Sunday congregation.

"They are called the 'Order of the Golden Dawn' and they are ushering in this brave new world. I know it sounds mad, but I have seen their magic myself. By drinking the blood of the dragon, as they call it, you can have eternal life! They have asked me to join them, Oscar."

Also, as my mother's son, I know that obscure folk tales about ancient orders are not always to be taken literally. "You are having me on, or they are having you on. This is but a pipe dream or a shared madness."

"No, I witnessed a ritual, just last week, in which a member of the Order was given the elixir. He was feeble and old, but after the ritual he was full of vitality and the strength of ten men. There are members of the Order who claim to be hundreds of years old. Of course, they have to be careful who they let into the Order. You wouldn't want just anyone to have immortality."

I must admit curiosity had now taken hold of me. Also, a glimmer of hope that the world was not as it appeared to be. Could death be cheated? Who would not be tempted by such a possibility, especially when offered by one so dear to them?

"They have asked me to be one of them. Come with me to the next gathering, Oscar. I will tell them I will not join their order unless you can join too. Think of it, we can be together forever, and forever young."

Against my better judgement, I acquiesced.

"The ceremony begins at midnight on Friday. Tell no one. I shall meet you at your house and we'll go together. Oh, and you will need this to gain access to the meeting." He took a handkerchief from his pocket, unwrapped a small object and put it in my palm. I was horrified to discover it was an onyx chess piece. A black bishop!

I let it fall to the floor. "Derrick," I cried. "I have seen this calling card before, in the hands of a monster, a vampire!"

He was not shocked by this and in fact gave a small shrug of his shoulders.

"Sometimes a monster is merely a creature that is misunderstood."

"And sometimes a monster is something that does monstrous things like suck the life out of innocent people!"

"I have not seen my friends do any such things. They offer life, not death."

I could scarcely believe what I was hearing.

"Friends? You don't know what they are capable of! Why, one tried to kill me once in Dublin."

"There are evil and good men, are there not? I am sure the same can be said of vampires. The Order has been empowered by God to control the forces of darkness for the good of the righteous."

He picked the chess piece up off the floor and forced it into my hand. "Come with me and see for yourself."

I looked into his cobalt-blue eyes and I was lost. All I wanted was for it to be true. To spend the rest of my life with him – and to have that life last forever – was, I have to admit, dear diary, a temptation I could not fight. If a serpent had entered our Garden of Eden, I had not the power to resist its fruit.

I turned the chess piece over in my hand and felt its cold weight. It was chipped from its fall to the floor, and it had cut my finger as I squeezed it. A drop of my blood disappeared into its blackness. I slipped it into my pocket, and for that I cannot help but feel a little ashamed. And as you know, shame and I have rarely been the best of friends.

I told him I would go. I fell into his embrace and felt all was lost.

Together forever. And forever young.

Will I be reading you a hundred years from now, dear diary? Do fairy tales come true?

TELEGRAM FROM BRAM STOKER TO RICHARD BURTON, 22ND OF JUNE 1879

To: Richard Burton, c/o Signet Hotel, Edinburgh, Scotland
   =Need help or advice re: dispatching creature of the type you faced in Crimean War=

TELEGRAM FROM RICHARD BURTON TO BRAM STOKER, 24TH OF JUNE 1879

To: Bram Stoker, Lyceum Theatre, London, England

=Cannot come. Leaving for India in the morning but sending expert to help. Dr. Martin Hesselius arriving from Holland on 26th June. Worked with him myself, you are in good hands=

LETTER FROM DR. NEIL SEWARD TO DR. WILLIAM GULL, ROYAL PHYSICIAN, 23RD OF JUNE 1879

Archivist's note: Correspondence related to the hospitalisation and treatment of Prince Albert Victor at Blyth Sanatorium during this time was ordered released to the White Worm Society by Queen Victoria herself. Her Majesty, while unable to publicly acknowledge the Society due to the secretive nature of our endeavours, has long supported our work.

Dear Dr. Gull,

Let me offer my sincere congratulations on your appointment as Her Majesty's personal physician. The royal family could not be under finer care.

This letter, I am afraid, is to report on Prince Albert Victor's worsening condition. As you may know, the prince, affectionately known as Eddy to the staff here, has been under my care for over a month now. His grandmother, the Queen, has requested weekly reports to you on his health and treatments.

He is sixteen years of age and in fine physical health, but his mental faculties continue to worsen. He is greatly burdened by hallucinations and emotional fits. There is much speculation as to the cause of his condition, but his ailment is most likely the result of being kicked in the head by a horse when he was a child and, later, a bout of typhoid fever.

As to his history, all seemed fine with the young prince for much of his life. Although his tutors say he was a slow learner, he did not show any of the symptoms he does now.

At fourteen, he and his brother were sent to the Royal Navy's training ship, *HMS Britannia*. There he continued his studies but returned home for the summer after he contracted the typhoid. Seemingly fully recovered, he returned to the ship for further training. It was at this time he nearly bludgeoned a fellow cadet to death with a cricket bat, claiming the cadet was trying to steal his thoughts. The ship returned to shore at the earliest opportunity and the prince was remanded to my care.

The most disturbing facet of his condition is that he is stricken with zoophagous mania. He has been caught on several occasions eating flies, spiders and even a bird that had flown to his window. He believes by consuming these creatures alive he absorbs the life force, making himself stronger.

Lately, he has told me of his desire to achieve his twisted objective in a cumulative way. He wishes to feed many flies to many spiders, many spiders to several birds, and the birds to one cat, which he will then consume to become immortal. He becomes very agitated that his dietary requirements are not being met, and often exhibits violence towards the staff. I am forced to keep him sedated with strong opiates.

Tomorrow we will begin administering ice-water baths, and a new electrical therapy that has shown promise in other patients.

Sincerely,

Dr. Neil Seward

LETTER FROM OSCAR WILDE TO RICHARD BURTON, 24TH OF JUNE 1879

Archivist's note: The letter below was written mostly in Greek, perhaps to keep its contents from servants' prying eyes. It is translated and transcribed below. Burton had just left for India and the letter was forwarded to him there. It would have taken weeks or even months to reach him.

Dear Captain Burton,

I am writing to you in the direst of circumstances, for you alone among my friends have the expertise, the courage and the fortitude to advise and aid me in this, my darkest hour. The tale I am about to relate to you will seem implausible, outrageous even, and many would call for my immediate commitment to Bedlam – or worse, the removal of my gin supply – were they to read it. I know that you will perceive the grim truth of the story and understand the grave danger we now must face.

Since moving to London, I have become close friends with a young man named Derrick Pigeon. While Derrick has many worthy attributes – he is a loyal friend, a witty and intelligent conversationalist and an exceptionally talented pianist – he is largely valued by himself and others for his youth and beauty. Where he differs from other young and beautiful people is in his realisation that this is a fleeting commodity. He often becomes morose at the thought of growing older, his dark hair peppering with grey, his flawless skin becoming lined and creased, his vitality dimming.

Recently, Derrick told me that he had discovered a way to never grow old and to never die. It involved participating in a ritual with a group known as the 'Order of the Golden Dawn'. I'm sure you have immediately realised that anything promising so unnatural a result can only be monstrous, but I confess that, despite my reservations, I was swayed by friendship to trust Derrick's assurance that the Order's intentions were pure. I agreed to go with him to the ceremony, where he planned to sponsor me into their ranks.

The night we were to convene was clear and cool. The streets seemed strangely hushed as we made our way to the appointed meeting place in Knightsbridge, almost as though the entire city and all its denizens knew that the evening was full of portent. "I wonder if this will all look different to us," Derrick mused, watching the parks and pubs and street lamps slide past. "When we've changed, I mean." I found myself uncharacteristically without reply.

As we alighted from our cab in front of a large but otherwise unremarkable white house, Derrick clapped me on the shoulder and bounded up the front steps. I followed, with somewhat less enthusiasm, and with a last grin at me, he rang the bell. Moments later, the door was opened by a butler. After we showed him the black bishop chess piece that would grant us entry, he ushered us into the drawing room, where a small crowd already awaited.

Clearly, immortality, like so many of the finer things in life, is reserved for the upper classes. The majority of the men and women – mostly men – in the room, would be familiar figures to anyone who frequents charity balls, opening nights of operas or the more exclusive London clubs. A few, like Derrick and me, seemed more likely to live by the fruit of our talents rather than the depth of our bank accounts.

A tall, thin man seemed to frown briefly as we came into the room, but excused himself from his conversation and came to greet us. He was middle-aged, with pale blond hair and eyes the colour of the Irish Sea in January. I've never been fond of the sea in wintertime.

"Derrick," he said, shaking my friend's hand. "So glad you could come. And you brought a friend." He turned to me with a smile that wasn't quite as warm as one might like.

"Yes, Lord Cavendish," said Derrick. "Lord Wotton and I have both spoken to you about my friend, Oscar Wilde. You said that a man of his sensibilities and talents would be a worthy addition to the Order. You marvelled at what he might create, with an eternity in which to work."

"So I did," Lord Cavendish replied. "Still, a formal invitation is the preferred way of doing things. I think perhaps your name will not be in the running for tonight's ceremony, Derrick."

Derrick blanched at this and I hurriedly interjected. "If my presence is a problem, Lord Cavendish, I will gladly excuse myself. I have no wish to disrupt your evening."

He turned those cold eyes upon me and smiled mirthlessly. "My dear boy, it is far too late for that. I think it's best that we get to know you. I'm sure when we do we will gladly welcome you into our circle. And you, Derrick," he continued, "do not look so stricken. You are still on the list. You will simply not be chosen tonight."

He excused himself, and Derrick quickly grabbed two glasses of wine from a passing servant. His hand trembled slightly as he passed one to me.

"I'm sorry, Derrick," I said. "I hope I haven't caused too much of a problem for you."

"My fault entirely," he answered. "It was I who insisted you come. He's right, I should have waited for them to issue an invitation. Still, I don't regret a thing. I'm glad you're here. It will all work out for the best." He raised his glass and drank, and the wine seemed to fortify and reassure him. "But you know, Oscar," he said, glancing at me out of the corner of his eye, "I would be grateful if you would do your utmost to make yourself agreeable tonight. I know how charming you can be when you try."

I forced a smile and murmured, "I am never less than agreeable. I find that it pleases my friends and annoys my enemies." I sipped my wine but still felt far from sanguine. I wondered what Lord Cavendish had meant when he said it was 'far too late' for me to leave. And what would happen if they didn't deem me worthy to join the Order? Or if I declined membership?

Derrick and I mingled after that. I had met some of the party at previous social events. There was a young woman who is the daughter of a friend of my mother's, a wealthy patron of the arts I'd met at a salon in Chelsea, and a middle-aged gentleman who I believe is a member of Parliament. With these acquaintances and total strangers, I played the charming raconteur, all the while keeping my eyes open for clues to the evening's true purpose.

As the midnight hour approached I could tell that I would soon find out. (Midnight: is there anything truly mystical about that hour, I wonder, or was it chosen only for effect?) I noticed that the servants had stopped circulating with their trays and discreetly left the room. The hum of conversation grew simultaneously quieter and more intense, as though an almost unbearable level of excitement was being forcibly restrained. The lights on the periphery of the room dimmed so that those in the centre seemed to shine even more brightly. The stage was definitely being set for something.

At the stroke of midnight, the arts patron I mentioned earlier, now looking solemn and ceremonial, struck a small gong in the corner twelve times and the room fell silent. A young man wheeled a teacart draped in red into the centre of the room, bringing it to rest before an older man to whom I had been introduced earlier in the evening. His name is Lord Alfred Sundry and I am told he has considerable land holdings in the West Country, an impressive art collection and a son at Oxford. But this night he looked more like an ancient druid, berobed in black, the candles on the teacart casting dramatic and sinister shadows upon his face.

Can you guess what else was upon the cart? I'm enough of an Irishman to take pride in the fine Waterford crystal pitcher and goblet I saw there, and to be appalled at how they had been desecrated. How many times have I heard wine described as 'blood-red', and yet nobody who has ever seen blood ready to be served up like wine could have made the comparison. The colour could not have originated with any grape, its deep red seeming nearly black in the flickering light.

And how the assemblage longed for it! I felt the slightest surge forwards as though I were in the sea and the tide was starting to come in. They were drawn to this blood, these members of the Order of the Golden Dawn.

Well, most of them. Some had withdrawn to observe from behind Sundry, standing politely back, hands folded in front of them. As I scanned their faces, I saw two men exchange glances. One smiled, baring fangs that had not been there when I had conversed with him earlier that evening about the theatre season.

So now I knew for certain what I faced. I don't believe I've ever told you, Captain, that Bram Stoker and I fought a vampire in Dublin before I left that fair city for London. I barely escaped that encounter with my life and now here I was among a gathering of such creatures.

Lord Sundry began to speak. "We, the Order of the Golden Dawn, meet this evening for our most solemn and yet most joyous ritual: the welcoming of new members into our ranks. We do not take this responsibility lightly. To be fully accepted into the Order means nothing less than eternal life and that blessing is to be bestowed only upon the most deserving among us. With eternity comes power. The world is ours, even if the world does not yet know it."

My blood chilled. Sundry continued. "We will build a new society, and those who would live forever must have something to contribute to it. Wisdom. Talent. Passion." Here he glanced at a lovely young woman who blushed and bit her lip but smiled in return.

Then he turned the program over to Lord Cavendish, to explain the terms and conditions. "To build that society, we must also have capital. Therefore, to be a full member, one must contribute to the Order a sum of five thousand pounds, in cash or property."

I was relieved. Neither one of us could come up with anywhere near this sum. Surely, we were now safe from becoming vampires. But, I thought, Lord Cavendish must certainly know this and he invited Derrick anyway. Did they have something else in store for us? My relief quickly turned back to panic.

"Some of you, I know, do not have such a fortune at your disposal," Lord Cavendish went on. "But you would not be here if you did not possess other qualities that we value." Sundry's eyes were drawn again to the young woman. (The lecher.) "You may still join the Order as provisional members, but you will not partake of the pure blood of the dragon." Lord Cavendish gestured to the crystal pitcher. "Instead, you will be welcomed into our ranks by a current member. This person will be known as your sire, and you will owe him or her your allegiance, and your gratitude."

"We shall begin," Sundry said, drawing a scroll from within his robes. Lord Cavendish and a woman I had not met took places on either side of him. Unfurling the scroll, he intoned, "Lady Millicent Demming." The woman in question, a society matron with sharp eyes and an elaborate hairstyle, approached eagerly. "Lady Millicent," he continued, "do you have the requisite offering?"

"I do," she replied. "It has been transferred per instruction." Sundry glanced at Cavendish, who nodded.

"Very well," Sundry said. He poured a portion of blood from the pitcher into the goblet. It was as thick as cream and clung to the side of the pitcher when he set it back down. Stepping around to stand in front of Lady Millicent, Sundry commanded, "Kneel." The lady complied.

Two attendants took places on either side of her.

"Lady Millicent Demming, do you accept membership of the Order of the Golden Dawn? Do you pledge fealty to the Order and vow to work with your brothers and sisters towards our shared aims?" It was like a perverse wedding vow.

"I do," she whispered breathlessly.

"Drink the blood of the dragon, Millicent, and be born into your new life." He handed the goblet into her trembling hands and after the merest hesitation, she drank its contents. I may have been mistaken, but from where I stood I swear I saw her tongue dart out to lick up the blood that still clung to the inside of the goblet before handing it back to Lord Sundry. Her body shuddered and she nearly swooned but steadied herself. She looked up at Sundry, who helped her to her feet. When she turned to face us, she was smiling and she looked stronger and more vigorous than she had before. She then fainted and fell back into the arms of the attendants.

The crowd gasped.

"No worries," Sundry assured us. "Now comes the dream state. For some, it lasts days but for most only minutes. For some it is terrifying and for others pleasant."

One of the attendants lifted her into his arms and carried her out of the room.

Lord Sundry took up his parchment again and the scene was repeated with a middle-aged man – military, by the looks of him – and a foppish young fellow with exceedingly good taste in clothes. Then the next name: "Miss Carolyn le Fey." The young woman who had caught Sundry's eye approached, with shaky step, I thought. Sundry looked at her, not unkindly.

"Miss le Fey," he said gently. "Do you have the requisite offering?"

"I do not," she answered, her voice barely more than a whisper.

"Are you willing to accept the terms of provisional membership?" he asked.

She wavered. When he spoke again, his voice was lower but I could still hear him. "You will be forever young and beautiful." Slowly she nodded, and he whispered, "You have to say it."

Clearing her throat, she said, "I accept the terms of provisional membership in the Order of the Golden Dawn."

He beamed at her. "I am so pleased, my dear. I believe I will welcome you into our ranks myself."

He stepped towards her, looming over her like a wolf about to seize a rabbit, and she was visibly trembling. He took her by the shoulders and pulled her to him, then curled one arm around her body while sliding the other hand into her hair. As he leant into her, I heard him murmur, "This is quite an honour for you, my beauty. I rarely sire."

Then, to my horror, his fangs emerged and he buried them into her neck.

She stiffened and cried out slightly. Her arms flew up as though to push him away, but instead, she grasped his shoulders and he pulled her even closer. She moaned softly.

I could scarcely believe what I was witnessing. I wanted with every fibre of my being to run away; only good sense kept me where I was. The crowd stirred but with excitement, not with the disgust that was boiling up in my stomach. I had to stand there with the same stupid look of wonderment on my face, or risk being singled out for the interloper I was.

Sundry is obviously a man of some breeding. There was very little slurping as he slaked his obscene thirst. After what seemed like hours but could only have been minutes, he withdrew his fangs with a contented sigh, daintily licked a drop of blood from the young woman's neck and eased her to her knees. Raising his wrist to his mouth, he opened a vein with his fangs and gently placed it to Carolyn's lips. She sucked at it greedily, gazing up at him like a babe being fed by her mother. He smiled down at her fondly.

When she was done, he raised her to her feet and proudly presented her to the crowd, who applauded the new monster in their midst. She fainted into his arms. And like the others, she was taken away.

I believe thirteen vampires in all were created that night, but I may have lost count. Most bought their way in, a few were sired by senior members. When the last name had been read and the pitcher nearly drained, Sundry concluded the evening's ceremony by assuring those of us who remained unchanged that our time would come.

As the crowd dispersed, Derrick said to me, "I wish I could afford full membership, but the siring process doesn't look too bad. A moment of pain and then you're in."

A young servant nearby snorted.

"Excuse me," I asked him. "Was that humorous?"

"Nah," he said, in a distinctly Cockney accent. "The siring ain't bad, your friend's right."

"You've been sired?" Derrick asked eagerly.

"Sure have. Hurts a bit, no doubt about it. Then it feels good, kind of dreamy like. Sort of like when you've had just a bit too much whisky and a bit too little food."

"See, Oscar?" Derrick said. "You're already used to that feeling!"

"Then what happens?" I asked the Cockney, ignoring Derrick.

"Well, that first night they treat you like a king, don't they? It's your coming out party, like, as long as you don't sleep through it. There's food and all. The second night, that's the one you've got to watch out for."

"What do you mean?" Derrick asked.

"Well, what do you think His Grace up there meant when he said you owe your sire your allegiance? Allegiance to this lot means you do whatever they say. If your sire's a decent sort, that might not be so bad. Me, I wouldn't know. And notice he didn't put a time limit on this allegiance. But, well, eternity is the point of the whole thing, isn't it?"

Derrick blanched. "What do you have to do?"

The man chuckled cruelly. "Best I don't get into it, but let me just tell you this: the Order of the Golden Dawn ain't all parties in posh Knightsbridge houses. Now if you gents'll excuse me, the party for the new lot is generally a corker, and even I get to go. I don't want to miss it." He tipped an imaginary hat and trotted off to another part of the house.

We looked at each other for a long moment before Derrick muttered, "I wouldn't say no to another glass of wine. Do you see any servants about?"

I didn't. "I expect they're serving 'the new lot'," I said.

"Yes," Derrick mused. "That bloke said there was food."

"Derrick," I said patiently, "vampires don't eat roast beef and Yorkshire pudding."

I convinced him it was best that we leave before we found ourselves on the menu.

That was two nights ago, Captain Burton. I have no idea when the next ceremony will be, nor do I know what Derrick intends to do. But I cannot let him fall victim to this obsession of his to remain as he is forever. I know I am but one man against a potentially vast and definitely powerful force of enemies. I would feel more confident of my task with your leadership and guidance. Please say you will come to London and help me. More may be at stake than one young man's life.

Sincerely,

O. W.

LETTER FROM ELLEN TERRY TO LILLIE LANGTRY, 25TH OF JUNE 1879

My dearest Lillie,

I am not sure if this letter will find you on your travels, but I must tell someone of the events that are transpiring. As if life in the theatre is not strange enough, I find myself thrust into a Gothic tale so morbid and fascinating I should think it the work of an overwrought playwright if I did not know better.

As I have told you before, I for some time have had my suspicions about Henry. He has all manner of odd habits and has given me pause as to his moral character. You will remember that I wrote you in the spring that I had gone to Bram Stoker with my concerns. He investigated the matter and assured me that my suspicions were unfounded.

It seems circumstance has brought on a change of heart.

He approached me today as I was preparing to leave the theatre and offered to escort me home. He knows my penchant for walking the entire way and I thought he had a misguided concern for my safety. Still, I enjoy his company and so accepted. We made small talk for the first part of the walk, though it became obvious to me that he had something more important on his mind.

As we passed by Regent's Park, he ushered me to a secluded bench, and for a moment I thought he may have had a romantic intention. I was wrong.

With obvious reluctance, he brought up my earlier suspicions of Irving. "Has anything happened since to cause those suspicions to recur?" he asked.

"Nothing at all," I said, somewhat taken aback. "Henry has been perfectly normal. Well, for Henry."

He surprised me even further then, asking, "Has he been to your home?"

"Yes, once," I said. "He stopped in to discuss...something.... The rehearsal schedule, I believe. Or perhaps it was costuming."

"Odd. Would not either of those topics been more easily discussed at the theatre?"

"Well, yes, I suppose so. Perhaps it was during a break when I had not been to the theatre for a few days. I'm afraid I don't recall. Mr. Stoker – Bram – what is prompting this enquiry?"

He ignored my question in favour of one of his own. "Did Henry meet Lucy when he came to your house?"

"Yes, he did."

This seemed to confirm some grim suspicion in his mind. "And did they...become friendly?"

I laughed out loud at this. "Are you asking if they have embarked on an affair, Bram? I can assure you their interaction was cordial and nothing more."

"And has she mentioned him since?"

"His name comes up in conversation, generally at my instigation when I am discussing my day at work. Bram, I really must insist that you tell me what this is about."

"I fear I must," he said, "though you are not likely to believe me. Miss Terry, I suspect that Henry Irving is a vampire."

I might have laughed at first had he not seemed so grim.

He continued, "I know this seems mad, and a few years ago I would never have entertained the idea, but I have encountered such a creature before."

When I asked for more details of this previous encounter, he demurred, saying, "I know you to be friends with Oscar Wilde – ask him if you don't believe me. He was there and remembers it all too clearly, I am sure. Right now, we need to focus on Lucy."

"Lucy!" I exclaimed, then the penny dropped. "You don't think...."

He nodded. "I fear that Henry is the cause of Lucy's ill health, that he is visiting her in the night and draining her of blood!"

I am not given to fainting, Lillie, you know this, but at that moment I came very close to doing just that. The thought of poor Lucy being victimised in this fashion – and that I might work side by side with her tormenter – was nearly too much to bear!

"I would not burden you with this knowledge, Miss Terry, were I not concerned for your safety and that of our mutual friend."

"Of course. But we must do something about this, Bram! Go to the authorities and tell them what we suspect."

He smiled. "And what do you think they would say?"

"Nothing," I admitted. "At least not until they finished laughing."

"Precisely. No, this is something I must deal with on my own." Grim-faced once more he was.

"I will help," I said. "Lucy is my friend and I will do what I can to stop what is being done to her. Shall we go tonight?"

He looked at me wonderingly. "My dear Miss Terry, you will be nowhere near when the time comes to dispatch Henry Irving. Besides, help is coming and we – I – shall await it." He told me that his friend Richard Burton has sent a noted physician, Dr. Martin Hesselius, who would arrive today. He specialises in exotic diseases and maladies and has hunted vampires with Burton.

Bram accompanied me the rest of the way home, swearing me to secrecy and making me promise to act naturally around Henry while we await Dr. Hesselius. "But be careful, Ellen," he admonished. "I shall take care to always be close at hand when you and Henry are in the theatre together, but if you feel you are in danger, remove yourself from the situation immediately." I assured him I would, taking his hand and squeezing it reassuringly. Which of us I was trying to reassure I don't know, but Bram blushed a bit, which made me smile.

Whatever happens, it must happen soon. Lucy's doctor has given her a blood transfusion. She has become so anaemic he fears she will not last much longer without intervention. The procedure is experimental and has had mixed results. Her fiancé, Robert Roosevelt, has volunteered to give his blood, and she seems to be responding to the procedure, even waking for a moment and talking to us.

Her condition has the doctors baffled, but now I suspect the real cause. I dare not share what I know for it may mean being carted off to the mad ward at Bedlam.

I shall write you again tomorrow. Until then,

Forever your friend,

Ellen

LETTER FROM ELLEN TERRY TO LILLIE LANGTRY, 26TH OF JUNE 1879

My dearest Lillie,

It has been a day since my last letter and things have taken an even more tragic turn. I am so saddened it is difficult to put words to paper but I feel compelled to make a record of the events, for Lucy's sake.

Earlier today, Bram and I met with our newly arrived vampire expert, Dr. Hesselius, in Lucy's drawing room.

Dr. Hesselius is a grandfatherly man, but very energetic in his manner. He strikes one at first glance as altogether ordinary – neither tall nor short, fat nor thin, neatly (though not particularly fashionably) dressed. Still, he has an air of quiet authority about him, and the poise of his head is indicative of thought and power. Although he is of German descent, he was raised in Holland and has a thick Dutch accent. He has a well-kept grey moustache and beard and wears small round spectacles with lightly rose-tinted glass.

After brief introductions, we withdrew to Lucy's room to allow him to assess the situation.

Her physician was giving her another transfusion of Robert's blood. Imagine one's blood actually flowing into another's veins! Have two lovers ever been closer than this? I think not.

"That's all I can do for her, I'm afraid," the doctor said, after removing the needle and bandaging her arm. "Now rest will be the best medicine for her."

He took the needle out of Robert's arm; he was lying on a cot next to the bed. "Do not get up for a few moments. The loss of blood makes even the strongest of men dizzy."

We waited until Lucy's doctor left to talk freely.

Dr. Hesselius examined the wounds on Lucy's neck. "Hmmm. Very interesting, ya?"

"Are my worst fears true, was she bitten by…?" Bram asked, but stopped himself from finishing the sentence. I suspect it was because Robert was not yet aware of the horrible truth.

Dr. Hesselius had no such compunction. "Ya, it is indeed a vampire, and by the looks of it he has fed on her three, possibly four times. It is unusual that he did not drain her in one feeding. Very unusual indeed. I have only seen one other case like this."

"You mean to tell me she has been bitten by a bat?" Robert asked, astonished.

"No," Hesselius replied. "By the creature of the night. The Un-Dead. The vampire."

Robert was incredulous, as I had first been, and gaped at Bram and me. "A vampire? Bram, Ellen, who is this man and why is he here?"

Bram made a brief introduction, then said, "Robert, I know this is hard to believe. But I have experience in such matters that aroused my suspicions – though not soon enough, I'm afraid."

"So, you actually believe this," Robert said. "That vampires are real?"

Hesselius nodded grimly. "Terribly real."

"And one of them is feeding off Lucy?" Robert sat up shakily. "I am a man of science, I cannot believe this."

"Do you not think that there are things which you cannot understand, and yet which are?" asked Hesselius. "Ah, it is the fault of our science that it wants to explain all, and if it explains not, then it says there is nothing to explain."

"It is true, Robert," Bram said. "And I think I have identified the vampire. It is none other than Henry Irving."

The shocking news and the loss of blood combined to make Robert look very pale indeed as he tried to make sense of all this. "But how is this possible? Why would she let him? How did he enter the house unseen?"

"The vampire has been known to turn into smoke and enter through a gap under a door," Hesselius said. "It can hypnotise its prey, making them willing victims, even through the glass of a window. After the first feeding, the victim is under its spell completely."

"I will kill him!" Robert said. He tried to stand too quickly and swooned a moment before finally rising shakily to his feet.

"My dear fellow, I understand your sense of urgency, but we must take care and do things properly," Hesselius said, his voice gentle as he helped Robert steady himself. "The monster may seem like a man, but he could easily overpower and kill all of us if cornered."

Bram added, "I have faced two of these things down myself, and nearly lost my life each time."

Dr. Hesselius took off his spectacles and cleaned them. "They have the power to cloud men's minds, possess the strength of ten men and cannot be killed by ordinary means. We must find the creature, stake it in the heart and cut off its head. Furthermore, we must do it in the daytime when it is at its weakest."

It was hard to take in all that I was hearing. Were we really going to kill Henry?

"It will sleep in the day. In a dark place," Hesselius said.

"I think I might know where he is right at this moment," Bram said.

"No time like the present, ya?" Hesselius said, retrieving his doctor's bag from the drawing room. From it, he pulled silver crosses, wooden stakes and a phial of liquid. "Holy water," he explained. "It burns them like acid. I am told lilacs and other purple flowers can render them immobile, but I have not yet tested this myself." He pulled a bouquet from the bag as if he were performing a magic act. "If it tries to enter your mind, recite the Lord's Prayer and force him out! Lead the way, Mr. Stoker."

As we all started to leave, Bram stopped me. "Ellen, this is men's work. Besides, I need you to watch over Lucy."

I was about to argue my point when suddenly Lucy sat up and let out a blood-curdling scream!

Robert rushed to her side to comfort her, but she struck him with the back of her hand with such force that it knocked him to the ground.

Hesselius started chanting something in Latin and waving the flowers over her.

She hissed and growled like a wild animal, her eyes darting about, taking us all in. She leapt out of bed and Bram and Robert tried to restrain her but she shook them off, throwing them across the room.

Dr. Hesselius confronted her, waving the flowers with one hand and sprinkling holy water with the other. She slapped him across the face and sent his glasses flying.

She tore at her nightclothes, ripping them to shreds. She then clawed at her naked flesh, scratching deep wounds that did not bleed. It was as if she wanted to step out of her skin as she had her clothes.

Robert started towards her again, then stopped, horrified, as she began to change.

Her open mouth looked more like the giant maw of a beast. I watched her teeth growing before my eyes, dripping with saliva. For a fleeting second, our eyes locked and there was a moment of recognition. The creature's gaze became Lucy's again as if she were trapped inside it looking out. The fangs retracted. She went from looking menacing to looking frightened.

"Ellen?" she gasped.

I started to move towards her, but at that moment Hesselius stumbled to his feet and ripped back the curtains. Lucy screamed and hid her face from the light. She withdrew to a shadowed corner, covering her face and whimpering. She began to convulse, flopping around like a fish thrown onto land.

"Lucy!" Robert rushed towards her.

"No!" Dr. Hesselius commanded. "Do not touch her!"

I don't think Robert would have obeyed, but there was no chance to find out. As quickly as it had begun, her fit was over. She collapsed to the floor. Her face was peaceful and human, but sadly, Lucy Mayhew was now dead.

My heart breaks. For poor, tragic Lucy. For Robert, who loved her. For her friend Florence; Bram is telling her now. Florence hasn't been herself lately either, as she fights a bout of melancholy. I am afraid the news will drive her into deeper despair.

I know not what will happen next, nor what part I may play in it. But I know this: he who corrupted and snuffed out this vibrant young life must answer for his crime.

Ellen

LETTER FROM ROBERT ROOSEVELT TO THEODORE ROOSEVELT, 26TH OF JUNE 1879

Dear Theodore,

I know you won't read this letter until you return from your trip out West, but I feel I must record these events and trust only you to keep these words safe.

I am sorry, Teddy, that I ever doubted your account of battling a vampire in Mexico. Can you ever forgive my mocking tone? As a naturalist, I should have been more open to the possibilities of unknown creatures. I now know these vile monsters are horribly real. One such abomination has corrupted and murdered a vibrant young woman and stolen away my last chance at true happiness. If I had accepted the truth sooner, would I have been able to prevent this tragedy?

Here in civilized London with its vast populace, it is apparently quite easy for a vampire to go about undetected. Paradoxically, at least one is able to live a very public life in high society while maintaining his dark secret. The famous actor Henry Irving is such a creature. I know this is hard to believe, but it is true. And this monster has killed my Lucy!

I have felt tremendous grief before, but never such rage. Being of gentle temperament my whole life, it is a feeling I cannot stomach for any length of time.

After my dear wife died, I never thought I would find love again. I had planned, as you know, to devote the rest of my life to my work and to my conservation efforts. Lucy Mayhew changed all that. Getting to know her gave me hope that the world was good and fair, and now that she has been so cruelly taken from me I see nothing but despair and darkness.

I pray for Lucy's soul and my own. Will God judge me should I give in to my own need for revenge? Or is it our duty to send this thing back to hell? Am I murdering a man, or putting down a rabid animal?

I can't help but recall my time with the Ojibwa tribe in the wilds of Northern Michigan, where a young brave lost his wife in a ferocious bear attack. Instead of hunting the bear down for revenge, he let the creature go. It was only doing what was in its nature, he explained. If his woman had been killed by lightning, would he hunt the storm? The bear had no malice in its heart and was not responsible for its actions any more than it could 'murder' a deer.

I wish I could find such peace from this hate welling up in my own heart. This thing is not a man, but some sort of creature controlled by the devil. Is it responsible for its actions? And yet, unlike the bear, it speaks, it reasons. In this case, it even enacts the works of Shakespeare. How could it not be held to account for what it has done?

I have joined forces with a vampire expert, Dr. Hesselius, and a young man named Bram Stoker, who works for Irving. As I write this, we are waiting for the sun to come up, at which time we shall leave to kill the fiend that murdered Lucy. Dr. Hesselius tells us they are much weakened in the daytime and must return to their coffins to sleep before sunrise.

I must go now. Bram has ascertained the creature's lair and we are off. Should I not return, I entrust you to take care of my children and my estate.

Sincerely,

Uncle Robert

SECOND LETTER FROM ROBERT ROOSEVELT TO THEODORE ROOSEVELT, 26TH OF JUNE 1879

Dear Theodore,

As I write this we have the foul creature in our custody!

My cheeks are still ruddy with the thrill of the hunt. I feel twenty years younger and recall the time you and I fought off that grizzly bear!

The sun was still low in the eastern sky but shining brightly when we broke down the door at Irving's apartment, scattering unclaimed post that was piled under the mail slot. Armed with wooden stakes and crosses, we slowly crept through the front hall and entered the sitting room, wrenching open curtains as we went to wash the rooms in as much blessed sunlight as possible. However, by the looks of the place, no one had used it for quite some time. A layer of undisturbed dust covered rich furnishings and the air was stale and stifling. A thorough search of the remaining rooms yielded no sign that the creature was there or had been recently.

After working myself up into a state of determined readiness en route, this was anticlimactic to be sure. Undeterred, Stoker spoke two simple words: "The theater," and we were off again.

As manager of the Lyceum Theatre, Stoker has complete access and authority. As it was by now mid-morning, the theater was a beehive of activity. The stage was dressed for *Cleopatra*, adorned with Egyptian gods, mummies and the like, and many craftsmen were about, putting on the finishing touches.

Stoker ordered everyone out of the building to make our search easier and safer. Staying together, we covered much ground as quickly as we could – the attic, the catacomb of backstage rooms and the cellar – to no avail.

"Perhaps there are clues to another location in his office," Dr. Hesselius suggested.

This triggered a revelation in Stoker. "Of course! He has a secret passage leading to the alley from his office. Perhaps there are more such passages."

We ransacked the office, pulling books from the bookcase, tapping the walls and turning over furniture. In addition to the passage Stoker had known about, we found a trapdoor hidden beneath the rug.

Upon opening it, all that could be seen was darkness. A stale, musty smell wafted up from the narrow passage, with a hint of cold, damp dirt behind it. Stoker lit a lantern and lowered it a bit into the passage, revealing a ladder attached to one of the walls, but how far down it went I didn't know, for we could not see the bottom. We knew we must descend, for surely our quarry must be at ladder's end.

After acquiring another lantern, Stoker descended first, followed by me, then Dr. Hesselius.

Through the very walls of the theater we crept downward. All of us were surprised at the depth the ladder was taking us.

"We are far below even the cellar now, I should think," Stoker said after we had been descending for several minutes.

Suddenly his foot broke one of the rungs and he dropped his lantern. It crashed below, its light briefly illuminating the bottom. I now held our only lantern, as Hesselius was clutching a doctor's bag with his vampire-fighting paraphernalia.

When we reached the bottom, we could see walls of stone by our flickering lantern. It appeared to be some ancient Roman aqueduct. Rats scurried from our light down a tunnel that opened before us, and I could hear the dripping of water ahead.

With much trepidation, we made our way into the damp darkness. Occasionally my lantern would spit and sputter, indicating that it was low on oil. The smart thing would have been to return to the surface for more lanterns and men, but Stoker pressed on before I could suggest it.

About forty feet down the tunnel, another room had been carved out to the right side. Mounds of earth were haphazardly piled here and there, with the tunnel ahead completely filled with dirt from the excavated room.

We could not see clearly inside the room, as the lantern's light was not being thrown far enough to remove the shadows. Entering it required our stepping up off the rounded stone floor of the aqueduct and onto loose dirt. I stumbled, almost dropping the lantern, and when I regained my balance and put the lantern high in front of me, we could see the outline of a coffin! It rested upon a pile of rubble.

"Bring the lantern closer," Dr. Hesselius whispered, as he opened his bag to retrieve a wooden stake and mallet. For, according to the good doctor, a wooden stake through the heart is a sure way to dispatch the creature.

With Hesselius's stake at the ready and my lantern shining the way, Stoker flung open the casket. For a moment, we were taken aback at its contents. Surely this was not a living creature. Even in the dim light, its skin was stone-white and waxy. Dark veins could be seen under the translucent skin. Its lips were dark and swollen, with a trickle of blood in the corner of the mouth. Its chest did not rise and fall with breath. It was recognizable as Henry Irving, but only barely, like a wax statue of the man that had started to decay.

Dr. Hesselius had placed the stake just above the heart and swung his hammer back to give it a good wallop when suddenly, the creature's hand shot up and grabbed the stake. It hissed and snarled, ripping the stake from Hesselius's hands. It flung the stake at me and, too late, I realized it was aiming for the lantern! With great force and incredible precision, the stake shattered the glass and snuffed out the flame, plunging us at once into total darkness!

I felt a gust of wind blow past me as I dropped to one knee and searched my pocket for matches. Dr. Hesselius had beaten me to it and I turned to see he was lighting a candle he had retrieved from his bag.

We jumped down into the tunnel once more and ran towards the ladder as quickly as we could without extinguishing our precious light. The creature was nowhere to be seen.

"He won't get far in the day," Dr. Hesselius said as we hurriedly scaled the ladder to the surface. "He will find a hiding place indoors, somewhere in the shadows."

It took us many precious minutes to climb back to the surface, a distance the vampire covered in mere seconds. I worried that he would have blocked the trapdoor upon his exit, trapping us in his lair until such time as he chose to return to finish us off, but chose not to share this concern with my companions.

Fortunately, he must have been in too much of a hurry to think of this, for the trapdoor was wide open. Daylight poured into the office and we knew the creature would need to seek cover downstairs, but where?

We searched the stage and backstage areas. Stoker climbed a ladder up to the catwalk and lit the limelight. The gilded Egyptian set glittered and produced a comforting glow. He swung the spotlight around and made sure the vampire was not hiding among the seats.

Stoker came down and met us once again on the stage.

"Come, there is a room below the stage accessible by trapdoor." He flung it open but before we could descend a streak of black burst up from below. In the literal blink of an eye, it had Dr. Hesselius in its grasp!

"Back," it commanded. "I could easily break his neck."

Stoker backed away until he was nearly in the left wing. He then suddenly disappeared into the wings, momentarily confusing the creature. There was a loud swooshing sound and it was then I knew what he had done. The heavy curtains on one side of the auditorium fell away, revealing large overhead windows. Daylight poured in and filled the stage.

Dr. Hesselius struggled and the creature lost its grip on him. I lunged forwards and together Hesselius and I wrestled the vampire to the ground. It struggled but now had only the strength of a weak, older man.

I slugged him in the jaw and he went limp. The fear and grief and rage that had propelled me through the hunt had now reached its peak. With the creature beneath me, I felt a thrill of righteous vengeance, and I wanted him to know I was no mere monster hunter but on a personal mission. "I'll kill you for what you did to my Lucy!" I shouted.

"I have hurt no one," it said. "Please, get me out of the light."

Stoker approached with a cross at the ready. "You murdered her and you will pay the price, demon!"

"I did not kill Lucy, and if you give me a chance I can prove it."

"Lucy was killed by a vampire," Hesselius said. "She transformed before our eyes into a vile creature such as yourself."

"By a vampire, yes, but not *this* vampire," Irving insisted.

"There are others, ya?" Dr. Hesselius asked.

"Yes, London is infested with them at the moment," Irving said, his voice weakening. "I am trying to hunt them down, like you, and destroy them. I am so sorry I was too late to save Lucy."

"How are we to believe you?" I asked, tightening my grip.

"I am afraid Lucy is one of the Un-Dead now. She will rise from the grave, feed, and then be compelled to return to the vampire that made her. She herself will lead you to her killer."

"Still, you are one of these things. Why shouldn't we kill you?" Stoker demanded.

"Because I am the only one that stands between you and a much greater threat. There is a nest of vampires in London under the control of a madman known as the Black Bishop. He will stop at nothing until the whole world is under his control."

"Black Bishop?" Stoker asked. It seemed to stir a memory in him.

A cloud moved between us and the sun and I felt the creature grow stronger. I was able to contain him for a moment more, then suddenly I was no longer holding him. It was as if he evaporated out of my arms. There was a wisp of smoke, then he was standing at the back of the stage where an Egyptian arch protected him with a dark shadow.

"As you can see, I could flee, but I will not," he said, with his authoritative actor's voice. "I will show you how to bind me so I cannot escape if that's what it takes to gain your trust."

So, now, my dear Theodore, we have the thing locked in a cage under the stage, its feet and hands bound by silver chains. Will this keep him contained? I know not, as we only have his word this will keep him our prisoner, though Hesselius seems satisfied by the restraints.

And tonight? Tonight, we go out and put Lucy to rest and hopefully find the one that desecrated her. May God protect us and have mercy on our souls.

Sincerely,
Uncle Robert

TRANSCRIPT FROM EDISON TINFOIL CYLINDERS RECORDED BY DR. MARTIN HESSELIUS, 27TH OF JUNE 1879

Archivist's note: One of the earliest sound recordings, certainly the earliest in the White Worm Society's collection. The transcript below was taken from twelve Edison tin cylinders. Four other cylinders had corroded and the contents were not recoverable.

From the Case Files of Dr. Hesselius, Number 354: The Siring of Henry Irving.

Hesselius: Hello, testing, testing. It is the 27th of June 1879 and I am interviewing an actual vampire. If you would state your name and birthplace and age.

Irving: I am currently known as Henry Irving, but my real name is Jonathan Harker. I was born in 1681 in Edinburgh, Scotland. I was turned into a vampire when I was forty-two years of age and have been a vampire for over a hundred and fifty years. (Pause) What else do you wish to know?

Hesselius: Oh, a great many things, ya? What powers do you possess?

Irving: I have incredible strength and swiftness. I can mesmerise people and control them, especially if they're feeble-minded, or drunk.

Hesselius: And turn to smoke, ya, we witnessed this?

Irving: I am not actually turning into smoke. It is more like slipping behind a curtain for a moment and then emerging in another place. Smoke is produced in the process, but I do not become it. It is difficult to explain, but when I do it, I sometimes see another world.

Brief images of other creatures and a sky that is not our own, and then I am pulled back into this world resulting in me being moved a few feet away.

Hesselius: Can you turn into a bat or wolf?

Irving: I cannot. I have heard tales of older, more powerful vampires that could do such things, but this may just be a legend. I have never witnessed it myself.

Hesselius: You have met others of your kind? I mean, besides the one that made you?

Irving: Yes. There are the mindless ones we call Nosferatu. They are said to have been made by vampires so ancient it was before humans developed rational thought, yet they possess an animal cunning that has allowed them to survive. More common are those like me: articulate, able to pass themselves off as human. I have met nearly twenty at last count. I have dispatched almost all of them; a few nearly killed me. Bram met one of them as well, in Dublin, last year. He hunted the beast, as did I. I found him first.

Hesselius: You are killing your own kind?

Irving: I…I prefer not to think of myself as one of them. I do not kill or feed from the unwilling. I kill those who do, to protect the living.

Hesselius: How do you kill a vampire, besides the stake in the heart?

Irving: Chopping off the head works, as does fire.

Hesselius: Sunlight?

Irving: Perhaps. I myself have spent brief periods out in the daytime and experienced only weakness and loss of my powers. A longer time in direct sunlight may produce death. I have not done it for long. It is very uncomfortable.

Hesselius: Other weaknesses?

Irving: Silver. It burns our skin and even our eyes should we look directly at it. Our images do not show up on mirrors backed by silver or on film, I think due to the silver nitrate. It is said most vampires also fear Christian symbols, although I myself do not. The savoury smell of cooked food we find repulsive, especially garlic. I cannot be in its presence for long.

Hesselius: Is it true you need to be invited into someone's home, that you cannot cross the threshold of your own free will?

Irving: It is. Somehow there is this odd feeling of…protocol.

Something I feel is inherited from the mistress that cursed me, something she in turn inherited from her master. It is a perverted sense of honour and civility that is normally missing from my kind, but I am compelled to obey it, even when confronted with my monstrous appetite.

Hesselius: How did you become a vampire?

Archivist's note: There is a long silence here and his voice trembles for a moment as if he is recalling a fearful memory. Irving's acting talents are also on display as he changes his voice when speaking for the characters.

Irving: I was once a man, of course. My mother was Hungarian and taught me the language. When a group of Gipsies from Hungary came through our village, I joined them with hopes of seeing the world. For the next twenty years, I travelled with them all through Europe.

Eventually, I left them and joined a group of touring actors and musicians. Our travels took us to Csejte Castle in Čachtice. There we performed for Hungarian soldiers and were offered food and shelter within the castle walls for the night.

With much of the castle taken up by officers and the rest in great disrepair, we were put up in tents in the courtyard.

It was a cold and rainy night and my tent leaked. Although we were told it was unsafe to enter the ruined part of the castle, I sought shelter there. I was surprised to find it pleasantly dry and free of rats. I found an empty room with a fireplace and set to building a fire with the broken furniture that was strewn about. It is funny how a nice roaring fire can make even an old castle seem warm and inviting, and how misleading that feeling can be.

The sounds of the soldiers breaking camp awoke me early in the morning before the sun was up.

As I settled back down for more sleep I heard a faint cry.

The wind, I thought. Then it grew louder and more forlorn. I lit a torch and made my way deeper into the ruins to find the sound. Down at the end of the hallway was a brick wall embedded with a large iron cross, gilded in silver, stretching from floor to ceiling and from wall to wall on either side. The crying was quite clear now.

"Who is there?" I called in Hungarian. I frantically searched for a door, which I was sure must have been there.

"Help me, kind sir!" a woman cried from the other side. "Some horrible men walled me up in here and I am half-dead of hunger and thirst!"

"How monstrous! Why would they do such a thing?"

"I am betrothed to a count and I refused to marry him, so he walled me up to make me bend to his will."

"I shall get the authorities," I said.

"No! They are all in the count's pocket. Please, break me free."

How could I resist such a request? I was adventurous, then, and prone to romantic heroism. After a quick search, I found a timber of suitable size and used it as a battering ram. I pounded at the bottom of the cross until it was free from the wall. I wedged the beam under it and pried it up. It was rusted and broke away from the wall, nearly falling on me in the process. I did not think to wonder how long it must have been there to suffer such corrosion.

I worked at the wall until I made a small hole all the way through. The smell of rot and death wafted from it. That poor creature, I thought. I could see her inside, though not clearly in the dark, with my torch on a nearby wall nearly burned out.

"Oh, thank you! Thank you! I never thought I would see outside these walls again. Come closer, let me see your face."

As I leant in, her hand shot out and grabbed my throat. She stepped through the bricks as if they weren't there, the trick of apparition, as I would later demonstrate myself to you. It was the cross keeping her trapped there and I had removed it!

She was a hideous old hag, skin and bones, her head covered with cobwebs and a few remaining wisps of white hair.

She unhinged her jaw like a snake and sank her teeth deeply into my neck.

There was a momentary pain, then the feeling was actually pleasurable, such an ecstasy as I had never felt before. I went limp and fell into her oblivion.

She drained me and I awaited the sweet release of death, but it did not come. She slit her own neck with the sharp claw at the end of her bony finger and pushed my mouth to the open wound. She tasted of dust and the foulest dirt, but I was compelled to drink.

"Drink your reward, my prince," she cackled. "We shall be together always."

I fell into a fevered dream from which I could not awaken.

I dreamt I was sitting on the ground, my back up against a tree. I was unable to move.

This dream world was not our own. Above me a large crimson sun filled the sky, bathing the world in a reddish light. The plants around me had black, leathery leaves. The grass that grew up around me was sharp and jagged and whistled as the hot wind blew across it.

Strange insects crawled on me as if I were part of the tree. Occasionally, a small animal would come up and sniff me and wander off, uninterested. These creatures were all unfamiliar to me, a menagerie of animals one might see in a book of Greek myths. Two-headed, furred turtles, winged lizards and birds that looked more like fish than creatures of the air.

Night fell and the sky above was filled with unfamiliar stars. Their Milky Way was a giant pinwheel of stars that filled most of the sky and gave off enough light to read by.

The next day it rained. It was hot and smelled like sulphur and all I could do was feel it pour over my body.

Then as the sun started to set, some insects buzzed about me, just out of my view. I could see nothing but their shadows. Three, perhaps four of them circled me.

Suddenly one of the shadows bit me. I could feel it burrow through my skin. Unable to move, all I could do was feel it seep into my blood. It flooded my body and burned my brain. I felt my heart stop.

I awoke with a gasp. I was tucked snugly in bed in a nicely furnished room. I was weak and felt very near death. I fell back to sleep.

I awoke sometime later in the night. A servant was in my room, watching over me.

He put a wine goblet to my lips and I guzzled the bright red liquid down. I had never tasted anything so wonderful. It was like the sweetest cherry wine and the most savoury meat at the same time. I instantly felt my strength returning and my head clearing.

He helped me out of bed. I followed him down the stairs to the large banquet room I had performed in just a few nights before. A woman was seated at the head of the table dressed in an elegant golden gown. She and the gown were adorned with jewels, and her raven hair cascaded over her shoulders. She had a strong, lithe body and dark eyes that held no trace of fear or pity or humanity.

The bodies of my theatre troupe were strewn about like carcases of meat. The stench of death filled the room and maggots and flies infested the corpses.

Waving her hand at the dead, she commanded her servants, "Take these away." An evil grin let me know she had wanted me to see them in this state, to see them as she saw them: as only empty sacks of food.

There were many male and female servants. Some were vampires themselves and some human. I could tell by smell which was which. For you see, all my senses were intensified. Colours were brighter, shapes were more in focus and I could hear the faintest sounds with clarity. I could hear the humans' hearts beating fast and could smell their fear in their sweat.

"Please, my prince, be seated." She pointed to a chair to the right of her.

I did as I was commanded, for I could not resist anything she asked, or even thought for that matter. It was like I was connected by invisible marionette strings. I knew then that she was the horrible hag who had bitten me, turned young and beautiful now that she was free to feast again on the innocent.

"I am the Countess Elizabeth Bathory de Ecsed," she said in accented English. She switched back to Hungarian. "You shall be my new prince. The knight who rescued me." She leant over and kissed me on the lips. Her tongue slithered into my mouth and tasted of the liquid in the goblet, which I then knew was blood.

My time with her was a blur, a drunken nightmare that plunged me into the very depths of hell itself. A hell I am ashamed to admit I found exciting.

Her debauchery knew no bounds. Night after night it was an orgy of sex, blood and death. Dozens of young maidens were brought in and slaughtered for our feasts. She would actually bathe in a tub filled with buckets of their blood.

Young men met a different fate. If she desired them, she would turn them into vampires and, like me, they became her unconditional slaves. If she did not like them, she tortured them for sport, seeing how long they could live without skin or some other even more heinous act.

With the soldiers off fighting in foreign lands, there was no force to protect the village. The townspeople mounted attacks on her castle, which her growing vampire army easily thwarted. Their only chance for survival was to flee or provide her with virgins from enemy villages.

One day word came that the army was returning to put an end to her reign of terror. She just laughed it off and went back to her feeding frenzy. It was apparent she was quite insane now. Maybe she had always been. Or maybe being walled up for decades drove her mad, but she had no fear of what was sure to come. By her own count, she had slaughtered over six hundred people. The cries of their families must have been heard across the country. Surely an army *was* coming.

Then one night, as she once again filled the castle with screams and blood, I heard a voice in my head. "Let me in and I will spare you."

I heard it again, this time louder and with direction. I went to a side door and felt his presence.

"Let me in and I will spare you."

I opened the door and a tall dark man stood there, shrouded in a cloak, his eyes glowing like hot coals. I knew at once he was the vampire that made her. Her master, therefore my master.

"Come in," I said, stepping aside.

He moved past me with such speed he was a blur of light and smoke. I followed him into the main hall, where he proceeded to take off the heads of any vampire in his way with his bare hands like an unruly child might lop the heads off of flowers. In only a few minutes every vampire in the room, save the countess, was destroyed and the humans were cowering in fear.

The countess screamed as she saw him coming for her. "No!" She fell to her knees and starting kissing his feet.

He kicked her off. "You are a spoiled, vain creature," he said. "You have made us known to the humans. Our greatest strength is that we are shrouded in legend. When they know they always come. They come with torches, and silver crosses. They come by the light of day and turn you out into the sun. An army is coming here and they will not find you."

"But, sire," she pleaded. "They walled me up for seventy-five years. They are only paying me what is owed!"

He pulled her screaming to her feet. She threw her arms around him and kissed him. He embraced her tightly and when he broke away from the kiss he plunged his hand into her chest and extracted her tiny heart.

It was dry and black as coal and he crushed it in his hand. She gasped and collapsed into a pile of ash.

I felt a terrible pain at her death as if I myself were having my heart ripped out.

"Come here," he commanded me. I had to obey, for now this was my new and only master.

I walked up to him, awaiting death. But instead of killing me, he put a finger to my forehead and I felt a burning sensation. I felt something inside me release, like the snapping of a taut piano string.

"I release you from her bond and from mine." He turned and started walking towards the door. "I have given you a rare gift for a vampire – free will. Use it wisely."

With that, he walked out of the room and I never saw him again in all my travels. From that moment on I began my search for others of my kind. I know not why. Perhaps at first, I wanted companionship. Later I wanted a cure for my affliction and thought maybe older vampires knew of one, so I travelled the world....

{End: last usable recording cylinder.}

FROM THE JOURNAL OF BRAM STOKER, 27TH OF JUNE 1879

6:25 p.m.

What a momentous day! Only yesterday morning my heart was heavy with the thought I must kill my friend and mentor. Now, not only have we forestalled that plan, but my heart and mind are burdened with even more troubling revelations.

The most disturbing of all is that there are many vampires in London, perhaps dozens, plotting some sort of mass attack under the leadership of the Black Bishop.

But the other discovery is far more personal and has left me shaken, questioning both my history and my future.

I stood before him in his cell, which is the property cage beneath the stage, where we had deposited him after his interrogation. He instructed us to bind his hands and feet with silver chains as this will hinder his powers of apparition, keeping him from leaving the cage. Whether this is true or not remains to be seen. He may very well be lying to me as he has since the very first day I met him. Even that, as it happens, is a falsehood, for I would come to learn we had encountered one another long before that dinner in Dublin.

He must have seen the wariness and betrayal on my face, for he said, "You must believe me, Bram, I would not and will not harm you, nor any of your friends."

"A creature from hell has no trouble lying," I said. "And I am apparently quite gullible, so I cannot trust myself to recognise the truth even should you present it."

"Search your feelings, Bram," he urged. "Remember when you were a frail, sickly boy? A man came to you and administered a remarkable cure."

The memory came flooding back. A man, I thought he was a doctor, gave me…what, medicine? The next day I was cured from my ailments. It was the dark of night, though, when the man came. And my parents were not the ones who brought him.

He could see the recognition in my eyes. "Yes, Bram. That was I. I gave you a bit of my blood, not enough to turn you, but enough to cure you. You would have died in a week's time had I not visited you that night."

I turned from him, steadying myself against a wooden chair painted to look like gold, a sham throne for some mad Shakespearean king. It was a moment before I could find breath to speak. "But why would you do such a thing?"

He smiled ruefully.

"I am afraid my motives were not purely unselfish. This curse was thrust upon me and I thought many times about taking my own life, but this thing inside me will not permit it.

"I have walked the earth for over a hundred years, searching for a cure to this malady. My travels led me to the Reverend Wilkins, who convinced me that I could cast out this demon.

"He introduced me to a Gipsy woman who told me of an ancient prophecy. That a half man, half demon could open the gates of hell and send back the creatures of the night, curing any who were cursed by them."

"So that's what I am, a demon?" I asked, mortified because it is what I feared most. I sank into the chair, gripping its arms to stop the shaking in my hands.

"No, not in the true sense," Irving said. "Siring a vampire is a more complicated procedure. If it were not, the world would be up to its hips in vampires. First, a vampire must drain the blood, and at the precise moment before the last heartbeat, feed some of its own blood to the victim. I fed you, Bram, but I did not drink from you.

"The blood of a vampire, freely given to you as an innocent child with none taken in return, gives you a foot in both worlds, fulfilling the prophecy. It appears it has also acted as a vaccine. You are inoculated against vampires and other evil creatures, and you have powers to see their true nature."

That reminded me of the inconsistency that had troubled me. "Why, then, could I not see you for what you are?"

"I am not sure. Perhaps because it was my blood that gave you your gift. I prefer to think it is because I am trying to stay on the righteous path."

I sprang from my throne. "Righteous? You fed on that poor girl right here in this very building!"

He backed away from the bars, slightly, but his voice remained mild. "I still need to feed from time to time, that cannot be helped. Prostitutes, for a price, are willing victims if one takes only a small amount, as I have learned to do. I haven't killed a human for over a hundred years."

"How noble," I said. "Desperate people will do many things for money, but we don't usually describe those who take advantage of that as righteous."

"I would stop if I could, Bram. As I cannot, I try to atone by hunting down others of my kind and killing them, if they are unwilling to join me in finding a cure and turning their lives back to God."

I found it difficult to stop the questions and accusations from pouring out, and yet I could not bring myself to ask those that truly troubled me: Who invited this monster into my life? What did this affliction with which he'd cursed me mean to my own immortal soul? It's true I would likely have died had he not intervened – my illness and miraculous recovery have become family legend – but at least I would have died in innocence. Had Irving's 'cure' damned me for eternity? I didn't ask these questions, partly because I thought he would not know the answers, partly because I feared he would. Instead, I asked, "How are you able to live as a man with a wife and children, or are they all a fabrication as well?"

He seemed relieved at this – perhaps he guessed how close I was to asking far more uncomfortable questions. "They are very real, as was Henry Irving. He died in a fire, leaving a widow and children. Through a financial arrangement with his wife, I assumed his identity. Our likenesses were close enough and I quickly moved them away from their village before any had a chance to refute the claim. It is in this guise that I began to travel the world, an actor by night, a hunter of vampires, well, also by night. I am truly sorry I was unable to stop Lucy's killer before tragedy struck."

The mention of Lucy brought me up short, and I shook off some of my petulant self-pity. Lives are at stake, and deeds must be done. If Irving is the un-monstrous monster he claims to be, we can help one another.

"You said I could break your curse. How?" I asked.

"According to the Gipsy, there are places in the world where the veil between the earth and hell are thin. If we find one of these places, your blood will open the gates of hell. Anyone possessed by a demon who stands near the doorway will have that demon torn from him and cast back into the pit of damnation."

"And what happens to your earthly body?"

His gaze never wavered. "I do not know. It is possible I will collapse into dust on the spot, having already far exceeded the number of years allotted to a man. But I suspect I *could* live out the rest of a normal, human lifespan, and then die a normal, human death. Except I shall feel obliged to continue hunting vampires, so the probability of a normal lifespan is somewhat lower than it might be otherwise."

I thought, then, about my own obligations: to Florence and our unborn child. To a world that is menaced by creatures it does not believe in. To one of those very creatures, strangely enough, who had – for better or worse – made me the man I am today.

"Well, then," I said, "why wait? Let's perform this ritual now."

He smiled regretfully.

"We cannot. The amount of blood required to open the gates is described as 'two goat stomachs' worth', which is more than you might think. A man cannot lose that much blood and live.

"Moreover, we do not know of a place to perform the ritual. The Gipsies say it has to do with ley lines and the alignment of the stars. A book with the maps of these places was stolen from my office the night Miss Terry encountered the burglar. The book is written in an ancient language that I had only begun to translate.

"In any event, even if we were able to open the gates of hell, I am unsure of how to shut them. We could unleash all sorts of terror on the world if we leave the gates open too long."

Now that my mind was made up, I was reluctant to abandon the idea. "Perhaps more blood will close the gate?"

"I cannot be sure and am not willing to take the risk without more information."

He was right, of course. Sighing, I returned to my wooden throne and sat heavily.

"Who is the Black Bishop?" I asked. "Some sort of vampire king?"

"It appears so. Vampires fear him and do his bidding. From what I have discovered, he is planning to create a vampire army that would enslave humanity, reducing you to nothing more than their cattle."

I thought back to the chess piece we found on Count Ruthven that night, a black bishop! That was over a year ago; how far their plans must have progressed in that time.

"My only ally in this fight has been Reverend Wilkins. And the Gipsies, for they also have cursed among them, werewolves, whom they wish to cure. Even as we speak they are travelling the world to find a place where the ritual can be performed. It is my duty to keep you safe until that day."

Safe. I felt anything but. "I hope what you are telling me is true, Henry," I said. "If I can lift your curse, I will."

"Thank you. But we have more pressing matters at hand. You must put Lucy to rest and hunt down her killer. After that, we can discuss what to do next."

Despite what he has told me, I cannot wholeheartedly trust him, for it is not only my life that is at risk. I will leave him locked up until we dispatch Lucy's killer. Irving tells us that Lucy will rise and be drawn to her sire. She may have already done so. I hope in our zeal to interrogate Henry we have not missed our chance to follow Lucy to her killer.

FROM THE CASE FILES OF DR. HESSELIUS, NUMBER 355: THE MYSTERIOUS CASE OF ABRAHAM STOKER, 28TH OF JUNE 1879

I have been summoned to London by Captain Richard Burton to help track and put down a vampire terrorising the city. (See Case 354: The Siring of Henry Irving.)

It seems Abraham Stoker, the manager of the Lyceum Theatre, had discovered his employer, the famous actor Henry Irving, was in fact, a vampire.

After a successful hunt and capture of said vampire, I was taken into Mr. Stoker's confidence. He came to me concerned and looking for a cure to what he saw as an affliction.

It seems he has the power to detect the darker forces of the supernatural. A power that was bestowed upon him as a small child by the vampire Henry Irving.

While suffering a blood condition that would have most certainly led to his death, Stoker was visited by Irving, who gave him some of his vampiric blood and did not feed on him in return.

I have never heard of such behaviour from a vampire. Indeed, the vampire Irving seems to be most unusual indeed. Perhaps his release from the lineage of the vampire king so many years ago had given him back his soul.

In any event, Irving's actions towards young Stoker were not purely altruistic. Irving was and is seeking a cure for his vampirism, and the ritual of inoculating the boy was to give Irving an ingredient for such a cure.

According to Gipsy lore, the feeding of vampire blood to a boy on his seventh birthday would give the boy a foot in both worlds – our world and that of the Other Realm. This would make the boy a key to open a doorway between those worlds. How this would help to cure Irving is unclear, as is the place and manner for opening the door. Irving's research continues and his time grows short as the day approaches when the veil between worlds will be at its thinnest.

It seems that Irving's blood both cured and cursed the young Stoker. His blood does indeed show unusual properties. For example, vampires are sickened by drinking from him. It may be that Stoker could never be turned. His blood could lead to a vaccine to protect us all from vampirism and I hope to study it further.

The blood has also given him the power to sense supernatural creatures.

"Especially," he told me, "if there is violence involved or the intent to do violence."

He became quiet and found it hard to continue but pressed on.

"It is as though their lust…their hunger sets something off in myself. I see a green glow around them and the things they have touched, as if they are giving off the scent of evil. If they commit an act that is extremely violent, I can see it days later. I can relive the violence as if I were the one perpetrating the crime."

I told him that this is known as clairvoyance, and it can be very disturbing to those who experience it. He seemed relieved that I had a diagnosis for his condition.

"Yes," he confessed. "I am frightened to give in to it, even when I could be helping to track down these monsters."

"You fear becoming a monster yourself," I said. "It is understandable and you are wise to keep yourself distant from it."

He confided that he'd had a few spells as a boy, but that it wasn't until he encountered a werewolf that it fully took him over. After that event he found it hard to concentrate, difficult to resist his baser self. He found himself carousing and drifting from his intellectual pursuits. He chalked it up to a failing of character, but with his recent contact with the supernatural the feelings have become worse. His temper has become short, his lust is harder to tamp down and he finds his mind drifting into dark fantasies.

I asked him what the contents of his dark fantasies were, but he said he was uncomfortable discussing them in detail.

However, he finally added after coaxing from me, "When I become aroused I feel as though I am not myself, as if I am watching someone else enjoy intimacies with my wife. Someone who delights in making me watch. I know that sounds vague and somewhat silly, but it is an unsettling feeling."

I told him that it may very well be a side effect of using the power and that he should trust his instinct about this 'vague' uneasiness.

"If this power comes from a supernatural place, the price may be that you leave a bit of yourself there to bring that power here," I explained.

I do not think he felt better after my advice; however, I feel honesty is the best medicine when it comes to protecting one's self from evil forces. How many men who have dabbled in the supernatural thought they could control its power and could not?

FROM THE DIARY OF FLORENCE STOKER, 28TH OF JUNE 1879

I am going mad.

Reality is collapsing around me. I know not what to believe anymore. The events of last night seemingly cannot be real, but I know they are.

Last night I awoke to find myself sleepwalking. I had flung open the French doors to the garden and was stepping outside, my bare feet coming down on cool, rough flagstone. My heart began to pound as I shook off sleep and realised I could have brought harm to myself or the baby in such a state. I knew, however, that something had pulled me out there.

It was a warm and breezy night. I stood there for a moment taking in the moonlight and the wind in my hair when I heard a voice whispering from the darkness.

"Florrie…."

She stepped forwards into the moonlight. I could scarcely believe it. It was a dream, surely. How could she be standing there in front of me?

It was Lucy! She was wearing a burial shroud and in her arms clutched something wrapped tightly in a blanket. She put the bundle down and ran towards me with open arms.

I did not care if I were dreaming, I happily embraced her.

"Lucy, my dear Lucy, this is a miracle!" I exclaimed. She was cold to the touch. "How can this be?"

"I awoke in a coffin in the family crypt," she cried. "Can you imagine my terror? Why did everyone abandon me?"

"We thought you were dead!" I clutched her tightly and my heart filled with joy as I realised this was really happening.

"I can hear your heartbeat," she sighed. "I can hear the baby's heartbeat."

She kissed me and I nearly fainted. Her lips were ice-cold yet sent a shock of warmth through my body. I could not deny her anything as my will folded into hers. I'm ashamed to say we kissed not as friends. She began fondling me as a man would. Part of me was screaming to break away, but another part was her willing slave. She buried her face in my neck and it was all I could do to remain standing as shivers of pleasure ran down my spine and into my legs. I was trying to convince myself to stop her when she let out a yelp and pushed me away.

"Your necklace! It burned my lips!" she hissed. It was then I remembered I was wearing the silver cross Oscar had returned to me after I broke off our engagement. Surely, she cut her lip on it, not burned it.

I felt as though I had drunk a full glass of whisky. The world was hazy now, my head swimming. I noticed the bundle she had been carrying had landed safely in the hedges. What could it be?

"Lucy," I said, "what is wrapped in the blanket?"

A large smile spread across her face.

Like an excited schoolgirl, she squealed, "I almost forgot." She retrieved the package and hurried back to me, unwrapping it. She held it upside down by one of its ankles. What was I seeing? At first, it looked like a rabbit or a suckling pig, but then, to my horror, I saw it was a baby!

"We both can be mothers now," she said, smiling.

My own baby began to kick violently inside me, breaking my spell, and I began to swoon.

She reached for me, dropping the baby as if it were no more than a rag doll.

I fell forwards but by some miracle, I stumbled and caught the baby.

I clutched the infant in my arms and made a mad dash for the doors.

"Bram!" I screamed as I fumbled the doors closed behind me. "Bram! Help, come now!"

The baby began to stir in my arms. It was alive! Revived from the heat of my body, it stirred and began to cry.

"Florrie, whatever is the matter?" a bewildered Lucy called out, tapping on the glass. "Let me in. Give me back the baby, I am ever so hungry."

"Bram!" I screamed.

Where was he? Why wasn't he here? I heard Mrs. Norris running down the stairs and saw the light from her lamp, coming quickly towards me.

The baby inside me was kicking so hard I thought I may give birth that very moment.

Lucy backed away. "That thing inside of you is a monster," she yelled, before fleeing into the night. "You should rip it out!"

Mrs. Norris entered with a lamp in one hand and Bram's pistol in the other.

"Dear God," she exclaimed. "Mrs. Stoker, you're bleeding."

The baby in my arms was crying very loudly now, but it was a happy sound to my ear for I knew it meant it was healthy.

"Whose baby is this?" Mrs. Norris asked.

She took the baby from me and put it down between two pillows on the bed. Then she put a washing flannel to my neck. By the light of the lamp I could see in the mirror that I was bleeding. The sight of my own blood made me swoon and I collapsed onto the bed.

"I'll fetch the doctor and a constable," Mrs. Norris said as I slipped into unconsciousness.

Later I awoke to find the doctor and Mrs. Norris over me. He sat me up so I could take a drink of water.

"The baby?" I enquired.

"Yours is fine," he said. "And the other baby was returned to his mother by the police."

"Some crazed fiend attacked the nanny and took the baby," Mrs. Norris said. "A neighbour saw her fleeing. The nanny is barely hanging on to life."

She brought me tea and sat with me. Later that night the constable returned to take my statement, though it was not to his liking.

"So, you are saying it was Lucy Mayhew who attacked you?" he asked, his pen poised over his notepad.

"Yes."

"And yet you also say that Lucy Mayhew died three days ago."

"Well, obviously she was not really dead," I said curtly. "You hear of these things happening all the time. Someone is thought to be dead, and through a physician's incompetence, the person is buried alive. She was very lucky to be in the family crypt and not in the ground."

"Indeed," the officer said with more than a bit of scepticism in his voice.

"And waking up in a coffin has driven her mad," I added. "The poor thing is out there scared out of her wits. You must find her before she hurts herself or someone else."

"Perhaps the perpetrator who attacked you last night just looked like her, and in your grieved state and being half-asleep you mistook her for Miss Mayhew."

So, that was it. The facts all nicely wrapped up in his mind, and a great deal of sense they no doubt make. It is unfortunate that I know exactly what I saw and experienced or I might believe them myself.

"I'll leave a constable at the door, in case she comes back," he said, standing and flipping his notepad closed like a coffin lid.

Now I sit waiting for daylight and Bram's return. Where is he? Why did he abandon me? And where is Lucy now?

LETTER FROM ELLEN TERRY TO LILLIE LANGTRY, 28TH OF JUNE 1879

My dearest Lillie,

The tragedy of Lucy Mayhew has drawn to a close. I am sure I will relive tonight many times when I sleep, or when sleep eludes me. Oh, Lillie, I had thought myself worldly, with few illusions about the cruelties that life can inflict upon the innocent and the powerless. I had no idea. The world is far more merciless than I ever imagined if it can produce creatures such as I have seen tonight.

After Lucy's funeral, she was laid to rest in a mausoleum purchased by her Aunt Agatha. Dr. Hesselius told us that on the third day Lucy would rise from the dead and return to the vampire that killed her. However, Henry tells us she could already be walking the earth. Her sire, the vampire that turned her, may not want anything to do with her, or he may summon her to be his bride. Furthermore, he informs us, a newly made vampire has not learned to control its appetites and she may go on a killing rampage.

Bram, Robert and Dr. Hesselius set out this evening to watch over Lucy's crypt in hope that she will lead them to her maker. However, obtaining the key to the mausoleum took more time than anticipated and it was already getting dark.

Bram forbade me from going, not wanting to expose me to any more danger. Besides, they needed someone trustworthy to watch over Henry, who is still our prisoner. It was a task I found myself woefully unfit for.

"Let me out, I can be of help," Henry pleaded, throwing himself against the cage. "The sun is already down and she is out hunting by now. Three men are no match for two vampires!"

"Back, you fiend!" I commanded, with my cross in hand. Thank heaven I am a trained actress, for I believe I managed to sound bold despite the fear that gripped my heart.

"Please," he said, calmly now. "Ellen, you know me. I'm not a bad person. I did not ask to become like I am, and I have tried to fight on the side of righteousness."

I must admit that the tale he told us earlier, of using his vampiric powers to rid the world of other vampires, rings truer to me than the idea of Henry Irving as a blood-sucking, murderous fiend. But I was not yet ready to take him at his word. "Bram wants you locked up for now, and locked up you shall stay," I said, and looked into his sad eyes.

Looking into a man's eyes has so often been my undoing.

"As an actress, you understand the human heart," he murmured. His voice was silky. "Surely you are in touch with all emotions in order to be so expert in your craft. Can you not perceive the truth about me? That I only wish to help?"

Of course, I saw that. It was all so clear....

"Open the gate and remove the chains," he said, a command that became a fervent wish the moment it reached my ears. And moments later he was free and it was I in the cage!

"Oh, damn you! How did you do that?" I cried, for my mind was now clear and yet I did not remember setting him free.

"Never look a vampire directly in the eyes, my dear," he said, not unkindly. "We have the power to cloud your mind and bend your will. As you see, I could have killed you and I did not. I am no threat to you. I only wish to reach the others before it is too late and all is lost."

"Then you will have to let me out of here," I retorted. "You don't know where they have gone. I do."

He turned and I shielded my eyes. "You won't get the information that way. I have learned my lesson."

He unlocked the cage and I emerged, warily. "Where are they?" he asked.

"I will tell you if you take me with you."

"It is too dangerous." He looked alarmed, which confirmed that I had the advantage.

"Time is running out, Henry. That is my final offer."

After a mere moment's hesitation, he relented. "So be it."

We left the theatre and I tried to hail a cab, but Henry stopped me.

"No, I am quicker than a cab. Climb on my back."

"What?" I nearly laughed, despite the situation. "No, that is preposterous."

"I can move like the wind. Climb on and tell me where we are going."

And that is how I found myself jumping on the back of my employer and wrapping my arms around his neck tightly, like a little girl getting a ride from an indulgent father. "They're at Pembroke cemetery, it's—"

"I know where it is," he said and with a great whoosh, we were off!

We moved so fast the houses looked as one solid wall. The air blew through my hair as if I were sticking my head out the window of the fastest moving train in the world and I was absurdly grateful that I had not spent overlong styling it this morning. It was hard to catch my breath and I had to shield my face against his back for the rushing wind stung me. It was terrifying yet exhilarating! And in what seemed only scant minutes, we arrived at the cemetery gates.

I climbed down from his back on wobbly legs. We found Bram, Robert and the doctor hiding behind a mausoleum with a good view of the Mayhew family crypt, a mere twenty-five yards away. The full moon provided much-needed light.

"Miss Terry!" Bram whispered. "What is the meaning of this?"

"No need to whisper," Henry said, surveying the graveyard. "There is no one, not vampire nor human, within earshot at the moment. I made her bring me here. You need my help."

"Obviously, we are powerless to stop you," Bram said. "At least get out of the moonlight."

We joined Bram and the others in the shadows.

"Are we too late?" Bram asked Henry. "Is she gone from here for good?"

"Perhaps. If she has already joined her maker she might not return here." He continued to scan the graveyard with his heightened senses. "Some turn in a night, some it takes longer."

"I was afraid of that," Dr. Hesselius said. "She could have led us right to the vampire that made her, if only we had arrived before sundown."

"If her master is miles away she will need to feed to have the strength to travel," Henry said. "We may need to fan out from here to find potential...." He paused and listened. "She comes," he whispered.

After a moment, we saw Lucy enter the graveyard hand in hand with a child, a little ragamuffin not more than five or six years of age. He was skipping along with her as she cheerfully sang.

"...Mary had a little lamb, little lamb, little lamb, Mary had a little lamb whose fleece was white as snow...." She stopped and lifted the child onto a nearby tomb. "My tasty little lamb." She tickled the boy and he giggled. She moved in for the kill but, with another whoosh, Henry snatched her away and brought her to us.

"No!" she screamed. "Release me!"

Henry forced her to the ground. "Stake her!" he cried.

Her spell on the street urchin was broken. He jumped from the tomb and ran with all his might out of the graveyard.

She struggled so fiercely I was sure not even Henry could hold her. Dr. Hesselius rushed forwards with mallet and stake.

"Don't!" Robert screamed. He stepped between them and held Dr. Hesselius back. "Lucy, repent! Pray to God to save your soul!"

She only bared her fangs at him and snarled in response.

"She isn't your Lucy anymore," Henry yelled. "Let us release her soul. It is the right thing to do." A confused Robert hadn't any time to ponder this. From seemingly nowhere a shadow swooped in and threw Henry off of Lucy, flinging him a great distance and crashing him into a large gravestone.

A brutish-looking vampire – for what else could he be with such strength? – was suddenly standing over Lucy. He struck Dr. Hesselius and Robert down with a single blow.

"You've come for me, Mr. Coal!" Lucy squealed with glee. She rushed over and threw her arms around him. "Take me away from all this death."

Bram rushed Coal, but in a great bound of speed Coal swept Lucy up into his arms and sped off.

Henry was on his feet now and gave chase. He caught up to them just as they were about to jump the cemetery wall. He tackled Coal around the legs and the three of them went tumbling in a tangle of limbs. They growled like animals as they wrestled. But Henry was no match for two vampires and they quickly pinned him.

Robert, Hesselius and Bram made a mad dash to Henry's aid, with stakes drawn.

Lucy, like a rabid cat, was clawing at Henry's face, tearing off flesh, snarling and laughing all the while. Coal had his arms around his neck and was trying to snap it.

They paid no mind to us in their frenzy and this gave us humans an opening. We rushed them and Robert plunged a stake into Lucy's back. "Forgive me, Lucy!" he cried. "Forgive me!" He threw his weight behind the stake and it burst out through her chest. She screamed and exploded into a pile of blood and gore!

Bram wrapped a silver chain around Coal's neck and brought him down like a dog. You could hear the vampire's flesh sizzle as he fell to his knees.

Henry was up and, surprisingly, did not appear to be in pain from the wounds inflicted by Lucy. However, his face was grotesquely deformed, with deep scratches. Part of his nose was missing and his left ear was torn clean off! Ridiculously, my first thought was that his acting days were certainly over.

Poor Robert was in a silent daze. He just stood there, mouth agape, holding the bloody stake he had used to dispatch Lucy.

Henry could see Bram was struggling to keep Coal down. He stalked over to Coal and struck him across the face, so hard a few teeth flew out of his mouth.

"Who is the Black Bishop?" he ordered. "Tell me or I shall stake you!"

"I…I don't know 'oo 'e is," Coal gargled.

"This is pointless," Hesselius said. "He is bound to his master and could not tell us if he was ordered not to."

"That's right," Coal said. Bram had let up a bit on the chain to make it easier for him to talk. "I can't. I'd like to, can't."

"All right then, let's stake him and be off," Bram said, tightening his grip on the chain.

"Wait, wait!" Coal pleaded. "The Black Bishop didn't turn me, so I could tell you if I knew. But I don't know! I swear! Me and Leech was 'ired by this count from Romania to get 'is 'ouse ready. Bloke showed up one day, introduced himself as the Black Bishop and offered us a lot of money to kidnap the count. I didn't know until that day the count was a vampire. Never even 'eard of vampires before then, truth be told."

"How did you become one?" Hesselius asked.

"I can't say who drained and filled me," he said. "I am forbidden to tell anyone."

"Where can we find the Black Bishop?" Henry asked.

"I don't know nothin'. I'm just one who looks after my master's 'ouse."

"Ah, are you forbidden by your master to tell us where he lives?"

"Car—" he said, but the words were choked out of his mouth. "Ca— Car—"

"He is worthless," Bram said. "He is an illiterate henchman at best."

With that, Robert suddenly snapped out of his trance. Before anyone could react, he rushed forwards with a heartrending wail of grief and rage and thrust the stake into Coal's chest, leaving another pile of bloody remains.

The rage quickly left Robert's face and he now looked horrified at what he had done. "Sorry about that. I wasn't thinking."

We found some shovels in a nearby shed and buried what was left of the vampires in separate graves. Robert was still wracked with guilt for having killed Lucy, and for killing our only lead to the Black Bishop, such as he was.

"You released her. It was a kindness," I said. "And we weren't going to get much more out of Coal."

"When I saw her taking delight in killing Irving, I knew my Lucy was no longer in that body," he said as he finished filling her shallow grave with the last shovel of dirt. "I thought killing Coal would bring me peace. It did not." I could only pat his shoulder, feeble comfort at best. There will be no peace for him, for any of us, any time soon.

"The older ones just turn to dust," Hesselius said to Bram, quietly so Robert wouldn't hear.

Henry was amazingly almost back to normal. His nose was intact once again and the scratches were completely gone. A bud of an ear was growing before my eyes. Imagine if he could perform that trick on stage, what a sensation it would be!

Oh, Lillie, I do hope you get these letters and write back soon.

Love,

Ellen

LETTER FROM WILLIAM (WILLIE) WILDE TO JAMES WHISTLER, 28TH OF JUNE 1879

Hope all finds you well, James. I am sure you are in shock at finding the enclosed twenty-pound note. Yes, I am paying back the loan and no, I did not rob a bank.

I am now a fully employed member of society. I am a reporter for the *Financial Gazette*, thanks to a friend of my father's, Lord Basil Wotton, who owns the publication.

I fully see the irony in my working for a newspaper that is concerned with finance, as money and I are rarely on speaking terms, but fear not, I shall be covering the theatre, opera, society parties and other sordid subjects only tangentially connected to money and those who have it.

Enclosed is an advance on my first month's salary. Thank you, James, for keeping me afloat and inebriated in lean times.

One would think Oscar would be pleased at my new position; however he seems to have a grudge against my benefactor. To hear him tell it, Lord Basil is some sort of monster who is only trying to exert control over Oscar through me.

Is it not interesting how all things circle back to Oscar? I am sure he feels my servitude to Lord Basil makes it harder for him to claw his way up the social ladder, which has been his obsession since childhood. When he is not mocking the upper classes behind their backs, he is grovelling at their feet.

It is a waste of time as far as I'm concerned. We were never part of their world and my father made sure we never would be with his scandalous behaviour. The best we can do is take their money when they are foolish enough to throw it at us.

Oscar being Oscar to be sure, but it was still upsetting that he could not be happy for me and support my new career.

In any event, I will be making enough to keep Mother in her house and myself in libations.

Why don't you get out from behind that easel and come out with me this Saturday night? We can paint the town red like we did in the old days.

Forever in your debt,

Willie

LETTER FROM FLORENCE STOKER TO PHILLIPA BALCOMBE, 29TH OF JUNE 1879

My dearest Mother,

I am sure by now you have heard the tragic news of Lucy's passing. I am shocked and saddened to the extent that I have been ordered to bed by my doctor. Fear not, he says the baby is in good health and this is but a precaution.

It saddens me greatly that the baby will never know Lucy, for she brought my life great joy with her sunny outlook.

My own disposition has been very melancholy even before Lucy's death, and now I have no light to shine upon this shadow hanging over me.

I cannot help but think there was more I could have done for her.

Bram and I are well and looking forward to your visit after the baby is born. It is a comfort knowing I will see you soon.

Your loving daughter,

Florence

LETTER TO FLORENCE STOKER FROM PHILLIPA BALCOMBE, 6TH OF JULY 1879

My sweet, sweet Florence,

You must pray to God and ask for forgiveness. Not for failing Lucy, for I do not think you have, but for failing yourself. Wallowing in despair is a selfish act at best and at worst is putting your soul into the hands of Satan himself. Cheer up, my little flower, and turn your face once again towards the sun.

It is the lot of women in life to be the emotional backbone of the family. Give up your silly notions of acting on the stage and redirect your efforts into being a good wife and mother. I think it will give you a greater sense of purpose and fulfilment; I know it did for me.

Your father and I will pray for you and the baby's good health.

Love,

Mother

FROM THE DIARY OF FLORENCE STOKER, 25TH OF SEPTEMBER 1879

Death haunts me.

Lucy's death hangs on me like a funeral shroud. What I have learned in its wake has left me shaken and at sea, untethered from the moorings that held me fast to the rational world I thought I knew. My logical brain and sceptical nature kept me from even considering what was before my eyes.

For Bram has told me that there are vampires in the world and Lucy became one. I would have thought him mad if his story weren't supported by Henry Irving, who apparently is one himself! He demonstrated this for me by suddenly sprouting fangs, a trick that I know to be beyond the skills of the theatrical artists of the Lyceum.

I would think myself mad even for writing this, that I had dreamt the entire conversation in my grief and fear, but at breakfast this morning I cautiously broached the subject with Bram and he confirmed that it had happened and that he stood by every word.

I am angry at Bram for not confiding in me sooner. Apparently, he has known of such creatures since before our marriage. Indeed, as a child, he drank from a vampire – none other than Henry Irving – in an act that saved his life and changed him forever, though he learned of this only recently. He shouldered the burden of this knowledge on his own, thinking he was protecting me; however, it only put me in more danger. I shudder when I think that Lucy could have turned me into one of those things that night.

I am still uneasy around Henry Irving. Bram assures me that he is no threat and, in fact, he offers us much protection. But I can't help but see him as a thing wearing human skin. I do my best not to be in his presence, for my blood runs cold at the sight of him. I can't help but feel he is somehow tangentially responsible for Lucy's death.

If I'm honest, I am uneasy with Bram as well. How can I trust him, knowing the secrets he has kept from me and the lies he has told to keep me in the dark? What sort of man is he, and how has his nature been formed by drinking the blood of a vampire? Will this nature be inherited by our unborn child?

What can I still cling to as truth? Is there a God and a heaven? My only comfort is in believing so, for if there is Lucy should surely be there, now that she has finally been put truly to rest.

But what of the wages of sin? I am haunted by that night in the garden. Did it condemn her soul to hell? Did she repent before her death? What sort of God would make us with human longing and weakness and then throw us into the fires of hell for giving in to them? I would prefer the cold, dark earth than to be at the whims of such a God.

I assumed I was witnessing a lustful indiscretion, but now I know there was more to it. She was slowly being killed before my eyes. Did I just assume I was witnessing willing participation, because that is what I wanted to see?

I have lost so much: My friend. My belief that we live in a rational world. My faith in my marriage. How I long to turn back the clock to the days when I felt safe, loved and confident in my future.

FROM THE JOURNAL OF BRAM STOKER, 28TH OF NOVEMBER 1879

8:25 p.m.

I am feeling much more optimistic as of late, for the vampire threat seems to have been contained at least for the moment.

Irving and Dr. Hesselius dispatched a nest of them last month. In addition, I have not sensed their presence in weeks. At the very least, Irving thinks we sent them into hiding and have disrupted their ranks.

Our lives have returned to a normal routine and for that I am grateful.

Florence has been ordered to bed rest by her doctor but he assures us she and the baby are doing fine and it is just a precaution.

FROM THE DIARY OF OSCAR WILDE, 3RD OF DECEMBER 1879

I feel my life descending into chaos. All around me corruption of the most hideous kind rages. And I, too, want to rage, to lash out, to scream profanities at the uncaring world. But I must not give in to the madness. I must find the internal strength to push it aside and deal with the matter at hand.

Frank's artistic nature perhaps has made him more susceptible to evil's influence than most. Sweet, gentle Frank has witnessed a horror and it has broken his mind.

As I write this, he has been institutionalised for his own protection. I am devastated, for it is I who brought this evil into his house.

Nothing that day was a portent of the violence to come. In fact, I was in quite good spirits. After our conversation with the Cockney servant at the ceremony, Derrick had quite cooled to the idea of becoming a vampire, a great relief to me. I was jotting down a few ideas for a play I am working on, and Frank was finishing a painting of a young woman named Ingrid. I had become accustomed to nude people in the flat night and day, to the point where it seemed quite ordinary.

Ingrid was becoming a Greek nymph through the magic of Frank's brush. She was a patient creature, maintaining poses for hours at a time, which included standing while holding a large bouquet of ferns and flowers.

A Swedish girl, she spoke little English but could convey much with a smile. She was truly an exquisite specimen of womanhood and had not an ounce of shame in her nudity.

A frustrated Frank threw down his palette. "I cannot for the life of me mix the proper blue to capture her eyes."

"I take break, now?" Ingrid asked hopefully.

"We might as well call it a day," Frank said. Ingrid did not understand the colloquialism, so he rephrased. "Yes, we are done working for the day."

As she laid down her burden and reached for her robe, our quiet evening was interrupted by a frantic pounding at the door.

I had barely opened it when Derrick came barging in, out of breath and in a panic.

"They are after me, Oscar!"

I shut and locked the door and hurried after him into the drawing room.

"Who are after you?"

"The vampires! Lord Wotton has become one and I am to be his!" His eyes were wild with fright, and I felt as though the world had suddenly turned upside down.

"Can he do that?" I asked, incredulous.

"Apparently so," Derrick said. "I have been summoned to his house to have 'the gift' bestowed upon me."

"What about 'accepting the terms' and all that rot from the ceremony?" I asked. "Can't you simply refuse?"

"I have, but was told by Lord Sundry that I cannot. In joining the Order, I entered into an agreement. And for the poor who cannot buy a spot at the top, our fate is sealed. When we are requested by an elder to be a servant, we must do so. Imagine, an eternity as a slave to that cretin!"

"We will go to the authorities," I said. "I have thought long and hard on this. These creatures must not be allowed to overrun London!"

"Don't you understand, Oscar? They *are* the authorities!"

I blanched, remembering the member of Parliament I had seen at the ceremony. How many other government officials might be in the Order?

"You must run then," I said. "Go to Europe or Canada, someplace they cannot find you."

He seized upon the idea. "Yes, yes, I will work my way across on a merchant ship if I have to. You will help me, Oscar, won't you? You will hide me for the night?"

I was assuring him that I would when suddenly the door burst open, the frame splintering as the lock was shattered. There stood Lord Wotton, flanked by Leech and Dripp!

"He can't come in unless you invite him," Derrick cried.

"I'm afraid I have purchased this entire block of apartments," he said, stepping inside and removing his hat and gloves. "So, I need no invitation. Enter," he commanded his two lackeys.

"I believe you are all acquainted with Messrs. Leech and Dripp," Wotton said. "They now work for the good of the Order, as will you, Derrick."

Frank appeared in the doorway to see what the commotion was.

"Run, Frank!" I screamed.

But in a flash, Dripp was upon him and had his hands around Frank's throat.

Just then, Ingrid's voice called out from the studio. "Frank? I come tomorrow again?" My heart sank for the young woman whose fate, I feared, was now sealed.

"You have company!" Lord Wotton exclaimed with a smile. "How rude of us to converse here without her. Let us all go and meet her."

Dripp sped off with Frank towards the sound of Ingrid's voice, while Wotton pulled Derrick along and Leech seized me.

Ingrid was dressed now and, though confused, knew things had taken a dangerous turn. She tried to make her exit but was stopped by Mr. Leech.

"Please, sit," Lord Wotton said. Dripp threw Frank, gasping for air, to the sofa. The rest of us sat, trembling with fear.

Wotton began pontificating. "I am a patient man, even more so now that I have all of eternity. But what I cannot stand are people who do not know their place in society. The British Empire is a well-oiled machine because all the cogs and gears work together." He intertwined his fingers to make the point. "Those of us who have the breeding and intelligence to run things, do. Those who are meant to serve and to entertain do that as well. Happiness is dependent on you doing what you were born to do."

"Go to hell!" Derrick said.

"Been there and back," Wotton said. "You will come with me now, Derrick. That is the way it is going to be."

"Never!" Derrick said. "The very sight of you makes me want to vomit."

"Why do you want to turn him if he is unwilling?" I asked. "Surely there are many who are eager to join your ranks."

"Because when I see something I want, I take it. The collector in me, I suppose. You will see, I am a fair sire, and in time you will come to thank me for the gift I give you."

He turned his attention to Ingrid.

"Come," he commanded. She stood as if in a trance and walked over to him. He took a penknife from his pocket and opened it. He handed it to her. "Feed me," he commanded.

To our horror, Ingrid slit her own throat. Blood spurted like a fountain. Lord Wotton pulled her close to him and her blood bathed his face as he clamped his mouth around the gaping wound and greedily drank his fill.

"No!" I screamed, as Leech held Derrick and me back.

"I'll kill you, you monster!" Derrick screamed. "So help me God!"

Frank was silent and catatonic at what he was seeing. No, more mesmerised. A stupid grin came to his face as if he were watching a play and none of this were real. I could hardly fault him for that; I too wished to retreat into my own mind to escape the horror I was witnessing.

Wotton released Ingrid and she collapsed to the floor, blood still spurting from her throat.

Wotton took out a handkerchief and tried to wipe the blood from his face, but there was so much of it he could not. He merely smeared it around, making him look like a horrific clown.

Wotton's lackeys tossed us aside and jumped on the body, lapping up the remaining blood like hungry rabid dogs.

"Derrick, you will leave here as my servant or as my food. The choice is yours. Come with me willingly and I will let your friends live."

Derrick hesitated a moment and Wotton took a step towards Frank.

"No," Derrick said. "I'll go with you."

I gazed at him in despair. I wanted to stop him, started to open my mouth to protest, but found I could not. For I took Wotton fully at his word: if Derrick resisted all three of us would die as poor Ingrid had. There was nothing to be gained by foolish courage when rational cowardice might leave me alive to fight another day.

"It's all right, Oscar," Derrick said, understanding all without a word from me. "It's my mess. You have done all you can for me. Just…remember me. As I was, not as I shall become."

"Of course, dear boy," I said, my voice breaking. "Always."

"A very moving departure," Wotton said, his voice dripping with malice. "Now come."

As Wotton left with his servants and Derrick, he stopped to say, "You might want to get rid of that body. It would be hard to explain to your cleaning woman in the morning." It was then he noticed Derrick's portrait hanging above my mantle. He looked quite annoyed. "Bring the painting," he said to Derrick, who took it down with shaking hands.

They left and I was alone with Frank and a corpse. I was paralysed for several moments, and when I regained my wits I ran out onto the street. They had already got into Wotton's cab and were off.

I ran after them for a block or two, thinking that if I could alert a policeman perhaps the day still could be saved. But the only people about were a startled elderly couple who hurried up their front walk as I passed. I quickly realised I could do nothing. Dejected, I returned to the apartment.

To my horror, Frank was at his easel painting as if nothing in the world were wrong.

He had flipped Ingrid over and slit her belly open, and her entrails spilt out as if she were one of the pigeons he had dissected to capture 'their inner nature'.

Her lifeless eyes were open and black now, like the glass eyes of a doll.

"I think I was worrying too much about colour," he said cheerfully. "I can capture her true essence if I use only one."

"Frank," I said. "We must dispose of the body. The police will never believe we did not do this."

I came around the easel to see that he was painting her in red, then gasped when I realised it was her own blood!

"I don't know why I never thought about cutting them open before," he said, dipping his brush on his palette of blood and returning it to the canvas. "Who knew it would be so simple? This, this will be the masterpiece I was meant to paint."

I grabbed him by the shoulders and shook him angrily. "Ingrid is dead! Don't you understand that?"

He shook me off and returned to his painting. "It's all right, Oscar. Don't you see? She will live forever in my painting."

I poured him a large glass of laudanum and persuaded him to drink it. When he passed out, I went to work.

I rolled up Ingrid in the rug and dragged it down the stairs to the cellar, where I buried her.

It took many more hours to clean the blood from the floor and furniture. The upholstery was ruined from the borax but that would be easy to explain to the cleaning lady come Monday. Spilt some wine, tried to clean it, or something like that.

After I burned Frank's painting of Ingrid in the fireplace, I collapsed in exhaustion and cried for Ingrid and Frank and Derrick. I cried for a more innocent time when I knew not of supernatural evil.

After my own dose of laudanum, I awoke late the next morning and for a moment thought it all a bad dream.

I found Frank at his easel, working on a new painting. He had a dead cat on the table and was again painting in his new medium of blood.

I took Frank to Bedlam hospital. He happily told the doctors of his new painting technique, and after a fanciful tale about vampires visiting him in the night, he was committed.

In the course of one night, I have lost Frank, Derrick and what was left of my innocence.

How I wish Richard Burton would write back to me! However, I cannot let this deter me. I will rescue Derrick and make that monster Wotton pay for his crimes, even if I have to beg Stoker to help me.

LETTER FROM DR. MUELLER TO LORD ALFRED SUNDRY, 11TH OF DECEMBER 1879

Dear Lord Sundry,

Success!

At last, I can make up for the werewolf Captain Burton killed.

Such elusive creatures, werewolves. Most only show themselves when they can't help it, under the light of a full moon, making them difficult to detect, let alone capture.

As a man, the werewolf has his full wits about him. He has all his morals intact. Yet the transformation to wolf strips him of all this; he sheds his human conscience like he sheds his human skin.

If God exists, why would he allow such a thing? Furthermore, why would a bite from a werewolf pass on the curse to one who has not sinned? Thank goodness most werewolf attacks are fatal, or the world would soon be overrun by them.

But back to the matter at hand. As promised, I have acquired a werewolf in the allotted time.

Once I found one and ascertained his nature, I befriended him. I learned he does not wish to kill and so I have helped chain him up during the change, earning his gratitude.

He has handed himself over to me fully. I shall bring him to Salisbury and present him to the Bishop. He is eager to help in any way he can.

I hope that he can aid the Bishop with his important mission. If there is anything left of the creature after the procedure I should be glad for the opportunity to study the remains. It would undoubtedly prove a fascinating avenue of research.

This concludes our business. Upon our arrival in Salisbury, please provide the requested materials to me as stated in our agreement.

Sincerely,

Dr. Mueller

FROM THE JOURNAL OF FLORENCE STOKER, 3RD OF JANUARY 1880

The old year has died, as has the old me. Gone is Florrie, the carefree, vivacious ingénue. It is now the year of our Lord 1880. The new decade will see the rise of a far more matronly Florence. The child that was within me emerged yesterday and I am a mother now, to Irving Noel Thornley Stoker.

The birth was the stuff of nightmares. Indeed, there were times I thought I was dreaming, so closely did it resemble the lurid crimson terrors that have plagued my sleep recently.

Bram was at the Lyceum, of course, when it became apparent that the time had come. I dispatched Emma to send a message to him and to fetch Dr. Ward. The wait for the doctor's arrival – surely no more than an hour, according to Miss Jarrald, the nurse we have engaged for the infant's care – felt like anxious days. Back home we would have sent for a midwife, but I am told in London it has become fashionable for a doctor to attend, especially at first births where more things tend to go wrong and require the hands of a surgeon.

At last he arrived and we prepared for the work that lay ahead of us. Dr. Ward is an efficient, skilful physician and he came highly recommended by several in our social circle. Nevertheless, I found myself wishing for Dr. Cullen, back in Dublin. He is a kindly man, inclined to jokes and hearty laughter and reassuring words. Dr. Ward always makes a point to smile at the end of every visit and tell you that everything is going along just fine and you shouldn't worry, but one gets the feeling that these are rehearsed words and actions, items to be ticked off on a list of things he does when seeing patients, right before closing his bag and gathering his coat and hat.

Yesterday afternoon, as he came to my bedside, I am certain the terror I felt was reflected in my eyes, for Dr. Ward said, "Now, now, Mrs. Stoker, you mustn't worry. After all, you are not the first woman to ever give birth, you know."

"Nor would I be the first woman to die in the process," I spat back. Mother would be appalled at my manners, but you simply cannot expect a woman to hold her tongue in such a situation. Well, I cannot, in any case.

Dr. Ward's eyes widened. "My, what a thing to say," was all he was able to manage, then he busied himself with preparations. After carefully removing his coat and rolling up his sleeves and donning a smock (a fine precaution as far as it went, but as things turned out perhaps he wishes he had brought a butcher's apron) he positioned me on my back with my knees raised and parted. Such humiliation! And yet an image sprang momentarily to mind of Lucy as I had seen her in the garden that night months ago with her legs spread and the man at her....

Then pain took me and I cried out an anguished, banshee wail. "Some chloroform, I think," I heard Dr. Ward murmur, and he took a bottle and a clean white handkerchief from his bag. He moistened the cloth and handed it to Nurse Jarrald, who held it to my face. I writhed away – if I were to die, I wanted to cling to every moment of consciousness I had left, painful though they may be. Jarrald did not persist, bless her, but I must have breathed in some of the drug for I found myself slipping in and out of awareness.

Maybe that's what gave the day such a surreal quality. I remember pain, though I didn't mind it so much anymore. I remember Jarrald holding my hand and stroking my brow and I remember fixating upon her face for a long time. I remember other times when I looked down past my bent knees at Dr. Ward, his gaze steadfastly and modestly focused on my face. I remember his smock, the part of it that I could see above the sheet that blocked my view of the birth, becoming stained with blood. (Surely this wasn't normal? The man would need a new smock every time he delivered a baby!) And I remember when he had to finally disregard modesty and look down at what was happening below the sheet, at the part of me that even I have not seen. At my child, who was painfully emerging. At my life's blood, that was pouring from me at an alarming rate.

"Doctor, is this normal?" Emma asked, frantically handing him towels.

"Get her out of here," he commanded Jarrald. Emma was quickly rushed out.

Even in my haze, I could see the doctor was panicking.

Jarrald returned as I felt the baby free itself from its nine-month prison.

I drifted in and out and with each awakening more pain.

"Florence," I heard Bram call to me. I opened my eyes and was happy to see him.

"The baby?" I asked.

"He is fine. A beautiful boy. We need to attend to you now."

I was so weak.

There were others gathered around me, though I could not make out faces.

I heard the doctor whispering to someone, "There is nothing more I can do for her."

"Out!" I heard an enraged voice shout. It was Henry Irving's voice! I remember thinking I should feel surprised at this but had not strength enough even for that.

"Help her, Henry, help her," Bram pleaded. "Save her like you saved me!"

Henry took my hand and suddenly the pain stopped.

"Drink," I remember him saying, but I do not remember drinking anything.

I lost consciousness completely then, though whether from more chloroform or from the loss of blood I cannot say.

I awoke two days later. Although I am sound in body, a melancholy has overcome me. I am so stricken with it I am almost unable to get out of bed and dress and feed myself, let alone feed the baby. Bram has hired a wet nurse. I feel ashamed the baby must take to another woman's breast.

I am told Henry saved my life. I had no idea midwifery was among his many talents, but even the doctor tells me it was Henry who stopped my headlong rush towards death. How could he be a vile creature when he saved my life?

I call the baby Noel, though he is named in honour of my saviour. He is a fretful child, and though I love him – I do – I feel he looks at me accusingly, as though I have already failed him in some crucial way.

Perhaps his birth was as terrifying for him as for me. Will I ever be able to make it up to him, this bloody beginning? I must try.

And so, my new life begins.

FROM THE JOURNAL OF BRAM STOKER, 4TH OF JANUARY 1880

Thank God Florence and the baby are all right. There was so much blood and pain. I should have recoiled at it, yet I am ashamed to say it was all I could do to not become aroused by it. Am I becoming one of those creatures? Was Irving's 'cure' just taking decades to turn me into a vampire?

I must put such thoughts out of my head. I owe Henry Irving a debt that can never be repaid. And to think I had almost killed him. He has earned my respect and loyalty. If I can help him regain his humanity, I will.

He assures me that the small amount of his blood he gave Florence will not turn her into a vampire. Whether it will give her the second sight that has cursed me so we do not know, though Henry doesn't think so. The prophecy referred to giving the blood to a child. I did not even think of such a thing in the heat of the moment; I only wanted her life saved.

I held Noel today and forgot about all the evil in the world. He is so small and innocent. Looking into his eyes I feel grateful to be his father, and a sense of responsibility like I have never known. I will protect him from the dark forces that swirl around me.

LETTER FROM DR. NEIL SEWARD TO DR. WILLIAM GULL, ROYAL PHYSICIAN, 12TH OF JANUARY 1880

Dear Dr. Gull,

I am afraid to report there has been very little progress in the prince's condition, and he may, in fact, be getting worse.

As of late, he is suffering from new delusions that he is to be rescued from this 'prison' and be installed on the throne. He claims he will rule over heaven and hell and bring a new world order.

Twice now we have found him out of his room and out of the building, roaming the grounds. How he made his escape is unclear and troubling to say the least. Once it was below freezing and he nearly succumbed to hypothermia.

His zoophagous mania continues and, short of sewing his mouth shut, we can do little to keep him from devouring insects and rodents.

He has taken to reading the Bible and praying for hours on end. We encouraged this behaviour at first, believing it to be a non-destructive outlet for his delusions. However, he has developed a complex fantasy world where he is the head of the Church of England and on a mission from God to purge the world through fire. Very disturbing thoughts indeed. He has drawn dragons and fire imagery all over the walls of his room, along with quotes from imaginary prophets. The language is blasphemous and profane, and many of the writings are from a mysterious figure he has named 'the Black Bishop', which I feel represents his relationship with his father. When ink and pen are taken away from him he draws on the walls with faeces and even his own blood. Twice now he has punctured his wrists to obtain this gruesome writing material. We have had no choice but to restrain him in a straightjacket for fear he will harm himself further.

I have been forced to stop administering opiates to keep him from growing dependent on them. Ice-water baths and electrical shocks to his body are the only courses of treatment left to us.

I shall keep you informed as to our progress; however, I have begun to fear we shall not make any.

Sincerely,

Dr. Seward

FROM THE JOURNAL OF FLORENCE STOKER, 15TH OF JANUARY 1880

It is a very cold but sunny day and my sadness continues, though it has been lightened some by a visit from Oscar.

I managed to dress and go downstairs to receive him for tea. It is hard to keep my sadness hidden from others, but I do my best.

"You are looking lovely, as usual," he said, smiling kindly as he lied. I could tell by the concern in his eyes and the way he scrutinised me while trying to disguise his doing so that he had heard about my difficulty in childbirth and possibly my condition since. I should have been embarrassed at this but could not find the energy.

I merely replied, "How nice of you to say," and forced a smile, which Oscar, of course, detected.

"You don't have to be happy on my account. People seldom are," he said. "So, where is this miniature person of yours?"

Miss Jarrald brought the baby down and, to my surprise, Oscar scooped him up in his arms.

"Oh, Florrie, he is beautiful. Thank goodness he doesn't look like Stoker."

"He does so, Oscar," I protested. "More than me, I think."

"Nonsense, he is a Balcombe through and through." He rocked Noel gently in his arms and the baby smiled and cooed. It made me sad to see what might have been had I made other choices. Oscar would have been a good father.

I started to cry. Oscar handed the baby to the nurse and tended to me.

"I'll put the baby down for his afternoon nap," Jarrald said.

Oscar waited until she left. "Florrie, whatever is the matter?"

"Oh, Oscar, nothing and everything. I feel I am an utter failure as a mother. I have no maternal instincts!"

"Instincts are for the animals. We have logic and reason and a strict code of etiquette to guide us. Maternal instinct went out with the joy and exuberance abolished by Queen Victoria. In exchange, we have stiff upper lips, soap and hot tea. A fair trade, if you ask me."

I laughed a real laugh.

"Seriously, Florrie, I have heard of this before. My mother suffered from this kind of melancholia. Not after having me, of course, but with Willie's arrival. She always had strong intuitions about people! She said it was quite terrible. Father had to drag her out of bed and into the sunlight every day. That's what cured her, lots of fresh air and sunlight. That and opium, which I would not recommend, for that's when she started cavorting with Gipsies and talking to spirits."

For the first time in a long time, I felt happy.

"Now, drink up your tea, stiffen that lip and let's go for a stroll in the garden."

"It's freezing out, Oscar."

"That does not stop the Eskimos or the Finns. It is a sunny day. We shall bundle up against the elements and walk across the tundra."

And we did.

"I do so wish you and Bram could put your differences behind you," I said. "It would mean so much to me. With vampires about I would feel better if you two could be friends, if only to protect Noel."

He stopped and stared at me. So now my accomplishments include rendering Oscar Wilde speechless, which is surely something.

"Yes, Bram told me about them," I said. "And that you helped him hunt one in Dublin. Oh, and that ludicrous story about the werewolf – that was true! And I thought you were just a gifted teller of fanciful stories."

He seemed uneasy, but said, "Well, I am gifted, but not nearly as fanciful as you'd imagined."

I took his arm again and we continued our walk. "Please think about what I said, Oscar. I would so like it if we all could be friends."

"I will make peace with Bram if he can make peace with me," he said. "I am sorry I have been away. I have been looking for someone who has gone missing and fear he is gone for good, taken by those wretched creatures; he may even be one himself by now. When I find him, I will be all yours again."

From what I could see of his face I knew that he too has been no stranger to melancholy of late. I took off the silver cross he had returned to me and put it around his neck.

"You need this more than I do," I said. He objected, but I told him I have a box full of crosses from Bram, and Dr. Hesselius has given me many phials of holy water.

"This cross saved me from Lucy. Now it can work for you."

It cheered me to know that Oscar might be a part of my life once more. We walked some more and I let him prattle on about nothing in particular.

The sun is setting now and my gloom is returning, but now I know it is something that can go, and that is heartening.

LETTER FROM RICHARD BURTON TO OSCAR WILDE, RECEIVED 15TH OF JANUARY 1880

Archivist's note: Due to the distance between London and India, Oscar Wilde did not receive a response to his letter sent on the 24th of June until the 15th of January 1880.

Dear Oscar,

I find the recent events you have found yourself in disturbing, to say the least. I have heard rumours about the Order of the Golden Dawn for years and thought it nothing more than legend. If what you say is true and they are dabbling in the dark arts, they must be stopped at all costs.

I am told you and Stoker are not on speaking terms. I highly suggest you put your differences aside for the sake of the Empire! Bram is investigating a recent vampire attack in London and he would find your information extremely valuable. Tell him immediately about the Order and expose those you know to be involved.

Had I not important business here in the Far East I would return at once to help you destroy these vile creatures, but I have my hands full with a black magic cult of Thugees who are killing thousands to appease their god.

I implore you, Oscar, join forces with Stoker. I have sent him a vampire expert to help track these demons down and destroy them. Swallow your pride if you must. The team of Stoker & Wilde is once again called forth by destiny to put down the forces of darkness!

Queen and country are counting on you.

Sincerely,

Richard Burton, Bombay, India

FROM THE JOURNAL OF BRAM STOKER, 18TH OF JANUARY 1880

10:15 a.m.

A full house this Sunday morn, and a full day ahead as I continue my investigation into the mysterious vampires and their even more mysterious scheme.

Florence's mother has come to tend to her melancholy. It has been three weeks and she still rarely gets out of bed. The baby seems to be her only sense of comfort when she does rise. I blame myself, for I have been distracted and not as fully attentive as I could be.

Along with Mrs. Balcombe is her maid. The poor thing is sleeping on a mattress on the floor of our housekeeper's room.

Still, I am glad Florence has others around to tend to her needs while I fret and fear about the vampire threat.

A fear kicked up again with a visit from Oscar Wilde. It seems I am never rid of the man for very long.

There he was on my doorstep in the pouring rain, like some wet alley cat. Oscar did not even have the sense to bring an umbrella, instead relying on his purple velvet top hat for protection. It was ruined now, of course.

There was an awkward silence, which I broke with an impatient, "What do you want?"

More silence followed, his face becoming strained at the words that would not come.

"For God's sake," I said. "Come inside before you catch your death."

"Thank you," he finally managed to stutter. He entered and took off his dripping hat and soggy coat.

The housekeeper appeared from wherever she had been hiding. "Get Mr. Wilde a towel, please," I asked her, before ushering him into the study to dry by the fire.

"First, let me apologise for my behaviour when last we met," he said, and to his credit, he did look quite contrite. "The best man won Florrie's hand and I should accept that." More silence. This was very much out of character for him and made me oddly uncomfortable.

I know I should have accepted his apology graciously, but to be fair I hadn't particularly liked the man even before he had attacked me in the street. "And second?" I finally asked.

"Ah, yes, there must be a second if there is a first."

He was interrupted by the maid with his towel. "And some tea," I said. She nodded again and scampered off.

He blotted his face and neck and dishevelled hair. It struck me that I had never seen Oscar dishevelled before. Well, possibly while under attack by a werewolf, but that was it. Finally, he met my eye and said, "Bram, I have come to ask you for your help. May I sit?"

"I suspect you will drip all over the furniture, but I suppose so."

Oscar actually smiled slightly at my brusqueness. I suspect for him it was something of a return to normalcy. Sitting, he said, "I am at my wit's end, which you know for me is a long journey. I would not inflict myself upon you if I had anywhere else to turn, but who else would believe me, much less be able to help? It seems a friend of mine has got mixed up with vampires."

He was visibly shaking now and told me his friend had been abducted by them and they killed a woman in his flat. He dares not go to the police for they will think him mad, and likely a murderer to boot.

I got up and poured two brandies. He took the glass but did not drink. It was the first time I had seen a Wilde not indulge in drink. This was almost as unnerving as his silence and unkempt appearance.

I sat across from him in my favourite armchair and told him about Lucy and how we killed her sire.

"Furthermore, we have learned that London is crawling with them, an epidemic of evil that could easily become the next plague," I said.

"I personally know this to be true," he said sheepishly. "I should have said something earlier, told someone, but I am ashamed to say I did not."

He told me of a vampiric ritual he had witnessed at a party in Knightsbridge. Apparently, there is some sort of hierarchy in this vampire coven – the Order of the Golden Dawn, it's called – and one either buys one's way into the ruling class or offers oneself up as a slave for eternity. His friend, Derrick Pigeon, was initially eager to join, but when he changed his mind they took him against his will.

We were interrupted briefly when the housemaid brought the tea, but by then he had started to drink his brandy and the pot was destined to grow cold.

I had something of my own to confess and told him of Irving and his visit to me as a child.

"Egad, one right under your nose, and you couldn't sniff him out?" The irony of this seemed to enliven him for the first time in the conversation.

"The same blood that gave me powers clouded my mind in his presence, I believe."

"About that," he said hesitantly. "When I returned to Dublin a few months back I had a chat with Bonnie Ashcroft."

I was taken aback. "My family's former maid?"

"Yes, that Bonnie." He looked down as if to avoid looking me in the eye. "She knew a vampire had saved your life. She didn't know it was Irving, but she told me of his curing you. I am further ashamed that I didn't tell you. You had a right to know. It could have helped."

"I don't understand," I said astonished. "How did you come to chat with Bonnie? Last I heard she was cloistered in a convent."

"Yes, she is. I tracked her down."

"Whatever for?"

"I am not entirely sure, myself. To get something on you, I suppose. And I was truly intrigued by your visions and wanted to know more."

I should have been angry with him for prying into my personal life, not to mention not telling me about what had transpired on my seventh birthday, but I was not.

"To think, Oscar, both of us had important information the other one needed but our petty squabbling kept us from communicating. There is too much at stake for us not to pool our resources."

"I agree wholeheartedly," he said. "I shall do so from now on."

"Good, I shall too."

"Bram, why ever did Irving cure you? Was it just out of altruism?"

"Not entirely," I said. "He does not wish to be a vampire and takes no joy in it, and somehow thinks infecting my blood will lead to a cure for his own affliction. The details are vague – they are in a book he was trying to have translated that went missing – but it apparently involves the spilling of great quantities of my blood."

"Intriguing," Oscar mused. "Though I imagine you would prefer not to have been a participant in his experiment. To do that to a child of seven." He shook his head wonderingly. "Why, it lends an entirely different colour to his Richard III." I laughed grimly at that. "Still, it saved your life."

"When you were at the ceremony, did you meet or hear of someone referred to as 'the Black Bishop'?"

He jumped to his feet, exclaiming, "Yes! Their club calling card is a black bishop chess piece like the one we found on Count Ruthven. I think he may be their leader."

"We had the same impression after interrogating Lucy's killer. I wish we hadn't dispatched the creature so soon. There are so many unanswered questions."

"Yes, pity he's dead. I should have liked to ask him about Derrick. However, I think I might know where the monsters are nesting," Oscar said. "I have come to ask you to accompany me and use your powers to see if my suspicions are correct."

I shook my head. "It would be dangerous for only us to go. Robert is out of town on business for the army and won't be back until tonight. Dr. Hesselius, our vampire expert, is in Cardiff for more research, and Irving is of little use to us during the daylight hours."

"Surely it would not be dangerous to just investigate the location. You could sense if they are inside and we could gather reinforcements later," Oscar suggested.

So, I have agreed to go with him later this afternoon to the Carfax estate, which he suspects the vampires are using as a base of operations, as it was Lord Wotton, now a vampire, who abducted his friend. I have sent word to Robert at his hotel, in case he returns this afternoon in time to accompany us.

It is a simple reconnaissance to be sure, but I can't help but feel a foreboding and not even crucifixes and wooden stakes are easing my fears.

1:25 p.m.

I decided to leave word of our whereabouts with Ellen as well, so that if we should go missing for any reason at least someone could alert the authorities. She still resides with Lucy's aunt across the courtyard.

I startled her with a rap on her French doors. Fear quickly turned to a smile as she invited me inside. We sat down for a cup of tea, but decided on stronger refreshment, an apple brandy, while I told her of our plans.

"Do let me come," she pleaded. "I wish to be a part of this adventure."

"It is not safe, and it is not an adventure," I said. "It is grim business, and I wish to God that it didn't fall to me. I am ill-prepared for heroics."

"I disagree," she said, smiling.

Yes, I blushed. "In any case, bringing you near to that vipers' nest would put you in unnecessary danger. Besides, I need you to keep watch over Florence and Noel."

"Have you told her of the vampires?"

"Yes. I did not wish to upset her in her delicate condition, but when Lucy came to her as a vampire it became a difficult secret to keep. Not knowing almost got her killed." I don't know why I continued to speak, but my words would not stop. "She has barely spoken to me in days, and I can hardly blame her. All this madness could not have come at a more inopportune time. Why me? Why did I have to get dragged out of my blissful ignorance of all things supernatural?"

"Perhaps it is your destiny," she said. "Men of destiny often have it thrust upon them, whether they will it or no. You have risen bravely to the challenge for the greater good of the Empire and, dare I say, all mankind." She paused a moment, then added, "You do not have to face this alone."

Then, without warning and to my total surprise, she leant over and kissed me full on the mouth, her hand reaching up to caress my face. In my mind, I pushed her away and jumped up to make my apologetic but entirely proper escape, but physically I did none of this. I took her in my arms and kissed her like I had never kissed another woman before, like I have been wanting to kiss her for many weeks. She felt different against me than Florence does – or at least than my memories of Florence, for how long has it been since she allowed me to hold her close? Florence is (Was? Will be again?) a loving wife, but her kisses are girlish, willingly acquiescent to my passion. Ellen felt strong in my arms, and pulled me closer, running her fingers through my hair and pressing her lips hard against mine.

It took me a while to come to my senses but finally I broke away.

"No, this isn't right," I said, my voice a hoarse whisper.

She smiled and remained strangely calm at my refusal. "I am not asking you to leave Florence. I am married myself, remember? People have needs, and why should yours go unmet when you are in such a terrible place? Let us give each other comfort."

She leant in once more but did back away this time when she sensed my unease.

"I am not the kind of man who could do this," I said, wishing I was. "Especially now that I know there is true evil in the world, I must regain my moral centre. Don't you see? We know there is a devil, so there must be a God. It is more important than ever to keep on the righteous path."

"I am sorry," she said. "I may not share your views of righteousness, but I did not mean to make things worse for you. I take no offence at your rejection, Bram, if you can forgive me for being so forward."

"I can. I do. If things were different...."

"No need to explain further," she said, but I could feel her disappointment. Had I led her on all this time? Had she picked up my attraction to her that I thought I was hiding so well?

I left without saying another word, but with another complication my life does not need.

Oscar has arrived with the carriage and we are off to find these monsters who have torn apart our lives.

FROM THE DIARY OF OSCAR WILDE, 19TH OF JANUARY 1880

Getting this all down is important, I suppose. If not as a catharsis for my troubled mind, then at least for history's sake. When England is overrun by vampires this diary may shed light on the beginning days of the end times.

Earlier I swallowed my pride, choked down my loathing and begged Stoker for his help.

He accepted my apology with all the graciousness I have come to expect from the man – which is to say as much as an irascible old bear would display towards a woodsman who had wandered too close to his den – but, surprisingly, he agreed to assist me in my quest. I am sure he would be the first to admit it was in aid of his own agenda. These creatures have plagued him nearly as much as they have me – though they have stopped short, to my knowledge, of framing him for murder. Joining forces, we might be able to rout them out into the daylight for the world to see.

I had my suspicions regarding where the villains might be, so it was decided we would do some reconnaissance and if that revealed the whereabouts of the creatures we would return to the theatre and garner stronger forces. Apparently, he has accumulated some allies since last we collaborated.

It was a cold and gloomy day, but what little sunlight there was brought me some comfort due to the protection it would afford. This cheering thought was difficult to embrace, however, as en route to the vampires' lair Bram insisted on driving the carriage himself and does not appear to be that skilled at it. My bottom is purple with bruises from his inability to avoid a single pothole or broken cobblestone.

We parked the carriage and made our way by foot up the long, winding road to Wotton's Carfax estate. We cautiously scaled the back wall into the topiary garden, far from the view of any windows. We made our way amongst the menagerie of shrubbery sculpted to look like animals of Africa and found cover behind the elephant as Stoker tried to invoke his powers of supernatural observation.

"I am getting nothing with my sixth sense. But I do not believe I have ever detected anything at such a distance, and if they are in the cellar that may interfere as well. Though I was able to track you and that Ruthven fellow to your wine cellar in Dublin, but I had already detected the fiend at that point, so perhaps…." He shook his head and cursed in frustration. "I may as well admit it, I have no idea how this bloody curse works." With that, he left the safety of the bushes and went to the window.

"Get back here," I whispered. He ignored me and stuck his big face up to the glass, cupping his hands to see through the glare.

"No, still nothing. I'm going in."

"What?" I cried in horror. "Are you insane?"

"Why not? Lord Wotton and I are acquaintances." He was behaving quite recklessly, most out of character for the stodgy curmudgeon I thought I knew and tolerated. Perhaps fatherhood makes one bold.

"Whatever will you say as to why you just happened to stop by?"

"I'll tell him Irving is inviting him to Tuesday night's performance."

And with that, he marched around to the front of the house and rang the bell. I remained hidden and could not hear him talking to the butler, but in a few moments he was led inside.

After what seemed like a fortnight, but was more like a quarter-hour, he emerged unharmed. He left through the front gate, which left me having to scale the wall once more, tearing a perfectly good pair of dove-grey gabardine trousers in the process.

He was waiting for me at the carriage.

"Wotton and most of his servants have left for the country and will not return until late spring," Stoker said. "The butler would not tell me where they went."

"Damn," I said. "So, the trail has gone cold." It was then I remembered the dilapidated estate adjacent, the one that had Wotton in such consternation the night we met. Hadn't Derrick mentioned something about Coal and Leech getting the house ready for their master? And now Coal and Leech seemed to be under the control of Wotton. (Well, only Leech now that Coal is dead.)

The road up to the eyesore was almost impassable by carriage. I was growing ever more uneasy as storm clouds darkened the sky. The horse became more agitated the closer we came to the house, finally refusing to continue past the old chapel.

"I guess we walk from here," Stoker said.

With only fifty feet to the front door, Stoker froze. His eyes glazed over and he held his breath for a moment. "There are vampires in there," he said. "We should go. We should go now!"

As we turned back there was a whooshing sound behind us. I had barely taken a step when I was struck to the ground!

The world went black.

Sometime later, I fought my way to consciousness. I could hear voices, but my eyes would not open.

"Keep Stoker alive, the Black Bishop needs him for something." It was Wotton! "Do what you want to the other one." A door slammed shut and I felt the stem of a hookah pipe forced into my mouth. My nose was pinched closed and I sucked in sweet smoke that pulled me back into sweet sleep.

Later, I am not sure how much later, I was awoken by a cackle, a hideous laugh full of madness and cruelty and anything but joy.

I was in a large bedroom on the biggest feather bed I have ever seen. What was left of my clothing was shredded beyond recognition. On top of me was a very naked female vampire, ample of breast and with long, flowing locks of raven-black hair.

"Wakie, wakie!" She laughed. "Time for fucky, fucky!" She had a thick Eastern European accent. The room was hazy with smoke; my head was swimming and I instantly recognised the smell of opium.

Next to me was a second naked female vampire fornicating with what my intoxicated mind saw as a ginger werewolf. As my brain started to clear I realised it was just Stoker's excessively hairy body. The vampire was writhing with ecstasy, as was Stoker. I assumed this was due to the opium, as I couldn't imagine Stoker taking any form of pleasure willingly.

I did my best to avert my eyes, but the room was covered in mirrors that reflected the appalling sight of a gyrating, grunting Stoker everywhere I looked. The vampire on top of him was invisible in the reflection, making the scene all the more revolting. Just Stoker bouncing up and down, his angry member in full view of all.

A third nude female vampire was sitting in a chair near the fireplace, puffing away on a hookah pipe and laughing maniacally.

The one on top of me rolled off. "Dis one smell too much of perfume, and is all floppy," she said, jabbing at me with her pointy finger. "Let me take turn on dat one."

She started pawing at Stoker.

"No! Mine," the other hissed.

"I am older, you must do vhat I say!"

Stoker's woman laughed at her. "Your master is my master's prisoner. You are lucky we let you live, let alone play with our new friends!"

"Your master left us here to starve to death!" She spat and turned back to me. "Fine, I just eat dis one!" She bared her fangs and lunged towards my throat.

"Wait!" I screamed.

She laughed and backed away for a moment. "I like it when they are afraid, it makes da blood sweeter."

I remembered the violent reaction Count Ruthven had to Stoker's blood. "Stoker there is a much better meal. Look at how plump and juicy he is," I said. "Look how pale and weak I am. Hardly a morsel. Besides, I've been subsisting on a primarily vegetarian diet recently, while Stoker eats almost nothing but meat – much more appetising, I should think."

"Mr. Dripp said we aren't to feed off the hairy one," the pipe smoker said in a Scottish accent. "Just you."

"Why do you think he told you that?" I said. "He wants him all to himself."

Stoker moaned disapprovingly as if he was finally hearing the conversation through his opium haze. He then tried to throw the vampire off him. She slapped him repeatedly across the face and into submission. "Bad boy! Ooh, he is strong! What could a taste of him hurt?"

The two on the bed looked at one another with contempt. They suddenly lunged at Stoker's throat simultaneously, jaws agape and fangs dripping with saliva. To my horror they bit into him like hungry dogs, greedily lapping up the blood. In their frenzy, they did not seem to find Stoker's blood immediately disagreeable.

The third vampire flew from her chair and joined in, sinking her fangs into his thigh! What had I done? I tried to pull them off but was thrown across the room with a single blow.

Then, just as all seemed lost, the first two sprang away from him in horror. Their faces contorted in disgust and shock. They fell off the bed and to the floor, choking and gasping.

The third one fell off to the floor as well, vomiting up blood. The first two were crying and screaming, clutching their stomachs in pain.

The pipe smoker must have managed to purge most of the tainted blood for she staggered to her feet and came for me. "You, you poisoned us!" She yanked me to my feet and tossed me across the room once again. I hit a wall and shattered the plaster. I closed my eyes and waited for the final blow.

Suddenly there was a loud cracking sound. I opened my eyes to see her head being bashed in with a chair. The chair shattered on impact, a blow so forceful it took her head clean off. She collapsed to the floor and burst into a pile of dust.

There stood Stoker, completely naked, covered in his own blood. In his hand was what was left of the chair, a single broken leg. His mouth hung open, whether in horror or simply as an after-effect of the opium, I could not say.

The raven-haired vampire was on her feet now and lunging towards him, woozy but enraged and swift. Turning quickly, seeming to operate on pure instinct, he plunged the jagged end of the chair leg into her heart. She exploded with a loud *poof* into a cloud of dust that enveloped Stoker but quickly settled to the floor.

The other was still writhing in pain on the ground. Stoker knelt down and rammed the makeshift stake into her and she exploded in a burst of gore. He turned to me, his eyes blazing with fury and loathing, and momentarily I feared he was not done wielding the chair leg.

"You...you bastard!" he stammered. Drained of strength and still woozy from the opium smoke and loss of blood, he collapsed against the bed.

"Now, Stoker, in my own defence, I knew they would choke on your blood. Your curse does have its advantages." He tried to glare at me but his eyes were fluttering closed. I pulled a sheet from the bed and wrapped him in it. He was shivering and just barely staying awake.

"We must get out of here," I said, pulling the big man to his feet with some effort. It was then I remembered my own nakedness. What little clothes had clung to me before were dislodged when I was flung about.

Stoker looked at my body, not with disgust so much as an indifferent disdain. I lowered him to the bed, hoping he would remain in a sitting position while I looked for something to wear.

"Twice in my life I have seen you naked, Oscar, and that is two times more than one man should have to bear." I thought, somewhat smugly, I'll admit, that there are men who would disagree, but said nothing.

I found some clothes in a nearby wardrobe. Fortunately, they were men's and fit me, although rather snugly. Unfortunately, they were at least five years out of fashion. Well, one must make do in trying times.

"How did my life come to this?" Stoker lamented, looking around the room. "I have fornicated with a demon. I could not become any more depraved than I am now."

With trousers on, I felt ready to return to my comforting duties and sat beside him. "You must not blame yourself. They have supernatural wiles, and besides, they had you doped with opium."

"Being doped on opium only adds to my list of failings for the day," he said. "First Ellen, now this."

I wondered what had occurred with Ellen but thought it best not to ask at that particular time.

"You saved my life once again and managed to dispatch three vampires. I'd say you have some tick marks in the good column to balance it all out."

"I would like to think so," he said. "But I must confess I enjoyed the fornication for a moment as I regained my wits."

I did not tell him it was more than a moment but shuddered a bit at the memory. There are some sights one simply cannot un-see. Instead, I said, "Why must you constantly fight your nature? Animal instinct, nothing more, and nothing to be ashamed of. Now, I shall find you some clothes and we will get out of here."

I resumed my search through the wardrobe.

"I suppose you will tell Florence," he said sullenly.

"Don't be absurd," I said. "Why would I do such a thing?"

"If she were to ask you directly, I would not want you to lie for me," he said sternly. Self-righteous prig.

"I seriously doubt the subject will ever come up. 'Did my Bram fuck a vampire?'" I chuckled at the thought.

I could not find any clothes that would fit Stoker's abnormally puffy body. "Nothing here will fit you. I shall search the other rooms."

I ventured out into the hallway with an oil lamp, only then realising there may be more vampires about. However, my fears were soon quelled as I found the house completely empty.

The house looked as though it hadn't been lived in for years, but was in remarkably good shape, aside from the cobwebs and layers of dust on everything. A perfectly fitting house for a vampire, I suppose, but I must remember never to hire Mr. Dripp and Mr. Leech to prepare a home for me. Hadn't Lord Wotton said that this property was to be occupied by an Eastern European count? Both Mr. Dripp and the wretched female vampire that tried to devour me had Eastern accents. Had he come to England for greener pastures only to get into a territorial squabble with the Black Bishop? Survival of the fittest extends to vampires, I reckon, and a naturalist would have a field day studying their behaviour. Or perhaps a supernaturalist.

In another bedroom, I found clothes for Stoker, even more out of date than mine were, I noted with some satisfaction. As I turned to leave I stopped, shocked. Derrick's portrait was leaning against the wall next to the door. I dropped the clothes and knelt down before it, reaching out to touch the canvas gently. It was like he was in the room with me, his eyes trying to tell me something.

As I gazed at it, Stoker wandered into the room, naked as a newborn babe, his eyes still glazed, clutching the broken, bloody chair leg. He bumped into the portrait and it fell forwards with a thud.

"I was worried you had found more of them," he said.

As I rushed to pick up the painting before he could stomp all over it, I noticed a note scrawled on the back in pencil.

Whosoever finds this painting, please deliver to Oscar Wilde, Salisbury Street, London.

Oscar, I hope this painting finds its way back to your possession. The Black Bishop has not given Wotton permission to turn me yet – I think perhaps he is being punished for the scene he created in your home, which was too much of a risk for the Bishop's taste – so for now, my humanity remains. I shall kill myself before I let him steal my soul, unless I manage to escape first.

Dripp and Leech are now under the employment of Wotton and torment me daily for their own amusement. It is only Lord Wotton that keeps them from eating me outright.

We are to leave in the morning, for I know not where.

For as long as my soul is my own, it belongs to you, Oscar. Please do not try to rescue me. All is lost for me and I do not want you to be lost as well. I could not bear knowing I led to your downfall. With love, Derrick.

My eyes welled with tears and my heart with anger. I vowed then to rescue him, even if it meant plunging a stake into the heart of the devil himself!

Stoker was struggling into the clothes I had found. "What's that written on the painting?"

"A message from Derrick," I said, showing him. "I am afraid we are too late."

"We'll find him," Stoker promised.

We returned to our homes, vowing to gather with Stoker's team to plan our next move. Derrick's portrait once again hangs above my fireplace. Is it wrong of me to get my hopes up, dear diary? For Derrick is not yet turned, and with Stoker and friends on my side, I feel we just might win the fight against these monsters!

FROM THE JOURNAL OF BRAM STOKER, 19TH OF JANUARY 1880

11:01 p.m.

Upon returning home, Florence was both confused and amused that I was wearing clothes out of date and too small for me. "There is a story here, surely," she said.

I told her of our vampire encounter, leaving out some of the more unsavoury elements of the story. She was very concerned for my safety and it made me feel closer to her again. We held each other and kissed tenderly. As we did, my thoughts drifted to Ellen and the kiss we shared. Was it just yesterday? I remembered how she felt in my arms and pulled Florence closer, kissed her more passionately. When I opened my eyes, I was almost surprised to see it was Florence in my embrace. She nuzzled my neck, whispered a reminder that she has not yet fully recovered from childbirth and regretfully pulled away. How can I think of another woman with my wife in my arms and our infant son in the next room?

Dr. Hesselius is staying with us. Fortunately, Florence's mother has returned to Ireland, freeing up the spare room. Florence is happy to have the company and seems to be in better spirits now that her mother has departed.

I invited Oscar to dine with us, at Florence's suggestion, to reinforce our newfound collaboration. Florence retired after supper and Oscar, Dr. Hesselius and I retreated to my study for brandy and cigars.

Oscar and Hesselius conversed in Latin and German for a bit and laughed at some bawdy joke Oscar told in French of which I understood only 'priest' and 'prostitute'.

"I never bothered studying Dutch, I'm afraid," Oscar said. "Although I once accidentally bought a horse in Amsterdam merely by clearing my throat. It seems a country that small shouldn't have its own language, especially one that requires one to cough up a lung." Fortunately, Dr. Hesselius did not take offence to this slight of his native tongue.

The good doctor told us of his travels and the many vampires he has hunted and killed. His hatred of the creatures was spurred by the death of his beloved niece at the hands of one.

"I was a country doctor at the time," he said. "I could not believe in vampires, so I did not see. I did not see my niece's life being drained away." There was much sadness in his eyes and anger in his voice. "She returned to life right before my eyes, a snarling, horrible creature – you saw the same, Bram, with the tragic Miss Mayhew. I vas unable to kill my niece, not that I even knew at the time *how* to do so. She fled into the night and killed innocent children, all because I did not stop her. I never did track her down. She could be out there still."

(With a sick feeling in my stomach, I thought of the three female vampires at Carfax. Had one of them had a Dutch accent? Surely not.)

He then related another remarkable story. He later gave it to me in writing, which I've transcribed here. I've cleaned up the English, but the story remains the same.

Dr. Hesselius's Account of Meeting the Vampire King

I was in a remote village in the Carpathian Mountains leading a hunting party. All legends had a common thread running through them: there was a vampire who was the first, a former king who lived in that region.

We were on our way to an abandoned castle on foot, for the terrain was too rocky for horses. We felt brave, for we had a large party of men with guns, torches and wooden stakes.

It was early spring and the weather changed on us abruptly, bringing a terrible blizzard. I soon found myself alone; I must have blundered off track thinking the group was just ahead of me.

For hours I fought against the blinding snow, but it was too much and I collapsed. It was a relief to lie there, to give up the struggle and let the storm rage around me. Soon I wasn't even cold anymore and waited peacefully for death to take me.

To my surprise, I awoke later in front of a roaring fire, wrapped in wolf fur.

I got to my feet and surveyed the room. I was in the banquet hall of a castle. A dining table in front of me was laid out with food and wine. A note written in German said, *Please, help yourself to supper.*

After I ate, a man appeared in the doorway. I stood to greet him.

He was tall and had a full head of white hair and a thick white moustache. He was dressed in silks adorned with jewels and looked as though he were a prince stepping out of a fairy tale book.

"Welcome. I am your host," he said in perfect German. "Please, sit down and have a drink with me."

He sat and poured me some wine, but none for himself, saying, "I never drink...wine."

I thanked him for saving my life and introduced myself.

"I know who you are, Doctor. Surely you know who I am," he said, his piercing eyes fixed on mine.

A chill ran down my spine. This, of course, was him, the vampire king I had been hunting. My hands began to tremble as I set down my wineglass.

"Why do you hunt me?" His voice was calm, but why shouldn't it be? I was unarmed; he had no reason to fear me. He could afford to toy with me for as long as he liked, or at least until the dawn approached.

"Vampires are an abomination. One killed someone I loved."

"One of my kind may have killed the one you loved; I did not. Some mortal men also commit murder. Do you then hold all men accountable for the actions of a few?"

"I see your point," I said. "But vampires are monsters and killing them is doing them a favour. It releases the soul."

"Perhaps," he said. "Maybe killing you would release your soul."

"I am sure it would," I said, trying not to show my intense fear.

He laughed at this, then said, "I don't care if you kill the others – most vampires are blundering oafs and there are far too many these days anyway. But you won't be killing me tonight."

"That would be rude of me after you've shown such hospitality," I said. I felt if I could keep him talking I could learn much about my foes, and even if the knowledge would shortly die with me I really had nothing to lose. So I asked, "How...how did you come to be a vampire?"

He laughed again. "In hundreds of years and thousands of conversations, no one has ever asked me that."

"Let me be the first then," I said.

"Very well." He grew silent for a moment, reaching back for his thoughts. "I was once a powerful ruler, but not a good or just one. In fact, I was a vicious, godless monster whose only enjoyment was torture. To me, the suffering of others was like drinking wine. The smell of blood intoxicated me and I revelled in inventing new forms of depravity. Soon, however, I became numb to all but the most outrageous horrors. I felt empty, my life meaningless. The greater my wealth and power, the unhappier I became.

"Then one day, my forces were destroying a village. I entered a Christian church and found a priest on his knees praying at the altar. I strode up to him, sword drawn, intending not just to kill him but to ensure he beheld me first in all my terrible glory so that he would die in fear. He turned his head slightly to look at me and smiled. No one who saw me coming at them with sword drawn had ever smiled before. It enraged me, and without a moment's hesitation or thought I lopped off his head with my sword. The head rolled to my feet but the body did not drop, it just remained there praying, blood gushing out of the severed neck.

"I looked into the face at my feet. A smile was still upon it and there was a peaceful light in his eyes. He was happy, even as he saw death coming for him. I decided I wanted to feel that. I converted to Christianity the next day and pledged my kingdom and army to the Holy Father. They were happy to have me, for though the Church preaches peace, it knows that strength and brutality have their uses.

"It was a dark time, then. The Turks were very powerful and angered by the Crusades. Their armies pushed into the eastern parts of the Empire and all seemed lost. Desperate for anything to help us win, the Vatican scoured their vast library for something that would help, even turning to the forbidden books. Books of spells and dark magic. One told of a way to bring forth dragons from another realm. Once they had that knowledge, how could they resist using it for their 'righteous' cause?

"The Order of the Golden Dawn was formed," he continued. "My ruthless past made me, shall we say, ideally suited for their purpose. I would be their weapon, my talent for death channelled for what they deemed the greater good. They summoned a dragon from the pits of hell and gave me the power to wield it. Fearsome, it was, and magnificent. An enormous beast, its wingspan broader than the Danube, with talons the size of gravediggers' spades and steel-grey scales armouring it from head to tail. Its golden eyes missed nothing and it could blow a plume of fire twenty yards long. It was enraged at being plucked from its world, but I controlled it and turned that fury to my ends. You should have seen the fear in my enemies' eyes when I came down from the sky riding a beast from hell!

"With every victory, I became more powerful and a greater hero to the Empire. But as you know, pride goeth before a fall and I was perhaps not so changed as I liked to think. The ancient books had told that there was power in the dragon's blood, and so I decided I would perform my own sacrament. I cut the beast – no easy task with a dragon, as you may imagine – and collected some of its blood. Then I knelt before God and my soldiers and I drank the dragon's blood in place of sacramental wine. I still remember the taste – sour and metallic. That single act of arrogance forever cursed me to drink blood and live in darkness.

"The thing that contaminated the dragon's blood took up residence inside me. It had an unquenchable thirst and compelled me to make other vampires, who went on to sire more vampires. It became apparent to me that vampires would soon outnumber the human population if left unchecked – and then what would we all eat? I learned to control my nature. To be selective about who I turned and who I did not. But just like any parent, I cannot control all my children. So, have at them as you will if they are so bold as to make themselves known."

He stood and I feared the worst.

"I have prepared you a bed and, in the morning, you are free to leave. I will give you a map and compass and food for your journey."

He was true to his word. The storm had passed and in the morning I left and by afternoon had located my hunting party. I convinced them we should turn back and search elsewhere.

I do not know why he let me go. Perhaps he wanted me to tell his story. Perhaps he really did want me to keep the vampire population under control. If that is the case, I have done my best to accommodate his wish. I have not encountered him since.

LETTER FROM BRAM STOKER TO DR. (WILLIAM) THORNLEY STOKER, 25TH OF JANUARY 1880

Dear Thornley,

I hope this letter finds you in good health. Florence and Noel are well, as am I. Florence continues to fight melancholy, which I have been assured by Mother is normal after a first birth.

Once again, thank you for your instruction regarding blood transfusions for Lucy Mayhew. Although her ailments were too great, the procedure did bring her comfort, and I think extended her life.

I find myself increasingly fascinated by your work in this new medical technique. A friend and I the other day were discussing its application in surgery.

I suppose it would behoove a patient to have a relative standing by for a transfusion should something go wrong during an operation. However, I was wondering if it would be possible to stockpile one's own blood the day or even weeks before?

I thought not, as it would spoil quickly outside of the body. Is this, in fact, true?

Bram

LETTER FROM DR. (WILLIAM) THORNLEY STOKER TO BRAM STOKER, 2ND OF FEBRUARY 1880

Dear Bram,

It's not like you to take an interest in medicine, especially blood, as I seem to remember you fainting at the sight of it as a child. Has this interest been set off by Florrie's difficult childbirth? I am so glad to hear she is doing well.

To answer your question, yes, it is true blood does spoil quickly; one only has to visit the local butcher's shop to see that. However, should the blood be put into airtight, sterilised glass jars and stored in an icebox, it can keep for several months without spoiling.

So, in theory, one could stockpile enough blood for several transfusions. The problem is the blood tends to clot in only a few minutes outside of the body. Efforts to strain the blood through cheesecloth and the like seem to be ineffective. Until this problem can be solved, only blood coming directly from a donor can be used in transfusions.

Please write again should you have further questions about blood or other bodily fluids.

All the best,

Thornley

FROM THE JOURNAL OF BRAM STOKER, 10TH OF MARCH 1880

1:15 p.m.

It seems my life is marked by neglect. I neglect my duties as husband and father and am in turn neglected by Florence. I cannot blame her. I am preoccupied by work and the troubles of the world. Distracted by my cursed second sight and the terrible knowledge it brings. And, if I am honest, distracted by other things as well.

For weeks now, I have been preoccupied with the search for Oscar's friend Derrick Pigeon and the gathering vampire threat that has taken him. Robert and Oscar have been scouring the countryside seeking word or evidence of vampiric activity. Striving to maintain an illusion of normalcy at work and at home, I help them strategise and, if a lead seems promising, go out with them to see what may be seen with my strange vision. We have had no success and I grow discouraged.

My only moments of dutifulness and concentration are when I gaze into Ellen's eyes. There I find peace and a joy I have never known. But it is only for a moment. I must look away before I fall into them.

I find myself thinking of the kiss we shared in her sitting room and fantasise about doing it again. In the fantasies, the kisses grow more insistent, our hands grope at one another, clothing is torn away and skin meets skin. I dreamt of her one night, and in the dream I had the strength and vigour I felt while channelling the werewolf in Greystones. She matched my passion, but in the midst of our coupling, my dream self felt darker urges. Thankfully, I awoke before I could act upon them. But the next day at the theatre, I could barely face her.

I must not give in to temptation, not now when I know for certain my soul would be in jeopardy. I must focus on my duties, even those I did not ask for.

I wish I could be more like Ellen. She takes vampire slaying all in stride as if it is just another part she is to play. No sweat upon her brow, no tears in her eyes for the simple world now lost to us. She sees every moment of life as an adventure and this is just one more.

I, on the other hand, struggle with my new destiny. Oh, how I wish I were a petty sessions clerk again and Florence, Noel and I were living little lives in a little cottage by a little stream. But that is not to be.

I fear the creatures know I am hunting them and in turn are hunting me. Twice now I have sensed their presence, once as I walked home for the evening. I ducked into pubs and shops and eventually lost them.

Once I saw one watching my home from across the street! I fetched a wooden stake, but the creature fled as soon as I opened the door.

It simply is not safe for Florence and Noel to stay in London, and so I have made a decision for the safety of my family. Mrs. Burton has kindly offered to take Florence and Noel into her home in Hertfordshire until the vampire threat is over.

Florence and I fought about it this morning. She refused to leave her home to stay with Mrs. Burton. I had to be firm with her and it led to my shouting and using words I now regret.

I am sure now she regrets her marriage to me. I have infected her life, and the life of our child, with my curse.

This battle may cost me my marriage, but by God, it will not cost my wife and child their lives.

FROM THE JOURNAL OF FLORENCE STOKER, 17TH OF APRIL 1880

I fear I have lost Bram's love and know not how to get it back. He loves another. When we were still in London, I would see his eyes brighten when she entered a room. Now that I have been exiled to the country, I have no doubt that she has many times entered rooms that are rightfully mine.

The worst part is I have no one to confide in now that Lucy is dead. Ellen would be the person whose shoulder I would cry on now. How she would love that! Playing the secret confidant, all the while having a secret of her own.

I have half a mind to put her in that position. Play stupid and blind and ask her advice. "Oh, whatever am I to do, Ellen? I fear Bram has been finding comfort with prostitutes and harlots. How can I win him back? You are an older woman of the world, surely you must know the art of love. You have played the part of the whore on stage, surely you can teach me how they tempt men away from their wives and children?"

To think, I fret about being a good wife and mother, all the while she steals husbands and abandons her own children. I will no longer fret. It is time to step aside or to fight. Now I have only to decide which it will be.

I am learning much from Mrs. Burton, who has had to endure such things herself in her long years of marriage.

She has given me a book, one she translated herself, the *Kama Sutra*. The drawings are very interesting, to say the least. I should be shocked, and am shocked that I am not.

I daresay I could give Ellen a run for her money with the instructions I have here.

FROM THE JOURNAL OF BRAM STOKER, 18TH OF APRIL 1880

9:17 a.m.

Robert sent word from Salisbury that several girls have gone missing in the area. This is the only lead we have had in weeks and we shall follow it. I fear there is little hope left for rescuing Oscar's friend, and believe we must act now or face far graver losses.

3:15 p.m.

Reverend Wilkins is in London. Over tea in my office, Oscar, Ellen and I told him of the latest vampire sightings in his area. He was visibly shaken.

"This lends credence to my darkest suspicion," he said. "I fear the Black Bishop is none other than the Bishop of Salisbury himself, John Moberly!"

He told us of Moberly's recent odd behaviour: secret meetings with lords and clergy in Amesbury, to which Wilkins, as vicar of Amesbury parish, would normally be invited but is not. Large sums of money diverted to special projects on Moberly's word alone.

"Mind you, I have no proof of wrongdoing," he continued. "It is possible that my suspicions are unfounded, and I dearly hope they are."

I reminded the group that we will need proof if we are to expose him. He is the second most powerful member of the clergy in England, and we cannot make accusations lightly.

"Indeed," the reverend said. "But the Archbishop of Canterbury has the power to unseat him and the two of them have no love for each other. Perhaps I could appeal to him to start an investigation."

"He is just the sort to be the Black Bishop," Oscar said. "He is a friend of my mother's and I have always felt he had an evil presence about him. Why, he once told Mother she didn't beat me enough. Can you imagine?"

If I could get an audience with Bishop Moberly, with one glance I could tell if he is a vampire. However, Wilkins is in his bad books at the moment. The Bishop refuses to see him; perhaps he knows Wilkins has been investigating him.

But Mrs. Wilde, as a friend, should be able to get us a meeting with him. So, it was decided that Oscar would make arrangements and we will continue our investigations in Salisbury.

POLICE REPORT FROM INSPECTOR FREDERICK ABBERLINE, 20TH OF APRIL 1880

08:00
Investigative Report from Inspector Frederick Abberline to Superintendent Thomas Arnold.

HIGHLY CONFIDENTIAL

– Subject –
On the kidnapping of Prince Albert Victor Christian Edward.

– Evidence –
On the morning of 19th of April 1880, an orderly of Blyth Sanatorium reported the prince missing from his room. The bars on his window were bent and the glass broken. Outside the room the footprints of two men wearing shoes were found along with bare footprints believed to be the prince's. There appears to have been no struggle.

– Statement from Dr. Seward, Head Physician Blyth Sanatorium –
"The prince was unusually quiet last night and in very good spirits. We were able to remove his restraints and he took solid food for the first time in weeks. I now fear his good behaviour may have been a ruse to have his restraints removed. In his mental state, he may have very well participated in his own kidnapping without understanding what was happening. As of late, he has had a delusion wherein he is broken out of jail and made king. I cannot help but think that this escape is somehow related."

– Investigation –

An hour before sunrise, a woman, Mary Ann Nichols, witnessed three men getting into a carriage outside the walls of the sanatorium. Although the woman admits to being intoxicated, she remembered that one of the men was dressed in bed clothes and was barefoot. The man was not forced into the carriage that she could recall and she said the men were laughing and talking in a friendly manner.

The carriage went west on Whitechapel Road. Constables are scouring the area for more witnesses and additional clues.

– Observations –

There has been no ransom demand. If this remains the case, it may be the prince arranged his own escape. There may also be a political objective on the part of the kidnappers, although even this scenario would have them contacting the royal family to make demands, which they have not yet done. If the objective was to kill the prince they would have done so already and made it known to the public.

LETTER FROM ELLEN TERRY TO LILLIE LANGTRY, 21ST OF APRIL 1880

My dearest Lillie,

I know you to be a woman of the world. Despite my years and experience with men I must turn to you for advice.

Something both wonderful and terrible has happened. Bram and I have become intimate. Despite my growing attraction for him – and, I daresay, his for me – I had resigned myself to the idea that we would never be together. He is married, and I know him to be a man who does not take that commitment lightly.

But some attractions are not to be denied, and Bram and I have given in to ours. It was not what I expected from the sweet, solicitous man I thought I knew. It was raw and savage. It both excited me and made me fearful.

With the death of Lucy, I have taken new accommodations, a small apartment above a haberdashery. It isn't much, a sitting room and bedroom. Bram visited me there one night. He wasn't himself and seemed distant.

When I asked him what was troubling him, he told me of a horrible encounter he and Oscar had with three female vampires. They were drugged and nearly killed by the monsters before gaining the upper hand and dispatching them.

Since the encounter he hadn't been able to sleep through the night for he was plagued with bad dreams. He was at the point of sheer exhaustion. He told Florence about the incident but has not confided in her how it continues to affect him, for fear of worrying her even more and further deepening her melancholy.

I did the best I could to comfort him and he fell asleep in my arms.

Just when I thought he might find some rest at last, he awoke with a fright, his eyes wide. It was as if he looked right through me to some past trauma.

"Bram," I cried. "What is it?"

He then kissed me hard on the mouth, more passionately than I have ever been kissed before! I responded in kind. He pulled me to him roughly, then rolled me onto the floor.

He literally tore off my clothes and ripped off my petticoat. It was all so savage and wild. We threw off all of our humanity and became beasts of the night. I was his completely, and I felt an ecstasy that I have never before experienced. Waves of pleasure passed through me with such intensity that when we finished I collapsed into the deepest slumber of my life.

When I awoke, I was bruised and scratched and yet felt little pain. A warm feeling of pleasure still coursed through me.

Bram was no longer by my side. It was dark in the room now and I lit a lamp. Bram was naked, curled up on the floor in the corner of the room, quietly whimpering.

"Bram," I said softly.

"How…how did I get here?" he asked. His voice sounded like a little boy.

I brought a blanket over, curled up beside him and held him. We eventually fell asleep.

When I awoke I found that he had dressed and gone.

I know I should fear him. At the very least I should not tempt him further from his wife. I know he feels terrible guilt and I do not wish to be the cause of it. But I cannot stop thinking about him. About the feel of him, the taste of him.

He fears he is becoming a monster. Am I too becoming one? Does contact with the supernatural lead to moral decay and corruption?

I fear now it is I that will have troubled dreams.

If you have any words of wisdom to share, dear Lillie, please do. I am surrounded by people but in many ways feel so alone.

Ellen

FROM THE JOURNAL OF BRAM STOKER, 24TH OF APRIL 1880

1:15 p.m.

Oscar and his mother are off to visit with the Bishop of Salisbury. It was hoped that I would get an invitation as well and would be able to tell straight away if he were a vampire. However, Lady Wilde said an invitation to me would be hard to come by due to my mother's activities against the church.

So, she and Oscar are off for their lunch with Bishop Moberly, and Ellen and I went to Reverend Wilkins' cottage as we wait for Oscar's report.

"I hope very much that Bishop Moberly is not this monster you seek," Wilkins said. "And yet I hope that he is, for that would mean we could expose him."

I hoped the latter, not wanting the Black Bishop to slip through our fingers.

"Now," he said, rising, "I would have liked to invite you to stay for lunch, but I am afraid I have some business to attend to in Rollestone."

We rose as well, saying we completely understood and thanking the reverend for his help, but he stopped us with a gesture. "Though I cannot share a meal with you, I did not wish to send you away hungry after such a long journey." He ducked out of the room and returned a moment later with a large hamper. "I've taken the liberty of preparing a lunch basket for you."

"Oh, you shouldn't have gone to so much trouble," Ellen said.

"No trouble at all. Just some sandwiches, cold chicken, grapes, scones and jam, a bit of leftover Beef Wellington and some apple pie and a jug of wine to help digest it all. Come, I will drop you off at the perfect picnic spot on my way."

The perfect spot turned out to be Stonehenge, which is a couple of miles out of town. I had heard of the stone circle, of course, but never had seen it with my own eyes. It is an eerie sight, these mammoth stones set around and on top of one another, alone in a large field. They form a circle over a thousand feet in circumference. Certain stones line up with the summer solstice and phases of the moon, so it most certainly was used as an observatory. There is no quarry for at least twenty-five miles and it is a great mystery as to how they came to be here and how ancient people with no technology transported them and hoisted them into place.

One could imagine all sorts of pagan rituals being performed there under the light of the full moon. Bones found during excavations indicate that human sacrifices may have been conducted there, a fact I would keep from Ellen so as to not spoil the beautiful scenery. The ruins are surrounded by tall grass and a sea of wildflowers, making it a perfect spot indeed for a picnic on such a fine, sunny day. I know we should be continuing our investigation, but we have completed our appointed task and what else have we to do until we meet up again with our companions?

The reverend promised to fetch us on his return trip, within a few hours.

The meal was excellent. Ellen and I talked of many things, never once mentioning or – for my part – even thinking of vampires.

As we lie here under the sky she has drifted off and I am taking the time to jot down this entry. I must put the pen down as I am feeling rather sleepy myself. Oh, why can't more days be like this?

FROM THE JOURNAL OF LADY WILDE, 24TH OF APRIL 1880

What was to be a lovely day in the country has turned into a social faux pas, the scale of which only Oscar could orchestrate.

I may very well be excommunicated for bringing him to meet Bishop Moberly. At the very least my social standing has been knocked down another peg, which it could ill afford, having already been seriously damaged by my late husband's scandals, Willie's carousing and Oscar's sharp tongue. (I suppose my own eccentricities may share a bit of the blame as well.)

Bram Stoker and Oscar confided in me that they suspect that Bishop Moberly is up to no good, and in fact might be a dastardly villain known as the Black Bishop – a vampire, no less, or at least in league with vampires!

At first, I thought the idea to be absurd, but the more I thought about my old friend's temperament and radical ideas, the more I could see him going down that dark path. Furthermore, their acquaintance, the Reverend Wilkins, offered proof of the bishop's obsession with the occult. The bishop had spent a large sum on collecting books of witchcraft and the dark arts and Wilkins had the receipts for these purchases.

Bram and Oscar asked me to arrange a visit with the bishop straight away. Although we have not seen each other in many years, our longstanding friendship would make such a request seem perfectly natural. I sent a note over to the bishop as soon as I arrived in Salisbury, explaining that Oscar was considering the priesthood. (Lying to a bishop is a sin to be sure, but it's not my first nor my worst.) I was quite gratified when he answered immediately and invited us to join him for luncheon.

Before we ate, he gave us a fascinating tour of Salisbury Cathedral, as he is quite knowledgeable of its history and architecture.

I thought Willie was the son who would embarrass me by

blundering about carelessly, but almost immediately, Oscar seemed to be playing detective in a most unsubtle way. I wanted to take a more delicate approach to our enquiries and not tip our hand, but as we toured he seemed determined to get the bishop to show his true nature in a mirror.

"Does this mirror have any historical significance?" he asked of one hanging in the cathedral's antechamber. There was nothing remarkable about this mirror, mind you.

"No, not that I am aware of," the bishop said. "I think it is there just to reflect the candles in front of it."

Near the end of our tour, there was a large ornate mirror down the end of an adjacent hall that was too much for Oscar not to notice. "How about that mirror?" he asked, scurrying down the hall to get close to it. "Surely it is from one of King Henry VIII's palaces. Fifteenth century, at least."

As the bishop was about to go over and humour him, a servant approached to announce lunch was ready. Foiled again.

It was an exquisite dining room, small, but well-appointed and tastefully decorated. The meal was potato soup, followed by roasted quail with pears.

My delicate palate noticed there was garlic in the soup and whispered the fact to Oscar. I was again doubting the bishop was a vampire.

"I taste only onions," Oscar whispered back.

I complimented the bishop on the silverware. "My mother's," he said. "We didn't have much growing up, but she insisted on fine silverware for company."

"Yet I notice you are eating with a wooden spoon," Oscar said.

"Metal hurts my teeth," the Bishop replied. "Always has."

As the meal progressed the Bishop and I engaged in delightful conversation about old times. He told Oscar about the time I encouraged him to publish a rather scandalous tract at Oxford. He smiled. "Nearly cost me a teaching position years later."

"Do tell, Bishop," Oscar replied. "I am intrigued by scandalous thought."

"I am afraid I fell in with the Oxford Movement," he said. "As you may recall, it promoted Anglo-Catholicism. Mainly we were for the reinstatement of lost Christian traditions of faith and their inclusion into Anglican liturgy and theology. I have to admit they took it too far in conceiving the Anglican Church as one of three branches of the Catholic Church."

"Oh, that does sound scandalous," Oscar said. "Asking us to be plunged back into the Dark Ages."

The Bishop did not look pleased with this remark. He became slightly agitated.

"Not our intent. We saw it as a reaction to the liberalism that was running rampant in the church. You have to remember at the time the Whig administration was gutting the clergy and seizing ecclesiastical property across Ireland. Not to mention, the Church was doing nothing to prevent the relaxing of morals and standards of decency. We saw returning to older traditions as the only way to keep the Empire on the moral path. We would still keep the Anglican Church intact, of course."

"So, no boiling people in oil for reading the Bible in English, or anything like that?" Oscar mused.

Oscar has a way of pushing people too far, almost immediately after meeting them. The Bishop, even with all his holy patience, was no exception. "No, of course not! Even a young man such as you must admit our country has fallen into a pit of depravity," he said sternly.

"One would hope," Oscar said. "For without the pit, there would be nothing to climb out of."

"Oscar!" I said. "That is quite enough clergy baiting for the day. For heaven's sake, this is not one of your salons; it is a religious institution."

"Sorry, Mother," he said, his eyes firmly not sorry. "I apologise, my lord, if I have offended you in any way. I am merely trying to ascertain the Church's position on such matters. One hears so many different takes on it."

And with that, Oscar pulled out something from his pocket and slammed it down on the table. It was a chess piece, a black bishop. He said nothing, but just stared into Bishop Moberly's eyes as if the chess piece were to provoke some reaction.

And it did. The bishop looked terrified. He reached out to touch the piece. "Where...what is the meaning of this?"

Oscar pulled a silver necklace from his pocket and suddenly

lurched forwards and pressed it to the bishop's head! The bishop fell back, tipping over in his chair and taking his plate of quail down with him in the process!

"Aha!" Oscar yelled, standing defiantly over the Bishop. Astonishingly, he pulled a wooden stake out of his coat! I sprang up to stop him before he could inflict any more damage.

"Mother, stay back. I am right – he is a vampire! He fled the touch of the silver cross!"

The bishop stood and brushed himself off, trembling with anger. "I fled your assault on my person! What is this nonsense?"

Oscar threatened him with the stake. "Back, or I'll stab you in the heart with this!"

I ran over to put myself between him and the bishop. "Oscar, you will do no such thing!"

"Get behind me, Mother. These creatures have a way of mesmerising you."

"If this some sort of joke, it is not a funny one," the bishop said. "I've heard you were a strange one, but I had no idea you were deranged."

"You were clearly upset by the chess piece," Oscar said. "Why?"

"One of my reverends, Wilkins, has been investigating some rumours involving the clergy. Something to do with a group of blasphemous dissenters led by an anarchist who calls himself 'the Black Bishop'. At first, I thought these allegations to be unfounded, but other rumours have come to my attention, and then you pulled out the chess piece. I thought you might be here to assassinate me."

"You aren't, Oscar," I said. "*Are* you?"

"He *is* the Black Bishop," Oscar replied, his eyes locked on the bishop with an anger I had never seen in him before. "You are the one who is running around turning people into vampires and killing people!"

"Vampires aren't real," the Bishop said, looking to me for support. "Tell him, Lady Jane."

I shrugged. "I wish that were true, but I have it on good authority that they are. Perhaps we could test the bishop," I suggested to Oscar.

I told him to touch the silver cross to his bare arm. He did and it did not burn him, much to Oscar's consternation.

"That proves nothing. He might not be a vampire, but he surely is the Black Bishop!"

"That is enough!" the Bishop yelled. He pulled forth from his pocket a small gun! "Drop the stake."

Oscar complied.

"I have been carrying this gun for days, just in case this Black Bishop's deluded followers were coming to kill me. I have let fear get the best of me, listening to a crazy, unfounded story straight from the penny crime magazines. Shame on me."

He handed me the gun.

"Please, Jane, take it. But whatever you do, keep an eye on your son. See, Oscar? If I were, in fact, a dangerous anarchist, would I give up my gun?"

Oscar paused, confused, then relented and apologised. He tried to clean off the bishop with his napkin.

"Stop it! Don't touch me, you imbecile. Get out! If I ever see your face again, I'll rip off my collar and pummel you within an inch of your life!"

"You see," Oscar said, "there *are* vampires and they are infesting London at the moment. If you could only help us...."

"Out!"

"Just listen to what he has to say," I pleaded with my old friend.

"You're as mad as he is," the bishop yelled. "Give me back my gun, before you accidentally shoot me."

I carefully handed it back to him.

"All you need to do is talk to Reverend Wilkins," Oscar said. "He will tell you I am not insane."

"I am sorry if Wilkins put these foolish ideas into your head," the Bishop said. "He is an old buffoon who likes to find conspiracies where there are none. I share part of the blame for humouring his delusions. In any event, the matter has been turned over to the Archbishop of Canterbury for further investigation. If there is any truth to these rumours he will get to the bottom of it. Good day."

Oscar raised his hand, "If I could just—"

"I *said* good day!"

Back at the cottage, Oscar told me of the horrific things that have been going on in London, right under my very nose. It seems we are knee-deep in vampires. Who will believe us? Who will help us? All seems lost.

We are off to gather up Bram Stoker and Ellen Terry and head back to London. I cannot wait to put this whole day behind me.

LETTER FROM ELLEN TERRY TO LILLIE LANGTRY, 24TH OF APRIL 1880

My dearest Lillie,

With so much horror in my life lately, is it wrong for me to enjoy an afternoon picnic? As I write this, Bram is busy shooing away a rather large flock of woolly sheep. I am sitting among the stones of Stonehenge on a carpet of grass and buttercups.

Stonehenge is a sight to see. Enormous rectangular stone pillars form a circle. On top of the pillars are stone slabs – how anyone hoisted them up there is a mystery, though I am told giants may have been involved!

We are alone except for the sheep. Dear Lillie, I fear I am falling in love with Bram. I am sick with guilt, for Florence is a dear, sweet thing and does not deserve to be hurt. Perhaps it is just the thrill of the danger we have found ourselves in that has me swooning like a schoolgirl.

I know I must suppress my feelings. The incident I wrote of previously has not recurred. He is a decent and moral man who is trying to remain steadfast to his marriage. A proclamation of love would only make things more difficult for him.

So, for now, my feelings must remain unspoken.

Bram returns, I shall pick up this letter later.

– Later –

Bram has fallen asleep next to me. I cannot help but think that we are soul mates, kept apart by the cruel stars. I am even more enamoured than before. Our afternoon picnic was platonic, I assure you; however, my heart does not think this to be true. I do not think I have met a man like him before. So strong, brave and such a troubled soul. One wants to save him.

We talked of literature, the theatre and mythology. He told me of his aspirations to become a great writer. Did you know he corresponds regularly with the esteemed American poet Walt Whitman, who finds his writing to be invigorating? I must say, I find everything about Bram invigorating.

– Later –

Oh, Lillie!

What a thrilling day! I have been shaken to exhaustion by romantic infatuation, intense fear for my life and a heart-soaring victory!

My earlier pages in this letter pale by comparison. I am very tempted to write this down as a play, it would make for thrilling theatre! I shall do my best to recall all that was said and done.

Our fine picnic was interrupted by Oscar and Lady Wilde arriving in haste by carriage. I woke Bram from his nap.

He sighed and said, "All good days must come to an end." He stood and brushed grass off his trousers.

The poor horses were sweating from a full gallop.

"Egad," Oscar said, climbing down from his seat. "Any further north and we would be in Scotland."

They recounted the tale of their lunch with the bishop; he is definitely not a vampire and by all indications is not the Black Bishop either. However, it sounds as if the bishop thinks the Wildes to be quite mad.

"It's not all bad news," Oscar said. "The food was excellent."

Bram was not convinced, pointing out that even if he were the Black Bishop, he would have hesitated to kill them in a cathedral full of witnesses.

"How did you know where we were?" I asked, still a bit put out by the interruption. "And why the urgency of your arrival?"

"Reverend Wilkins left word at the cottage that you would be here. And we thought your life may be in danger," Lady Wilde said. "Is that pie in the basket?"

"I do not understand," Bram said. "The reverend knew we were in no danger. Why would he say we were?"

"No, no, man," Oscar said, rummaging through our picnic hamper. "He simply said you were here should we be looking for you. And knowing the business we're about, danger was a natural assumption at a locale such as Stonehenge. Who could have suspected it was merely a spring idyll on a grassy plain?" He cocked an arch eyebrow at Bram, who turned away, clearly embarrassed. When he turned his wry smile to me I defiantly refused to blush, but I was not too proud to change the subject.

"Reverend Wilkins told us of some very suspicious actions of the bishop," I said. "I think he still bears watching."

"We assumed the Black Bishop is a vampire, but maybe he is not," Bram speculated. "He doesn't need to be a monster to rule the monsters."

Oscar agreed, adding, "If the Right Reverend Moberly is the Black Bishop, and I am still not convinced he isn't, then he knows we are on his trail. He and his vampires may be nearby. That is why we thought it best to come find you. Safety in numbers and all that."

"Well, I can assure you we were quite safe. It is a sunny afternoon and we are miles from Salisbury," Bram said. "Wilkins should be by any moment now to take us back to his cottage."

"I would hope so. As you can see, it is no longer a sunny afternoon, but dusk." Oscar said. "And eerie Stonehenge is not where one should be in the dark. Why, I can just picture a druid strapping us to a stone table and sacrificing us to…. Whom did they worship, Mother?"

I could see a cloud of dust off in the distance: yet more people on horseback. Our private picnic spot was becoming a crowded village.

It was six fast riders. I could not make out their faces but suddenly I saw them leap from their horses at a full gallop! It was then I knew they were unearthly creatures. "Bram!" I screamed, but in that very instant they flew at us at a tremendous speed. We had no time to react before they were on top of us!

We were instantly in their clutches. Four vampires each held one of us from behind as a fifth struck Bram and Oscar hard across their faces.

"That is enough," a sixth one said, calmly standing before us. He was well-dressed, upper-class, and clearly the others' superior. He slowly took off his riding gloves. His horse trotted up beside him and he took an apple from his pocket and fed it to him. "Marvellous creatures, horses," he said. "They live to be obedient."

Oscar spat out some blood. "Sundry! This is one of the Golden Dawn I told you about, Bram. He leads the vampire ceremonies."

"That is Lord Sundry to you, Wilde. You and Stoker here have been particularly irritating thorns in my side. You, Mr. Stoker, killed one of my men. There is a price to pay for that. And you, Wilde," he said, looking Oscar up and down. "You really just wear upon one's nerves, don't you?"

"I have been told that before, though there is far from a consensus on the subject," Oscar replied coolly.

"I killed no man," Bram said, struggling to free himself from the clutches of the vampire. "Coal was a monster like you."

"Well, I suppose you are right about that," said Sundry. "In any event, a price will be paid. One for one seems fair. I will not kill you, for I am told you have something we may need. So, pick one of the others and be quick about it or I will kill all three."

"Kill me, you bastard!" Oscar yelled. I must confess it seemed out of character for Oscar. So often he plays the callow narcissist for amusement, I was touched by his willingness to give his life for others.

Sundry smiled. "On second thought, I suppose Wotton will want to kill Mr. Wilde himself. So, Stoker, choose one of the women."

"Go back to hell!" Bram commanded.

"Fine," Sundry said, nodding to the vampires holding me and Lady Wilde. "Have your fill."

"No!" Bram cried.

"Choose now!" Sundry screamed, baring his pointy teeth.

"It is all right, Bram," Lady Wilde said. "I have lived a long life. It is only logical it be me."

"No, you do not get to choose," Sundry said. "Kill the other one."

I could feel the fiend's cold breath on my neck. Terrified, knowing the next few seconds would be my last, my legs gave out and I slipped momentarily from the vampire's grip. My mind raced as I steeled myself to make a run for it and wondered whether there was anything in the hamper I could use as a weapon when suddenly – I do not know how to write this any more delicately – the vampire's head exploded! Blood spattered onto Lord Sundry's fine clothes, and the vampire who had been about to end my life collapsed into a pile of sludge, making a frightful *sploosh* sound.

A stunned Lord Sundry scanned the horizon, looking for an assailant. Then the vampire holding Oscar released him and made a run for it. His chest exploded outwards from a bullet to the back. Bram broke free and pushed the vampire holding him away, and in the confusion, that one too took a shot to the chest.

The others fled for the cover of the stones. *Poof!* Another one exploded. Sundry took a shot to his leg and collapsed. The remaining vampire sped away at high speed. Oscar and Bram started to give chase, but the vampire was gone.

"He's getting away," Lady Wilde screamed. Lord Sundry was crawling along the ground, trying to make his escape. Lady Wilde ran over and sat on him. Facedown, with his arms pinned beneath his body, he snarled and hissed and twisted his neck to snap at her like a wild animal, any vestige of his previous humanity gone.

Oscar and Bram secured him with silver chains, which, apparently, they've taken to carrying around with them. It is amazing the habits one can cultivate when pressed.

Way off in the distance, at the top of a hill, a man stood and waved a rifle. It wasn't until he was closer that I could see it was Mr. Roosevelt.

He ran up to us, panting and holding his rifle in the air.

"Buffalo…rifle…silver bullets. Two-hundred-yard…range." It took him a moment to catch his breath, as it did us all.

Apparently, he had run into Reverend Wilkins in Rollestone. The reverend's carriage had broken a wheel and he sent Mr. Roosevelt to fetch us.

Bram pulled out a stake and pressed it against Sundry's chest. "Who is the Black Bishop?"

"I am," Sundry said, a predatory grin on his face.

"Why you're never!" Oscar exclaimed. "You're not even clergy."

"Not Church of England, perhaps," Sundry said. "But there are other faiths, other gods. Some grant more power than yours, if one proves worthy. Perhaps it is now time to see what else my god has in store for me." Hands and feet bound by silver, he still managed to bend his knees enough to launch himself forwards onto Bram's stake. Bram instinctively pulled away, but not quickly enough. Sundry's weight overbalanced him, and the two fell together, Sundry landing firmly upon the stake to complete his intended suicide. He let out a hideous scream and exploded into a puddle of foul-smelling sludge.

"I so hate it when they do that," Bram sighed, wiping the sludge from his face. His clothes were soaked, however, and smelled putrid.

We looked about at the piles of dead vampires among us and started to laugh from sheer relief as the truth sunk in. We had won. The Black Bishop was dead!

So, that was my day, dear Lillie.

Bram, Oscar and Mr. Roosevelt remain in Amesbury to seek Oscar's friend. Lady Wilde and I are now on the train heading home to London. She will ask Mrs. Burton to keep Florence and Noel at her home for a while longer until Bram is certain none of the Black Bishop's minions will seek revenge, while I am to inform Henry about our victory. My heart soars just thinking about it, but sinks when I think of returning to the theatre and to keeping my love secret from Bram, who will soon have his wife by his side once more.

Please write back soon to let me know if these letters are finding you on the frontier.

Love,
Ellen

FROM THE JOURNAL OF BRAM STOKER, 25TH OF APRIL 1880

Archivist's note: Events covered more thoroughly in Ellen Terry's previous entry have been omitted here.

8:13 p.m.

When we set out for Amesbury we had hoped to confront the Black Bishop and resolve this matter, but I'll confess I had not thought we would dispatch the villain so quickly. However, our work here is not yet complete; Oscar is more concerned than ever about his friend. There are still more vampires about and they have Derrick. Without the Bishop's leadership, I fear they are likely to eat him. I am honour-bound to assist with his rescue, if such a feat is even possible.

My 'gift' had not alerted me to the presence of any supernatural element, so we decided to make some discreet enquiries in the village. We began, as is Wilde's wont, in the pubs.

One thing that can be said for Oscar is that he is able to make himself agreeable when needed. He quickly ingratiated himself to publicans and patrons alike, discussing the weather, the merits of the local beer and national politics before eventually working his way around to asking if they had noticed any unusual activity or strange visitors in the area. While beer and politics could provoke heated discussion, on this point they all agreed that, no, life in Amesbury had been proceeding quite as usual.

As we staggered from our third pub, Robert recklessly decided that discretion was not giving us the results we needed. He approached a police constable making his rounds and introduced himself, then asked whether there had been any reports of mysterious activity in the vicinity.

"Mysterious activity, sir?" the constable asked, affecting the bland politeness that is the hallmark of his profession.

"Yes. A young man of our acquaintance has been kidnapped, you see, and we have reason to believe that the villains have hidden him here in Amesbury."

"I can assure you, sir, that had we heard inklings of an abduction we would have mustered our forces straight away," the constable said.

"The chaps would likely only move about at night," Oscar contributed helpfully. "Perhaps you're more familiar with criminal activity on the day shift."

"Well, sir, it's not such a large village," replied the constable, an amused smile spreading beneath his greying moustache. "We of the constabulary do tend to keep one another informed of such things."

"Yes, yes, of course," Oscar said, disappointed. "Thank you for your time, constable. If you should happen to hear anything, perhaps you would be good enough to let us know? We are staying at the inn. The name is Wilde."

Heaven knows why the man asked; he couldn't have possibly intended to share any information with us. But he helped us out immeasurably when he enquired, "What inn would that be, sir? The Boar's Head near the village green or the Lamb and Whistle out on the way to the old Wotton estate?"

We all froze for a moment. Finally, I broke the silence. "Wotton estate, did you say?"

So, with our confidence in our own investigatory skills shaken, we made our way directly to the Wotton estate, which is located on the road heading north out of town. It's a monstrous old thing, well-kept but stark, and I couldn't help but feel that even had there been no monsters within, I would not have wished to visit.

We approached on foot, each carrying a pack with our meagre tools: wooden stakes, holy water and the like. Robert also carried his buffalo rifle. Though it was still full daylight, we cautiously kept to the trees and circled the property until we found a side entrance that we could get to without crossing too much open ground. If this vampire coven is as organised as it seems, I would not be surprised to learn they have human henchmen about to guard their interests during daylight hours.

We sprinted across the narrow stretch of lawn and flattened ourselves against the stone wall of the house. Robert readied his gun, then nodded at Oscar and me. We positioned ourselves on either side of the door, stakes clutched in our fists. I twisted the doorknob, expecting to find it locked. It wasn't. I pushed the door open and Robert swiftly and stealthily moved through, his rifle leading the way. Oscar and I followed, eyes darting around a small sitting room, which was quite uninhabited.

Following the same pattern, we moved from the sitting room into the hallway with still no sight of man nor beast. Yet my senses tingled for a moment, then nothing. My sixth sense does diminish with distance, and it was a very large house.

We continued, penetrating deeper into the house. There was some evidence of recent habitation – a discarded newspaper, muddy boot prints on the hall carpet – but we found nobody to rescue or to kill. Finally, we had searched the entire ground floor and were faced with the choice of looking either upstairs or below ground – neither would afford easy escape should it become necessary. And the day was growing late.

The cellar seemed the less desirable choice, and therefore that is where we headed first. I followed Robert down into a gloomy hall, which led to a kitchen in one direction and what appeared to be storage for wine and other household goods in the other. The kitchen was the most disused of any of the rooms we had seen. If Derrick was here I am not sure what they could have been feeding him because the only food in evidence were some withered apples and a pint of soured milk. We turned to explore the storage area, but it was then we realised that Oscar was no longer with us!

"Damn him," I cursed as, abandoning stealth, we hurriedly searched the rest of the cellar. There was no sign of him. We sprinted back up the stairs and burst out into the back hallway, frantically looking for some indication of which way he had gone. We spent precious minutes on our search, fearing to call out loud for him as it might attract hidden vampires to our presence.

An open door was our only clue and we followed it through the formal dining room, then on to the drawing room and front hall. We could complete the loop of the ground floor again but going up seemed more promising and we mounted the grand staircase. When we were halfway up, a door opened in the hallway above and Oscar emerged with his brother Willie!

He had told me Willie was working for Wotton, but I was still astonished to see him there. Robert and I hurried the rest of the way up to meet them in the hall. I was immensely relieved to sense nothing untoward about Willie. I had feared I would have to plunge my stake into the heart of my oldest friend.

"What are you doing here?" I asked him in a fierce whisper. Robert was standing with his rifle at the ready, his eyes sweeping the hall, waiting for anyone – or anything – to emerge from a doorway.

"No need to whisper, they are all gone," Oscar said. "Willie has confirmed it."

Robert lowered his rifle and I introduced him to Willie, who nodded but remained strangely silent.

"Any word of your friend?" Robert asked.

"Yes," Oscar said. "I am afraid we are too late. He has become...." His voice trailed off.

"And you, Willie?" I asked. "Are you unharmed?"

He laughed harshly at that, which I found most alarming. "I am well at the moment," he said. "Quite sorry I ever joined their ranks, and I will continue to be sorry for a long time to come."

"No reason for us not to return to London now," Oscar said. "It will be dark soon and I, for one, would like to be on a train by then. Preferably with a drink in my hand."

Now, here we sit on that train to London and Oscar does, indeed, have a drink in his hand, not his first of the evening either.

It is a hard thing, the loss of hope, the certainty of defeat. But at least he now knows. He is bearing up surprisingly well. I know that he will mourn his friend, but I find myself, to my own astonishment, hoping that the loss will not change Oscar too much. The darkness of this world can crush a man, but if Oscar can face it and emerge still as arrogant and vaguely ridiculous as he started, perhaps there is hope for us all.

Willie is also drunk, though it has done nothing to lift his morose mood. I wonder what he has been through here with the vampires. He is not one himself, of this I am certain. Perhaps once settled back in London I can persuade him to confide in me.

FROM THE DIARY OF OSCAR WILDE, 25TH OF APRIL 1880

Dear diary,

I don't know what drew me to the attic; perhaps I am developing Stoker's second sight. I felt compelled to go, leaving the safety of our rescue party in the process.

We were searching the Wotton country house, which appeared to be empty, for clues to Derrick's whereabouts. Stoker's vision had not been triggered and I was growing more anxious that this was another dead end when I wandered off on my own.

I climbed the broad staircase, past portraits of Wottons from generations past – hard-faced men and bored-looking women and the occasional pampered child. The upstairs hall was richly appointed and lined with doors – so many, how would I choose? As I wandered slowly down the hall, I passed a small open door from which a warm, musty breeze flowed, followed by something floral. It triggered something in me, and before I knew it I was climbing the narrow staircase to the attic.

And to think I was giddy and full of confidence after our victory at Stonehenge. The Black Bishop has been thwarted, and the discovery of the Wotton estate nearby had raised my hopes to new heights that we would find Derrick. Instead, I found only despair and heartache.

The faint, sweet smell of opium was in the air, the attic dark except for tiny amounts of daylight coming through narrow windows.

To my shock, Willie was sitting on a cot in the corner, his back against the wall. He looked rumpled and bereft, lacking coat and cravat, with his shirtsleeves rolled up and his legs drawn up in front of him, his arms wrapped around them.

"Hello, Oscar," he said. He did not seem at all surprised to see me.

"Willie!" I exclaimed. "Whatever are you doing here?" I rushed over and sat beside him, sensing he needed help but having no idea what that might entail. Up close, I could see the desperation in his eyes and the sheen of sweat on his brow.

"I am Wotton's employee, remember?" His eyes met mine only briefly before looking away again. "He has taken to helping me in my career, but he decided that journalism is not my strong suit, so for a time, I became his personal secretary. Turned out to not be much of a promotion. I think I shall resign."

"Why are you hiding in his attic then?"

"I thought I'd have a go at killing myself, but I have run out of opium so I may have to find another method."

"What have they done to you?" I feared the worst. "Oh, Willie, they haven't turned you into...a vampire?"

He laughed. "I should be so lucky! No, nothing as glamorous as all that. They merely cursed me and left me to die. They have all gone. When you killed Sundry, that sent them scattering like rats. I think they are afraid of you, Oscar. Good for you!" He laughed weakly.

"Have you seen Derrick? Derrick Pigeon?" I asked him.

"Yes. He is one of Wotton's vampires now," Willie said.

My heart turned to stone in my chest, then, traitorously, back into a heart that ached.

He saw the pain in my eyes. "Have you really been looking for him?"

"Yes," I said. "Where did they go?"

"They were talking of leaving the country. Italy, I think. Apparently, that is where vampires go on holiday."

I forced my brain back to the here and now. It was too late for Derrick – too late! simply writing those words fills me with bitter regret – but my brother was still here and needed my help. "You said they cursed you," I said. "What do you mean?"

Willie laughed bitterly. "It's a funny story. You like funny stories, Oscar. Seems they have been trying to open a portal to hell, or some such thing. There is a ritual that requires the blood of a half man, half monster. They have been trying different man-monsters – you would be surprised how many there are. I will have to let Mother know so she can update her books. They felt a werewolf just might do the trick. Didn't work. But there was a bit of a tussle when we were moving the animal into place and the damned thing bit me."

"My God, no!"

"My God yes, and it was a painful bite. One that will hurt me every time the moon is full. So that is why I am doing the proper thing and killing myself, although I have several weeks yet in which to do it so I am taking my time. Perhaps I'll drink myself to death; it's how I've always wanted to go, really. And, yes, I see the irony in the fact that I helped kill a werewolf in Greystones and now I am one."

"That is the first time I have heard you use the word irony correctly," I said. "Perhaps the bite has improved your grammar."

He chuckled. "Can things be so bad if you are still insulting me?"

I grasped his arm. "Willie, we can break this curse. I hear tell the Gipsies are working on it even as we speak. We can return you to normal," I said.

"Not an incentive, Oscar. I wasn't much of a person when I was uncursed."

"Stop that, you are stealing my lines. And you know I only mean half of what I say."

He smiled faintly, then we heard Stoker calling my name. I started for the stairs to call down to him, then realised he might be able to see Willie's condition. How would he react? Or Robert? Well, I would just have to take a chance and find out. I returned to Willie's side.

"Don't do anything rash," I said. "You have nearly a month to the next moon. Please keep yourself alive until then. If not for me, then for Mother."

"I am all bark and no bite, Oscar. I haven't the courage to actually kill myself. In any event, they say you learn to enjoy being a wolf."

"Stop talking nonsense," I scolded. "We shall bring you back to London. You can stay with me at my flat and we shall decide what to do next. If we have to chain you up once a month, then so be it. It can't be any worse than how we tortured each other as boys."

He gave me an unexpected and uncharacteristic hug. "Thank you, Oscar," he said, his voice breaking a little.

We went downstairs and I told the others we were too late to save Derrick. With that, we returned to London.

Willie came with me to my flat. I was happy to have the company now that Frank was in the sanatorium. But when I awoke the next morning I found Willie had gone. He left a note simply saying, *I can't put you or others in danger, Willie.*

I fear I will never see him again. And even worse, I fear that one day I *will* see Derrick again. It is almost as if I can sense him, circling my soul like a vulture.

FROM THE JOURNAL OF BRAM STOKER, 27TH OF APRIL 1880

11:13 a.m.

I am in the grips of great joy and tremendous guilt.

I am in love.

I am married.

These two facts do not fit together as neatly as one would hope.

I have feelings for a woman who brings out the best and worst in me and I feel myself lost in both extremes.

After that day at Stonehenge, perhaps it was inevitable. When we encountered the vampires, I felt certain we would all lose our lives. I have never known greater fear. And yet, never have I felt greater joy than when we survived and defeated the Black Bishop. More than that, it felt like it was a sign from God that, together, Ellen and I could achieve anything.

Arriving home in London after the search for Derrick I felt like a soldier returned from battle. My ordinary life seemed foreign to me and I felt a hunger for something I could not name.

I brought Florence home from Mrs. Burton's care and we embraced, but without the warmth that either of us deserves. I told her that we had killed the Bishop and she seemed pleased but distant. I know she has never truly forgiven me for the supernatural secrets I kept from her, and likely regrets having married a man who has brought such darkness into her life. She excused herself, saying she was exhausted and wished to retire for the evening. As she was departing, she laid a hand on my shoulder and said, "I really am happy for you, Bram." Then she kissed me on the cheek and walked away.

The unnamed longing in my soul grew feverish and I paced restlessly about the house. From my window, I saw a light shining warmly behind the closed curtains of Ellen's sitting room and decided that I should tell her of the events at the Wotton estate – a perfectly normal thing to do, after all. Only polite, really, after all she had been through on our monster hunt.

I strode across the courtyard, my pace quickening the closer I got. I rapped on her French doors and after a moment her hand drew back the curtain and, seeing me, she quickly opened the door and stood aside to let me in. As she closed the door behind me, I turned to her and started to say, "I wanted to tell you about what we found...."

But the look in my eyes told her far more and in a moment she was in my arms. Her hands were in my hair and my lips were on her mouth and my arms were around her waist holding her tightly. Before long, both hands and lips started wandering and, as clothing became an obstacle, it was pulled aside. I protested feebly that her sitting room wasn't the place for such actions, but the curtains were closed tight and she assured me we were quite alone in the house and so that is where we stayed. She undid her hair and it tumbled around me as we coupled before the fire. But with this ecstasy came something darker. Soon I found my will and humanity burning away!

The monster in me started to take over, filling me with primal urges and animal instinct. I no longer cared if I physically harmed her. I saw fear in Ellen's eyes and it only increased my pleasure.

Horrified, I fought the demon within and it is only by the grace of God that I was able to pull my humanity back before I was fully consumed. I forced the monster to retreat into the shadows. Still, it grinned at me, knowing it had almost taken over fully.

She claimed I did not harm her physically, yet even by the firelight I could see scratches and bruises on her alabaster skin. I began to cry uncontrollably like a lost child.

She comforted me and this only increased my guilt, yet I knew that I needed her and had not the strength to end our newly kindled affair.

Eventually, I had to leave and told her so regretfully. She smiled, with only a hint of sadness, and said she understood. I left through the front door – in case Florence happened to be looking out a back window – but not before Ellen kissed me again and said, "Bram, I have no wish to hurt Florence, but you and I can still be something to one another, can't we?"

"Everything," I murmured into her ear as I held her close. "I feel you could be everything to me."

At that moment, I felt not a shred of guilt for what I had done. That came later, as I stopped in the nursery to kiss my sleeping son.

I know I have betrayed my vows and my family. It would be easy to blame my fall on the curse I bear — a little bit of demon nature forcing its way out. But I know this failing is all too human. And besides, what I feel for Ellen is too pure, too joyful to be demonic.

Florence and I married in haste, I know that now. I do love her, but it's not the same as what I feel for Ellen.

What I will do about this, I do not know.

FROM THE DIARY OF OSCAR WILDE, 29TH OF APRIL 1880

Dear diary,

I was too late to save Derrick's soul, but my search for him continues. He was last seen in Salisbury, en route to God knows where, and I know that it's a near impossibility that I would get some clue to his whereabouts here in London.

But I must do something. I am sure other vampires are still in the city, perhaps having fled here when we killed the Black Bishop in Salisbury. Derrick may be among them. I dare to hope – foolishly, I suppose, and yet I cannot help myself – that he may be on the side of good as Henry Irving is, and I wish to meet this new incarnation of Derrick to see for myself. If he is a monster, I owe it to my friend to kill him and release him from this existence.

My hunt has taken me throughout the city, from the posh gentlemen's clubs of Knightsbridge to the seamier parts of the East End. Today I found myself in Whitechapel.

It was there I spotted that vile creature, Leech! He was coming out of a butcher's shop on Goulston Street, in one of the less seamy parts of Whitechapel. Although it was a cloudy day, he was dressed to protect himself from the sun, in a filthy trench coat, a ridiculously wide-brimmed straw hat, and rose-tinted glasses like Italians wear for a day at the beach.

I recognised his slimy, pale face straight away as he wove through the pedestrians on the busy pavement. The large burlap sack he carried wiggled, so I am sure it held something living.

His presence gave me both fear and hope: fear that these hideous monsters were once more in London, and hope that Derrick may be among them.

I followed him for quite a long way, being careful to stay far back and hidden in the crowd. I was almost too good at this for I lost sight of him from time to time and he almost slipped away entirely.

The comfort of Goulston Street was far behind me and the buildings were becoming more dilapidated as we went on. The crowd was still thick, but now it was full of the unwashed and poor.

He eventually stopped at an abandoned building, a former 'Dry-Cleaning Factory', according to the faded sign. One could still smell the solvents and it was most unpleasant.

Knowing vampires are acute of hearing, I did not venture over to the building to peek into the windows. (I still have nightmares of the three vampire women that attacked Bram and me so viciously.) I am off now to gather forces to destroy this foul nest.

Once again, I must ask Stoker for help.

FROM THE JOURNAL OF BRAM STOKER, 29TH OF APRIL 1880

9:12 p.m.

Well, thanks to Oscar my life has once again been put in danger, and to top it off I spent a good part of a day in jail!

Not all is lost, however; we have dealt a blow to the vampires and valuable information is now in hand. We know Wotton and his lackeys are once again in London and for some nefarious reason other than feeding.

Oscar came to me early yesterday with the whereabouts of the vampire Leech and by association his boss Wotton.

Robert was away and Irving was sleeping, so that left just Oscar, Dr. Hesselius and myself as the hunting party. This made me very wary as we had no idea how many vampires were waiting for us, or what our plan of attack would be once we arrived there.

Dr. Hesselius insisted we stop at a Catholic church to stock up on holy wafers. He assured us we would be undetectable to vampires with fists full of holy wafers in our pockets, and this gave us more courage than we should have had otherwise.

We entered the old dry-cleaning factory stealthily through an alley door and found the main floor to be empty. However, there was a crack in the floor big enough to peer into the cellar and we could see two of the creatures moving about below.

We went onto our stomachs and crawled to the crack to listen. We suddenly heard a piglet squealing with much fright. Oscar cautiously peered into the crack and reported there were two vampires below.

"Dripp and Leech," he whispered. "They are the ones that took Derrick. Leech has the pig."

Perhaps Oscar's voice was covered by the sound of the piglet's squeals or maybe the wafers in our pockets did offer some sort of protection, but in any case, the vampires did not hear us.

I peered into the hole ever so briefly and recognised the one not holding the pig as the vampire that had attacked me my first month in London. His flinty face was forever burned into my memory. Dripp was as dry and dusty as Leech was slimy and greasy. Each had the look of a corpse to them. Had I not known they were the Un-Dead I would steer clear of them for fear of typhoid or cholera.

"I ain't eatin' pig blood again, it tastes awful!" Dripp protested. "Besides, it does nothing to fill my belly."

"His lordship says we can't be feeding off the locals, at least not yet, or we could give ourselves away," his partner replied. "After Saint George's Day, it will all be different. It will be a banquet and we'll be able to feast on whoever we wish. Me, I've got my eye on the butcher. Some rich, meaty blood in that one, you can count on it."

"Yes, well, grand plans for tomorrow are all easy to talk about, but they don't do anything for the here and now. Where is 'his lordship' anyway?" Dripp asked, in a mocking tone. "You can bet he's not eating pig."

"Back up north to get it all ready," Leech said. "He'll be back tonight. Maybe he'll bring us food." Leech bit into the pig's throat and there was a loud squeal and then the piglet went silent. We could hear Leech's disgusting slurping as he sucked the poor thing dry. "Aww, you're right, that is terrible. And if anything it has made me more hungry!"

"There's plenty around here no one will miss. I won't tell his lordship if you grab a snack on your way out to keep an eye on Stoker," Dripp said. I froze as Oscar and Hesselius looked at me warily.

"On my way? It's your turn to watch 'im!"

"You work for me. I'm in charge when Wotton's away, and I say you'll go."

Leech growled at him then relented. "Awww, all right. I wish we could just kill him."

"What would be the point when we can't even eat that disgusting blood of his? Save it for the ceremony," Dripp said. He spat as if remembering the bad taste left in his mouth by our encounter months ago, and I felt a small surge of satisfaction.

"I have a plan," Oscar whispered. "Get up, get out of here."

As quiet as we were getting to our feet, the vampires had heard us.

"What was that?" Dripp said.

"I dunno," Leech said. "Rats upstairs?"

Oscar went over to a large metal can that had *Petrol Solvent* written on the side. He dumped its contents and it spread over the floor.

Hesselius and I bolted back out into the alley, for that must surely have alerted the vampires to our presence.

Oscar followed with an oil lamp in his hands. He took a match from his pocket, lit the lamp and tossed it inside. The petrol burst into flames remarkably fast.

We heard Dripp yelling as he reached the top of the stairs.

Hesselius pulled a wooden stake from his bag. "Let's wait here and stake them if they come out."

Then we heard the police whistle. I turned to see a police detective glaring at us. He drew a gun and spat out the whistle. "Hold it right there!"

Had it been a constable with a billy club I am sure we would have continued to make a run for it, but we weren't going to outrun a bullet. We froze in our tracks.

The police detective took us down to the station and 'processed' us for arson.

"When did police start carrying firearms?" Oscar asked me. "It's downright uncivilised. This isn't America."

A constable was going through Dr. Hesselius's bag and describing the objects as another constable wrote them down in a big ledger.

"Three wooden stakes, two bottles of water, fifty digestive biscuits...."

"Eucharist wafers," Hesselius corrected.

The constable rolled his eyes and continued, "Fifty Eucharist wafers, four silver chains, two heads of garlic and a ham sandwich wrapped in paper."

The arresting detective led us down the hall towards the holding cell. He took off our handcuffs. "You lot seem pretty well-dressed for arsonists. Why were you burning that building down?"

"Rats," Oscar said. "It's infested with them and as you know they are thought to carry the plague."

A street urchin ran up to us and pulled on the detective's jacket. "Please, sir, let my da' go, he didn't do nothing wrong."

"Tomorrow, son. Let him sleep it off today and give your mother time to recuperate from the beating he gave her."

"I say, child, how would you like to earn a shilling?" I asked him.

"A whole shilling?"

I directed the child to the carriage we'd left waiting at the corner of Whitechapel and Commercial Road and instructed him to tell the driver where we were and to fetch Henry. The lad dashed off.

The detective put all three of us into an already overcrowded cell, packed with every kind of unbathed miscreant one could imagine. Not even the smell of Oscar's cologne could overpower the stench.

A slight, handsome young man approached us. Even in jail, Oscar knew someone, for the man addressed him. "Ay, Mr. Wilde, sir, good to see you again."

"I don't know what you are talking about," Oscar said, turning away from the young man in embarrassment. "I haven't seen you before in my life."

"It's Joseph Smalls, sir. I talked to you the day they brought Frank Miles to the asylum," he said. "And when you visited him a few times."

Oscar turned back to get another look at the man. "Oh, sorry. I do remember you now. Glad to see you are…better."

"Just had the DTs is all. Thanks for asking. Frank is doing well; he was out of the straightjacket when they kicked me out."

There was a fight at the back of the cell and we all got pushed forwards against the bars.

"Hey, watch it!" Smalls yelled. "We gots some gentlemen up here." He shoved back with all his might and that bought us some room.

Meanwhile, I was fuming. Once again, I found myself in a precarious position at Oscar's hand, and I told him as much. He scoffed at my concerns.

"You could have said no to coming along. We could have waited for Irving to awaken, but you were the one that wanted to go straight away. Why, I just killed two vampires with my quick thinking! Isn't that what we do now?"

I reminded him that his 'quick thinking' has landed us in jail and most likely for a very long time! And we don't even know for certain that the vampires went up in flames.

"I am sure my mother or your vampire can get us out of this," Oscar said calmly.

"Your mother's and Henry Irving's connections will have little sway with the court. We were caught red-handed by a high-ranking detective."

"You are always doom and gloom, aren't you?" Oscar said. "Perhaps this is why you attract evil like cats to dead fish."

I know not why this infuriated me so, but it got my dander up. I grabbed him by his purple waistcoat and shoved him against the bars.

He groaned dramatically. "Help! Constable, I'm being manhandled by a ruffian!"

"It does us no good to be arguing among ourselves," Hesselius said, breaking us apart. "Even if we go to jail forever we must get word out that the vampires are planning something."

"That's right, Stoker, didn't they say they needed you for something? Possibly your miracle blood again." Oscar said. He wasn't chiding me with this, though it felt as though he was. "A ceremony? What could that be?"

"But they mentioned Saint George's Day. That was last week," I said.

"Ah, but that's according to the Church of England," Hesselius replied. "Perhaps they are using the Eastern Orthodox calendar. That would place it on the 6th of May."

"Next week," Oscar said.

It was then we realised Smalls was privy to our entire conversation. He looked at us with bewilderment, fear and avid curiosity. Perhaps he thought we too belonged in the asylum.

We waited in that cell for what seemed like days but was only a few hours. Then the detective came with the keys. His eyes were all glassy as if he were drugged on opium.

Henry entered behind him.

The detective silently opened the door.

"You must hurry," Henry said. "Step out of the cell, calmly now. I don't know how long I can keep him mesmerised."

Smalls and several other prisoners also took this opportunity to escape.

We made our getaway to a waiting cab.

"See, Stoker, your vampire did rescue us," Oscar gloated. I grudgingly conceded this was true.

"I've wiped the detective's and the other constables' minds of the events. I hope that is enough to avoid the pressing of charges,"

Henry said. "It doesn't work on everyone and sometimes the memories come back."

It has been a full day with no visit from Scotland Yard, so I am hopeful that we are free and clear.

However, once again I fear for my life. What could Wotton possibly want with me? What is this ceremony they speak of? Saint George's Day is but a week away. Am I safe until then?

Hesselius has vampire-proofed our house by hanging garlic and wolfsbane around the windows. I have taken to wearing extra silver crosses and carrying a pistol with silver bullets. I pray I won't need it.

LETTER FROM BRAM STOKER TO OSCAR WILDE, 1ST OF MAY 1880

Oscar,

Something most dreadful has happened, and I turn to you in my hour of need. The Black Bishop is not dead as we thought, and he has taken Noel! Why did we allow ourselves to believe that our foe was defeated so easily? I cannot let Florence and Noel pay for that mistake!

Three of the Bishop's men came in while I was at the theatre, struck Florence down, took Noel and fled. They left a black bishop chess piece and a note, which I have enclosed for you alone to read.

Florence is hysterical and has had to be sedated. I am to go to Amesbury immediately. A carriage waits for me outside and a boy waits at the back door to deliver this when I am gone. I must keep this from the police but wanted you to know the truth.

I know not what I shall find in Amesbury. Do not try to rescue me; Noel is my priority and I do what I have to do. But once he is safe, you and the others must carry on our work, if you are willing.

I have sent for your mother to sit with Florence. Tell her there is hope I can negotiate Noel's return and that it is of the utmost importance that Florence not contact the authorities.

Florence and I are counting on you, Oscar. I am sorry to place this burden on you, but I know you will shoulder it for Florence's sake. Tell no one of this but your mother. As you can see by the ransom note, discretion is vitally important here.

Forever in your debt,

Bram Stoker

BLACK BISHOP'S RANSOM NOTE

Mr. Stoker, I realise you are very upset right now; however, you must follow these instructions carefully if you are to have your son returned alive.

A carriage will arrive on the hour to take you to the railway station. You are to get on the train to Amesbury. There an associate of mine will be waiting to bring you to me. You are to come alone; do not contact the authorities or your troublesome cohorts.

I have a simple proposal. When you fulfil its terms, your son's life will be spared. Follow my directions and you have my word that Noel will be returned into his mother's arms unharmed.

You can rest assured he is being properly looked after. I have hired a nanny and wet nurse to attend to his needs. We wish him no harm, but we do need you to perform a task for us, indeed, for the benefit of all humanity. It involves a bit of your special blood.

Sincerely,

The Black Bishop 🕯

LETTER FROM ELLEN TERRY TO LILLIE LANGTRY, 1ST OF MAY 1880

My dearest Lillie,

My heart is still racing as I write this – forgive my trembling hand. So much horror for one afternoon! I am heartsick and fretful. We have been dealt a great setback in our efforts against the Un-Dead.

First and foremost, my beloved Bram's son Noel has been kidnapped by 'the Black Bishop'! We did not kill the fiend as we had thought; that was all a ruse.

In exchange for his son's safety, Bram has been summoned by the Black Bishop to perform some task. I cannot describe the dread and foreboding I feel now. I wish I were the type of woman who faints. Unconsciousness would be a sweet oblivion.

Secondly, we were attacked by vampires and one of our comrades is dead! My heart is heavy at his loss, but his bravery saved my life and has given us hope that we can rescue Bram and Noel.

It started late this morning. It is Monday, so the theatre was empty except for myself and Anthony, a craftsman who was fixing the lift built into the stage. We are currently performing *Romeo and Juliet* and the lift is supposed to bring up the tomb set for the final death scene, but it malfunctioned at Sunday's performance. The set came up but would not drop again.

"Drat," Anthony said, wiping grease from his hands with a rag. "Needs a new gear and I don't have the right size. Back in a bit."

As he left, Oscar and Robert came rushing in, alarmed to find me there by myself.

I didn't tell them I was there to meet Bram, as it was the only time during the week we could be alone, opting instead for the half truth that I often rehearse by myself on Mondays.

They told me of Noel's kidnapping and showed me a letter from

Bram to Oscar as well as a ransom note from the Black Bishop. Bram himself is the ransom! He has rushed off to Amesbury to trade his life for Noel's.

I have not been feeling well lately and nearly became sick to my stomach at the news. Robert helped me to a chair on the stage near Juliet's casket. I did not fail to see the irony in being surrounded by the final scene in the story of star-crossed lovers who died rather than be parted. I felt at the moment that I would never see Bram again.

Oscar, who has taken to carrying a walking cane wherever he goes, pulled a hidden sword from it, pointed the blade to the sky and proclaimed, "We will kill the bastard for good this time!"

We sent for Dr. Hesselius, awoke Henry from his sleep and set about developing a rescue plan. The note was very specific that we were not to go to the authorities, so we were on our own.

"I should go and do some reconnaissance," Irving said. "Perhaps I could even join their ranks."

"Not bloody likely!" a voice yelled from the balcony, startling us all.

We looked up to see four vampires in the balcony.

"Dripp!" Oscar yelled.

"Surprised to see us?" he laughed. "Thought you roasted me and Leech in the fire, did ya?"

"Takes more than a little fire to kill us," the one I guessed was Leech said.

With Dripp and Leech were a ginger-haired vampire and one that could not have been much more than a boy when he was turned.

They leapt down onto the stage, more swiftly and gracefully than I would have imagined. Before any of us could react, Dripp plunged a silver dagger into Henry's chest, barely missing his heart, for I thought for sure he had struck it! Henry staggered back and collapsed.

The other vampires were fighting Robert, Oscar and Dr. Hesselius. My dear friends were no match for vampire strength. The monsters could have quickly killed them but took great joy in toying with their opponents, like bullies slapping small children.

The ginger-haired vampire was laughing as he absorbed Robert's punches to his face.

The young vampire kept pushing Oscar down every time he got

to his feet. He did this with only his index finger. He too found it most amusing.

Leech was merely holding Dr. Hesselius back and watching the others, egging them on.

"That's right, it's fun to play with your food!"

With their attention away from me, I rushed to the house curtains.

Dripp stood over Henry and gloated. "This is for killing Mr. Coal." He slowly removed the dagger, causing Henry to writhe in pain. He brought it up to show Henry he was about to die.

Was there enough daylight left to weaken them and make it a fair fight? I pulled the ropes and the curtains rolled up and let in a bright, beautiful beam of sunlight, blinding the vampires.

Henry rolled away into the shadows and covered his eyes. Dripp fled from the light, first trying to leap into the balcony, but finding his strength gone he climbed back upon the stage and looked for a shadow in the wing.

Robert pummelled the ginger vampire, attacking him with great fury, pounding him deeper into the sunbeam. He is very strong for an older man; I was quite impressed with his use of fisticuffs.

Oscar dived for his cane, jumped to his feet and started beating his attacker across the head with it. The vampire grabbed it and tried to yank it from him, only to pull away the sheath and reveal the sword.

The bullies were not smiling now!

Oscar sliced his vampire across the neck, nearly cutting his head off. Black blood gushed like oil from a well. A second blow took the head clean off and he exploded into dust. He must have been older than he looked!

Oscar then went to the aid of Hesselius who, at his advanced years, was no match even for a weakened vampire. Leech had Hesselius around the neck from behind and was using him like a shield. "Back or I'll snap 'is neck!" the monster cried.

Dripp came to the aid of his cohort and together they were winning against Robert.

Oscar turned sharply and stabbed the red-haired vampire in the back through his chest. The fiend exploded in a great gush, as if he were a boil being lanced. Robert now turned his fury on Dripp.

Dr. Hesselius let out a horrifying scream. Leech had broken his arm so severely that a sharp bone protruded from his wrist! Hesselius nearly fainted from the pain and Leech had to hold him up. "Stop or I *will* kill him!"

Robert and Oscar did as he commanded and stopped. Oscar tossed his sword away.

"You, drop the curtain," he shouted at me. I complied. Once the sun was gone, their smiles returned.

Dripp took me hostage and gave a nod to Leech, who sank his teeth into Hesselius and drained him nearly to the point of death. Pausing for a moment, he asked, "Do you want to be my slave?"

Gasping, Hesselius said, "You will not require a slave in hell." Then, mustering the last of his strength, he threw his ruined arm forward, plunging his broken bone deeply into the monster's heart, screaming in agony at the effort. The vampire barely had a moment to look surprised, then burst to death. Bone, it seems, has the properties of wood as far as vampires are concerned. Hesselius collapsed to the floor.

Oscar and Robert turned to Dripp.

I retrieved Oscar's sword.

Outnumbered, Dripp sped away at great speed and, leaping up onto the balcony, made his escape through a rear door.

Henry was too weak to give chase and I could see the frustration in his eyes.

We rushed over to Hesselius. I held his head in my lap. We could tell there was nothing we could do. He was so drained of life. Tears filling my eyes, I thanked him. "We would all be dead now if it weren't for you," I said. He smiled weakly.

"I only wish I could continue to fight by your side," he said. "Destroy them at all costs."

Then he was gone.

There was little time to cry over our friend's death. We must now find a way to save Bram and Noel.

– Later –

Dear Lillie,

We have hatched a plan.

We are off to Amesbury, where Henry will get himself captured by the Black Bishop. Oscar and I will try to find where they are keeping Noel and Bram, and Robert will find reinforcements, and join us with what he calls his 'secret weapon'. He is quite resourceful.

We leave in the morning and if you do not hear from me again, thank you for being my friend. Please tell my children I love them and wish I had been a better mother. If I survive this, perhaps I shall be. But for now, my duty lies in Amesbury.

All my love,

Ellen

FROM THE JOURNAL OF FLORENCE STOKER, 1ST OF MAY 1880

I am being driven mad with fear and guilt. I feel as though I have been torn in half by my grief. I am so ashamed when I think back on how I wished I had never become a mother; now all that I want in the world is to have my Noel returned to me, to hear him gurgle contentedly as I rock him in my arms, to kiss his precious little face.

It is God's punishment, I know, for my lack of gratitude. I have been a terrible mother and wife, a spoiled child throwing tantrums because life hasn't progressed as I wanted it to.

Lady Wilde is here – to keep me company, she says, but I know she's really here to look after me. I pray Bram and Noel return safely, and when they do I vow to be all that they deserve.

I managed some fitful sleep last night and Lucy came to me in a dream. The Lucy I knew, not the foul creature she had become. She came to tell me she is happy in the afterlife. Is her visit meant to reassure me that Noel also will be safe and happy, in this life or the next? Or is it merely a reminder of another person I cared for who I failed to protect?

FROM THE JOURNAL OF BRAM STOKER, 2ND OF MAY 1880

It is done. I am in the hands of the Black Bishop. I've been given pen and paper to write a farewell missive to Florence, an act of kindness that only demonstrates my captors' true cruelty. I have written my letter and now write an account of my imprisonment. I shall hide the pages in my shoe; perhaps after my death, someone will find my body and these notes. Or will my captors burn or bury me so that I take these words to my grave?

I have been selfish and arrogant, thinking I can use my cursed ability to confront evil. All my best intentions only served to corrupt me and drag me down to hell. And worst of all, I have brought this danger and despair home to my wife and child.

But for all my regrets, I cannot now change the course of events that led to this horrific day, and so I did as the ransom note instructed.

I was taken by train to Amesbury, to have my audience with the Black Bishop. Night was falling as we arrived, and a young woman approached me as I stepped off the train. She smiled, though there was little warmth in it, and extended her hand. "Mr. Stoker, I believe? I am Carolyn le Fey. I shall escort you to your appointment with the Bishop."

I ignored her hand and she shrugged and led me from the station. A carriage waiting outside took us to the inn on the outskirts of town, the one on the way to Lord Wotton's estate. We went directly to a room on the upper floor. A fire blazed in the fireplace and dinner was laid out on a table.

"Do make yourself comfortable," Miss le Fey said, then exited. As comfort was not top of my mind, I paced the room, wondering what would happen next.

As I looked out the window, speculating about where they might be holding Noel, I heard the door open behind me and turned to face my nemesis. I felt certain there must be some mistake when *he* entered. Reverend Wilkins! Miss le Fey and a male vampire accompanied him and I thought he had also been captured until he said, "Leave us now. I am in no danger." His minions obediently departed.

I was dumbstruck. His jovial nature and friendship had been nothing but a cover for his nefarious agenda! How he must have laughed at me all the time he was playing the good-natured ally. I have been an utter fool.

He greeted me warmly and said, "You must be famished after your long train ride. Please join me for dinner."

Outrage helped me find my voice. "I will not sit and break bread with you as though we are friends," I said. "You have already done that quite enough for the two of us. Now, where is my son?"

"Please, sit and eat something, Bram. You will need your strength if you are to rescue your boy. Let us discuss the terms of his release."

And so I sat, and stated the obvious. "You are the Black Bishop. Not Lord Sundry as we were led to believe."

"Correct. You see I staged that little picnic, including sending Mr. Roosevelt to rescue you. You were all so persistent, and I was not yet ready to perform the ritual. To get the full effect, it has to be done on Saint George's Day – inconvenient, but there it is. Leading you to believe you had killed the Black Bishop was a stroke of genius, if I dare boast. Sundry was my most loyal follower; it grieved me to sacrifice him, but any good chess player would have done the same. It had to be someone who could credibly be in charge. You would have only kept searching otherwise, and what good would that have done any of us?" He smiled benevolently. "This way, your last days were spent in peace and happiness, not in a frenzied hunt for someone who was always several steps ahead of you. You should be grateful, really."

He noticed the doctor's bag I had brought with me on the floor next to the table.

"My men tell me you have jars of blood in there. Whatever for? Did you think you could bribe the vampires with it to release your son? I'm afraid they only like fresh blood."

"It is my blood," I said. "I have been collecting it for weeks and storing it in an icehouse. If it is my blood you need for your ritual, you may have it."

He seemed genuinely surprised. "Very clever, Bram. You may have found a loophole that will keep you alive. Yes, I can see no harm in trying. However, I will still need you for the event. Should the jarred blood not work, I will need to slit your throat." He told me all this while stuffing his fat face with greasy roast chicken and calmly munching away as if this were any ordinary supper.

"What will this madness bring to you?" I asked.

He grinned in genuine delight. "It brings me a dragon!"

I actually laughed. "Surely not," I said. "Or do you mean that as a metaphor?"

He started babbling quite excitedly. "No, no, I am speaking literally. If your jarred blood works – and I do hope it does, Bram, please believe me – you will soon see an actual, flesh-and-blood dragon. An honest-to-goodness giant, winged lizard. It may or may not breathe fire, that part is not clear in the literature – I'm quite torn, actually, on which I would prefer, but it will be as it will be. The ritual lets me open the gates of hell, summon the creature, and – " here he banged his hand upon the table, " – shut the gates. You are a key, Bram, nothing more. Half man, half demon, that is what I need. I tried vampires, werewolves and all manner of man-monster combinations. I even imported a skinwalker from America. Nothing worked.

"I was getting desperate. The ritual opens a portal between worlds, you see, when done at the right time. Those times are rare enough, but when you're looking to find a dragon on the other side, well, the opportunity comes around perhaps once in a lifetime, and it was approaching quickly. Then I was told of your remarkable powers by my friend Henry Irving. What luck! I took a sample of your blood a while back. Remember when you were attacked on the street and I saved you?"

He could see the recollection in my eyes.

"Yes, I see you do. Sorry about being so rough with you, but I had to be sure. You see, vampire blood has these little thingies swimming about in it. I took a look at your blood under a microscope and it has the same thingies, but only half as much. Voila! Half man, half monster. You have a foot in this world and a foot in theirs."

No wonder it seems I belong nowhere. But I couldn't brood on that. "What do you mean to do with this dragon?" I asked instead. I pictured a dragon flying above Parliament, Wilkins on its back declaring himself the new head of state.

"Excellent question," he said. "It will help me create my new ruling class. Drinking the blood of the dragon makes one a vampire, you see, without any of that business of being sired. And with no sire, my new vampires will owe allegiance to nobody but me."

"How can you be so sure they will follow you? What's to stop them from simply disposing of you and 'ruling' on their own?"

"Most people like to be told what to do, I find," he mused. "At least I certainly observed so in my role as a pastor. Besides, I have a secret weapon. It's served me well so far."

I had to concede that was true. He was no vampire himself, certainly, and yet they followed him.

"I like you, Bram," he continued. "In fact, if this collected blood of yours does the job, I don't see any reason I could not let you live. I will have to turn you into a vampire, of course, but I think you would make a valuable member of our order."

"I would rather die than become one of those vile creatures!" I exclaimed hotly.

His smile turned colder. "It is not entirely up to you. However, I can be benevolent, and if all goes well may be inclined to leave it as you wish," he said. "Now, eat your last meal and I will let you write to your wife and tell her Noel is coming home. After all, there is no need to make her worry any more than she has to. Don't bother writing to your whore, Ellen."

"How dare you call her that!" It was all I could do to not grab a knife from the table and stab him in the heart.

"She chose to live the way she does, tempting married men and conceiving bastards. All that will end under my reign, I can assure you."

A big smile spread across his fat face. "You needn't worry about her sullying your good name, even posthumously. I have despatched my vampires to deal with her and the rest of your gang. They have been a thorn in my side for too long. I will leave you alone with your thoughts and send some stationery and a pen so you may set your affairs in order. Now thank me."

As I sat silently, the smile left his face; all sanity left his eyes. "Thank me!" he bellowed.

"Thank you," I said, seething with anger.

FROM THE DIARY OF OSCAR WILDE, 3RD OF MAY 1880

Dear yours truly,

Our clandestine operation to rescue Stoker has begun!

Ellen and I are incognito. Our disguises, designed by myself and brought to life by the Lyceum's fine makeup artists, are quite good. My own mother failed to recognise me (although her eyesight isn't what it used to be).

I am posing as a peddler, wearing moth-eaten clothes and donning a grey wig and a face full of wrinkles and warts. I pull a cart full of my wares and have even managed to make a sale or two. Ellen is posing as my wife, also artistically aged and embodying the part with the verisimilitude I have come to expect from her performances. And now I can say I've acted alongside one of the greatest talents of the London stage!

We move about Amesbury unnoticed in a crowd of all sorts of poor and nefarious people.

We have found lodging at a boarding house, which is surprisingly clean and comfortable. We have sent word to Mr. Roosevelt of our whereabouts. He is procuring armaments as well as additional troops. We fear to confide in the constabulary or military as they may have been infiltrated by the vampires – and if not would quite possibly lock us away as lunatics. However, Roosevelt is seeking mercenaries to help us free Bram and Noel.

I shall keep you informed, dear diary, as we progress.

Dear yours truly,

We have already gathered some important – and troublesome – information!

Irving was making enquiries at a local tavern while Ellen and I sold our wares just outside.

He was inside for only a moment when he was hauled out by three men. He struggled, but in the daytime he has only the strength of an ordinary man and was greatly overpowered. This is all part of our plan, of course, but it was disturbing to see him hauled off nonetheless.

They stuffed him into a hansom cab and he was whisked away. It was all I could do to hold Ellen back from running after him.

"You cannot catch them on foot, and besides, this is precisely what we wished to happen. We must stay on our mission," I said. "We have to find out where the Black Bishop is holding Bram, as that is where I suspect they are also taking Irving."

"You are so wise in these matters," she said, or something to that effect. "Whatever should be our next move?"

"Reconnaissance," I said. "We shall seek information among the lower classes, as they often know what the upper class is up to."

We moved about the marketplace, among the other cart vendors. The hushed talk on the street was that there was money to be had in selling to lords and ladies who had recently arrived in town for a festival of sorts. No one knew what this festival was about, but it was bringing people with money to town like never before.

"I sold fifteen kerosene lamps," one vendor told me. "I thought I'd never unload those things. They make a bright light, but the kerosene is too expensive for folks around here."

I enquired who he had sold them to, and he told us it was to Lord Wotton's estate. I could barely contain my revulsion at the memory of that horrid place.

We made our way to the estate to find many merchants had set up camp around the property in hopes of selling goods to the new arrivals.

The place was bustling with aristocracy and bore little resemblance to the abandoned property Robert, Stoker and I had visited earlier. A seemingly endless stream of carriages was arriving at the estate.

Then, to my confusion, a carriage arrived and was greeted with much pomp and circumstance. It was a humble carriage and seemed to not warrant such attention. Footmen lined up, a carpet was rolled out; this must truly be an important person, I thought.

I was astounded when out stepped Reverend Wilkins! He was carrying an old spear as if it were a sceptre. The vampires milling about bowed down before him as if he were the king. Following out of the carriage was Prince Edward, the grandson of the Queen. (I recognised him from when he posed for one of Frank's portraits.) They paid him no mind at all, still fawning all over Wilkins.

"I don't believe it," Ellen whispered. "Wilkins must be the Black Bishop!"

I must confess this had not yet occurred to me until she said it. (Don't judge my lack of acumen, future Oscar. Things were happening at a rapid pace.) From the way he held the spear, I would wager that it is the source of his power over the vampires. Indeed, a few of them seemed to be glaring at it rather resentfully, though when Wilkins turned their way they made sure their expressions showed only adoration.

A few servants approached us and our fellow merchants.

"You," one yelled to the peddler I had spoken to earlier. "You got any more of those lanterns?"

"No, but I have plenty of torches and pitch," he said. "Back in my storehouse. I can give you a good price."

"All right, that'll have to do. You stay. The rest of you, clear off! There will be no more selling or buying today."

The peddler went up to him and they talked for a moment, although I could not hear what they were discussing. The crowd was noisily moving off.

Ellen and I each took a handle of the cart to start the long walk back to town, but before we could begin the torch merchant called out to us. He trotted over and asked whether we had a horse to go with our cart.

"Not at the moment, but I can procure one," I said. "Why?"

"I need to deliver a load of torches to Stonehenge Friday night. I'll cut you in if you help me get 'em there."

"Oh, we would be happy to, dearie," Ellen said in her best Salisbury accent. We made arrangements to meet on Friday morning.

"This is a very good day, indeed," he said, smiling. He trotted off with his nearly empty cart, leaving us to our own journey back.

"What a stroke of luck," I said. "We know where it is happening, whatever it is, and we will be in the thick of it when it does."

"And we know where they are holding Bram, Noel and Henry."

"Er, we do?" I asked.

She nodded her head towards the estate.

"Oh, of course," I said. "I am sure I knew that."

"I hope Robert brings an army of mercenaries," she said, picking up the pace to the point where I could almost not keep up. "It's about time we sent these demons back to hell."

LETTER FROM THE BLACK BISHOP TO HENRY IRVING, 4TH OF MAY 1880

My dearest Henry,

I apologise for not coming to see you in person. I am at the Stonehenge site overseeing last-minute preparations.

Please forgive me for locking you up, but it is for your own protection. I am also greatly sorry that I had to take the Stoker boy, but that too is for your own good, and the good of all, as you will see.

I was quite touched by how you ran to Bram's aid. You are a true and dear friend; I have always valued this quality in you, and that is why it is important to me that you understand the truth.

I am not the monster you think me to be – quite the contrary. I have been chosen by God to rule the thousand years of peace, after which Christ will return to judge all. He has given me the Spear of Longinus – the actual spear that pierced Christ's flesh. The blood on the blade gives me control of the wretched creatures of hell – vampires, werewolves and the like. I, of course, do not mean that *you* are wretched. In fact, the spear does not control you. (Yes, I confess, I have tried.) I have no idea why you are immune to its effects. It might be because your creator's creator set you free all those years ago. Perhaps it is because you have devoted yourself to God. You are proof that vampires can possess free will and therefore fall under his watchful eye.

I must thank you, Henry, for you showed me a world I did not know existed. It was my research into a cure for your condition that led to my discovery of a once-great order that served God by controlling the powers of the underworld. I alone resurrected the Order of the Golden Dawn and recovered the last of the pure dragon's blood currently in this world – and determined how to obtain more.

Unlike the tainted blood of vampires, this blood allows those who drink it to keep their free will and gain the immortality that is our destiny. The upper class shall rule, as that is our burden, and we shall serve God until his return.

Thanks to you, I have the key to open the very gates of hell. The Stoker blood was the final ingredient I needed. We took some previously and tried to perform the ritual; unfortunately, it was not enough and it must be given willingly. So you see, I needed Noel to make Stoker comply. With his blood, I shall bring forth a dragon, giving me an ample supply of the magical elixir for all the aristocracy.

As I write this, noble men and women are coming from throughout the Empire to become part of our new world order. They will become an army that I alone control.

The royal house shall also come under my command. Prince Edward has joined our cause and will be crowned king. He will, in turn, enthrone me the Archbishop of Canterbury. I will use this power for good, Henry, I assure you. We shall usher in a new era in which we can save many souls before the Second Coming. The common folk will comply. As in the olden times when they feared what lurked in the dark woods, their fear will lead them to righteousness.

Join me, Henry! You are my friend and, I believe, sent to me by God to rule by my side.

I must go now to continue preparations for the momentous event. I leave you pen and paper to reply with your answer. And, if you would, give some thought to what sort of role you would like to play in history. With your oratorical skills, I think you would make a fine prime minister.

Your friend, always,

Rev. Richard Wilkins

P.S. I, of course, cannot free you until after the ceremony. I am no fool and leave nothing to chance.

LAST WILL AND TESTAMENT OF HENRY IRVING, 5TH OF MAY 1880

Perhaps writing down my thoughts in these – my final hours – is a waste of time. Wilkins will find these pages and destroy them. I shall do it nonetheless and hide the pages somewhere in my cell in hope they will be found one day. Most likely anyone who does find them will think them a discarded work of fiction, but there is the possibility that they may make their way to someone who will understand the truth of them.

I am being held in what must have been a monk's sleeping quarters, loosely chained in silver – over my clothes so it does not burn, and slack enough that I can move about in the narrow confines of my cell, but it is enough to keep me restrained. Only a slit in the wall for a window and a bare wooden platform that serves as both bed and seat. Hardly room to get on my knees and pray in here. Bars separate me from the rest of the dank cellar.

I will not become part of the Black Bishop's plans. I have spent so many years trying to live a righteous life; to turn to evil now would make a mockery of my efforts. It is bad enough that I have unleashed Wilkins' madness upon the world, albeit unwittingly. If not for me, he would never have discovered this underworld or been corrupted by it. I thought I knew him and could trust him, that he was a pious man. Perhaps no man is completely immune to the lust for power. And yet still I believe in the good

– Later –

Something remarkable has happened. As I was trying to write my last testament, I was interrupted by the sound of a voice, deeply resonant, with a European accent. "I can smell your despair through the wall, my friend," it said. I froze, my pen still poised above paper.

The voice sounded familiar, yet I did not think I had heard it among the Bishop's henchmen.

"Who is there?" I called back.

"A friend. Like you, I am a prisoner of the so-called Black Bishop."

I wondered if together we might be able to formulate an escape and said as much to my new ally.

"Do not bother. He will just summon us back with the spear," he said, his voice edged with bitterness.

So, my neighbour was a vampire then, but not on the side of the Black Bishop.

"So, he does have some sort of magical talisman?" I asked.

"Yes. I suppose if you were to get far enough away, its effect would diminish," the voice said. He sounded Romanian, or perhaps Hungarian. "If I ever get the spear away from him, I will use it to stab him in the heart. Trapped like a rat," he growled. "No one has ever controlled the Dark Prince!"

"Wilkins says the spear has no control over me," I told him. I heard a scraping sound from beyond the wall, as though he had leapt off his own sleeping platform, causing it to slide against the stone wall.

"If you could get us both out of here, we could take the spear from him," he said.

Did I dare trust this new ally? 'Dark Prince', one must admit, sounds a bit menacing. "If he can control you, why does he keep you locked up?"

"He is frightened of my strength. He fears that, like a trained wolf, I may one day reclaim my nature, turn on him and tear out his throat, for I am *the* vampire! The first to drink the dragon's blood. I led an army against the Muslim invasion. I made them flee the Holy Roman Empire forever! The pope himself kissed my ring in gratitude, then betrayed me, hunting me down like a dog.

"Now, it appears that history is repeating itself once again," he said. "Self-proclaimed holy men in pointy hats trying to wield a power they do not understand and cannot control."

His voice burned into my brain and ignited a memory – it was him! The one who freed me from the clutches of the vampire queen so long ago! But, the first vampire? Could it be true? And if so, might he have the knowledge to free me from the demon inside me?

"What is the ceremony for which he is preparing?" I asked.

"They need fresh blood."

He told me of how he became a vampire by drinking the blood of a dragon summoned from some place he called 'the Realm', which sounded very much like hell.

"With each generation of siring, the blood becomes weaker, the vampire more mindlessly brutal. Go far enough down the line and the vampire is nothing more than an animated corpse."

I thought of the mindless creatures I'd seen in the Crimean. "So, with blood from a fresh dragon...."

"These fools will unleash an epidemic of vampirism they will not be able to stop," he said. "The Bishop might be able to control a handful of vampires with the spear, but can he control a hundred, a thousand, a million?"

"But what if this *is* the will of God?" I asked. "The pope successfully used this power. Maybe God *did* lead Wilkins to the spear. Not to rule, but maybe all this is part of the end times."

He laughed. "The creature, the so-called *demon* that lives inside you, do you know what it is in the Realm?"

I remembered my fevered dream. Had I been in the Realm?

"In its world, it is a harmless insect," he continued. "A parasite that feeds on the blood of fellow creatures with no harm. Dragons shake them off like fleas. But here, it takes us over entirely. It reproduces by compelling us to pass on the parasite."

"Is the Realm what we would call hell?"

"I think not. It is a place where the laws of nature work differently. Sometimes our worlds open up to each other and something spills in or out. Supernatural creatures are merely visitors from this undiscovered country. Imagine being the first person to see a firefly, or the honeybee if you knew nothing of honey. Would not that seem magical?"

"It must be more than that," I argued. "For the cross and the power of Christ turns them. There must be supernatural elements at work."

"Perhaps. Or maybe he is from there as well."

"He? Do you mean our Lord and Saviour, Jesus Christ? That is absurd! There is no way he was a vampire!"

"Not a vampire, but something else from the Realm. How else do you explain the magical powers?"

"The powers of God! That is how I would explain it!" I could not believe I was arguing such a blasphemous point with a creature from hell.

"I have been there, the Realm," he said. "I walked the ground there as I do here. It was a strange place filled with unfamiliar creatures, but it was a place like here. Trees and plants, animals and insects. Two suns in the daytime, but suns like ours, and stars at night. No people damned in lakes of fire."

"How did you get to the Realm?" I asked, incredulous.

"There are places on the earth where you can merely walk through and back again. I travelled to such a place in the New World with a Spanish guide. I sought a cure for my...our affliction. I did not find it. That was many years ago, and now I am not sure I want to be human again. I have seen their wars. I have even been their weapon! Their atrocities are greater than anything vampires have done."

My hopes fell. This man – this monster – had no cure for me. I turned my attention to our immediate problems to keep from falling into despair. I asked him how he came to be the Black Bishop's prisoner.

"I was betrayed by people I hired to set up my new home in London. The Black Bishop promised to make them vampires in exchange for helping to kidnap me. Once I was brought within the power of the spear, I was powerless to resist him."

"The spear alone should tell you the power of Christ is real," I said, still arguing, I know not why.

"The blood on the spear, you mean," he said slyly. "Strange how it is always the blood that holds supernatural power."

We both were silent with our thoughts for a moment, then he asked me, "Why does the Black Bishop let you live?"

"He wants me to be a part of his madness," I said. "He sees me as his friend."

"Maybe you can use your friendship to your advantage. Get that spear away from him and I will do the rest."

A chill went down my spine, for I know his power. Would it be a mistake to unleash him back onto the world? Still, I am considering the option.

Can I act the part of the loyal follower and be Brutus to Wilkins' Caesar? Having played both Brutus and Caesar in my career, I believe I could.

LETTER FROM BRAM STOKER TO FLORENCE STOKER, 5TH OF MAY 1880

My dearest Florence,

It is with a heavy, yet resolute heart that I write what will be my final words to you. By the time you read this I will be dead. My hope is that this will mean Noel will be alive and safely returned to you. At least that is the promise the kidnapper has made to me. I have no choice but to believe him.

Giving up my life for his is the only way. I cannot tell you what this is all about, a restriction placed on me by the kidnappers. They would not allow this letter to be delivered if I did.

In these final moments of reflection, my thoughts are only of Noel and you. I know that in these past few months I have not been a model husband and father, and I am sorry. My biggest regret is that I will not be able to make amends.

I live under a curse and should have told you this in the beginning. I had thought my problems were in the past and that I could provide you with a safe and happy life. I love you very much and hope you will always remember me and tell Noel that his father loved him.

You are young and beautiful. Do not let your period of mourning go on for too long. It is my wish for you to love again and find a worthy man who can be a good husband to you and father to our son. (It would be best if this were not Oscar.)

There are dark times ahead for Christendom. Hold tightly to your faith and stay close to your friends. Ellen, Henry and Oscar will be there for you and Noel, of that I have no doubt.

Goodbye, my beautiful flower.

Love, for all eternity,

Bram

LETTERS FROM ROBERT ROOSEVELT TO THEODORE ROOSEVELT, 5TH OF MAY 1880

Dear Theodore,

Once more into battle I go! We must be victorious, for if we are vanquished, so much more may be lost than our lives. Bram Stoker and his son Noel have been kidnapped by a villain who calls himself the Black Bishop. This blasphemous reprobate is the ringleader of the vampire uprising and must be stopped at all costs.

I have procured arms and soldiers and am heading off to Amesbury momentarily. I did not garner the troops I would have liked, managing to hire only three mercenaries. However, they come highly recommended and are reputed to be fierce fighters.

Mikael is an enormous Russian who could easily be mistaken for a bear in both body and spirit. He even claims to have experience fighting vampires and I have no reason to doubt his veracity, or perhaps I simply choose not to.

Tom and Tim are Scottish twins, whom I am told fought valiantly in India and Africa. They are covered with tattoos, even upon their faces, and as they are identical it is the only way to tell them apart. They proved their usefulness to me by shooting out candle flames at fifty paces.

It is a small but fine force and we have ample rifles and handguns loaded with silver bullets and an ace up my sleeve. I hope it does not come down to me bringing out the big gun. I shall strive to make this a simple extraction with little bloodshed.

Teddy, if we fail in this, if the Black Bishop achieves whatever nefarious goal he has in mind, it can only mean trouble, not just for England but for the rest of the world. I leave it to you to warn our government and urge them to make ready. They may soon have a foe unlike any they have faced before.

LETTER II FROM ROBERT ROOSEVELT TO THEODORE ROOSEVELT, 6TH OF MAY 1880

Dear Theodore,

Success! Partial success, in any event.

When I arrived in Amesbury with my men we met up with Mr. Wilde and Miss Terry in the market square and they told us the prisoners were being held on an estate on the outskirts of town.

Ellen told us that Bram had been taken to Stonehenge. They believe he is to take part in a ritual. She seemed upset but very much in control of her emotions for a woman. As far as they knew, Noel and Henry Irving were still being held at the estate.

"Bram would want us to rescue Noel at the expense of his own life," Oscar said.

"Then we shall," I said. "Leave it to us." The Scottish brothers let out a banshee war cry that took us all by surprise, particularly a woman passing nearby with a young boy. She hurried him away, but the child stared back at us as he was being dragged along by the hand. He reminded me of you as a boy, Teddy, always so inquisitive and afraid of nothing. It gave me courage.

When we arrived at the estate, we took up position in the woods to observe.

There was a steady stream of carriages leaving the property and heading off to the east. This went on for a good two hours.

"With any luck the place will be near empty," Tim said, as the last carriage rolled through the gates.

"Aye. Time to make our move," Tom said. (At least that is what I think he said; his accent is rather thick and hard to decipher.)

Mikael grunted in approval.

Before I could say another word, the three of them were storming the house! So much for my hopes of a stealthy approach!

Like a fool I followed.

Mikael kicked down the door and Tim and Tom shot two vampires in the foyer straight away, hitting them right between the eyes. They exploded into goo, as I have learned the newly created ones often do, and we fanned out.

Tim took control of the situation and ordered Mikael to take the ground floor while he and Tom searched upstairs. They rushed up the stairs and I followed, if for no other reason than to ensure they didn't accidentally shoot the child in their zeal.

Two more vampires rushed towards us at the top of the stairs, but in short order they were nothing but sticky puddles on the richly carpeted floor. A vampire was guarding a door, but he fled in terror as he saw the redheaded brothers screaming towards him. It was actually cheering to realise that not all vampires were willing to die for the Bishop's mad scheme.

Nevertheless, I fired my Colt revolver, hitting him in the back, and the bullet exploded through his chest.

I kicked in the door and found a nursemaid holding Noel. She was cowering in fear in the corner and seemed human enough.

The two brothers continued to run up and down the hallway kicking in doors and screaming. I didn't hear any shots fired so I reckon they didn't find anybody behind them.

"You need not fear us, we are the rescue committee," I told her. I could see a wave of relief come over her and she hugged the infant closer. I asked her where the other prisoners were being held and she told me she thought they were in the cellar. I herded her out the door and called to my Scotsmen.

Mikael was already in the cellar when we arrived. Barred cells lined one end of the room. The piles of goo on the floor indicated he had killed at least three vampires.

"Two vampires are locked away. I kill dem now?" Mikael asked.

"Not yet," I told him. "Mr. Irving, are you down here?"

"Yes," he called from one of the cells. "I'm over here."

I had to retrieve the key from one of the disgusting piles of guts to free him.

"Release me as well," a foreign voice called from the other cell.

"Do not let him out," Irving warned.

"Me kill?" Mikael asked eagerly.

"No," Irving said. "He too is an enemy of the Black Bishop, but I don't know if we can trust him."

"Let me out or you will regret it," the unseen vampire said. "I am a valuable ally. More importantly, you do not want *me* as your enemy."

"I'm sorry, but Wilkins can control you," Irving replied. "He will just make you turn on me whether you want it or not. If I can get the spear away from him, I will come back and free you."

As we left, the prisoner starting yelling what I took to be obscenities in a foreign language.

Then, in English, he said, "I gave you freedom, Irving. You owe me the same!"

"And I shall repay you if I can," Irving said, then ushered us out of the cellar.

"We must get word to Stoker that we have freed his son," I said. "He needs to know the Black Bishop no longer has anything to hold over him."

I sent Mikael to accompany the wet nurse and Noel back to London. I wanted the baby far away from the place as soon as possible.

Tim, Tom and I will now meet up with Ellen and Oscar at Stonehenge. But first I must retrieve my Gatling gun.

I feel we may just win this thing, Teddy!

LETTER III FROM ROBERT ROOSEVELT TO THEODORE ROOSEVELT, 6TH OF MAY 1880

Dear Theodore,

This will be my last letter before our final rescue. I am on a hill overlooking Stonehenge with Oscar, Ellen, Henry and my Scottish mercenaries. I suspect the ceremony will begin at sundown, which is about an hour away. All attempts to send Miss Terry off to safety have met with her adamant refusal.

Since learning the nature of our foes, I have invested a considerable sum in silver bullets, much to the amusement of the armorer who made them for me. We have them loaded into rifles and the Gatling gun, which is set up in its wheeled cart. We are too far away for the Gatling gun to be useful in our assault, but it should fully protect our fallback position on top of the hill.

Irving can move, literally, in the blink of an eye. The plan is for him to grab Bram and make a break for the top of the hill. Any vampires pursuing us are in for a nasty surprise when they face a hail of silver bullets from our gun.

The sun has set and at least a hundred people (vampires?) are surrounding the ruins. For what purpose, I know not.

A round stone table has been brought in and placed to the side of the structure. I fear the worst as it looks like the stone table we saw atop that Aztec temple, the one used for human sacrifice! Channels are carved around its perimeter leading to a spout, like a mortician's table used to drain a body of blood. Workers are digging a small trench from the table into the center of the ruins and lining it with clay pipes.

Now that we are here, the task seems more daunting than it did back in Amesbury. Wish me luck, Teddy, and if I don't come back, remember me fondly, and take care of my children.

Uncle Robert

WHITE WORM SOCIETY BLACK BISHOP REPORT, 6TH OF MAY 1880

Operative: Anna Hubbard
Location: Amesbury, England

So much to report; I fear I cannot possibly do justice to the events I have seen, but I will try.

My attempts to infiltrate the Order of the Golden Dawn and ascertain the Black Bishop's identity have been successful.

The Black Bishop is the Reverend Richard Wilkins, a vicar at Salisbury Cathedral. How a low-level member of the clergy has come to garner and wield so much supernatural power I do not know, but it would be a worthwhile subject of investigation for the Society.

Reverend Wilkins has single-handedly managed to create dozens of first-generation vampires by resurrecting the dark arts we of the White Worm Society have tried so hard to wipe from the face of the earth.

In addition, he has accomplished what we fear most: he has opened a door into the Other Realm. He thinks it to be hell, which makes his motivation even more chilling. Of course, he was unable to control its terrible power.

Following is an account of the ceremony and its immediate aftermath. There are still many unknowns that bear further investigation.

The ritual took place at Stonehenge, a place known to have a particularly close connection to the Other Realm. The moon was nearly full. Perhaps this was needed for opening the portal, or possibly the night was chosen just for the light the moon provided. (The Occult Ceremonies Division is investigating this question.)

Wilkins addressed the crowd dressed in flowing white druid robes. I think this was mostly for theatrics, but it is possible the robes held some supernatural significance. (I have referred the matter to the Magical Properties of Objects Division.)

"Come forth, the twelve," he commanded. I must say, he has a powerful voice when he wishes to employ it; I am a bit surprised he hasn't risen further in the Church, but perhaps it has been to his advantage to appear unassuming.

Twelve men took up places around the ruins, spaced evenly apart. They were clothed in the normal, modern fashion. They began to chant in unison in an unknown tongue. At the completion of their chant, they knelt before the stones.

"Tonight," the Black Bishop intoned to the crowd. "Tonight we open the gates of hell and bring forth the dragon of everlasting life."

A young man – who appeared to my eye to be not quite in possession of his faculties – was brought to him by two black-clad minions.

"All hail the future King of England, Prince Edward!" the Bishop proclaimed.

I was shocked at this introduction. It was all I could do not to run away at that very moment and alert the authorities to rescue His Royal Highness.

The crowd cheered in unison, "All hail the future King!"

Another man, apparently a prisoner, was brought through the crowd to a round stone table outside the circle of stones. I recognised him at once from my investigations at the Lyceum Theatre as Bram Stoker. He clutched an ample leather physician's bag. The men who brought him forwards – I believe they were vampires – handled him roughly, though he did not struggle.

The Black Bishop turned to him and said, "Bram, we thank you for your blood, freely given to usher in a new era of peace and righteousness for all mankind. It is only fitting on such a momentous night that some of your friends have come to wish you well. I hope you will be as pleased as I am to see them."

Vampires dragged a woman and a man, whom I recognised as the actors Ellen Terry and Henry Irving, before the Bishop. Irving was bound in silver chains, which I can only assume means he is a vampire! (Imagine, a vampire right under our noses running the most prestigious theatre in London. At least he appears to be on the outs with the Bishop and a foe to his plans. Could there be 'good' vampires? The Supernatural

Creatures Division assures me they know of none such in the past.) Irving fell to his knees, the effect of the chains too much to bear. I could hear his skin sizzle where the silver touched his wrists and neck.

More henchmen brought two other men through the crowd to stand before the Bishop. One was Oscar Wilde; the second I had seen at the Lyceum, but never learned his name. Another vampire followed, pulling a Gatling gun in a cart.

"I fear, however, that they have not come with pure motives." The Bishop looked down at them, smiling. "Oh, Oscar, Oscar, when will you realise that I have been and always will be one step ahead of you? I knew you would try to free Stoker and Henry. I admit I was surprised you decided to use brute force. I thought you more of a strategist. However, all it took was to offer a reward for your capture and within hours your own mercenaries showed up at my door to collect."

Two red-headed, heavily tattooed identical twins waved to the crowd, grinning.

"They told me what your merry band had up your sleeves." He turned to the twins. "However, perhaps it was unfair of me not to tell you before that I hate turncoats, especially those who have killed my people." The fools' grins faltered as the Bishop commanded, "Mr. Dripp, Miss le Fey, give them their rewards."

Two of the vampires pounced on the twins, and their smiles and lives were quickly drained away to much delight from the crowd. They fell dead at the Bishop's feet within moments.

The Bishop walked over to the Gatling gun to admire it. He addressed the man with Wilde. "I must admit, Mr. Roosevelt, you have some very big sleeves. I take it you planned to mow us all down with this toy?"

The crowd laughed and booed.

"Stoker, Noel is safe! You don't have to do this," Wilde yelled, as he struggled to free himself from the clutches of a large vampire. The monster forced him to his knees.

The Bishop smiled. "Safety is an illusion, Mr. Wilde. I allowed the Russian to take Noel back to his mother as a sign of good faith. I can get him back anytime I choose. But Bram and I have an understanding, don't we, Bram?"

"Go to hell, Wilkins!" the one named Roosevelt spat. (Note: He is an American. Ask the U.S. chapter of the Society to check their records for the name Roosevelt.)

"No need, not when I can bring hell here." Wilkins smiled at his own joke.

The crowd roared with laughter and shook with thunderous applause.

The Bishop raised his hand and silenced the crowd. "Mr. Stoker has a plan that might save his throat from being cut. While I realise this may disappoint some of you, I admire his initiative. I hope it works, for his sake. Go ahead, Bram, pour your blood onto the stone, the way we rehearsed it."

Stoker took a bottle from his bag, spoke something in what sounded to be Latin and then proclaimed in English, "I, Abraham Stoker, do give this blood willingly." He uncorked the bottle and poured it into a channel carved into the surface of the stone table. The blood flowed halfway around the perimeter of the table, slowed to a crawl and stopped.

"Not quite enough," the Black Bishop said.

Stoker pulled another bottle from the bag, uncorked it and poured its contents onto the table. The blood flowed around then down a spout and into a trench laid out to the centre of the stone circle. Still, the blood did not reach the centre. The Bishop smiled patiently.

Stoker took yet another bottle and added its contents to the table. This was enough liquid to push it all the way to the centre.

The crowd became eerily silent as it waited with anticipation for something to happen. And they waited. Nothing. Finally, Wilkins spoke.

"Oh, I am sorry, Bram, truly," he said, and he did sound it. "It does appear that we need fresh blood. This is often the way with magical forces, I have found. A bit old-fashioned, but there you are." He snapped his fingers and two vampires grabbed Stoker, threw him onto the table and tied his four limbs to it, securing the ropes through holes carved near the edge of the table. The Black Bishop approached, drew a knife and put it to Stoker's throat.

"No!" Miss Terry screamed.

"Ellen," Stoker yelled. "Please, this must be. For Noel's sake and yours."

"I will make it quick, dear lady," the Bishop said. Someone in the crowd yelled, "Not too quick!" and some laughed, though the Bishop looked irritated. When there was silence again, he started to chant in Latin.

Then something happened. Perhaps the bottled blood only needed a few moments to properly soak into the earth, but suddenly the ground trembled with such force that everyone lost their footing.

Plumes of smoke and beams of light started to come forth from the ground, as though subterranean pressure was building and forcing its way out through small cracks in the earth. A glowing red ring appeared all around the stone ruins.

Then, a shaft of the most intense light, I swear as bright as the sun, shot into the sky. I could no longer see the stones and had to shield my eyes or go blind.

A few moments later the ground ceased its shaking. The pillar of light was gone. The stones were gone. Only a hole remained, about thirty feet in diameter, emitting the foul smell of sulphur. An eerie red glow emanated from its depths. Humans and vampires got to their feet and cautiously approached the gaping pit.

The red glow intensified and brightened.

"It comes! Quick, the net!" the Black Bishop yelled.

A flame shot out of the hole – followed by a large red dragon! Its torso was the size of a baby elephant and its head protruded forwards on a long, writhing neck. The hole was too small for it to flap its wide, leathery wings, so it clawed its way out, screeching and belching fire.

Several vampires threw a silver net over the creature and pulled it out of the hole. Though the silver did not appear to burn the creature, it did seem to weaken it.

One of the vampires manning the ropes was hit by a blast of fire and went up like a Roman candle. A lasso was thrown around the cruel-looking beak to force it shut.

They wrestled the beast all the way out of the hole and someone rushed over and put a silver stake through its webbed foot. It writhed in pain.

Many vampires descended upon it and tied body and neck to the ground with ropes and stakes. The Bishop himself muzzled the creature with an extra silver chain. It quickly learned that breathing fire out its nostrils earned it another jab with a silver stake so, once bound, it collapsed in defeat and remained still, except for heavy, laboured breathing and tiny puffs of smoke from its nose.

The crowd cheered once again.

With the creature subdued, Wilkins patted it on the snout, as if it were his pet. "With this dragon's blood, we usher in a new Golden Age."

He took the dagger he had only moments before had at Stoker's throat and made a small incision in the soft flesh of the beast's neck. A robed vampire handed the Black Bishop a chalice and he collected some of the blood.

He gave the cup to the prince, who guzzled it down. The crowd cheered and the prince stumbled around as if drunk.

Wilkins filled the vessel again and held it high to the crowd, proclaiming, "I now join your ranks."

He muttered and gestured over the cup (praying?) and the crowd cheered. And then, the noise of something else. A small rumble. The crowd was too transfixed on their leader to notice what I saw plainly; there was dirt falling away into the hole. It was rapidly becoming bigger. Then the ground shook violently, shaking the Bishop's cup so hard it spilt its contents before he could drink it.

A monstrous roar shot from the hole, a sound so loud and horrible I had to cover my ears for fear of bursting an eardrum. Dirt exploded into the sky and an enormous white worm shot out like a whale breaching an ocean of earth. It was truly the largest white worm I have ever laid eyes on – at least twice the size of the one we encountered in Nevada – as long as a locomotive and as wide as a house.

Many, including the Black Bishop, fled in terror. Others were too stunned to move or fainted outright. Some ran towards it, compelled, perhaps, by something in its nature calling to something in theirs.

Part of the creature, I knew not how much, remained underground while the top part writhed and flailed over a terrified crowd. It had no eyes, only a gaping, circular maw of teeth, dripping with saliva. It hungrily scooped up all in its reach, swallowing humans and vampires whole as if they were flies feeding a frog.

I retreated to what I thought to be a safe distance, hiding behind a row of now-tipped carriages. I freed the horses and they ran off into the night. I thought for a moment of joining them but realised how important it was for me to record these events.

Its hungry mouth snapped just feet away from where Stoker was tied to the table, just out of the beast's range. It sniffed and quickly discovered that he was the only live thing left nearby – aside from the dragon, which was so close that the worm seemed unable to contort itself enough to reach it.

The ground was loosening, and more and more of its grotesque body was wriggling its way out. With each lunge and snap of its mouth, it moved closer to Stoker, who was struggling fiercely to free himself.

I had lost track of the prisoners in the chaos of so many people screaming and fleeing. But then I heard gunfire. Mr. Roosevelt had got to the Gatling gun and was firing at the fleeing vampires. Dozens exploded at once.

"Robert, the worm!" Wilde screamed.

Roosevelt turned the big gun on the worm. The bullets pierced its flesh and it roared in pain, but then the gun jammed.

The creature continued its frenzied attempts to snatch up Mr. Stoker as Mr. Roosevelt turned his attention to unjamming the gun.

"Help me, Oscar!" Miss Terry pleaded, running towards Bram who looked at her in alarm.

"Ellen, no!" he cried. "The worm is too close, you'll never untie me in time. Free Henry – we need his speed and strength now."

With an agonised look at Stoker, Miss Terry rushed over to Irving and tried to remove his chains, but his ankles and wrists were manacled and locked. She picked up a rock and started to pound at the locks.

"I have an idea," Wilde yelled. Then he just stood there, paralysed in fear as we all were.

"What?" Ellen yelled. She had managed to break the lock on Irving's ankles and was working on the wrists.

"You won't like it," Wilde said. "Could make things worse."

"How could they possibly be *worse*?" Stoker yelled. The worm was so close to him now he was being sprayed with the creature's spit.

"It's now or never, Oscar," Roosevelt yelled. He stopped trying to unjam the gun as it was apparent it was not going to happen.

"Oh, bloody hell," Wilde yelled (or some such expletive), and started to run. He was going for the dragon!

He pulled the stake out of the beast's foot and began yanking up the roped stakes. After only a few were loosened the dragon broke free, casting off the silver net. It used its talons to rip the muzzle off its beak and let out a roar of flame that nearly hit Wilde, who dropped to the ground and covered his head.

It took to the air, circling the worm. I could tell it was looking to go home and was upset the worm was blocking its way. It screeched and cried.

Wilde's plan worked. The worm's attention turned to the dragon.

The dragon let out a huge roar and blasted flame onto the worm, producing a nauseating smell of brimstone and burned flesh. The worm screeched in pain, the noise terrible and deafening.

"Hooray for the dragon," Roosevelt yelled. He ran to Stoker.

Wilde sprang to his feet and grabbed the dagger that the Black Bishop had dropped. He and Roosevelt started cutting Stoker free.

The dragon flew past the worm and turned back for another attack. The worm gave one large heave and freed itself further, enough for it to extend itself in the direction of the dragon and grab it with its jaws.

With a quick flip of its neck, it tossed the dragon down its throat, snapped its mouth closed and swallowed. The worm belched a plume of fire and then swooped down to finish off Roosevelt, Stoker and Wilde.

Wilde ducked under the table, cowering in fear. Stoker was partially free and he and Roosevelt were frantically trying to remove the remaining ropes.

The worm snapped again, hitting and crumbling part of the stone table. Wilde rolled away in the nick of time, but Stoker collapsed with the table. A large piece of broken stone now pinned his leg.

Wilde and Roosevelt tried in vain to remove the stone and free Stoker's leg.

"Save yourselves," Stoker commanded.

"Any of that blood of yours left?" Wilde asked. "Maybe it closes the hole as well as opening it."

"As you can see, Oscar, the hole is currently blocked," Stoker said.

"Maybe we can unblock it! Where is the bloody blood!"

"In the bag. It fell somewhere over there!" Stoker yelled, pointing to the doctor's bag just a foot away. Unfortunately, it was a foot closer to the worm's grasp.

Wilde dived for the bag, and the worm dived for Wilde!

Wilde pulled a bottle from the bag and was frantically trying to unlatch the stopper. Then, in one quick gulp, Wilde was swallowed up!

Ellen screamed and ran towards the worm. Roosevelt sprinted forwards and grabbed her, holding her back.

The worm lifted itself up straight and swallowed. You could actually see the shape of Wilde moving his way down the throat and disappearing into the depths of the worm's stomach!

Then the worm suddenly grew still, stiff almost. It became eerily quiet.

After what seemed like minutes but was probably only seconds, it lurched forwards and vomited up Wilde at Stoker's feet. Wilde had the remains of the broken bottle in one hand and the dagger in the other. Bloody drool dripped down from the worm's maw. Its skin sizzled wherever a drop of blood touched it, and it flailed, apparently trying to rid itself of the noxious substance.

The earth shook once more. The glowing light returned and encircled the hole. The ground closed up like an iris on a camera, snapping the worm in half! What remained aboveground collapsed to earth with an enormous thud.

A blinding light once more shot into the sky, obliterating our view. The rumbling stopped and all was silent and then the light vanished as quickly as it had appeared. The stones were returned, undisturbed from their previous locations, every blade of grass and pebble replaced as if they had never been gone. All would have seemed as normal, except the top half of the worm's bloody body was coiled among the ruins, twitching and pulsating as the last of its life force oozed out of it.

Ellen and Robert ran over to Stoker and Wilde. Wilde was stunned and covered in saliva and vomit but appeared unharmed.

"Bloody hell, Stoker, you are paying for this suit," he said, shaking off the goo.

"Good job, Oscar," Roosevelt said, patting Wilde on the back. "What was it like in there?"

"Overly hot and unpleasantly wet, but I have been in worse places for longer."

Oscar and Roosevelt pulled off the stone pinning Stoker's leg and helped him to his feet. Ellen threw herself at him, nearly knocking him off his feet again, and enveloped him in a hug, which he gratefully returned.

"See, I told you it was your destiny to be a hero," she said.

"I did very little," Stoker complained. "It was Oscar who saved the day and my life."

"Once again it was your disagreeable blood that did the trick," Oscar said. "I was merely the hors d'oeuvre that delivered it."

"We can go home now," Ellen said, finally breaking her hug with Stoker.

"Not quite," Roosevelt said. He pointed over to a nearby area of thick grass. Prince Edward was hiding there, sobbing uncontrollably. "We need to get the prince back home."

A pistol made quick work of Irving's shackles and he was freed. Roosevelt rounded up a horse and they all loaded into a carriage.

When they had gone, I collected samples of the worm and its saliva. I also managed to gather a few drops of the dragon's blood that remained in the chalice and some of Stoker's blood from the stone table. All have been sent to Cardiff for testing. I set the worm on fire with kerosene, reducing it quickly to ashes.

May I also add that Supervisor D'Aurora agrees with me that Messrs. Stoker and Wilde would make valuable additions to the White Worm Society and its work. I feel recruiting them into our ranks should be an utmost priority.

– End Report –

THE EVENTS DISCUSSED HERE HAPPENED ON THE NIGHT OF THE 6TH OF MAY 1880

Archivist's note: This letter was delivered to the White Worm Society on 21st of April 1912. Is it a coincidence the letter was written just a day after Bram Stoker's death? It is unknown what motivated this unprecedented correspondence, but it does provide unique insight into the aftermath of 'the ceremony'. The details it contains match what we have learned from other sources, but this is certainly the most flamboyant account of that night.

So many lies written about me: lies in history and lies from the poison pen of Stoker.

I know you hunt me, obsessed with killing me as a trophy to add to your wall of monsters. But what is a monster? A cat is a monster to a sparrow. You are *my* monsters.

True monsters walk among you and they are men. They bring war and famine, slavery and death, yet you do not move against them. You should. A great war is brewing and the four horses of the apocalypse will be ridden by men.

The Black Bishop was one such man. You have no idea how close he came to the destruction of your entire world. The world of the Realm is like water and yours like oil; mixing them will just push your world aside. The Realm will burn your world off and take its place.

I have read the documents in your archive, for I have minions everywhere, even among the ranks of your 'secret society'. I have read the accounts of that night the door opened among the stones. More lies.

You give Stoker accolades, yet it was he who opened the door to the Realm because he was too weak to sacrifice himself and his son to keep the world safe. Fool. What good would it have done to save his son only to have him destroyed along with the world? My father sacrificed me as a hostage to the Turks to keep the peace of a kingdom. Stoker could not even muster the courage to sacrifice one child to save everyone in the world.

You hunt me? Fear me? Then blame Stoker for setting me free.

Here are the true events of that night.

After Wilde closed the hole to the Realm, the Bishop came to my prison cell in a rage and commanded me to chase down Stoker's carriage and rescue the prince. The blood on the Spear of Longinus gave him this power. I was no more than a dog on a chain and had to obey him, even as my hatred for him crouched taut in my chest like a tiger waiting for its moment to pounce.

We were off into the night. Like a common beast of burden, I carried him on my back and the vampires called Dripp, Leech and Wotton followed.

We quickly caught up to the carriage, near an old stone church and cemetery.

The vampire Irving felt our presence, but it was too late for I move like the wind. We descended on them. Dripp leapt upon Roosevelt, who was driving the carriage, while Wotton and Leech killed the horses, then dragged Wilde and Irving from the carriage and held them. I held Stoker. He went limp in my arms as if he knew all was lost.

Irving struggled and broke free from Leech.

"Mind yourself, Henry," the Bishop said to Irving, who was clearly gauging the best strategy for attack. "Your friends' necks could be so easily broken." Irving stayed poised but made no move. Fool. Had he freed me when he had the chance, it would never have come to that.

The Bishop helped the woman out of the carriage. (I forget her name; she is not at all important to history, in any event.)

The prince was sprawled across the seat of the carriage, unconscious, as he dreamt the dream of the vampire. The fools were unaware that he was only moments from waking and would have slaughtered them all when he did.

The Bishop stomped about like a petulant child.

"Do you know what you have done?" he screamed in Stoker's

face. "I was to lead the world to righteousness. You have condemned millions of souls to eternal hell! The stars must be aligned just so. We cannot open this gate again for another hundred years."

"That is a relief," Wilde said. "Now we need only hope that the twentieth-century megalomaniac who tries to open it is every bit as incompetent as you." (His whiny little voice rings in my ears to this day! I should have crushed his windpipe!)

The Black Bishop walked over to Wilde and slapped him across the face, the only action I would ever thank him for. "You may think you have beaten me, but you have not. You have just made things more difficult. The second part of my plan will continue. The prince lies in that carriage in a fevered state because he is becoming a vampire even as we speak. And such a vampire he will be, made from the pure blood of the dragon!"

"You monster," the woman shrieked.

The Bishop smiled and continued. "After the prince turns the royal family into vampires I will control them with the spear." He held it up for the prisoners to see. It was old and tarnished, yet at such a close distance its power set my blood on fire. It was almost too much to bear.

"Then it will only be a matter of time before all the royal houses of Europe will fall under my control. My vampires are everywhere."

Suddenly a shot!

The fool Wotton had become so enthralled by the Bishop's prattling that he had loosened his grip and Wilde had pulled a pistol and shot at Dripp, who was clutching Roosevelt tightly from behind. He was as incompetent at shooting as he was irritating to listen to, for the bullet instead hit Roosevelt in the shoulder.

Wilde looked horrified at what he had done. Another weakling, afraid to make the sacrifices necessary to save the world.

Dripp laughed. Then a look of dread crossed his face and he let Roosevelt drop. The bullet had gone through Roosevelt and into Dripp. It must have just nicked his heart, for he stood for a few more seconds with a stupid look on his face before exploding.

Wotton pulled Wilde closer but Wilde got a second shot off, just as Wotton snatched the pistol away. The bullet hit me in the neck and Wilde looked at me in terror as I turned my furious gaze upon him. I staggered and Stoker slipped from my grasp and rushed to the woman, standing in front of her as if he could protect her. I fell to my knees, the pain of the silver bullet radiating through my body from the wound on my neck.

Wotton tightened his grip around Wilde's neck to the point I thought he would break it.

In the confusion, Irving made his move. He plunged his hand through Leech's chest, grabbed his heart and yanked it out. Leech had a moment to look at his death and actually laughed. "See all of you in—" Then he exploded, but I could hear a faint echo of, "…hell."

Wotton spun Wilde around and slammed him against the carriage.

In the chaos, Irving grabbed the wounded Roosevelt, made a run for the church and kicked down its door. Stoker and the woman seemed poised to make a stand against me. Foolish. They would not have been able to stop me had I turned my wrath upon them.

"Kill them!" the Bishop barked.

I was still shaking off the pain and healing myself. This only took moments (for my healing powers are great), but I was momentarily unable to give chase. Oddly, the pain broke the spell of the spear, and I was hoping to use this to my advantage.

Wotton was preoccupied with Wilde.

"First I'm going to drain you to the point just above death. Then I will kill your friends so you can hear their screams as you lie here, helpless. Then I will come back and torture you some more, just for amusement, before turning you into my slave. I shall have centuries to torment you!"

"Give me the damn gun," the Bishop commanded. "I'll finish them off myself."

Wotton tossed the gun to him and the Bishop came over to me.

"Get up!"

"Still too weak," I lied. By then I was almost back to normal.

Wilde, still held against the carriage by Wotton, remained defiant and silent.

"What, cat got your tongue?" Wotton asked. "Normally you can't shut up. Where is your great wit now?"

Wilde shrugged his shoulders and smiled.

Wotton opened his mouth wide and bared his fangs, dripping with saliva.

Wilde took a deep breath through his nose then spat a tiny silver cross he had been hiding in his mouth down Wotton's throat. Clever, I must admit.

With a look of shock on his face I found to be quite humorous, Wotton stumbled back, releasing his grip on Wilde. Stoker and the woman took the opportunity to make a break for the church.

The Bishop raised his gun to shoot him, but Irving rushed out of the church at full speed and knocked him down. Damn it all, he managed to maintain his grip on the spear.

"Help me!" the Bishop screamed. By now my strength was back and so too was the spear's influence. I was compelled to help him and attacked Irving.

Wotton fell to his knees choking, frantically trying to cough up the cross, but it was all in vain. He must have swallowed it further, for a small hole burned near his sternum. The cross pushed its way out, clinging to the singed flesh of Wotton's chest for a moment before dropping to the ground. A look of relief came across Wotton's face. Then a big, evil smile. He staggered to his feet, triumphant, not noticing the flames starting to smoulder in the hole in his chest.

Wilde, who had stopped, mesmerised by the scene, shouted, "That is for Derrick Pigeon, and for Frank Miles! You shall destroy no more lives, you pompous, depraved, vulgar wretch."

"I shall squash you like the bug you are," Wotton bellowed. However, before he could take another step forwards, his stomach belched out a large flame and it ignited his clothes.

Wotton ran towards me and Irving, screaming in agony. He nearly stumbled into us, almost setting us on fire in the process. Irving and I broke apart.

Irving took that moment to grab Wilde and rush back into the church.

Wotton fell to the ground and collapsed into a pile of smouldering goo.

"Into the church," the Bishop commanded me. "Kill them all!"

Into the church I went, dragged against my will by the invisible force of his anger.

The humans scattered like rats, except for Roosevelt, who was lying between pews, barely conscious. Irving attacked me and I sent him flying with a slap of my hand. He smashed into a pew and it shattered. A large piece of splintered wood impaled his lower back, emerging through his stomach. With the vampire down, the rest of them had no chance against my great strength.

The Bishop entered, waving that damned spear like he was a Roman emperor.

Irving writhed in pain, much to the Bishop's satisfaction. "You could have had so much, Henry, and you threw it all away." The Bishop turned to me. "Kill the rest of them, now!"

Hatred flared inside me, and its power helped me regain a bit of my own will.

I cornered Wilde by the altar. He cried in fear like a lamb before a wolf.

I saw a glint of silver from a dagger in Wilde's belt. "Stab me," I whispered, for anything would be better than being a fool's slave. I held myself back as long as I could, giving him time to recover his celebrated wits.

"I said kill him!" the Bishop barked again.

But I had given Wilde enough time to grab his dagger and stab me in the chest. The clumsy fool missed my heart by a good six inches.

I fell to the ground with the dagger in my chest. It was enough to break the spell momentarily. "Get that spear away from him!" I yelled. The pain was quickly leaving my body and the wound closing up and pushing out the knife. When the dagger fell to the ground, I would be back under the spear's influence.

Stoker, the woman and Wilde all rushed the Bishop at the same time. Stoker grabbed hold of the spear at the shaft just below the blade. But it was too late; the Bishop had raised the pistol and fired, hitting the woman in the leg.

Wilde grabbed the gun, but the Bishop held on tightly.

Stoker cried out the woman's name (Helen?) in vain.

"Back!" the Bishop yelled, firing another shot, this time at Stoker, and missing him by inches.

Stoker and Wilde did as they were commanded.

"And you, Henry," he said to Irving, who had freed himself and was struggling to his feet. "Stay where you are," he said, pointing his gun more squarely at Stoker. He held the spear tightly in his left hand.

Seeing the woman crying in pain, Stoker took a step towards her.

"Stop!" the Bishop yelled. "She will be out of her misery soon enough, as will you all."

"Think of what you are doing, Wilkins," Stoker said. He held his palm out as if he could stop another bullet from hitting the woman. "Is cold-blooded murder part of your new world order?"

"It is for those who try to stop me," the Bishop screamed.

Suddenly Stoker rushed towards him, his arm out squarely in front of him, and purposely plunged his open hand onto the blade of the spear. The tip pierced through his palm and out the back of his hand. He did not wince in pain. His eyes held only a steely determination of which, I will admit, I would not have guessed him capable.

"You don't scare me, little man," he said. Blood dripped from his pierced hand.

Wilkins yanked the spear away, ripping the blade out of his flesh. Stoker took a step back, his hand now gushing blood.

The Black Bishop laughed. "Now what did that accomplish, Bram? Who's the little man now?"

What Stoker had accomplished – whether through brilliance or a foolish accident I do not know – was to cover the blood on the spear with his own, taking away its power. I suddenly found myself completely free of it!

Wilkins spat. "Kill this one first," he commanded me, pointing at Wilde.

"Maybe second," I hissed, sinking my fangs into his neck. I tasted surprise, fear and despair in his blood. I drained away his arrogance. Nothing had ever tasted sweeter, to my living or Un-Dead tongue. The spear clattered to the stone floor, no more a threat to me now than the arrows shot at me by doomed villagers all those centuries ago.

"Turn me," he gasped when I paused for a moment to savour his defeat. "Please. Together we can still reshape the world."

"I do not seek to change the world," I said. "Nor would I need a partner to do so. The only thing we will share, Mr. Wilkins, is this."

And I drank again. I drained him until his heart fluttered its final beat, then ripped his head off out of spite and tossed it into the baptismal font.

The humans looked at me, terrified, and Irving got to his feet, readying himself to defend them to the best of his ability. I should have killed them – at least Stoker before he could write his damnable book.

Few people learn my true nature and live to tell about it. But it is what Wilkins wanted me to do and I would not give him anything, even in death. I wiped the blood from my face and, with a dismissive wave, urged them about their business. "You are safe from me. Tonight," I said.

Wilde and Irving rushed to Roosevelt's aid, while Stoker tended to the woman's leg. The bullet had not gone through the bone and she was surprisingly brave about it, not even losing consciousness as women so often do at the sight of blood.

As I left, I told them, "Stoker's blood will turn the prince back into a human, but you must hurry before the demon takes hold. After that, it might kill him."

"So, his blood is not my salvation," Irving said, dejected.

"No," I said. "There is no cure for us. We are doomed to walk the earth forever, thirsty for life."

I paused again on the way out of the church. Roosevelt lay on the floor before me, barely alive from his gunshot wound. Wilde was pressing a handkerchief to the wound futilely.

To this day I do not know what came over me. Perhaps it was gratitude for my regained freedom. I bit my wrist and pressed it to Roosevelt's lips.

"Drink, it will save you."

He refused.

"It will not make you a vampire to take a small amount of my blood, but it will save your life."

He sipped and it revived him; my last act of charity, I can assure you.

This is the true account of what happened that night. You have *me* to thank for killing the Bishop.

As for your little Society, I continue to let you live because I do not want the Realm opened any more than you do. You serve me, even if you think you do not.

This is my world, and *my* world it shall stay.

LETTER FROM DR. SEWARD TO DR. WILLIAM GULL, ROYAL PHYSICIAN, 22ND OF MAY 1880

I have thoroughly examined the prince and must say he has made a remarkable recovery. The madness that ravaged his brain brought about by his head trauma and childhood typhoid fever has subsided.

Gone are his delusions and his manic behaviour. He is able to speak with us in a coherent manner, though he has no recollection of the last two years. Perhaps that is for the best.

I do not know what led to this cure. I wish I could say it has something to do with his treatment here, but alas I cannot. I can only attribute it to an act of God.

I see no reason he cannot return home and to his studies. I turn his care over to you, Dr. Gull. Please let me know if his odd behaviours return.

Sincerely,

Dr. Seward

FROM THE *LONDON TIMES*, SOCIETY PAGE, 25TH OF MAY 1880

WILDE ANIMAL FOUND IN ZOO

25 May 1880 – Regent's Park
This morning, a keeper at the London Zoo discovered a new exhibit, of the Homosapien-Drunkard type. The zookeeper was shocked to discover a naked man in the wolf cage 'sleeping one off'.

The man, later identified as William 'Willie' Wilde, is the son of Lady Jane Wilde.

Well known for his carousing, Mr. Wilde has taken it to new heights.

"Found him curled up among the sleeping wolves. Why they didn't eat him is anybody's guess," said zookeeper Peter Butcher.

Wilde was fined five pounds and released into the custody of his brother Oscar, who, when asked to comment on the incident, would say only, "My brother has always been fond of dogs."

This comes after reports of a wolf loose in Mayfair last night, but Mr. Butcher insists all the zoo's wolves are accounted for. If Mr. Wilde did let any of them out they have returned to their cages without incident.

LAST PAGES OF OSCAR WILDE'S UN-PRODUCED PLAY

Archivist's note: The White Worm Society has been unable to locate any source material that explicitly details Derrick Pigeon's actions, location or fate beyond the night when Willie Wilde saw him leave with the other vampires. What follows is an excerpt of an unfinished play by Wilde titled, Eternal; or Death of a Fallen Angel. *Though the play was never completed, it was dedicated 'To DP, always'.*

MAURICE'S FLAT, NIGHT

A storm rages outside, rain, thunder and lightning. It is dim, lit only by the light of the fireplace and occasional lightning strikes.

Maurice enters with a lit lamp held out in front of him.

Maurice: What kind of hell has broken outside? *(He goes to the window to watch the storm.)* I fear a flood has begun.

A knock at the door. Maurice hurries to open it and is stunned to see Christopher outside, carrying a large framed painting; it is the portrait of Christopher that George had painted. After an agonised moment, Maurice makes a decision and steps back, holding the door.

Maurice: *(his voice resigned)* Christopher. I suppose you had better come in.

Christopher: *(entering)* Aren't you glad to see me, Maurice?

He drops the painting and embraces his friend. After a moment, Maurice returns the embrace, then steps back, studying Christopher, trying to discern the change in him.

Maurice: I suppose I am. But I would have been happier had I found you weeks ago. I searched for you. I enlisted friends, we tried to rescue you.

Christopher: I was rescued. Rescued from the spectre of death, and the depravity of human nature.

Maurice: So I heard. You have been turned. I shall kill Willingham for this.

Christopher: You'll have to go through me first.

Maurice: You are under his control, Christopher, I understand that. But when I kill him, you shall be free. You will still be…as you are, but perhaps we can find a cure. I know someone who is searching for one, and….

Christopher: I do not wish to be cured. No one forced me to submit, it was my choice. Immortality is what I always wanted, after all.

Maurice: But I don't understand. They dragged you away, screaming in the night.

Christopher: Foolishness. I was frightened. Too timid to take so bold a step and embrace the power and destiny that was being offered to me.

Christopher begins to slowly circle the grief-stricken and horrified Maurice, like a venomous snake circling and mesmerising its prey.

Christopher: But you know in your heart, Maurice, that I could not accept an ordinary life of ageing, decrepitude and death, a menial existence among menial folk. I am meant for so much more, for life and adventure, glory and eternal youth, and a seat among the powerful. It has always been so that the wise and bold rule over the stupid and meek. The Black Bishop, he has given me everlasting life. Let me give it to you, Maurice.

Christopher stops behind Maurice, running a hand over Maurice's neck. Maurice is frozen in agonising indecision.

Christopher: Eternity, Maurice, for the two of us. It's what we talked about, what we both wanted. I know you've thought about it, dreamt about it. How could you not?

Maurice: *(weakening)* I have thought about you. Dreamt about you.

Christopher: Then this is the way. The only way.

He leans in to Maurice's neck, but at the last moment, Maurice pulls away.

Maurice: What good is everlasting life if one loses one's soul?

Christopher: The soul weighs so little, Maurice, you hardly miss it at all.

Maurice: And yet it keeps me tethered to something greater than myself.

Christopher: *(growing annoyed)* It keeps you tethered to the dirt of the earth. It keeps you tethered to death.

Maurice: Death is the only thing we all share, the only thing that binds us together and makes us human. The poorest man and the richest king all share the same fate.

Christopher: And you think that makes them nobler, somehow, than I?

Maurice: It makes them human, as God and nature intended them to be.

Christopher: Do you know where I grew up, Maurice?

Maurice: No.

Christopher: In the East End. My mother was a whore who sold her body for gin. And do you know where she plied her trade?

Maurice remains silent.

Christopher: She would wait at the side door of St. Paul's Cathedral. The human churchmen did nothing to save her, they just watched her go off with man after man. Many of them were clergy themselves. When she went mad from syphilis they put her down like a dog. The Black Bishop sees the folly and corruption of men and means to make them pay for their lack of humanity!

Maurice: Those men were hypocrites, but no more so than your leader; he wants them to have humanity but also wants to take it away. As he took yours away.

Christopher: As a human, I was like a child. I have grown up and have become so much more.

Maurice: A slave to that which made you. You have become less than what you were; a servant can choose to be a servant, but you have lost your free will.

Christopher: We are all someone's slave and someone's master. I chose to serve Willingham and he serves the Bishop.

Maurice: A chain of monsters leading all the way down to hell!

Christopher: The Black Bishop is no monster. He isn't even a vampire. He has chosen to keep his humanity.

Maurice: So, he is king of the vampires by election then? What is this power he wields over them?

Christopher: He has been chosen by God to lead. He has been given a talisman, the very spear that pierced the side of Jesus Christ. The blood on the spear calls on us all to help him rule.

Maurice: So, if I held this spear I would be king? There is no divine provenance in that.

Christopher: God showed him where the spear was and how to use it. The Black Bishop does not wield the spear, it wields him.

Maurice: To what end?

Christopher: A glorious rebirth of the world. A thousand years of peace, then the Second Coming. Let me turn you and you can witness the return of Christ for yourself.

Maurice: To watch the humans ascend to heaven while we who waited get thrown into hell?

Christopher: Those who serve the Bishop will be saved, so it is written in the secret bible, the Book of the Dragon.

Maurice: Oh, the secret bible, why didn't you say so? Listen to yourself, Christopher! You've thrown away your humanity, your free will and your soul because some madman told you it is the will of God?

Christopher: And you would turn down eternal life because some other madman convinced you that you have a soul! Become one of us, Maurice. You have no idea what it's like. All fear is gone, giving me such peace as you could never know. I experience things you can't imagine. Sensual pleasures are heightened; the night is alive with sounds I've never heard before. Even the wind on my face feels different, like the breath of a lover.

Christopher picks up the portrait from the floor, admiring it.

Christopher: I will not face death. I will live forever. This portrait George painted of me will decay and rot away long before I do.

Maurice: The eyes in that painting display more life then those gazing upon it!

Christopher stares at the painting and knows this to be true. It angers him and he smashes it against the mantle, shattering the frame into pieces.

Christopher: I shall not burn in the fires of hell – this wretched picture will!

He rips the canvas away from what is left of the frame, wads it up and stuffs it into the fire.

With Christopher's back still turned, Maurice grabs a splintered piece of the frame from the floor, rushes over to Christopher and plunges the wooden shard into his back.

Christopher screams in pain and falls back into Maurice's arms.

Maurice: Forgive me!

Christopher: (*dying breath*) You fool! You could have had immortality!

Maurice: I know. I will live a short life full of pain and misery. But it will be my choice.

For a moment Christopher regains his humanity.

Christopher: Maurice? Is that you?

Maurice: Yes.

Christopher: Thank you for freeing me from that soul cage. One second in your arms and I'm gratefully drawn to heaven.

Stage goes black.

Archivist's note: The last line spoken by Christopher is struck out, with a note written in the margins: 'Drivel. I shall never be a writer until I can write the truth!'

LETTER FROM HENRY IRVING TO DR. VICTOR MUELLER, 31ST OF MAY 1880

Dear Dr. Mueller,

I regret to inform you that Reverend Richard Wilkins is deceased. As his closest friend, I was tasked with going through his unfinished correspondence and other personal business.

I was quite intrigued to read letters from you that were forwarded by the estate of his acquaintance, Lord Sundry. I hope I am not invading your privacy, but I can assure you as executor of his will I shall keep the strictest confidence.

From his journals, I know he was quite taken with your work regarding the life-giving properties of electricity. By the contents of your letters, I take it he has sent you blood samples to be examined. I, too, am quite curious as to the properties of said blood and would be very interested in helping you with your experiments and research. You see, the blood in question comes from myself.

This ailment from which I suffer does have life-extending properties, but its other symptoms are such that I would prefer to be cured.

Please contact me if you have any thoughts on how such a cure might be possible.

Also, I see by this correspondence that Sundry sent you a map you had requested to certain locations in the American desert, specifically in the Nevada territory. May I enquire as to what was contained on the map?

Forgive me if I am too bold or asking you to betray confidences. However, Reverend Wilkins and I shared similar interests and I would be forever grateful if you would assist me in developing those interests further.

Sincerely,

Henry Irving

LETTER FROM FLORENCE STOKER TO ELLEN TERRY, DATE UNKNOWN

Dear Miss Terry,

Oh, to be a free spirit such as yourself! To throw all care to the wind and follow one's baser instincts; how freeing it must be. Necessary for your craft perhaps, or merely a character flaw; it matters not to me.

Leaving a trail of broken hearts and illegitimate children behind seems not to bother you, for you are always looking forward, a trait I can admire from a distance but not when it strays so close to me and mine.

Having almost lost my son and husband to monsters has given me a fresh perspective. We all lead such petty little lives that we try to fill with drama to keep ourselves distracted from the mundanity of it all. I forgive you your transgressions, I honestly do. I can understand how being so close to death would drive you to seek Bram's love.

I am partly to blame for pushing Bram away. I was having difficulty adjusting to married life and envied his 'glamourous' life in the theatre. I feel childish and foolish for not appreciating what I had. One day I will return to the stage with a new understanding of life and I hope it makes me a better actress.

All has healed now. We all get a fresh start. It is time for you to move on to your next conquest. I hope you find what it is you are looking for, but I assure you it is not my husband.

With best wishes,

Florence Stoker

LETTER FROM BRAM STOKER TO ELLEN TERRY, DATE UNKNOWN

Ellen,

Florence knows. I have confessed all. And yet she forgives me all my transgressions. This, along with the good Lord saving my life (even if at the hands of Oscar Wilde!), has given me a second chance at the life I had planned for myself and my family. A life I cannot refuse a second time.

I am sorry.

I will forever be grateful for your concern and affection in my time of need. If you wish to never speak to me, except in theatre matters, I shall understand, but I am and will always be your friend.

Florence says she also forgives you and I believe she does. She wanted me to tell you that you and I have been in a war. The spectre of war causes people to do things not in their nature, or perhaps because of it. In any event, she would step aside. It was up to me to choose.

I choose her and hope you will understand.

A part of me dies today.

Forever in your debt,

Bram Stoker

One thing alone we lack. Our souls, indeed,
Have fiercer hunger than the body's need.
Ah, happy they that look in loving eyes.
The harsh world round them fades.
In the sweetest music bids their souls rejoice
And wakes an echo there that never dies.

LETTER FROM ELLEN TERRY TO BRAM STOKER, DATE UNKNOWN

Dear Bram,

I cannot say I am not disappointed and heartbroken in your decision, but I do understand and bear you no ill will.

I have told Henry that I need some time off to tend to personal matters.

One must keep up appearances and it is time I return home to my husband for a while.

It has been ages since I have seen my children, and I will visit them as well if their father will let me. I shall return next year to the theatre, for I cannot be away from it for long. My husband has agreed to move to London so I can continue my career.

Farewell for now, Bram. I send my best wishes to Florence and Noel. They are very fortunate to have you.

Sincerely,

Ellen

FROM THE DIARY OF OSCAR WILDE, 3RD OF SEPTEMBER 1880

Dear yours truly,

I am glad to be done with monster hunting and am turning my attentions to a new horror: the terrible artistic tastes of my countrymen. I have written some essays on aesthetics that the *Strand* has taken an interest in publishing.

I must say it is quite nice to make a living again, but it is keeping me very busy and I haven't much time for a social life.

I have visited Frank in the sanatorium and he is making good progress. The doctors tell me he will be getting out soon. He seems fine to me, although he has taken to calling himself 'Jack', which I find to be a horrid nickname. The doctors say it is all part of rejecting his old self for a new one or some such nonsense. However, if that is the only scar he bears from what he has witnessed, I will be happy to live with it.

I haven't seen much of Stoker and Florrie, which I suppose is just as well. We all are trying to put the horrible Black Bishop episode behind us and I am sure socialising would do little to help with that. Still, I am surprised to find that I miss them – both of them.

I was entertaining the notion of writing it all down, as I think it would make a riveting tale. I would fictionalise it, of course, as I would not want others to think me even more mad than they do now.

But this notion has been quashed by something called the White Worm Society if you can believe it, dear diary. An 'operative' named Miss D'Aurora called upon me the other day.

"We are a clandestine scientific society charged by the Queen to keep the world safe from those things that go bump in the night," she explained over tea. "As a literary man, you may want to publish your accounts of what took place at Stonehenge, but we, and your Queen, are respectfully asking you not to. Our main objective is to keep the doors between our world and the Realm closed. Any knowledge that these doors exist, and particularly any instructions on how to open them, must be suppressed at all costs."

When the Queen asks one to do – or not do – something, it is understood that it is not actually a request, so I agreed and gave my promise never to speak of the matter to the public. (She does not know about you, dear diary, and I shall not tell her.)

"We have told Mr. Stoker and the others the same thing and they too kindly agreed to keep the secret," she said. "Also, we would like to extend to you an invitation to join our society."

I tactfully refused any official membership. "I am often on thin ice with polite society. I am sure the same thing would eventually happen should I join yours. However, I will keep my eyes and ears open as I mingle with the masses. Should I discover anything out of the ordinary – a monster here, a madman there – I will be sure to let you know."

"We would be grateful," she said, then took her leave.

I shan't tell them of Willie's affliction, of course. Aside from a recent incident with no harm done we have that all under control.

I stopped by the Lyceum a few days later and asked Stoker if he had joined the White Worms.

"Good God, no! I am trying my best to forget all that has happened. I have no desire to attend meetings where monsters are discussed at length."

"You don't have the itch to pen a novel?" I asked him.

"I make a vow this very day to never write or speak of vampires again," he said, crossing his heart.

"That might be difficult," I said, "considering you work for one."

"Indeed," he sighed.

MEMO FROM HENRY IRVING TO THEATRE

DATE: 12 October 1880
FROM: Henry Irving
TO: Please post this for the entire company to read, and distribute as necessary.

Travel! It broadens one's horizons. I would like to take this time to announce we are going on tour. Not Europe this time, but a whole new continent!

Next summer we shall tour America. I hope to start in Boston and make our way across the country all the way to the Pacific Ocean. Dates are not yet set, but we shall perform in many cities, even bringing a touch of civilisation – dare I say art? – to the Wild West.

More details will be forthcoming. Until then, see Mr. Stoker with any questions.

LETTER TO BRAM STOKER FROM OSCAR WILDE, 1ST OF MARCH 1881

Dear Bram,

Now that I have made England safe from vampires, I think I can leave it in your capable hands for a time.

My lectures on aesthetics have become so popular that I am taking the show on the road. I have been invited to tour America and will be out of the country for at least half a year.

The timing is poor on my part. Perhaps you read about me and a certain Constance Lloyd in the gossip columns. (I certainly hope so; I went to great lengths to put us there.) But alas, I must leave to make my way in the world and have no time to settle down, though I surprisingly find that I wish to. A man is not complete until he is married, then he is finished.

When one leaves for the wild places of the world, one's mind turns to thoughts of mortality. In case I am stricken with smallpox or am scalped by Red Indians, I want you to know that I hold you in high regard and am forever in your debt.

If I make you the subject of jest it is only because I feel inferior to you in some ways. (Small ways.) (There, I did it again.) Truly, Bram, I strive to be a better man because of your influence and guidance.

My mind often turns to the horrible events of last year: the deaths of Derrick and Dr. Hesselius weigh heavily upon me. However, I also think of more positive things. I discovered I could be brave when required. (Though I do hope it will never be required again. It is quite exhausting.) And I value the friendships I formed in the mystery of the hunt and the heat of battle, none more so than yours.

Give Florrie and Noel a hug from me.

I shall forever be your friend and confidant.

Yours truly,

O.W.

P.S.

Remember to enjoy yourself from time to time. I think God owes you a little sin in exchange for saving all of mankind. And you can tell him I said so.

P.P.S.

Shave off the beard.

LETTER FROM BRAM STOKER TO OSCAR WILDE, 2ND OF MARCH 1881

Dear Oscar,

This is an astounding coincidence: someone else will have to protect England from the forces of darkness for I, too, will be travelling to America soon. The entire Lyceum company will be touring Canada and the United States.

I am looking forward to expanding my horizons with travel, but not to the logistics involved in moving forty-some actors and stagehands – plus assorted sets, props and costumes – across the Atlantic, nor to arranging lodgings, trains and stagecoaches across the continent.

It should be a ripping adventure and not the supernatural kind to which we are accustomed. Florence and Noel are coming with me, although Florence refuses to go west of the Mississippi River for fear of bandits and savages. Henry has promised to cast her in some of the productions, so I am sure that will be enough to lure her into the Wild West.

It will be pleasant to get away from England and from the harassment of the White Worm Society. They continue to pester me to join their ranks and use my 'powers' to help their cause. It seems they acquired some of my blood at Stonehenge and find it 'most intriguing'.

The curse has not visited me since that awful night. I think it may have passed. Or perhaps, even better, evil supernatural elements are no longer among us. Captain Burton has been rounding them up from what I am told. Either way, I am not an eager recruit for the likes of the White Worms.

I was touched by your last letter. I must admit I am not a man who is good at expressing his feelings, but I shall try. I am the one who should be grateful, Oscar. You saved my life that night at Stonehenge, at a great risk to your own. And it was not the first time.

As troubled as I am by the events that took place, they have given me a new perspective on life. I would like to think I appreciate it more and want to be grateful to God for all he has given me. We have gained a valuable insight, Oscar. We know there must be a God, for we know hell and creatures from it exist. Conversely, heaven must exist. This is not knowledge I will squander. I have redoubled my efforts to be a good husband, father, son and friend.

So, it is with great humility that I call you my friend, Oscar. If I seem exasperated with you at times it is only because you possess so much potential. I do not wish to see you waste it pursuing the fleeting things in life. I know, I have done it myself to much regret.

I envy you because you are much more worldly and educated than I. I am jealous of your razor-sharp wit and your comfort in talking with people in all walks of life. But I promise you, I will no longer let these petty feelings get in the way of our friendship.

I hope our paths cross in America. I know it is a big place and we will be running in different circles, but fate has brought us together against all odds before and I feel it will do so again.

Sincerely,

Bram

P.S. Stop wearing clothes made of velvet. It is the fabric of seat cushions and curtains; it was never meant to be fashioned into a suit.

LETTER FROM THEODORE ROOSEVELT TO ROBERT ROOSEVELT, 15TH OF MARCH 1881

Dear Uncle,

You must return to America at once.

Why, you ask?

Vampires! Filthy, stinking vampires!

I learned about their existence here in America a few months back. I was asked by President Hayes to discreetly look into rumors of a Mormon uprising in Utah and made my way out West.

I met up with a mountain man they call 'Liver-Eating Johnson'. (An explanation of his name I will not put forth here.) He claims he was attacked by a group of vampires in the Colorado territory, and only his skills at scalping saved his life.

"They just kept coming," he told me. "I had to hack their heads clean off to stop 'em. I took out four on one night, then two more that jumped me the next night. I would show you the scalps but they turned to slime in my hands."

The cowboys with me that day laughed it off as the ravings of a madman, but I think we know better.

As I traveled on to San Francisco, I heard more tales of such attacks. One would think we are up to our hips in the wretched things.

In one of his first acts in office, President Garfield has asked me to stay in the West and look into the matter, now that my investigation of the Mormons is done.

Is it at all possible you could meet me in St. Louis, Missouri? I know it is a long journey, but I fear the worst. Now that you are a bona fide vampire hunter, I want to put you to good use.

Theodore

ARCHIVIST'S AFTERWORD

This concludes the collection of Bram Stoker and Oscar Wilde's involvement in the Greystones and Black Bishop incidents.

For additional material pertaining to Mr. Stoker and Mr. Wilde, see the collections The California Incident *and* The Amazon Affair.

While both men kept their promises to not reveal any information that could lead to the opening of the portals between worlds, they each incorporated their experiences into their writing. For Mr. Stoker see Dracula *and* The Lair of the White Worm. *For Mr. Wilde see* The Picture of Dorian Gray.

All books of fiction were cleared by the White Worm Society before their publication.

—Foster Giles, Head Archivist for the White Worm Society, 1938.

ACKNOWLEDGEMENTS

A million thanks to the Blue Moon Writer's Group: Anna Cherry, Denise D'Aurora and Rob Hubbard. Without your insight, support and encouragement we would have never pushed through to the end.

Thanks also to Jane Gferer for the proofreading, to Brent Mitchell for being our first reader, to the Minnesota Speculative Fiction Writers for help with the second draft, to Deborah Meghnagi Bailey for invaluable editing advice, and to the supportive community of the Horror Writers Association.

FLAME TREE PRESS
FICTION WITHOUT FRONTIERS
Award-Winning Authors & Original Voices

Flame Tree Press is the trade fiction imprint of Flame Tree
Publishing, focusing on excellent writing in horror and the
supernatural, crime and mystery, science fiction and fantasy.
Our aim is to explore beyond the boundaries of the everyday,
with tales from both award-winning authors and original voices.

•

Other titles available include:
Junction by Daniel M. Bensen
Second Lives by P.D. Cacek
Thirteen Days by Sunset Beach by Ramsey Campbell
Think Yourself Lucky by Ramsey Campbell
The Hungry Moon by Ramsey Campbell
The Haunting of Henderson Close by Catherine Cavendish
The House by the Cemetery by John Everson
The Toy Thief by D.W. Gillespie
Black Wings by Megan Hart
The Playing Card Killer by Russell James
The Siren and the Specter by Jonathan Janz
Wolf Land by Jonathan Janz
The Sorrows by Jonathan Janz
Savage Species by Jonathan Janz
The Nightmare Girl by Jonathan Janz
The Dark Game by Jonathan Janz
House of Skin by Jonathan Janz
The Widening Gyre by Michael R. Johnston
Will Haunt You by Brian Kirk
Kosmos by Adrian Laing
The Sky Woman by J.D. Moyer
The Gemini Experiment by Brian Pinkerton
Creature by Hunter Shea
Ghost Mine by Hunter Shea
The Bad Neighbor by David Tallerman
Ten Thousand Thunders by Brian Trent
Night Shift by Robin Triggs
The Mouth of the Dark by Tim Waggoner

•

Join our mailing list for free short stories, new release details,
news about our authors and special promotions:

flametreepress.com